YELLOWSTONE FAREWELL

Wayne M. Sutherland

Judy Sutherland

Wayne M. Sutherland
Judy M. Sutherland

YELLOWSTONE FAREWELL

Spur Ridge Enterprises
P.O. Box 1719
Laramie, Wyoming 82073
United States of America

www.yellowstonefarewell.com

Cover graphics by Jesse W. Sutherland from a photograph by
Wayne M. Sutherland

YELLOWSTONE FAREWELL

This is a fictional account of events that may only be speculated upon, but which are geologically possible. The locations described in this story are real, for the most part, and some groups and organizations mentioned are based on real entities in order to lend authenticity to the account. If any real group, organization, or entity is mentioned, it is used fictitiously and without any intent to describe their actual conduct. All characters and their actions are the invention of the authors and have no basis in reality. Any resemblance between these characters and any persons, living or deceased, is pure coincidence.

Copyright © 2003
Wayne M. & Judy M. Sutherland

ISBN 0-9723999-0-9

Printed by Pioneer Printing, Cheyenne, Wyoming.
United States of America

First printing, January 2003

For further information, please contact the publisher:
Spur Ridge Enterprises
P.O. Box 1719, Laramie, Wyoming 82073
www.yellowstonefarewell.com

For

Jesse

Acknowledgements

The rock outcrops of Wyoming, along with the beauty of geology that is so prominently displayed across the state, provided the initial ideas for this story. Our love for geology was first instilled in us during our college years by such people as Don Blackstone, Harold Bliss, Don Boyd, J. David Love, Samuel H. Knight, Brainerd Mears, Jr., and Richard G. Reider. Inspiration also came from a multitude of friends, hams, cavers, dogs, and horses, whose lives have touched us in many ways.

For help with our writing journey over the past two years, we are deeply grateful to those who gave generously of their time to aid us in the development and completion of this story. We especially thank W. Dan Hausel and William H. Wright for plenty of constructive criticism, along with encouragement; to Nancy R. Sutherland for writing valuable directional suggestions in our manuscript; and to Milt and Karen Mydland for devoting considerable time and effort to review, analyze, and provide detailed ideas that pulled our story over the threshold of loose connections into what we hope is a seamless and entertaining flow.

Wayne M. & Judy M. Sutherland

Table of Contents

List of Illustrations

Prologue

"In the beginning God created the heavens and the earth," (Genesis 1:1). God, in His infinite wisdom, created with logic and purpose. Science, through its evolving wisdom, tries to decipher the order and complexities of that which God created. Science is often successful in bringing to us great understanding of the world in which we live—our world being but a tiny part of the universe. However, where science fails to bring to us clear comprehension of what we call "natural events," humans then relegate such happenings to the realm of "the whims of God," or as the insurance companies say…"an unforeseeable act of God." Humans usually seek to find a scapegoat for large-scale natural catastrophes, such as those caused by severe weather disturbances, or by the sudden and dramatic activities of geologic forces.

Fact and *fiction* can often become so intertwined as to be inseparable. When that occurs, fiction is usually found to be more believable because it is more easily embellished than fact. Yet, fact itself often becomes unbelievable when its scope reaches almost unimaginable proportions.

In this story, the *geology of Wyoming* is the focus of the human characters' lives, and it is almost a character itself, with which they interact. For readers with little geological background, or for those who would like to learn more, we have included a brief *appendix* at the back of this book, suggesting information sources and supplementary reading material. A *glossary* is also provided in the appendix to assist those who are not familiar with the science of geology.

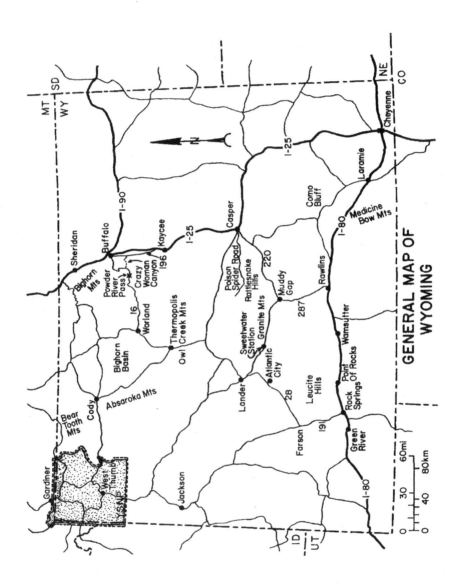

GENERAL MAP OF
WYOMING

CHAPTER 1

First Movements

▼

You have made the earth to tremble and have torn it open. Mend its fractures, for it is shaking. - Psalm 60:2

The frozen high desert of southwestern Wyoming rested in deep silence as a star-studded sky slowly brightened before sunrise. On this particular Thursday morning in February, a small group of antelope cautiously emerged from a shallow ravine onto the flat, icy surface of a frontage road along Interstate-80. Before crossing, they stopped and stood quietly alert, sensing some vague predatory presence. The distant drone of an approaching semi-truck broke the pervading silence, but the unseen menace lingered, not behind the familiar clumps of sagebrush, but within some indiscernible restlessness beneath the earth. All at once, the tensed-up antelope reeled in retreat and fled back through the hollow of the gully as if sucked into an invisible funnel.

Struggling eastward up the icy grade of I-80, a lone tractor-trailer rig reached the area abandoned minutes before by the wary antelope. Isolated in the confines of the truck's cab, the fatigued driver was unaware of any potential hazard on this lonely stretch of road. He had left San Francisco sixteen hours earlier, and his brain was now locked in a struggle against unconsciousness. Trying to arrest the descent of his drooping eyelids, he mentally retraced his route, from cluttered California out across the ranges and basins of Nevada and Utah, and on into the emptiness of Wyoming. He liked traversing Wyoming with its un-crowded horizons and easy driving. His only real enemy on the open highway was that lurking rogue *drowsiness*. It was only a few more miles to that rest area east of Point of Rocks; there he would pull over to sleep as the sun rose in the east. A practical man, he often timed his sleep periods to coincide with the rising or setting sun, depending on his direction of travel. This ritual allowed the sun to gain height and substantially reduce his eyestrain. Now he looked forward to that long rest just ahead.

But as the driver's drifting daydreams rode atop the truck's massive rubber wheels, he was oblivious to the dangerous current rising beneath him. Suddenly, the underlying pavement of I-80 cracked with a sharp sound like that of some ultra-modern high explosive, coupled with a long reverberating rumble. Startled for only a brief moment, the driver and his truck, along with its contents, were blasted upward and outward in every direction, shattering and disintegrating, then falling back to earth. The only vehicle remnants found later were a few of the major steel components and some of the wheels that had been scattered over a wide area. Analogous results might be obtained if one placed a toy plastic truck on a pile of mashed potatoes and blasted it with a twelve-gauge shotgun.

This unforeseen virulent renting of the earth's surface, on the west side of a long hill five miles east of Point of Rocks, propagated instantly southeastward and northward, severing both the east- and west-bound lanes of I-80 and the adjacent frontage road. That sharp linear break in the earth's crust also sliced through major power and telephone cables, oil and gas pipelines, and a bundle of high-speed fiber optic data transmission lines.

Simultaneously, a frothy cement-like mixture of rock debris launched skyward to a height of 4200 feet above ground, then fell back down to briefly mix with a still emerging ooze of roughly the same composition. The height attained by the rocky material was limited by its lack of cohesive strength, combined with excessive degassing, fragmentation, and air resistance. However, dust-sized particles swirled upward in turbulence to as much as 22,000 feet, eventually drifting back to earth as far as 150 miles downwind. This long and narrow eruption, no more than 450 feet wide where it crossed I-80, solidified quickly, leaving a three mile long ridge of new rocky material across lands owned by both the federal government and private interests. The newly formed solid barrier of rock, commonly referred to as a dike, totally stopped all traffic on that part of the interstate for more than a month, jeopardizing Wyoming's allocation of federal highway funds.

People generally assume volcanic eruptions are accompanied by fire. However, this outburst was unique. It differed not only in its composition from any other historical eruption, but in its temperature as well. Even though a major gas line had been severed, the eruption's low temperature, coupled with its high carbon dioxide content, prevented the rapid oxidation known as combustion, or fire, from occurring, at least immediately. The semi-fluid mixture, which extruded from beneath and to the sides of the highway, comprised a material somewhere between lamproite and kimberlite in composition. With an appearance similar to that of concrete, it was highly charged with carbon dioxide gas. The melt rose through the earth at close to twice the speed of sound, churning and accumulating bits of other rock debris as it pushed upward. The carbon dioxide gas expanded in response to rapid pressure reduction as the fluid ascended toward the earth's surface, causing rapid cooling of both the gas and the associated mixture. The rocky fluid breached the surface at a temperature near the freezing point of water, or thirty-two degrees Fahrenheit, which is not a stable condition for such material. The fluid hardened almost immediately, forming a tall but very weak irregular wall that wobbled momentarily, then collapsed, tumbling down into the still rising tail of the eruption and mixing with it until the process ended.

From start to finish, the entire surface eruption lasted only about three minutes—not the very slow geologic processes that go unnoticed by most people—but *catastrophism* in terms of geologic activity. Beneath the surface, however, the eruption began twenty-four hours earlier at a depth of about ninety miles, working its way upward with steadily increasing speed as the over-lying rock pressure decreased. Somewhere near a depth of forty-five miles, minor earthquakes began to accompany the magma movement as the surrounding rocks increased in brittleness. Then, at a depth of about ten miles, substantial fracturing began, and with pressures exerted by the overlying and surrounding rocks decreasing, the upward movement became a race. The eruption increased in speed and intensity until it broke the surface like a rifle shot. Fifteen minutes later, remnants of the new rock wall, none taller than 120 feet, were disintegrating slowly amid the rocky debris and dust. The crumbling continued for the rest of the day, with a relative stability reached about a month later.

The rumbling noise of the eruption and the associated earthquake startled people in surrounding towns as far east as Wamsutter and as far west as Green River. Workers in the Jim Bridger Power Plant and the Black Buttes Coal Mine were brought to waking attention, while train crews on the Union Pacific main line were jarred by the intense blast. At the rest area eleven miles east of Point of Rocks a Wyoming highway patrolman had stopped to recycle his early morning coffee. He was just getting back to his car when the sudden shaking of the ground caused him to flinch and stagger as he grabbed a door handle for support. The ensuing thunderous reverberation that assaulted his eardrums focused his eyes westward toward the direction of the sound. He stared in breathless bewilderment as a part of the earth heaved itself skyward to unknown height, creating a phantom-like wall that was illuminated in the pale gold of the early morning light. The bizarre sight was so unknown and inconceivable to him that it just did not register as a fact.

Startled people to the west of the eruption watched as an ominous, dark spectral shape vaulted upward, was silhouetted against the brightening eastern sky, and then collapsed. One onlooker later described the volcanic dike as "the devil's long row of jagged teeth, taking one last bite out of heaven before its fire was quenched by the breath of God."

When the ground finally ceased its shaking, and the showering debris from the sky subsided, the reality of the event gripped the minds of the onlookers. A violent eruption had occurred in their midst, with no warning whatsoever! Wyoming highway patrolmen and rescue units were called to the scene as a variety of trucks and cars piled up tight against one another on both sides of the dike. The icy pavement of I-80 contributed to a number of rear-end collisions, while causing other vehicles to be deflected into the snow-drifted ditches. Concurrently with the eruption, a series of deep gouges split the pavement of the interstate just west of Rawlins, causing several car wrecks that included three fatalities. Chaos and confusion rode the corridor of I-80 that cold winter day, and word of the fantastic event spread swiftly throughout the state.

A segment of Wyoming's news media hurriedly jumped into action when a recently hired reporter, from Casper's television station KWYN, chartered a helicopter without his station manager's approval. Vance Trounce was a young, overly enthusiastic news zealot who didn't mind breaking a few rules, as long as he created a lively story. Vance had graduated from a Chicago journalism school and had worked for a couple of years in a large eastern city. The novelty of a new job in the western United States had appealed to his sense of adventure. Upon learning of the puzzling disaster from his scanner, set to receive highway patrol and emergency services, Vance hoped to be first on the scene with live television coverage. He ordered a station camera operator, Liddy Hill, to accompany him on the flight.

Liddy was an attractive twenty-eight-year old woman whose gleaming red hair fell in a braid to her waist. She had worked at KWYN for three years as a station engineer and camera technician, and she had been instructed to assist and take orders from the new reporter when her shift required it. Liddy was dedicated and competent, but unlike Vance, she preferred reporting pure *facts* separate from *opinion*, as KWYN was in the process of gaining a reputation for doing. She too had experience in television reporting and she did not like Vance!

As she and Vance strapped themselves into the helicopter, Liddy wondered whether he had actually obtained the *go-ahead* for this endeavor from the station manager, Eric Larson. She hadn't remembered seeing Eric at work this morning.

"Well, Vance, are you going to fill me in on what's going on...where exactly we're headed and all that?" inquired Liddy as she wiggled into a comfortable position. Liddy hadn't heard about the eruption before Vance snatched her and her gear a few minutes earlier.

Vance responded, "From what I gathered, some unknown demon popped out of the ground and is eating cars and trucks along I-80, somewhere east of Rock Springs. So that's where we're going now, Liddy."

"Oh, is that all? Doesn't sound like a story worth the price of this helicopter!" Liddy wondered if this chopper trip would be smooth or not. She recalled her first helicopter ride many years back when her high school boyfriend invited her on a short blue grouse hunting trip into the nearby Bighorn Mountains. "We'll just take the bird for some birds," he'd said. Thinking he'd meant his dad's Ford Thunderbird, she was surprised when a helicopter landed in her parents' pasture to pick her up. *His father was a pilot*, she'd remembered. They had flown only two miles when she had become so nauseated that she demanded they set her down immediately. She walked back home and swore she'd never set foot in a helicopter again! But now her job required it, and she just hoped for the best.

"So what's really going on, Vance? I heard the word *"eruption"* flying through the hallway at work. A volcanic eruption or what?"

Vance nodded, "That's what it appears to be. I'll need you to get some good cover with your camera. Live coverage, Liddy...don't make any mistakes! I just hope there's enough wrecked cars and dead bodies to make a worthy headline!"

Infuriated by Vance's insensitive remark, Liddy snapped back, "Vance, we need to discuss something! Ever since you started working with us your dark side has been glaringly evident, and you've irritated everyone at the station. You distort every story you report...screw up the facts...add your own spin on things. I'll admit you're good at what you do, but your *focus* is wrong. You won't last, and if you want to keep your job, you'll relay the plain old truth and nothing more. People in Wyoming don't tolerate fantasy in the news! You'll be roasted before you know it, Vance!"

Liddy usually didn't get angry and blow up, but his

attitude that life and death were entertainment to be exploited for the promotion of sensationalism and personal gain had struck a raw nerve! However, she was already regretting the way she had spoken to him, and she was now concerned that their working relationship might suffer for it in the future.

Vance wasn't used to being cut up and insulted by *lowly* camera operators. He knew he was better than these country bumpkins, and maybe he was just *too* good for small town reporting. After all, nothing newsworthy ever happened out here in *no-man's land*—too much peaceful co-existence. If he couldn't jazz up the news a bit, maybe he'd pack up and head for the west coast—they'd appreciate him out there! But meanwhile, a story was waiting for him, and he hoped to be the first reporter on the scene. He might even get *national* attention for his footage. "Get your camera ready, Liddy! I think I see what we came out here for!"

⇆

KWYN's station manager, Eric Larson, had been a few minutes late getting to work that morning. He had only learned of the eruption upon entering his office quarters. Eric was considerably upset when he was informed that Vance had taken the initiative to visit the site without prior approval. He particularly expected permission be obtained by employees before incurring a major expense, such as a chartered helicopter. On the other hand, he would accept the scoop on this story and chew Vance out later.

Until Eric heard from Vance and Liddy, he would attempt to locate someone who could possibly explain what this *eruption* thing was all about. Eric had met a few geologists and knew of several who might offer some explanations. He remembered that the Wyoming Office of Mines and Geology (WOMG) in Cheyenne had recently tried to splash the media with press releases for "Geological Awareness Week." This had appeared to be a thinly veiled attempt to save their budget from cuts in the current legislative session. For geological insights, Eric could call the WOMG, or Wyoming State University's geology department in Laramie. But his dedication to the

Casper community suggested that the power of the press could be more skillfully applied through his selection of *local* talent. Eric remembered a fellow from Casper Technical College (CTC) who had recently impressed him with his seemingly extensive geological knowledge and communication skills. He telephoned Sam Westone, a locally known geologist who had begun teaching at CTC a few years earlier.

Eric quickly introduced himself, noting that he had listened to one of Sam's public lectures on diamonds some two months earlier. He informed Sam of the 5.4 earthquake, depicted on a United States Geological Survey (USGS) website, and of the mysterious eruption that had just occurred near Point of Rocks. He asked Sam if he could come by the station at nine-thirty that morning to offer any answers as to why this event had occurred. The USGS website had also shown a smaller 5.2 quake near Rawlins and a 4.8 quake near West Thumb in Yellowstone National Park, both of which Eric had failed to notice.

"That really sounds interesting!" responded Sam. "I hadn't heard the news this morning. The timing conflicts with my morning class, but I think I can get a fill-in. If you could round up as many details as you can, that would really help. I'll be there!"

"Great!" replied Eric. "I'll see you here at nine-thirty sharp. Thanks!" He hung up the phone while thinking that this just could be a *two-way coup*: one for our informative cover of the news, and one for publicity for our college. Eric was locally supportive of many things, although at times he could have been more sympathetic toward his own employees. He had been tight on wages and often required long hours, resulting in a greater staff turnover than would be expected from such a long-established television station.

Sam Westone had acquired a fair amount of field and consulting experience in precious gems and metals exploration. He was also interested in geomorphology, Precambrian geology, and volcanism. Sam cared little for oil and gas or coal, but while consulting, he had gained moderate experience in their exploration and development. Sam was currently concentrating on imparting his knowledge and experience to his students at CTC. He also spent his spare time writing articles and booklets on prospecting and geology. Sam received some decent remuneration from his writing efforts, but the college teaching job paid the bills, was gratifying to him, and suited his energetic lifestyle. He thoroughly enjoyed bringing an understanding of geology to anyone who showed an interest. Sam lived alone, just a few blocks from campus. Although only thirty-three years old, his dark brown hair and moustache were starting to show some premature graying around the edges. His broad shouldered, but lean, tall frame depicted a man who was physically active, while an easygoing manner attested to his calm disposition.

Sam was anxious to find out more about the eruption. He needed to brush up on the geology of the Point of Rocks region before rushing into his interview. He didn't have much time, and he kept asking himself *why* he had agreed to be interviewed at KWYN on such short notice. He drove to his office at CTC and made arrangements for his brief absence. Sam had never been one to jump into the spotlight for anything, but he usually took the initiative when he perceived that something needed to be done. Besides, he considered that the CTC Geosciences department might benefit from positive public exposure. And who knows? *This could be extremely interesting.* Or was he just rationalizing a poorly thought-out snap decision, made before he had sipped his morning cup of coffee?

The last time he had jumped on some unknown path was just after he began teaching at CTC, when the college's cave exploration club was in danger of being eliminated for lack of a faculty sponsor. Two of his geology students had asked him to sponsor their group, since there was a tie-in with geology. Sam accepted the position at the persuasion of his students. That had turned out to be an enjoyable adventure. He had learned a new perspective on limestone geology and had even accompanied the group on caving trips to Mexico. However, at the moment, he could not rationalize how a KWYN interview could develop into a similar adventure.

Sam found another instructor who would activate a video on gemstones and lead a brief discussion in his absence. Sam had been saving the video just in case he needed to miss a class. And come to think of it, he had not missed a class in two years and had filled-in numerous times for other instructors. Sam's dedication to geology and to teaching was well known among the CTC staff. Geology was not only Sam's occupation, but his greatest *avocation* as well, often provoking remarks that he "get a life outside of geology." Yes, he was dedicated to his chosen science, but he *did* have other interests.

Sam's biographical sketch, placed beneath his picture at the entrance to the CTC Geosciences building, along with those of the rest of the staff, mentioned that he enjoyed a wide variety of outdoor activities, including cross-country skiing, hiking, hunting, and cowboy action shooting. He still enjoyed those activities, although he was less involved in them now. He participated in his church, was active in amateur radio, and occasionally attended random social gatherings of various types. However, maybe the other staff members were right, in part. When CTC was in session, Sam found that he just didn't have enough time for his other interests. In fact, when he thought about it, his other interests almost always took a back seat to geology. He socialized much less now than he had when he first began teaching.

Sam's reflective thoughts faded as he now focused on class preparation and the hasty research he needed to do immediately. Sam really did not like to miss a class because it disrupted his interchange with students. Those interchanges helped him gauge how well they were learning the material he presented. But for some unknown reason, he felt that today's situation just might be important in the long run, or maybe it was CTC's budgetary concerns that caused him to agree to KWYN's request? He went to his empty classroom to write assignments on the chalkboard for his students.

After completing these preparations, Sam walked briskly back to his office and did a rapid scan of several geological references related to southwestern Wyoming. In particular, he looked for references to active faults or landslides, but there was not much detailed or reliable information available on these subjects. A small, but noticeable, earthquake had occurred outside of Green River in the mid 1990s, resulting in one death when part of an underground trona mine collapsed. After the dust had settled, part of that 1600 foot-deep mine was overlain by a surface depression more than one and a quarter mile long by a half mile wide and a couple of feet deep! Debate and follow-up investigations never fully determined whether the earthquake had caused the mine collapse, or whether the collapse had caused the earthquake.

More in his area of interest were reports published in the late 1900s by Louis Pease on the geology of the Leucite Hills, just north of Point of Rocks. Sam was familiar with Louis, and had even talked with him concerning a few consulting projects. Louis had been a dedicated geologist and prolific writer, working with metals and gemstones for the WOMG, but his interest had waned as the bureaucracy increased. Louis had retired from the WOMG and from geology, shortly after the turn of the twenty-first century, and was now entirely occupied with other interests, although he did occasionally converse on geologic projects that caught his interest. The WOMG no longer had expertise in metals or gemstones, and their current budget emphasized computerized studies related to expanding industrial minerals markets and coal mines.

Sam's brief research brought forth a lot of general information, but nothing that he wasn't already familiar with, although he may not have remembered all of the details from his previous investigations.

The Leucite Hills are a geologically young volcanic field along the east and north sides of the Rock Springs uplift, and they received their name from the potassium-rich mineral *leucite* ($KAlSi_2O_6$) found there. The volcanic field consists of several lamproite dikes, necks, plugs, flows, and cinder and pumice cones. Each individual eruptive center is very limited in extent, but conditions at the time of eruption allowed flows to build up to 122 feet thick at South Table Mountain. Although there are many variations in chemical composition and in xenolithic and xenocrystic inclusions, all of the volcanic material is classified as *lamproite*.

Xenoliths are rock pieces that have been incorporated into a melt from surrounding rocks and are included in an igneous rock, even though they may have no direct relationship to that particular igneous melt. Similarly, *xenocrysts* are crystals that are genetically foreign to the igneous rock in which they occur.

Lamproites are potassium-rich and silica-poor igneous rocks, generally containing many of the dark iron- and magnesium-rich minerals. No known eruptions of lamproites have occurred during the course of recorded human history. These represent some of the rarest rock types in the world, and act as hosts to extremely rare minerals. In addition to the mineral leucite, lamproites may contain potassium feldspar, diopside, apatite, olivine, and many other minerals. Some of these minerals, such as *armalcolite*, are hardly mentioned, even in mineralogy texts. In fact, armalcolite is so rare that it was first identified in lunar basalts brought back to earth by the Apollo 11 astronauts, before it was identified in lamproites on Earth. The mineral was named for the Apollo 11 crew—ARMstrong, ALdrin and COLlins, as it was thought to have been a unique discovery restricted to the moon.

Sam was familiar with lamproites, which have similarities to *kimberlites*. He had examined many kimberlites—the world's best-known host rock for *diamonds*. He also knew that both rock types originate at great depth and may bring to the surface nodules of rock from the earth's mantle that may include diamonds. Rich diamond deposits were mined from lamproites in Western Australia beginning in the 1980s and mining has continued to the present. Sam had explored for diamonds in the Leucite Hills, but he had never found any. However, some unconfirmed reports of diamonds, a few years earlier, centered near an olivine-rich lamproite that was found buried beneath dune sands near Hatcher Mesa.

The geologically young ages of the Leucite Hills lamproites had always intrigued Sam. The oldest lamproite there was dated at about 3.1 million years before the present, using potassium-argon radiometric dates on grains of the mineral phlogopite. That is the age of the *Boars Tusk*, a well-known, 300-foot high volcanic neck, or pinnacle, at the northwest corner of the volcanic field. The Boars Tusk is about twenty-eight miles north of Rock Springs.

Potassium-argon dates for the volcanics generally decrease toward the southeast with dates of 2.4 million years at Steamboat Mountain, 2.2 million years at Spring Butte, 1.6 million years at Zirkel Mesa, and 1.4 million years at Emmons Mesa. The youngest age was measured at 1.1 million years, plus or minus 0.4 million years. Sam knew that *plus or minus* could put the last eruption as young as 700,000 years before the present, or as old as 1.5 million years. The volcanic field also had a distant outlier at Pilot Butte about six miles northwest of Rock Springs, suggesting that a neat, orderly progression of the volcanics in both time and space, from the northwest to the southeast, may not be true.

Reviewing the geology of the area put Sam's mind in the right frame to accept and evaluate new information as it was presented to him. He just didn't know which information would prove to be useful, and which would not. Enroute to KWYN, he heard on the radio a brief mention of the blockage and closure of I-80 near Point of Rocks, which is just south of the Leucite Hills. He also learned of the traffic accidents at Rawlins and a report of a minor earthquake near there. Radio station KRAW in Rawlins had been on the ball reporting local happenings, but like many small stations that had been taken over by large broadcasting corporations, their flexibility in local reporting, and their availability of personnel to do so, had been severely reduced.

Casper Technical College, through a grant and cooperative study with Wyoming State University's Department of Geophysics and Geology, was in the process of installing a seismograph that Sam would eventually be able to make use of. Unfortunately, the unit was still at least a week away from being functional. A local earthquake would have been a nice test for that new piece of equipment. And it would have been something to intrigue his students. Earthquakes are uncommon throughout most of Wyoming, except for Yellowstone and the western Wyoming mountain ranges.

Sam had acquired much less knowledge on what had happened than he had hoped, and he was regretting his snap decision to appear on television. He liked to be one step ahead and did not like *winging it* with inadequate information. However, given a few facts, he was quite capable of realistic interpretations. Sam was also able to clearly convey to his audience, no matter what their background, the distinctions between known facts, interpretive projections, and pure speculation. Sam figured that KWYN wanted *interpretive projections*, even though they referred to it as *speculation*. The English language provides marvelous opportunities for the same words to have different meanings to different people. Sam arrived at the KWYN studios just before nine-thirty.

⇌

As the helicopter reached the sight of the eruption, Liddy shuffled her gear around and gazed out of the left cockpit window at what appeared to be the shiny double ribbon of I-80, cut in two by a long string of jagged rubble. It reminded Liddy of oppositely flowing tubes of some vital fluid that were suddenly cut and blocked. The tubes, or driving lanes, now slowly dribbled out their contents of vehicles against the sides of what severed them. "Looks like your subterranean monster shoved his rocky knife upwards across the highway. And the pieces of his blade are still stuck there, Vance." Liddy's sarcasm had no effect on the preoccupied reporter.

Vance ordered the helicopter pilot to slowly circle the dike several times so that Liddy could record an overall picture of what had occurred. The helicopter, because of its periodic rental by KWYN and by other television stations across Wyoming, sported an external uplink antenna so that Liddy's digital video and audio signals could be relayed, via satellite, directly back to Casper. The absorbed reporter, with his microphone against his mouth, could offer no clear explanation as to *what* had happened or *why* it had happened. This did not stop him from babbling incessantly with his uninformed ad nauseam opinions, more typical of popular national television talk shows than of the usually concise and informative statements made by KWYN's veteran reporters. Although not a religious person, Vance actually prayed that he would someday get to be in the spotlight of the national news.

⇌

Back at the station, Eric Larson met Sam Westone in the KWYN reception area and led him to one of the smaller studios, used for pretaping interviews. The studio was also occasionally used for splicing in live commentary, particularly during sporting or community-wide events. Here Eric briefed Sam on all that KWYN currently knew about the event, explaining that the interstate was blocked, and that traffic was now being rerouted either south to I-70 in Colorado, or to the north across South Pass. Eric also showed him the video that was now coming in from Vance and Liddy's airborne camera. The audio was also on, but the commentary, with the volume lowered, served no useful purpose for Sam. As the helicopter moved in for a landing, Sam carefully studied the aerial views with undivided attention, taking in the overall situation and noting some details. Sam was fascinated by what he saw! He realized that this would be of major interest to all geologists. *He would have to see it for himself.* Eric interrupted Sam's train of thought and explained that he would now interview him for the ten o'clock news.

⇌

Upon completing aerial views and commentary, Vance ordered the pilot to land near a hillcrest to the east of the eruption. Liddy quickly set up her ground-based satellite uplink and then mounted her camera on a heavy tripod downwind as a light breeze began to blow. The wind in that part of Wyoming is almost always from the west and usually gets stronger as the day progresses. Liddy zipped up her bulky, down-filled, hooded parka while Vance, in his polyester sport coat, attempted to look unaffected by the cold. As Liddy adjusted her audio and video, trying in particular to attenuate the wind noise, Vance wandered over toward the edge of the hill about thirty feet away and began to light a cigarette. This was a very bad move. Although the ruptured gas line had automatically shut down when its computerized sensors detected the break caused by the eruption, the large pressurized line still contained a lot of gas to leak after the shut-off. A substantial pocket of gas, from the ruptured pipe, had accumulated beneath the solidified volcanic debris and was escaping steadily. It was also being carried by the west wind up the slope of the hill to where Vance stood.

As Vance's lighter sparked, flames exploded from where he was standing just west of the hillcrest and flashed down to the new rock ridge, then expanded skyward and outward in a fireball. Vance's clothing ignited instantly and began melting. The force of the blast caused him to lean into the hill, his feet flying out from under him, due to ice that had built up on the ridge. The video camera recorded him as a ball of flames crashing headfirst into the rocky ground, before sliding backward on the ice and disappearing from view. The incident treated those who were monitoring KWYN's unedited video feed to incendiary activity, reminiscent of Buddhist monks in southeast Asia during the 1960s.

The flames arched up past the edge of the hill where Vance had been, causing a minor singe to the camera, the nose paint on the helicopter, and to Liddy's long red hair. The explosion happened so fast that no reaction or evasion was possible. Intense flames continued for several minutes after the pilot and Liddy had run for their lives. Because of the strong updraft from the fire, the rush of flames arched high above them, so damage to them and their equipment was minor. Vance was lucky only in that when he fell, the blow to his head rendered him unconscious. He felt nothing in what would otherwise have been an agonizing death. The scene recorded by Liddy's camera showed that Vance had fallen out of view below the hillcrest, and his position in the video was replaced by a wall of flames of sufficient intensity and duration as to leave no doubt about his demise.

A highway patrolman was at that time parked on the hillcrest about one hundred yards south of where the helicopter had landed. When the gas ignited near the helicopter, he had felt the heat, but was too far away across the wind to be in any great danger. He saw people running and immediately ran to their aid, bringing them back to his patrol car for treatment. It was ten minutes later before either dazed Liddy or the pilot thought to ask about Vance. The patrolman responded as quickly as before, but upon returning to where Vance was last seen, even a casual glance left no doubt that little remained of the incinerated reporter.

Eric's fifteen-second introduction of Sam was followed with aerial footage of the I-80 blockage. Sam's commentary was superimposed as audio instead of Vance's, with the exception of Vance's initial exclamation at how thoroughly the interstate had been blocked. Although only a short amount of time had been allocated for Sam's interview, it progressed smoothly with only one brief interruption.

"Dr. Westone, isn't this blockage of the interstate near some coal mines and the Bridger Power Plant?" inquired Eric. "Could you give us some details of the geology of the area?"

"The *Rock Springs uplift*, where this happened," explained Sam, "is an *anticline*…where rocks are bent convex upward, and the structure is of *Laramide* age, which is roughly sixty-five million years old. In the uplift, sedimentary rock layers have been bent and in some places broken. The rocks were then worn down or eroded over time by the actions of water, frost, and wind. This erosion exposed rock units ranging in age from Late Cretaceous to Paleocene. Oil, gas, and coal are found within the rock layers of the Rock Springs uplift. The Bridger Power Plant, just northwest of the recently blocked I-80, burns coal from nearby Paleocene coal beds mined south of the Interstate."

"Sam, could you define some of your terms?" interrupted Eric.

"Oh, sorry," apologized Sam. "*Cretaceous* and *Paleocene* are the names of geologic ages…"

The interview was suddenly interrupted when a studio technician shouted, "*What the blazes!*" Everyone in the studio looked up as Liddy's camera recorded a fireball engulfing Vance, accompanied by a scream from Liddy, and something unintelligible from another voice, probably that of the helicopter pilot. The brief excitement was followed by silence, and a view of the edge of the hill was accentuated for several minutes by intense, but diminishing flames. The video feed continued to run without commentary, causing much worry and frantic attempts by station personnel to communicate with the helicopter pilot and news crew.

Due to quick editing by Eric, the fireball recorded by Liddy's camera was not a part of the morning news. Eric did not believe that violent death, either graphic or strongly suggested, should be brought into his viewers' homes unannounced, even if most details are omitted. It was clear from the video that Vance's lighter had sparked the fire.

Taking a couple of minutes to calm down, Eric continued

GEOLOGIC TIME CHART

ERA	PERIOD	EPOCH	Millions of Years Ago	Events
CENOZOIC	Quaternary	Holocene	0.01	
		Pleistocene	0.6	Last Major Yellowstone Eruption
			2.0	1st Yellowstone Eruption
	Tertiary	Pliocene	12	
		Miocene	26	
		Oligocene	38	
		Eocene	54	
		Paleocene	65	Laramide Orogeny
MESOZOIC	Cretaceous		136	
	Jurassic		190	
	Triassic		225	
PALEOZOIC	Permian		280	
	Pennsylvanian		320	
	Mississippian		345	
	Devonian		395	
	Silurian		430	
	Ordovician		500	
	Cambrian		570	
PRE-CAMBRIAN	Proterozoic Eon		2500	
	Archean Eon			
	Estimated age of Earth		4700	

with the interview. *Interview* may not be the best term, since Eric's questions were cut out, leaving only explanations and interpretive projections by Sam, coupled with a state map showing the location, which then faded into the recorded aerial views.

Sam, too, was shocked by what he had seen in the fireball, but continued from where he had left off. He explained that the Paleocene generally encompassed the time from fifty-four to sixty-five million years ago, and the Cretaceous preceded it, extending back as far as 136 million years ago.

Sam's first look at the aerial views suggested several possibilities to him. His initial thought, which he found intriguing, was that the *first ever* lamproite eruption in recorded human history had just occurred, extending southward the progression of past eruptions through time in the Leucite Hills. Since such an *historical* event had never happened before, this would be unique in geology. Sam carefully explained this concept, but emphasized, "Proof of that would require field examinations coupled with the collecting of samples for analyses."

Sam's second possibility was that over-pressured gas, mud and water, probably from underlying Cretaceous strata, had vented through a fracture creating a *sand dike*. In his explanation of a sand dike, he noted, "The minor earthquake at Rawlins occurred at the same time as the new dike, and both quakes may have been related to a regional stress adjustment. Therefore, the stress adjustments and quakes possibly involved the creation of a new fracture through which a sand dike had been emplaced."

"Just how common are these sand dikes?" questioned Eric.

Sam continued, "Occurrences of sand dike injections are well-documented to accompany earthquakes in soft sediments. The geologic record shows similar dikes in more indurated sedimentary layers as well. Some over-pressured gas layers are known from Wyoming's Cretaceous oil and gas reservoirs, and some were reported in nearby oil and gas fields. As noted from the aerial views, there appears to have been little, if any, heat associated with the eruption; snow adjacent to the new intrusion has not been melted. The presence of flammable gas also supports the possibility of a sand dike, with the gas venting from some underlying reservoir."

No one thought to check with the regional gas transportation company to see if they had a line crossing that area, or if such a line was present, whether it had ruptured. The disruption of fiber-optic data, although noted in some areas, had not yet been commented on.

Sam found that the eruption, whatever its type, was *terribly* exciting! He knew that within the United States, no volcanic activity had occurred away from the west coast during historic times! The geologic record, however, is filled with volcanic activity across the west over the course of the last few tens of millions of years. If it *is* a sand dike, the structural implications would also be intriguing. Sam was wound up enough that he immediately decided to visit the site over the weekend, dragging any interested students along. This would nicely supplant his previously arranged introductory field trip to Bessemer Mountain and Muddy Mountain, south of Casper.

Summarizing his televised commentary, Sam took the conservative approach and addressed his second possibility first, with the slight hedge of noting, "A lamproite eruption is possible, but not expected." His final remark was, "On-site investigation is really needed before true causes can be determined." Hedging on bets and broadening the field of possibilities diminishes the impact of an interpretation, but sometimes it is better than placing all of your eggs in one basket. The Wyoming Office of Mines and Geology later took Sam's lead, but put all of their eggs in the *sand dike* interpretation basket.

⇋

An endless half hour after her camera recorded the fireball, Liddy reestablished audio contact with the studio in Casper. A sigh of relief then flowed throughout the worried staff at KWYN.

Sam's explanation of the possible geologic causes was picked up by the national news networks and was aired on their afternoon and early evening programs. They edited KWYN's five-minute take to less than two minutes, keeping Sam's words about "regional stress adjustment" and "sand dike," but emphasizing, "possible lamproite eruption" and "such a thing had not happened before in recorded history," because it sounded a bit more exciting for the national viewers.

Vance's prayer for the center-stage spotlight was answered when the national news media took an item from a later KWYN feed that afternoon. They noted that "one of our own" had died trying to bring news of this event to the world. It was a nice subject change for their news reports. Besides, it took some of the heat off of the most recent in a barrage of political scandals that had shaken the U.S. Senate for a month and a half.

Sam was not pleased with the national evening news programs that day. He did not like being quoted out of context, particularly when it was made to appear that he was making wild and unproven statements, even *if* a lamproite eruption was a definite possibility. KWYN's local evening news was a repeat of Sam's morning interview, with the addition of Vance's death in a natural gas explosion, the cause of which was under investigation. Liddy's and the helicopter pilot's escape from major injury was also included, along with pictures of them and the singed helicopter nose. In addition, the late newscast mentioned the accidents and fatalities resulting from the cracks in the interstate near Rawlins. It further related that temporary repairs near Rawlins had been made, but no estimate was given as to when the I-80 blockage near Point of Rocks would be cleared.

That afternoon, the pipeline company noted that the ruptured gas line had, indeed, been the source of the explosion. This information was relayed immediately to emergency personnel on the site to allay any fears of additional fire or explosion. But that did not make the news until the late evening program. Other details trickled into the news over the next week.

$\leftrightharpoons$

The Wyoming Office of Mines and Geology had been at a

disadvantage. Their access to the USGS earthquake information had come via a dedicated link through the now severed fiber-optic cable. That link had been set up as part of an earthquake hazards investigation grant for rapid retrieval of data, without the congestion found in typical internet links. The WOMG could access the same information over the internet, but if a large database was being retrieved there could be a substantial delay, hence the dedicated link. However, as with any system that gets relied on too heavily, when it breaks it often takes a while to remember how things were done before the newer system was installed.

Mismanagement for more than a decade, under the direction of half a dozen politically connected but incompetent (and a couple of rogue) office chiefs had pruned the WOMG of the competent staff geologists and mining engineers that had made it the geological force of note in earlier times. The rapid management turnover was perceived by a state government oversight committee as a problem with the existing staff, rather than with their poor choices for office chiefs. Independent thinkers and self-motivated problem solvers just did not mix well with the bureaucracy of the "just smile and say *yes* crowd." The *yes-men* and *-women* were the ones who remained employed, while the real workhorses generally resigned in frustration or disgust.

The WOMG now retained only one or two experienced geologists and several who, although they were titled "geologists" and "mining engineers," lacked both field experience and inspiration. However, these specialists were smooth at projecting an air of importance while talking about their chosen fields of expertise. For them, on-the-ground analyses would be a challenge. Other publicly funded agencies and more large private businesses than one would care to believe also suffered under similar *modern* management concepts. The general public, along with several prominent state legislators with their own agendas, noticed a lack of productivity from the agency—there had been no significant WOMG publications in more than four years. With the tighter state budgets caused by declining oil and gas production, the Wyoming Office of Mines and Geology was close to being eliminated entirely.

All other things aside, the geologist whose job it was to keep abreast of happenings such as earthquakes almost always checked the USGS Earthquakes Information Center, before he did anything else when he came to work. Bill Burnhard, fifty-five years old and looking forward to retirement, was in charge of Engineering Geology and Geologic Hazards at the WOMG. *Engineering Geology* encompassed anything that might be related to strengths of geologic material for any construction, outside of mineral production. *Geologic Hazards* addressed all natural movements of geologic materials, outside of groundwater. Groundwater was managed under a separate division of the WOMG. Geologic hazards primarily included landslides, floods, and earthquakes. Bill had been around almost as long as anyone at the WOMG could remember. He was frustrated because he could not access the USGS data link that morning.

Newer satellite links that would make the fiber optic connections as outdated as a Model-T Ford were coming to southeastern Wyoming soon, and they were currently being installed in several state agencies in Cheyenne and in some buildings on the WSU campus in Laramie. Earlier attempts at such a system had not worked well, but new breakthroughs in data transmission, switching, and signal enhancement were making this happen. However, if its budget was cut, the WOMG might not be around long enough to benefit from the technology. Casper Technical College got a good plug for their Geoscience Department with Sam's introduction on KWYN, and the WOMG first heard about the eruption from one staff geologist's wife who saw it on KWYN's mid-morning news.

⇆

The Wyoming State University Department of Geophysics and Geology (DGG) received several calls seeking explanations. However, those faculty members capable of providing answers were out of town and would not return until Monday. Several members of the faculty were presenting papers at a meeting of the National Association of Geologists and Geophysicists in Atlanta, Georgia. Although not considered a black eye for not having the first answers to an unexpected geological question, the department lost its chance to be first on any immediate interpretations. The spotlight was now shining elsewhere—at Casper Technical College.

Several calls were received by the WOMG after KWYN's morning news, and amidst the scramble to prepare a presentation of their endangered budget to the legislature, the WOMG moved rapidly. The current WOMG Chief, Gordon Aughey, made the snap decision that Bill Burnhard would not accompany him to the budget presentation, but would instead take a vehicle immediately to the eruption site to investigate. Bill would have rather sent one of his assistants, but they were all tied up in other important matters. Before eleven o'clock, most WOMG employees had all seen a replay of Sam's presentation, available on KWYN's web site.

Protesting the sudden change of plans made for him, Bill prepared to go to the field. At least he would not have to leave the Interstate, and traffic was certain to be light since the road was closed at Rawlins. Bill even thought to call ahead to the Wyoming Highway Patrol to make sure that they knew he was on official business and would not be stopped at the roadblock.

Not liking to travel alone, Bill persuaded a Computer Mapping Systems II technician, thirty-one-year-old Debby Johnson, to travel with him. They would be late getting back, but she would get overtime. With her low salary and the high cost of apartment rentals in Cheyenne, she could use all the overtime she could get. None of the other staff geologists or engineers were available to accompany Bill; they all seemed to have plausible excuses. Bill and Debby were on the road before eleven-thirty, after grabbing some prepared sandwiches at a convenience store as they left town. Bill very much preferred a leisurely restaurant meal to a sandwich, to which his overweight condition attested. He was, in striking contrast to his assistant, terribly out of shape. Any kind of fieldwork, or physical labor for that matter, was something that Bill avoided as much as possible.

Just before one o'clock, Chief Aughey headed for his budget meetings with the added ammunition that a field team from the WOMG was currently investigating the geologic causes for the blockage of Interstate-80.

Sam Westone found this new geologic conundrum that had jumped into his life terribly interesting, but it also worried him. What caused subsurface pressure to blow out a sand dike at *this* time and in *this* place? Were more of these likely to occur? And what if it really was *magma* instead? That would make things much more complicated to try to understand. What could cause a rupture in the earth clear down to the mantle? Or was new magma forming at a shallow depth because of some unknown geologic activity?

Compared to the historical geologic perspective of slow, but steady, processes shaping the earth over long periods of time, this recent *violent* movement seemed to be only an isolated occurrence. However, that paradigm of geology would soon be called into question.

CHAPTER 2

Investigations

▼

Speak to the earth and it shall teach you...that the hand of the Lord has wrought this. - Job 12:8-9

Surya Ganisalim was a young graduate student at the Wyoming State University Department of Geophysics and Geology (DGG). Geology interested him, but geophysics made everything come to life. How else could one peer into the depths of the earth and make sense of rocks and structures so deep and hot that no drilling rig could ever penetrate them? The interior regions of the earth held the secrets responsible for the actuation of all geological events and structures that can be observed at the surface. Geophysics fascinated Surya; it was his life's passion.

When Surya was in fifth grade, he and his parents moved to the United States from Kalabahi, on the island of Alor in Indonesia. His English was particularly good because his father, who wanted him to succeed in business, began teaching it to him when he was very young. His father was aware that English was *the* language for international business. Kalabahi, just southwest of the Banda Sea, was repeatedly jolted by plenty of earthquakes and was located near several active volcanoes. Indonesia hosts the largest number of historically active volcanoes of any country in the world, with more than sixty of them having erupted during the twentieth century. Indonesia has suffered the highest number of eruptions resulting in fatalities of any country on earth. Many of the volcanoes there have high explosive potential and include historically infamous eruptions such as Tambora in 1815 and Krakatau in 1883. The dominating influence of volcanoes and earthquakes strongly affected the culture that Surya had grown up with.

In Kalabahi, Surya's father and mother had owned a small hotel with an attached restaurant. His father had tried to enter into local politics in order to raise their standing in the community and to perhaps secure a minor government position. His efforts were an attempt to supply a higher quality education for his two sons. Unfortunately, his political savvy was not the best. His youngest son had died in an accident from mob violence, associated with lingering animosities related to East Timor's independence from Indonesia, during the previous century. In fact, it had been Surya's father's political feelers that had put his family in jeopardy, causing him to sell his business quickly and flee from his country of birth to the United States.

The Ganisalim family settled in the San Francisco area where Surya completed high school with honors. Surya received a bachelor's degree in geophysics and volcanology at a California technical school. He then got a full scholarship to attend graduate school at Wyoming State University to study geophysics. This was the most secure position he had ever been in. He was happy, energetic, and deeply interested in his studies. His parents, in good health and financially stable, still made their home in the San Francisco area.

Surya was not very interested in seismology as a mineral exploration tool. This tool highlights the cutting edge of modern oil and gas exploration, and more recently, has found applications investigating metals deposits. From these mineral industries, the users of seismology funded both the Department of Geophysics and Geology and Surya's research. However, Surya studied the equipment, methods, techniques, and interpretations—the better to apply the same to more deep-seated investigations of the earth. For his dissertation, he was trying to develop a new generation of three-dimensional seismic analyses that should yield previously undreamed of detail—and to much greater depths beneath the earth's surface than anyone else had believed possible. This increase in detail, using the latest generation of computer hardware, could revolutionize seismology in a way similar to that in which the CT-scan had replaced the simple x-ray machine in medicine during the last century. CT-scan or *computed tomography*, also known as CAT-scan or *computerized axial tomography*, is a method of using a computer to combine images from multiple x-rays to produce sophisticated cross-sectional or three-dimensional pictures of a body's internal organs.

Current 3-D seismology, with a method referred to as *seismic tomography*, uses hundreds of seismograms to develop three-dimensional pictures of subsurface geology. This is accomplished by measuring the speed of seismic waves from earthquakes or from artificial sources, such as explosives and heavy vibrators. The information is then computer-enhanced to compare seismic wave velocities, deviations, and reflections, from which an interpretation is developed. Uncertainties in data quality and interpretation increase rapidly with depth and with distance from the source of the seismic waves. At depths much greater than a couple of miles, these 3-D interpretations become extremely fuzzy.

Seismic analyses in Surya's system required a minimum of three points of data collection, although more was better. These needed to be dispersed in a roughly triangular or other polygonal array and separated by a distance similar to, or greater than, the depth to be examined. In other words, instead of generating fuzzy traces to depths of a few miles, clear three-dimensional structural views might be achieved extending into the earth's mantle. Surya's data collection array was simple, but what made the analyses possible was a complex series of algorithms and electronic filters applied repetitively to incoming bits of data. The algorithms and filters were *tunable* such that data already received from a calibrated array could be examined in an almost infinite variety of ways, emphasizing particular aspects of the otherwise hidden geology.

Surya was now in the process of setting up a calibration sequence, for an eventual total of seven seismograph stations in and around Wyoming, to be used in his thesis research. Precise locations of these stations, relative to each other within one centimeter, and synchronization of received signals to a one-millisecond base, were necessary for calibration. The locational accuracy had been available since the end of the twentieth century. Synchronization, once initiated, could be maintained with self-correcting chronometers overprinting their timing marks on the data. Surya hoped to have the calibration of his array completed by the end of March. The mathematical gyrations, used by Surya in his algorithms and filters, required that his dissertation committee include representatives from both the Mathematics and the Computer Sciences departments, along with those from Geophysics and Geology.

The new seismograph, installed recently in the basement of the DGG, was very sensitive and included state of the art computerization. Surya himself had designed certain aspects of both the hardware and software for his project, and he had also assisted with the construction and installation of the department's seismograph. This was "Station #1" in his current array of three. The Wyoming Office of Mines and Geology (WOMG), only fifty miles to the east in Cheyenne, was not aware of this new seismograph installation at the DGG.

Coordination between the DGG and the WOMG had been an essential component of both organizations two decades earlier. But it had been almost nonexistent for the last several years due to personality clashes between key personnel, coupled with WOMG policies of internal focus rather than outside cooperation. The almost symbiotic conflict was a natural outgrowth of the opposing perceptions of narrowly focused self-importance on both sides.

On the morning of the Point of Rocks eruption, as he was getting his office coffee started, Surya noted the recorded earthquakes from less than an hour earlier. His instrumentation, already holding preliminary synchronization links with seismographs at Dillon, Montana and Boulder Colorado, showed three earthquakes registering magnitudes of 5.4, 5.2, and 4.8 on the Richter scale. Their times of initiation began with Point of Rocks, followed 1.5 seconds later by a quake at Rawlins, then an additional 3.1 seconds later by a third quake at West Thumb, in Yellowstone National Park.

The *Richter scale* for earthquake magnitudes is a logarithmic scale, and each whole number corresponds to a change in amplitude of seismic waves by a factor of ten. The seismic waves in a magnitude 5.0 quake are ten times greater in amplitude than those of a magnitude 4.0 quake. Damage to man-made structures generally begins at about magnitude 5.0, with excessive to near total destruction in earthquakes greater than magnitude 8.0. The scale tops out around 9.0, limited by the strength of earth materials. Seismologists still debate the exact values at the top end. An earthquake's magnitude and the resulting damage relates to the amount of energy available, usually from rocks held in some kind of distortion and then suddenly released.

The energy released by 1.3 cubic yards of elastically strained rock is about seventy-four foot-pounds, or about the same as an average firecracker. Unconfined, this is a small amount of energy, but when focused, it is almost as much as the muzzle energy of the bullet from a .22 caliber rim-fire pistol. When the total energy released by a major earthquake is calculated for a very large fault, one must consider the total volume of rock that was being strained prior to release. This could take in an area several hundreds of miles long by fifty or sixty miles wide, extending to a depth of forty miles or so. That amount of energy may then be approximated by the simultaneous detonation of a major portion of the world's nuclear arsenal, spread out across the volume of rock affected, but focused in the area of the fault surface. The energy released by such a large volume of rock, suddenly unstressed, is analogous to a giant spring being allowed to snap. Even if the distance that the rock snaps is small, there is a lot of power behind it, and it is easy to understand why large fault movements can be so destructive.

Surya's preliminary seismic array of three stations, in a rough line, was not set up for the three-dimensional type of analysis he wanted. The array needed to be more of a polygon, but it gave some general information for him to play with. Other locations in his test array of seven stations would eventually include Salt Lake City, Utah, and Rock Springs, Sheridan, and Casper, Wyoming. These sites, while not the ideal spread, had other necessary characteristics. They had colleges or universities with cooperatively minded faculty, and Surya's grant was funding a couple of new seismograph units now being installed at these locations. Most importantly, these sites were also interconnected with a redundant system of fiber-optic and the newer satellite data links. The seismograph in Salt Lake City was a part of the United States Geological Survey (USGS) system and provided a control link to their data (as did Boulder, Colorado). The seismograph at CTC in Casper was now being installed, and it would be functioning before the month ended. Surya carefully looked over his new seismic data before heading off to class, but not until Monday would his computer be ready to provide interpretations from the data.

⇆

As Bill Burnhard and Debby Johnson drove west on I-80, they were pleased that the highway was in such good shape for the middle of winter, especially in the vicinity of Elk Mountain, located on the north end of the Medicine Bow Mountains. Much of the heavy cross-country truck traffic was now being rerouted across I-70 in Colorado. They passed over the hastily filled cracks in the pavement west of Rawlins around two o'clock. The Wyoming Highway Department's large maintenance facility, on the east edge of Rawlins, had initiated temporary repairs as soon as the wreckage from the early morning accidents had been cleared. If time allowed, Bill and Debby would investigate these cracks on their return trip. Their primary objective was to examine the new dike, of whatever type it was, just east of Point of Rocks.

They arrived at the eruption site around three-thirty, after stopping briefly at the nearby rest area. As they pulled over on the crest of the hill to take pictures, they gazed at the long rubble pile that was interrupted by tall vertical sections of rock. The grayish-brown debris stretched from across the hill to the south, down the slope, across I-80 and its frontage road, then beyond the hill to the northwest and out of sight. Bits of smaller material were scattered across the barren landscape in all directions, and the wind continually picked up fine dust that swirled around larger blocks and piles. Low angle winter light accentuated the angular rock shadows and dust plumes, creating an ideal situation for taking good photographs. Debby snapped several pictures from their hilltop vantage point.

Below them a host of personnel stood by at the scene, representing the Wyoming Highway Department, news organizations, the pipeline transportation companies, a fiber-optic cable company, the power transmission line company, the coal company, the power plant, state and county emergency personnel, the Sweetwater County Sheriff's Office, and the U.S. Bureau of Land Management. All of these people left a wide assortment of vehicles scattered about. The dispersion of people and vehicles gave good indications of scale for Debby's photographs. Other assorted individuals, too numerous to list, had also come to the site with a wide variety of reasons as to why they should be there. This was probably the largest collection of people in recent history to converge on this remote high desert location in southwestern Wyoming.

After taking in the overall situation, Bill carefully guided his vehicle down the icy highway to a point near the debris wall where he parked. The temperature was twenty-seven degrees F, but the west wind, steady at twenty-two miles per hour, swirled minor amounts of old snow mixed with abundant fine dirt across the debris, creating rather chilly and gritty conditions. Bill and Debby bundled themselves in their heavy coats, hats, and gloves, and then climbed out of the warm cab to examine some of the chunks of rock debris. Debby had never taken any courses in geology, nor had she read any geology books, but she knew her *Computer Mapping Systems II* very well. She could easily troubleshoot software and hardware problems related to that system.

Bill looked at a small fist-sized piece of rock, his eyes watering in the cold wind and swirling dust. There were variations in the particle sizes and colors. Sizes ranged from about an eighth of an inch down to that of very fine silt, with colors varying from light gray to brown and black. The material reminded him of massive Cretaceous mudstones and sandstones, with scattered larger particles, but with no layering that he could see. To him, it appeared to be similar to a fine-grained *turbidite*, often observed in Cretaceous marine deposits in Wyoming. The *rock* was soft enough to break apart when two pieces were sharply knocked together with his hands. He kept his gloves on, not only because of the cold, but also to avoid getting his hands dirty. In his haste to leave the WOMG in

Cheyenne, Bill had forgotten both his notebook and rock hammer at the office. He could write up his notes from memory when he returned to the office, but the rock hammer on his belt would have marked him as a geologist—an important consideration for Bill.

Bill examined some of the larger pieces of debris, noted a few small chunks of other rock types included within the soft rock, and decided it must be a sand dike as proposed by Sam Westone on the KWYN news report. A favored hypothesis, when once implanted in the brain, is hard to shed. Bill saw no indications that he could interpret any of this as volcanic rock, even though he had only examined two small pieces. There wasn't any pumice, scoria, or flow-like material where the debris littered the highway, at least none that he could see. The extrusion of material appeared to have been cold, such that even the adjacent snow and ice had not melted, except where the gas explosion had occurred just north of the highway. Bill didn't think to use a hand lens or small pocket magnifier to determine the shape of the mineral grains. He did bring his Brunton compass and measured the general orientation of the dike; he would remember the bearing and write it down when he returned to the office. He instructed Debby to note their location with a *Global Positioning System* (GPS) unit. He then wandered around a little bit talking to others, and he learned that wheels from an eighteen-wheeler had been scattered around the site, presumably caught when the dike erupted. Confirmation of this, along with freight company identification of the missing vehicle, would not come for another four days.

Just before four o'clock, Bill and Debby headed back east toward Cheyenne. When they reached the filled cracks in Interstate-80 west of Rawlins, it was getting dark, and the wind had increased noticeably. By then the temperature had dropped to nineteen degrees F. Bill didn't feel like examining the cracks in the highway under these conditions. However, at Debby's suggestion, he did pull over long enough to take a compass bearing on them, and she noted the location on her GPS. They stopped in Rawlins where Bill bought supper at a small, but well-known Mexican restaurant that served large portions of inexpensive fare. They finally arrived back at the WOMG offices in Cheyenne around nine o'clock. Bill hastily wrote down the compass readings as he remembered them, and he resolved to write up his report first thing in the morning.

⇌

Sam Westone began laying the groundwork for his field investigation as soon as he returned to the CTC campus from his television interview. His first priority was to secure permission from the Wyoming Highway Patrol to use the closed interstate for a visit to the eruption site. As a representative of Casper Technical College, and having appeared a few hours earlier as an *expert* on KWYN, he found this task easier than expected. Final approval would have to wait until Friday afternoon, but Sam could still return to his original field exercise on Saturday, if this arrangement fell through. The interstate would open this afternoon for local westbound traffic as far as the rest area, and it was already open from Rock Springs to Point of Rocks, although for limited area traffic only. More local traffic than most people realized used I-80, including ranchers, residents, service personnel for oil and gas fields, pipeline employees, and others.

Sam then secured permission for the trip from the CTC Geoscience Department Head, Ralph Escobido, with the built-in flexibility to change to his previously planned Bessemer Mountain / Muddy Mountain excursion, if necessary. Sam's rationale for visiting the site of the eruption, beyond his own intense curiosity, was that an uninvestigated geologic event would not only provide his students with the opportunity to learn field techniques, but they might also get the ego boost of contributing to the acquisition of new geologic knowledge. Sam knew that such a boost could inspire students to pursue further studies with greater vigor.

Sam sold his plan to Ralph *too* well! Ralph planned to call KWYN television to see if they would like to send a camera crew along for a human-interest follow-up to Sam's earlier interview. Sam preferred to be a bit lower key on field trips and would rather not have the news media hanging around, but said nothing, realizing that CTC really could use the publicity.

Sam announced his change of the field trip destination to his Thursday afternoon and Friday morning classes. Both of the classes were enthusiastic and all seemed to pay closer attention to his lecture and demonstrations on basic field techniques. Twenty-two of his students would participate in the field trip. Those unable to attend would be given a local, but less exciting make-up field exercise to complete. Two of the school's fourteen-passenger vans would be more than adequate transportation. Sam would drive the first van, and he asked one of his older students, Brent McKay, to drive the second.

As Sam finished his Friday afternoon class, he was given a message that a camera operator from KWYN would accompany him on the field trip and would be waiting at the south door to the CTC Geoscience building at seven o'clock the next morning. Although there would be extra room in the vans, Sam kind of hoped that whoever it was would be too late to come along. He had a reputation for punctuality that he expected his students to follow. They knew that he would wait no more than about five minutes for latecomers before heading out. Sam secured final permission from the Highway Patrol to use the closed section of I-80, provided he stay clear of the various crews attempting to clear the highway and reassemble the severed pipelines, power lines, and other utilities.

⇌

Saturday was one of the nicest days in two weeks. It was about as perfect a day as one could hope for in late February. The temperature was almost thirty degrees, the sky was a clear pale blue, and the air was dead calm. All of Sam's twenty-two students arrived on time. Liddy Hill, with her camera and cold weather gear, had arrived ten minutes early and introduced herself to Sam and some of his students. At five-foot, eight inches tall and 137 lbs in sturdy hiking boots and blue jeans, she blended in well with the geology students. She appeared physically fit and hosted an indelible smile, unhindered by makeup. After brief introductions, Sam decided that Liddy seemed like a pleasant person, and he somewhat regretted his earlier thought that anyone from the press could be detrimental to an enjoyable field trip. Besides, *she was sort of cute.*

Due to the loss of Vance, Liddy was the only KWYN employee available for this job. Liddy had previously demonstrated her abilities to fill in on reporting assignments, but Eric Larson was concerned that the memory of Vance's death might be hard on her, particularly when returning to the same location. *"It will not be a problem!"* she had assured Eric emphatically. Sam allowed Liddy to take a seat next to him so she could not only pick up on some of his rolling geologic commentary, but could ask more questions if she wished. Sam's commentary would be spoken into a microphone, and it would be heard from several speakers in the second van and through one in the back of his van. Liddy would also be able to look at some of the maps he brought along for reference.

It was 117 miles from Casper to Rawlins, via Muddy Gap. This portion of the trip would take two hours, and Sam had prepared geological commentary that would use up almost forty minutes of the trip. As he finished loading the students and gear, he told Liddy, "Ms. Hill, I hope that you either have an interest in geology or have brought a book with you to read. My lecturing will be intermittent from here to Rawlins."

"Thanks for warning me, Dr. Westone," she replied. "I *do* have a book. I usually carry one as a way to fill in time if I have to wait for something. That happens often in my job. I've also learned that according to *Murphy's Law*, if I plan on reading, other events will preclude it. In this case, I know very little about geology, but I *am* interested, and I'd like to hear your lecture. And by the way, it's *Miss* Hill, *not Ms!* But I'd prefer to be called *Liddy.*"

"Okay, Liddy," responded Sam as he drove the lead van westward from the CTC campus. "I don't have a Ph D, and I would prefer to be called *Sam.* However, I'll answer to anything that you're comfortable with. Several of my students came up with *Dr. Sam.* That's okay for a classroom, but I still prefer less formality. If you have any questions or don't understand something that I mention, just ask me to explain. We'll have plenty of time for extra discussion as we go along."

"Thanks," answered Liddy with a smile. "I'm sure I'll have loads of questions. I've already seen the blockage of I-80, Sam. I was a part of the TV news crew that investigated on

Thursday, and I'm really curious about what actually did happen there."

"Oh!" exclaimed Sam. "Then *you're the one* who was videotaping from the helicopter!"

"Yes, that was me."

"I'm sorry about your co-worker," sympathized Sam. "I didn't recognize your name, although I probably heard it mentioned at the station. I must have been too focused on trying to figure out what was going on geologically. I hope it's not too stressful for you to return to the scene of such an accident."

"Thanks for your concern, Sam," replied Liddy appreciatively. "It was really unpleasant, but other than the shock of the moment and a few recurring thoughts, I've been too busy to dwell on it. Today I'll just focus in on some geological enlightenment and ignore any memories of what happened."

"Well, I hope I can provide the explanations you want," continued Sam as he shuffled his notes with his free hand. "My goal is to unlock the puzzle of what caused the eruption. If there's anything I can do for you, don't hesitate to ask."

"Thank you, Sam," replied Liddy as she adjusted her seatbelt and settled in for the ride.

⇌

Sam began his commentary by explaining, "The geology of Wyoming is some of the most exposed, varied, and easily examined of any in North America. Geologic units and structures found near the route we're taking range from the very recent to some of the oldest Precambrian. Our first observed geologic features are Quaternary in age. The *Quaternary Period* in geologic history extends from the present back to about two-and-a-half million years ago. Erosion by streams can carve broad planar surfaces, called *pediments*, across bedrock. These surfaces are generally veneered with gravels transported by the streams and represent periods of relative stability in the erosional history of an area. Analogous long and narrow erosion surfaces within stream valleys are called *terraces*. Erosion surfaces at the lowest elevations within a drainage are the most recently formed, and each higher level is relatively older. A good example of this type of sequence can be seen on our left as we pass the Squaw Creek drainage flowing down from Casper Mountain."

Sam continued lecturing as he led them southwestward on Highway 220. "Casper Mountain is a block of Precambrian basement rock that was bowed upward, along with overlying younger sedimentary rocks, to form an anticline, which was subsequently faulted along it's northern edge and tilted southward. The 5000-foot vertical displacement on the fault brings Precambrian granite into contact with the much younger upper Cretaceous Cody Shale. The granite also over-thrusts the southern end of the Emigrant Gap anticline."

Sam's commentary followed their progress along the highway, explaining the erosion of the Bessemer Narrows canyon that contains both Highway 220 and the North Platte River, which cut the canyon. Sam pointed out economic developments such as oil fields and quarries as they were passed by, as well as outcrops of various well-known oil reservoir host rocks, including the Lower Cretaceous-age Muddy Sandstone and the Jurassic-age Sundance Formation. Between lecture segments, Liddy chatted with Sam and his students and asked several thoughtful questions.

While driving several miles east of Independence Rock, Sam described a meteor impact crater that penetrated Quaternary pediment gravels and the underlying Miocene Split Rock Formation. It lay only a mile and a half north of the highway, and a half mile from the Oregon Trail. The crater, almost three-quarters of a mile long, a quarter mile wide, and one hundred feet deep, was discovered by one of Sam's professional associates, just after the start of the twenty-first century. It was the *first* confirmed impact crater to be found in Wyoming. To encourage careful observation, Sam emphasized, "This crater lies adjacent to a travel route that has been in use for almost two centuries. The fact that it was not identified earlier tells us that one has only to look carefully, with unbiased eyes, to make new discoveries in geology. For those of you who have a religious background, biblical teachings say, 'knock, and the door will be opened to you; seek, and you shall find', and geologically, if you don't *seek*, you aren't going to *find*. You can look at all kinds of images and data to interpret geology, but you can never be certain of what you've found until you see the actual rocks in the field. Be optimistic like a prospector, and you'll find a lot of geology to pique your interest."

Liddy was intrigued with the rugged beauty of the Granite Mountains that contained some of the oldest rock outcrops in the west—over three billion years old. Prominent rounded gray hills, crossed by occasional streaks of black rock, protruded above a flat, bright snow-covered expanse of ground on either side of the highway. These were accentuated by the harsh shadows and pale yellowish glow of the low winter sun. The complex Precambrian history, responsible for a host of economic and exotic minerals in the Granite Mountains, was laid open like a book being read to a child as Sam's hypnotic voice caught and held Liddy's concentration. Sitting in the sunny front seat of the van, she could visualize the geological events and scenes, from the distant past, as they drove by Independence Rock and Devils Gate on the Sweetwater River. Her mind could, in response to Sam's tales of geology, almost see Archean volcanoes spreading out layers of material that became deeply buried in erosional debris. These were then rotated and turned upward, torn and heated, then broken again and injected with mineral-laden fluids.

Liddy's visualization of the complex geologic processes made her think of trying to bake a marble cake with ground nuts sprinkled thickly on top. But before the cake was done baking, it was pulled from the oven, folded over on itself and partially broken into pieces. Chocolate or some other flavored syrup was then poured over the mess, filling the gaps between pieces. It was then put back in the oven to bake further. A few more interruptions in the baking allowed pieces to be removed, and the remainder would suffer more pokes, folds, and breaks, before baking was complete. Not quite the same as real geology, but a reasonable analogy nevertheless.

Sam summarized the ages of the rock types that they now observed, representing the Precambrian history he had just finished describing. "The Granite Mountains appear as bare Precambrian hills, cropping out from a sea of Tertiary and younger sediments in central Wyoming. *Precambrian time* began with the earliest development of the earth around 4.7

billion years ago, and it lasted until about 570 million years ago. The outcrops here are primarily made up of granite, granitic gneisses, and a few areas of metasediments, some of which are as old as 3.3 billion years. Those rocks are sometimes referred to as *basement* rocks because they are the oldest and lowest rocks found within the earth's relatively stable crust beneath the continents."

Continuing his explanation, Sam elaborated, "*Granite gneisses* are coarsely-banded metamorphic rocks that were changed by intense heat and pressure and have compositions similar to granite. In this area, they also include scattered pieces of sedimentary and volcanic rock layers that have been only partially metamorphosed, such that their original characteristics may be interpreted. The basement rocks were intruded by granites a few hundreds of millions of years later. A few million years after that, northeast trending mafic dikes cut across the area. More subtle geological disturbances again altered this area about 1.65 and 1.5 billion years ago."

"How do geologists figure out the ages of rocks?" asked Liddy.

"The ages of the rocks and geological events are determined by measurements of radioactive decay of elements within minerals found in the rocks," explained Sam. "Whenever the rocks are heated or squeezed, causing melting or mineralogical changes related to pressure, their radioactive mineral clocks are reset to give a new date. It's a progressive field of study, as are most sciences. The ages that I've mentioned are taken from several studies that were done by various geologists. Geology is dynamic and rock ages, as well as other geologic interpretations, are always subject to change through more recent research, new ideas, and new methods of measurement."

Temporarily distracted from his driving and his lecture, Sam glanced over to see Liddy examining a geology text. She was contorting her mouth as she silently tried to pronounce some of the new and unfamiliar words she found there. At that moment, Sam made two decisions: first, he would pay more attention to the road; second, he would move Liddy from *cute* to *pretty*, and maybe even *beautiful* in his estimation of her attractiveness.

As they approached Muddy Gap, Sam lectured about Cenozoic tectonic events, some of which are graphically displayed at that location. "The Granite Mountains began to rise during a period of mountain building called the *Laramide Orogeny*, about sixty-five million years ago, with accompanying erosion exposing their core of Precambrian rocks during Paleocene time. The Granite Mountains again pushed up even further during the early Eocene, forming a major east-west trending fault-bounded mountain block about ninety miles long and thirty miles wide. Along the north side, the North Granite Mountains fault is interpreted to have shown upward displacement of about 5000 feet; and along the south side, the South Granite Mountains fault showed a rise of about 3000 feet. This uplift may have caused a pressure decrease in the lower crust sufficient to favor magma generation, resulting in middle to late Eocene volcanic activity."

As Liddy listened to Sam's discourse, the chapters of the book on Wyoming's geology unfolded, one geologic period after another: the mountains rising and falling, faulting, folding, and eroding; local volcanic eruptions and distant ones burying mountains, then leaving isolated reminders of their activity in partially exposed ash beds tucked away in gullies, after another cycle of erosion. *Geology came alive for Liddy today*! Her mental picture of almost three billion years of geologic time reminded her of lying on her back, watching the weather change over the Bighorn Mountains. As the clouds and thunderstorms would build up, shift, tumble, and then fade over the course of an afternoon, so too did the rocks move over the vast expanse of time in Liddy's vivid imagination.

"The movement of the rocks is essentially continuous," explained Sam. "It's just that the nature of our short-term human perspective makes it seem like they hardly move at all." A skilled geologist such as Sam could not only visualize those complex three-dimensional movements of the earth over the scope of time, measured in hundreds of millions of years, but he could convey that same sense of logical, almost poetic movement to his listeners. Never again would Liddy think of mountains as unchanging and everlasting! She knew that God had created it all, and that humans, no matter how hard they tried, would never fully comprehend it, although they would have fun attempting to unravel the mysteries.

Upon reaching Rawlins just before nine, the vans stopped at a fast food restaurant on the east edge of town for snacks and drinks and to use the restrooms. Sam would have preferred to stop at *Sally's Station & Convenience Store*, which they passed on the way to the fast food establishment, but Sally's restrooms could not handle such a large crowd. *Sally's* did have better coffee, but Sam would drink the more pale brew found close to the interstate today.

They were back on the road by nine-thirty, making note of the filled cracks in I-80 as they bumped over them five minutes later. Sam continued with a less extensive geologic commentary as they traveled west on the interstate. He discussed the Rawlins uplift, the Great Divide Basin, and the oil and gas fields near Creston Junction, Wamsutter, and Table Rock. They paused briefly at the rest area east of Point of Rocks and then stopped again, just after eleven o'clock, on the crest of the hill overlooking the eruption site.

Liddy began videotaping while the students took photographs. Sam gave a short explanatory lecture on what he already knew and on what the students should be looking for. He also admonished them, "Take detailed notes on your observations. Details on paper are always better than faded memories." That was one of his favorite pedagogic expressions that he related to field classes. After about five minutes, they boarded the vans and drove west down the hill on the eastbound lanes, avoiding equipment and crews working on both the westbound lanes and the frontage road to the north.

As they tumbled out of the vans, Sam assembled his students near the base of the new talus slope below the dike. He warned them to observe and examine, but to avoid climbing on the fresh debris that was still unstable and crumbling. Students worked in small groups to examine grain sizes and shapes, noting mineralogy, xenoliths, and any unusual structures. They also sketched and attempted to characterize the dike overall. Photocopies of the 7.5-minute topographic map of the area had been given to each student, preparatory to the field trip—they needed to locate themselves on the map with some degree of accuracy. Sam assisted the students and took his own notes, while collecting samples representative of as much variety in the dike as he could detect.

Liddy videotaped Sam and the students, including a few shots of the work crews to the north. It was now a beautiful and sunny thirty-five degree F day, devoid of any wind. But Sam had noted falling pressure on his office barometer before they had left Casper; he knew the nice weather would be short-lived. He had picked the right day for fieldwork—a winter storm was approaching the region, and tomorrow's weather would be dramatically different!

Sam and several students struggled up the snowy north-facing hill on the south side of the highway and took bearings on the dike. Their locational measurements were supplemented by Sam's old GPS unit, which had accompanied him on all of his field trips for the last seven years. They also noted one section of rock at the top of the hill that appeared to be *vesicular*—containing many small voids caused by gasses that had bubbled through the magma. Sam collected a sample of this rock and was convinced, beyond any doubt, that this dike was *indeed* of igneous origin, rather than a sand dike as he had first suggested. He would not verbally present this observation until after his students had worked to arrive at their own conclusions.

However, Sam's mind began moving in high gear, trying to figure out *why* a volcanic eruption had occurred here and what the future implications of this amazing event might be. Geologic awareness had never made Sam feel uneasy, but it did now! Was this a dangerous precedent for Wyoming geology? Could this happen *again*? And if so, *where*?

After an hour of investigation, everyone gathered at the vans to compare notes. The dike rock was grayish-brown, varying from soft with crumbly edges to slightly harder, with angular breaks. Matrix grain sizes ranged from one quarter of an inch down to silt size, with the mode of distribution about 1/16 to 1/32 inch. These grains appeared to be mostly angular. The students identified several mineral grains in this interstitial material that included phlogopite, olivine, minor ilmenite, and several unknowns. Xenolithic grains, up to several inches in diameter, included asphalt from the road, granite, sandstone, limestone, quartzite, and possibly peridotite. The presence of peridotite suggested a *deep* source for the magma.

The dike appeared to show some fine layering and

preferred orientation or zoning of mineral grains towards one edge of some blocks. The youngest exposed stratigraphic unit into which the dike had intruded was Quaternary alluvium, located in a draw on the north side of I-80. The Lewis Shale and Fox Hills Sandstone, upon which the interstate rested, were both of Cretaceous age and cut by the dike. The Cretaceous Lance Formation, overlying the Lewis and Fox Hills, was also sliced by the dike on the hilltop to the south of the highway.

Clearly, Sam's investigation had several advantages over the brief field visit conducted by Bill Burnhard: Sam was not under any time constraints; he had excellent weather; and he had the additional help of twenty-two extra sets of eyes, or twenty-three, if Liddy was included. Also, Sam had been able to research literature on the area before his visit, and he was not limited by any favorite hypothesis. In fact, when Sam went into the field, he always tried to clear his mind and let the field evidence determine his conclusions, even if his first ideas might turn out to be entirely wrong. *"Never second guess an outcrop until you've actually crawled over it!"* was another bit of geologic wisdom that he preached during field exercises.

The dike was vertical, with a strike of 167 degrees where it crossed I-80, curving another five degrees toward the east as one followed it south. Avoiding a hazardous route across the loose dike rock, Sam and a few of the students climbed up to a southerly hilltop vantage point. From there, they estimated that the dike was 380 to 480 feet wide, with scattered debris extending as much as 3000 feet or more on either side of the actual dike. Its thickness appeared to narrow drastically in the distance and then swell slightly, before being lost to sight beyond a hill to the south.

As his students grouped together to compare notes, Sam lectured, "You should form your own conclusions, then write them up and bring them to class for discussion next Tuesday and Wednesday. Your ideas *must* be supported by field observations. Supportive geologic concepts, from previous readings and lectures, need to be referred to appropriately to strengthen overall conclusions based on your field observations." Typical of most teachers, Sam often repeated directions and concepts to his students. He learned long ago that the *department of redundancy department* functioned well to infuse ideas into the brains of students.

Sam wrapped up the field exercise by summarizing observations made by his students. He suggested that a preliminary write-up be prepared during their drive eastward, while the details of their field notes were still fresh in their minds.

The entire group re-boarded the vans before one o'clock and motored east toward Rawlins. They stopped again along the almost vacant highway west of town to examine the filled cracks in the pavement. The cracks were actually in a section of fill material under the highway, on top of the Cretaceous Lewis Shale. The size of the cracks was more related to the instability of fine material used for highway fill than to the underlying geology. Only minor ground cracks, of about one inch maximum width, were observed extending outward across the Lewis Shale from beneath the highway fill. The orientation of the cracks was 358 degrees, almost due north. Sam, Liddy, and the students followed the cracks for one-quarter mile to the south between patches of snow cover and then another 1.4 miles to the north of the highway before losing them under snow that covered the Almond Formation in the Cretaceous Mesaverde Group. Sam and his students again took notes, and Liddy videotaped the activity. They finished their examination an hour and a half later and headed for the same fast food restaurant in Rawlins that they had stopped at previously.

This stopover lasted almost an hour, with a food and restroom break, followed by a gasoline fill up at *Sally's* where Sam finally got some *real* coffee with cream. During the return trip to CTC, the tired students asked few questions, and many slept. Liddy and Sam conversed with each other during most of the return trip, exchanging the explorative pleasantries of newfound friendship.

"Sam, thanks for allowing me to come along on your field trip. I think I got some good footage for a follow-up special to your interview the other day," stated Liddy.

"Glad your video efforts went well," answered Sam as he briefly glanced over at her. He needed to keep a watchful eye open for mule deer that seemed to materialize out of nothingness along roads and streams at dusk. "Did you find my lectures interesting enough? I didn't notice you reading your book."

"Oh yes, I really soaked in your lectures. I guess I never realized I had any interest in geology," she reflected as she shifted her position in the seat to look at him. "Or how much geology is in everything we see. How long have you been teaching?"

Looking first at the borrow ditches for deer, then at her, and allowing a warmhearted smile to creep across the corner of his mouth, he began, "I started teaching about three and a half years ago when a position opened up at the college. I decided pretty quickly that I liked teaching, and I've enjoyed it ever since. How about you and your television work?"

"Well, Sam," her eyes sparkled as she reflected, "I got my bachelor's degree in broadcast media engineering at Wyoming State University. Then I went to a technical school for six months in broadcast computer systems, followed up by another six months of television technology in Huntsville, Alabama."

A warm feeling came over her, and actually surprised her, when she realized that Sam was paying close attention to what she said. "When I finished training, I was hired right away as an engineer for a small local station near Huntsville. But the hot, humid climate with its awful noisy bugs and lack of open spaces never really appealed to me. I missed the intense change of seasons of the north. There just isn't anything that can invigorate the body and soul like a good winter storm. I guess I'm just a *northern girl* at heart!"

"I know exactly what you mean," interjected Sam. "Judging from my office barometer this morning and the last weather report I heard, I think tomorrow should be real invigorating. Were the people down there good to work with?"

"Oh yeah…the people were friendly enough, but I missed my prairies and mountains and the dry western air. I always felt smothered by the heat and humidity. And on top of that, they have bugs down there that you *would not* believe! I *hate* bugs!"

"So how did you end up in Casper?"

"Just about a year later, the job came up at KWYN, back near my home country, and I jumped at the chance. I've worked for the station ever since. What'd you do before teaching?"

"I worked as a geological consultant out of Casper," he replied thoughtfully, keeping his eyes on the road as it crossed a small stream with several deer moving nearby.

"Did you work or go to school in Casper before you started consulting?" she asked, following his gaze as the deer were suddenly passed by.

Entering a long straight stretch of highway, Sam accorded greater attention to her. "No, I went to college for two years in Dickinson, North Dakota. I then spent five years at the South Dakota School of Mines in Rapid City, where I got my bachelor's degree in geology and my master's in Precambrian and economic geology. My first job was in Butte, Montana where I worked in metals exploration and mining for two years, followed by another year near Kellogg, Idaho, doing similar work."

"Look at the fox!" he interrupted himself, pointing as a small red bushy-tailed canine ran across the road a hundred feet in front of the van. "I usually see more coyotes than foxes until I get close to Casper Mountain," he remarked.

"I like watching them," added Liddy. " I've seen one near my house northwest of town several times. What brought you to Casper from Idaho?" she queried, leaning slightly in his direction.

As he quickly glanced towards her, he continued, "I got an offer from a Canadian company, working out of Casper in diamond exploration. It sounded interesting, so I ended up working for them for two years in parts of Wyoming, Colorado, Montana, and western Canada. They even sent me on an educational trip that toured diamond mines in South Africa and Western Australia. I never was in any one place very long during that period. Unfortunately, the company bureaucracy started to get too overbearing for my tastes, so I decided to try consulting on my own."

Although he did not elaborate on any of his personal biases or his independent streak, Liddy would learn of these later. Her chat with him now had already given her an inkling of them. Sam was a throwback from an earlier generation, and he was typical of many people who grew up in the sparsely populated areas of Wyoming, Nebraska, the Dakotas, and other western states. He was a product of his western culture; maybe even classified as a *hick* in some circles. In fact, he had been called a hick on a number of occasions, but it never bothered him. Sam believed in honest hard work, and he would not bow down to the pecking orders that seemed so important to others in both business and government bureaucracies. He had just never developed the ability to form with his mouth those little round "Os", such as seen in comic strips, that were necessary to subjugate one's self to *higher level* management personnel. If his honest efforts were not sufficient for success in an organization, he wanted no part of it, hence his eventual migration into self-employment and consulting.

The winter sun set an hour before they reached Casper. As they drove, Liddy gazed backwards toward the west to watch the brilliant colors fade into darkness. The brightly illuminated crescent moon was seen floating in sharp profile above the horizon, fighting the growing brightness of Venus for dominance in the night sky. Other stars soon made their appearance, and then constellations that Liddy recognized. The stars seemed to have new meaning for her as she thought of the vastness of geologic time. Liddy felt at peace and wanted to learn much more about geology, and about Sam.

After a long period of silence, Liddy probed Sam further, "Was consulting and being your own boss fun?"

"You bet it was," Sam continued. "But the economics weren't as good as I'd hoped. I bought a home on the south side of Casper over near the college and consulted from there. My first year was very successful, but during the second year things took a bit of a downturn, so I started writing articles for several magazines. I lucked out and sold some to a couple of popular prospecting periodicals. Since then, I've sold several articles and have written a couple of small books on various aspects of prospecting and geology. I was almost making enough money from writing and my dwindling consulting to get by, but not quite. Then this teaching job came along and really seemed to fit the bill. So here I am."

"You mentioned Dickinson. That's not a very big place. How'd you pick that as a place to start college?" asked Liddy, adding, "I once went to a ranch camp west of there when I was in junior high. I was horse crazy then. And I still am."

"That's easy," replied Sam, watching the road and resting his arms on the steering wheel. "I grew up there." Glancing at Liddy in the transient brightness from the headlights of the few oncoming vehicles, he elaborated, "My father ran a feed store in Dickinson, then later a hardware store. He also sold insurance. Mom worked part-time with Dad's business, raised me and my brother and sister, and kept track of family finances. We spent Dad's days off camping and hiking in and around Teddy Roosevelt's old stomping grounds of the North Dakota badlands. We even managed occasional trips farther west to the Bighorn and Beartooth Mountains in Wyoming and Montana."

Thoughtfully, he slowly added, "I went horseback riding once, but don't remember much about it. I'd need a bunch of instruction before I'd get on a horse again."

Sam was silent for a moment as he thought about the home where he grew up. He treasured the wide-open spaces, watching the towering thunderstorms of summer, and venturing outside for brief periods to endure the fierce winter blizzards, like the ones that Theodore Roosevelt had written about during the 1880s. The storms would swoop down out of Canada and across the prairie, burying everything in picturesque drifts of sculpted snow. He could still visualize the stark white prairie and distant buttes accentuated by sub-zero temperatures as the storms passed, leaving a transparent veil of sparkling ice crystals floating in the air in the pale orange glow of a setting winter sun.

Sam continued, "I've always been obsessed with the outdoors. I sometimes write poetry about it, although my poetic efforts aren't generally known. Then after a pause, he queried, "So where did you grow up, Liddy?"

"I think we share some common ground in our appreciation of the outdoors, Sam," offered Liddy. "I was raised in Buffalo."

"Wyoming?" asked Sam.

"Of course! Is there really any other Buffalo of any importance?" she laughed. "I was born there, and my parents still live there. I was an only child, so I grew up in a pretty quiet household. You talk about liking the outdoors! My fondest memories are of growing up at the base of the Bighorns where my parents and I did almost everything outside. We hunted, fished, hiked, camped, cross-country skied, and rode horseback, and a few other things besides."

When Liddy got excited about something, she would

laugh. She was laughing lightly now. And when she talked of things she loved, her smile seemed to those around her to be as wonderful as the smell of sweet clover in springtime or as pleasant as a soft chair by a welcoming fire. "I still look forward to going up near Buffalo to watch the summer storms build up over the mountains. When I was small, I thought the storms rolled out across the Powder River Basin, flashing and rumbling, because they had gotten too top heavy to stay on the mountains and each flash was a piece of cloud banging into another. Buffalo and the Bighorns are my real home! Do you get home to visit your parents very often?"

"Uh...no," responded Sam with hesitation and a look of longing and sadness. "My parents died in a car wreck just after I came to Casper...killed by a drunk driver."

"Oh, I'm so sorry!" offered Liddy sympathetically. She detected dampness in his eyes in the dim light, and she knew that he must have loved them dearly. She said nothing more until Sam broke the silence several minutes later.

"I always enjoyed going home when I could, Liddy. Some of life's changes just take a lot of getting used to." Then, sensing Liddy's empathy, he gave her a warm look and told her, "Thanks for understanding. I haven't thought about it for a while, and the memory just hit me a little hard. My brother and sister are both married now and are busy raising their own families. Ben is in California, and Mary is in upper Michigan. I don't see them too often, but I call or write to them every few weeks." He smiled again at Liddy, "Thanks for coming along on the field trip."

It had been a long drive of almost 400 miles by the time they returned to Casper, and Sam was ready to get out of the van for a stretch. However, the time for him had actually passed rather quickly, more so than on other similar trips. His conversation with Liddy had seemed to shorten the drive and he felt that, with her company, he could have driven the same distance again.

The vans pulled into the CTC parking lot in the early evening. Heavy clouds were beginning to drift in from the northeast on a rising wind, and a moist hint of snow drifted through the night air. The temperature had dropped noticeably since they left Rawlins. Sam and Brent would park the vans in a fenced lot, three blocks away, after all of the other students had exited. Liddy volunteered to follow and give them a ride back to the Geoscience Building, where Brent's personal vehicle was parked.

The field trip had ended too soon, and Liddy was reluctant to let go of the most remarkable day she had spent in a long time. Brent was in a hurry and agreed to the offer of a ride. Normally, Sam would have preferred to walk, but he was now savoring Liddy's company, so he quickly accepted her offer. For him, the day had been very satisfying, but way too short. They returned to the main parking lot to let Brent out. Determined to get to know Liddy better, Sam then invited her to join him for a late supper at his house.

"It won't be anything fancy," Sam told her. "I have some fixings for a quick Mexican meal, including some home-made tortillas. You could tell me how your final videotape will be compiled."

"Don't go to any trouble on my account," said Liddy, thinking that maybe she had been too forward in asking Sam about himself.

"No trouble at all," replied Sam. "I'd enjoy the company."

"Thank you," she smiled. "I'd love to come over!"

They spent a quiet evening visiting, while relishing Sam's simple meal, complemented by homemade apple pie that he had purchased at a bake sale.

"What caused the dike to erupt?" asked Liddy, turning the conversation to her newfound interest in geology. "Do you think it's volcanic?"

"Yes," answered Sam. "I'm sure it's volcanic. But we won't have any idea as to why it erupted when and where it did without a lot of research and evaluation; that is *if* we ever can figure out the *why*. There's always a reason for geologic events, but often the complexity of geology only provides descriptions and guesses rather than definite answers. I'll be researching it, and I'll let you know what I find. But don't look for any *quick* answers!"

Around nine-thirty, Liddy excused herself to head for home. Her weekend shifts began at five in the morning, and this Sunday would be no different. Her shift would rotate again in March to give her Saturdays and Sundays off, but for now,

Mondays and Tuesdays were her free days.

As she was leaving, Sam suggested, "Perhaps we could get together again sometime...that is, *before* I come up with some geologic answers?" He was feeling a little awkward. This newfound friendship was like a door just beginning to open, shining a warm light through a small crack and beckoning him to enter somewhere he had never been before. He didn't want to seem pushy, but he was loath to let that door close without ever knowing what might lie beyond.

Liddy responded warmly, "Perhaps we can."

The predicted snow was beginning to fall in earnest as she drove away. Sam's mind was soothed with a coating of thoughts from the enjoyable evening he had just spent. However, his deeper thoughts churned over rock analyses and the geologic implications of his recent discoveries.

CHAPTER 3

Analyses

▼

As for the earth, out of it comes food; but below, it is turned up as by
fire. Its stones are the place of sapphires, and its rocks contain
nuggets of gold. - Job 28:5-6

Bill Burnhard began his write-up on Friday morning after first
relating to his co-workers the harshness of the field conditions,
the spectacular size of the intrusion, and the fact that at least one
eighteen-wheeler had been caught in it. The wandering around
in-person explanations and telephone descriptions to more
distant associates took over an hour and a half, making him
slightly late for morning break. He was *busy*, and he tried to
make sure that everyone knew it. His brief write-up took most
of the day. Gordon Aughey then had it turned into a press
release that was e-mailed to all newspapers and broadcast media
in the state. The e-mail was late getting out, but would probably
make the Sunday papers. These electronic press releases were a
lot faster than the paper copies that used to get mailed out,
sometimes taking a week to reach their destinations.

Bill subscribed to Sam's initial *sand dike* hypothesis that
Bill had, he thought, verified by his field inspection. The soft
sandy chunks that he had examined seemed to fit with that
premise. He believed that the material's present resistance to
collapse, where the dike still stood up above its rubble, was a

transitory thing that would disappear with a small amount of weathering. Bill should have consulted with the highway department; they knew that it really was *rock*, although relatively soft rock, as they were in the process of trying to excavate parts of it. Bill believed that the earthquake and fractures near Rawlins were probably related to regional stress relief. With Debby's assistance, he had developed colorful electronic maps to accompany his report and to verify that assertion. Debby had taken good digital photographs that were included, along with her by-line, for the press release. Gordon hoped that the public exposure would have a positive influence on the legislative session. He needed to continue with his budget presentations next Thursday; it would be the last of his scheduled appearances.

⇌

On Sunday and Monday, a major storm dumped more than ten inches of snow on eastern and central Wyoming, accompanied by winds of thirty to forty miles per hour. That weather system shut down highways across much of the area as well as in surrounding states. All government offices, roads, and schools, including Casper Technical College and Wyoming State University, were closed on Monday, as was the Wyoming state legislative session. On Monday afternoon, the storm moved out rapidly to the northeast. It was followed by relative calm and by temperatures plummeting to near zero. Major highways began opening Monday night, but many secondary roads would not be passable until Wednesday. Those faculty members of the WSU Department of Geophysics and Geology, who had been in Atlanta, were not able to return home until Tuesday afternoon, having spent a day and a half stuck in the Denver airport terminal.

On Sunday afternoon, Surya and several other geology graduate students cross-country skied through the snow-blocked streets of Laramie. They took photographs of the snowdrifts and visited each other's apartments, eating snacks and sipping hot drinks at each stop. An occasional nip of brandy or tot of rum contributed to a boisterous atmosphere within the wandering party. Hard-working graduate students often have abundant energy to vent at the slightest opportunity, such as that provided by the blizzard.

Although Wyoming State University was officially closed on Monday, Surya found that the emptiness of the labs and classrooms provided him with an excellent opportunity to work undisturbed. He began in earnest to combine the recent seismic data in his computer program, while making repeated adjustments in order to bring out as much detail as possible. His analyses allowed him to observe the data as a three-dimensional display progressing over time. However, he was not entirely happy with the results. Some of it made sense, but other parts did not fit with his expectations for an interpretation. He had read the WOMG press release about the sand dike and its probable origin in over-pressured Cretaceous sedimentary rocks. *Over-pressured* is a term used in drilling to indicate that down-hole pressures are excessively greater than those normally expected for a given depth.

Surya was not familiar with the WOMG or its personnel, and he would have to talk to his advisor, Chris Felsen, about the poor match he had achieved. He was enthusiastic about his work, but was still uncertain as to his own abilities. After all, who was he, a *mere student*, to challenge a professional's interpretation?

Surya's analysis showed that the quake near Point of Rocks began as a weak disturbance, within the earth's mantle, at a depth of about seventy-eight miles, almost twenty-four hours before the dike broke the surface. This initial disturbance, with a magnitude of less than 2.5, progressed upward from north to south in a curve. The curve was gentle in the lower 15.5 miles, then almost vertical for the upper part. The origin was some thirty-five miles north of where the dike breached the surface. At a depth of about forty-five miles, earth tremors greater than a magnitude 3.0 began, and the focus of the tremors moved ever more rapidly upward. Then at a depth of 8.3 miles, the disturbance suddenly shot upward as brittle rock cracked, and the 5.4 magnitude earthquake sent its shock waves outward in all directions. The narrow curved trace, as enhanced by seismic reflections from the later quakes, appeared to be loaded with material. If it was filled, then the dike was *not* a sand dike.

Contrary to Mr. Burnhard's assertion, it was almost certainly filled with some igneous material. The thinness of the dike and the linear positions of his partial seismic array prevented the use of P-wave velocities to determine the composition of the dike material.

Two types of seismic waves are *compressional* waves (P-waves) and *shear* waves (S-waves). Sudden movements of earth materials, such as with the slippage of rocks along a fault, generate these waves within the earth. P-waves propagate as volume changes or compression-decompression sequences; the particles within the rock move back and forth in the direction of wave propagation. P-waves may be thought of as similar to sound waves moving through air. On the other hand, S-waves move as particles within the rock vibrate back and forth, perpendicular to the direction of propagation. The S-waves are similar to waves propagated in a rope under tension. Such a rope, when struck, displays ripples moving along its length from the point of disturbance. P-waves are faster than S-waves, and both reflect off the boundaries between different densities of materials, with a small part of each wave penetrating each boundary. This is similar to the reflection of light as it encounters a piece of glass, with some reflected, and some passing on through. P-waves can transmit through liquids, but S-waves cannot, since fluids elastically resist, then recover from, compressional squeezing, but give no resistance to shearing.

P-waves travel at about 3.7 miles per second in granitic igneous rocks, about 4.35 miles per second in mafic igneous rocks such as gabbro, and 4.97 miles per second in ultramafic rocks such as peridotite or dunite. The velocities become faster as the rock densities increase. These velocity changes identify the chemical and lithologic boundary between the earth's crust, which is made up of mostly granitic rocks beneath continents, and the underlying mantle, which is made up of denser ultramafic rocks. The boundary between the crust and the mantle is called the *Mohorvicic discontinuity* (MOHO). It was named after the Yugoslavian seismologist who discovered it in 1909. Oceanic crust, consisting mostly of basalt and gabbro, also contrasts sharply with the underlying mantle.

The second quake, occurring near Rawlins, also had a

curved but more narrow trace, beginning at a twenty-five mile depth within the earth's crust, rather than in the mantle, and 6.2 miles to the north of its surface expression. Reflections from the trace of the Rawlins quake showed no fill material within its fracture. The third quake was detected just after the Rawlins quake and was the most shallow of the three. It began at a depth of 3.1 miles within the Yellowstone caldera, near West Thumb in northwestern Wyoming, and appeared as a horizontal fracture, radiating outward no more than two miles in an irregular plane. Surya rechecked his data and computer solutions, but he came up with the same results each time. He would talk to Chris later to be sure of what his interpretations were telling him.

Surya had not yet heard Sam Westone's Thursday morning television interview on either the local or national news. Surya did not watch television unless it was incidental to a social gathering, such as when visiting with friends. On Friday, the two southeast Wyoming newspapers had only mentioned the quakes and the I-80 problems, but had not elaborated on any possible explanations by someone from Casper. They were saving that opportunity for their local experts. The *Cheyenne Gazette* was aware of the WOMG's funding concerns with the legislature. Although the agency was small, its disappearance from the local economy could have a noticeably negative impact. The WOMG could use any help it could get, and the *Cheyenne Gazette* would supply that help if it could. Fifty miles to the west, the *Laramie Post* was saving its space for their favored institution, Wyoming State University and its Department of Geophysics and Geology.

⇌

Sam awoke Sunday morning to near blizzard conditions. After a bite of breakfast and a cup of coffee, he headed into his basement radio shack and turned on his equipment. Sam, *call sign* KC7QE, was an amateur radio operator, often referred to as a "*ham.*" He became licensed when he was in high school and had maintained his interest through the years. He had changed callsigns a few times as he upgraded his license and again when he moved from the *zero* call area of the Dakotas to the *seven* call area that included Idaho and Wyoming. It was an especially good wintertime hobby for him. Sam would at times indulge himself intensely in radio operating, and then he would creep through periods of dormancy where he might just visit (rag chew) with friends on regular schedules. Ham radio activities provided Sam with a variety of social outlets ranging from potlucks, picnics, and coffee shop gatherings to club meetings, emergency communications exercises, and conventions.

This morning, Sam particularly wanted to check into a local Sunday morning informal *net* in order to learn of regional weather conditions. Nets are organized *on-the-air* meetings between amateur stations at specific times and frequencies. Sam's favorite, the *Wyoming Cowboy Net*, met Monday through Friday at 0045 UTC, or *Universal Coordinated Time*, also known as *Greenwich Mean Time*, or GMT, on or near 3.923 MHz. The net served as a meeting place for hams around Wyoming. It also supported emergency communications when needed, and was a source of information on local weather conditions and other happenings. This morning at seven-thirty, Sam visited with several friends around the state on 3.850 MHz. He learned that light snow had fallen in Cody; Sheridan had three inches with light snow now falling; and Laramie and Torrington both had near blizzard conditions similar to Casper. Sam chatted, in his turn, about his field trip and about recent poor DX (*long distance*) radio propagation. His friends mentioned happenings in their jobs and talked about some of the new ham radio equipment being advertised. Sam signed off at eight o'clock and then headed for an early church service where he was scheduled to help as an usher.

Visibility was poor as Sam slowly maneuvered his small four-wheel drive pickup truck through drifts that were already developing as much as a foot and a half deep. He planned to pick up a few groceries after church and then spend the afternoon writing up his field notes and summarizing his observations. He would also compile a list of questions for his students and detail some lecture points for those who missed the fieldtrip. Sam was one of only a handful of people who attended church this morning because of the blizzard. After the service he visited with several members of the congregation and was congratulated on his recent television appearance on KWYN. He wondered how Liddy was coping with the storm. When Sam left the church, he found the streets mostly empty of traffic. The deep drifts made his drive to the grocery store and then to his house difficult, even in four-wheel drive.

After a quick lunch, Sam eagerly went to work on his geology project. His analysis of his field notes brought him to the conclusion that the dike blocking the Interstate *was in fact* made up of mantle-derived material. Determining its exact classification as *lamproite, kimberlite*, or other rock type would require some careful mineralogical and chemical investigations. Kimberlitic-appearing diatremes of Eocene or Oligocene age, about thirty to forty million years old, were found several years earlier, sixty-five miles southwest of the Leucite Hills near Cedar Mountain. They had been intensely studied since the mid-1990s, but no resolution had yet been arrived at as to how they should be classified. Those particular rocks carried a few diamonds, although the quantities found so far were not sufficient for commercial mining. Geological mysteries are not always easy to unravel. If one becomes too certain of a theoretical conclusion, some other person will invariably demonstrate the error.

Sam had his own microscope and other laboratory equipment set up in his basement from the time when he was actively consulting. His house also contained a reasonably inclusive library that covered most aspects of geology as well as several other subjects that interested him. However, many of his geology references had migrated to his CTC office after becoming useful for one class study or another.

As Sam examined his collection of samples, he noted the presence of vesicular scoria in the rock from the southern part of the I-80 dike. He also noticed some small peridotite nodules with pyrope garnets, along with tiny yellow spinels. Peridotite and pyrope garnets could only have originated within the earth's mantle. Pyrope garnets were not known to exist in the Leucite Hills, but yellowish-orange ones, accompanied by chromian diopside, were abundant near Cedar Mountain. Sam's pyropes were a deep purple color and no chromian diopside was observed in any of his samples. Sam picked out abundant olivine crystals that also indicated a source from within the mantle. Many of these were a beautiful clear pale green, up to one half inch in length. These were *gem quality* olivine, known also as *peridot*. Sam now realized that the dike had obvious economic potential!

When almost finished examining his samples, Sam found an octahedral, eight-sided bipyramidal crystal nearly one-quarter of an inch in diameter. Detailed examination indicated a tiny hint of a greenish inclusion near the edge of the otherwise clear bluish-white crystal. The crystal faces showed tiny triangular patterns under his microscope. Sam became excited; the triangular patterns known as trigons were common on *diamonds*. However, triangular patterns could also be found on other mineral crystals.

Sam tested the crystal's specific gravity and found it to be 3.52, rechecking it twice to be sure. He also tested it with a black light to see if it fluoresced—it fluoresced a moderate white. Sam carefully cleaned the crystal with a degreaser solution, then rinsed it with alcohol and placed it in a shallow dish with distilled water. The surface of the water curved upward on the glass at the edge of the dish, but curved downward around the edge of the cleaned crystal—the crystal was non-wetting. Sam then took a piece of corundum from his collection. Holding a flat surface of the corundum up in one hand, he carefully pressed one point of the octahedral crystal on the flat corundum surface. Drawing his crystal across the flat surface, the corundum, with a Moh's hardness of *nine*, was easily scratched by Sam's octahedron. Diamond has a hardness of *ten* on Moh's hardness scale. Sam's crystal was in all likelihood a *diamond*!

Diamonds! *Diamonds and peridot*! The dike definitely had a mantle origin, and it certainly could prove to be financially valuable. *What a discovery*! The only thing that really bothered him now was the fact that he needed to classify the dike host rock. If he could classify something, he could properly define it and put it in a descriptive box for others to mentally pick up and handle. But the rock was defying any immediate classification without the benefit of sophisticated chemical analyses. It occurred near a lamproite field, but the abundance of carbon dioxide suggested that it was more closely related to kimberlite. The cold temperature of the dike when emplaced also conformed to theories of kimberlitic volcanism. However, olivine is not generally present in kimberlite; it is usually replaced by serpentine. The dike rock-type would have to remain *unknown* for the moment.

Other types of crystals have often been mistaken for diamonds, but Sam was convinced that this was a diamond. However, before he spoke too loudly about it, he wanted someone else or some other technique to confirm his conclusion. The easiest and best test would involve an x-ray diffraction pattern. Around the turn of the century, the WOMG in Cheyenne used to have x-ray diffraction capability in their lab, but now they didn't even have a lab. However, the WSU Department of Geophysics and Geology in Laramie did have the x-ray equipment, and he might be able to convince someone there to run the analysis for him. He would call and make arrangements to visit the department in person; he did not want to send his crystal through the mail to someone he had never met.

Sam also did not want to start a *diamond rush* in the middle of winter, particularly along the interstate. The subtleties and politics of mining claims had stayed with him since his consulting days. He had scheduled a few of his classes to cover mining claims and mineral law a bit later in the spring. Perhaps that might provide an opportunity for education and maybe even for some economic gain, if he and the students were to stake a few claims when the weather mellowed out. But for now, he would not mention the diamond discovery to his class.

Sam looked at his notes describing the cracks in I-80 near Rawlins. He also checked references that showed previously mapped local geologic structures. It appeared that the small open fractures, traced by him and his students, were probably related to the reactivation of a Laramide-age fault along the west flank of the Rawlins uplift. The *Laramide Orogeny* was a period of mountain building in the Rocky Mountains that took place about sixty-five million years ago. That age is rather non-specific, since the actual mountain building was spread out over a period of several million years, beginning in the Late Cretaceous Period, and lasting at least until the end of the Paleocene Epoch, about fifty-three million years ago. Some geologists extend the term into the Eocene Epoch that began about thirty-eight million years ago. Most mountain ranges in Wyoming are of Laramide age, with several notable exceptions such as the Tetons.

Whatever the exact definition, the fault noted was of that general age and had just recently shown renewed activity along its length. *Faults* are planes of weakness or fractures that have experienced movement between the rocks on either side of the fault. If stresses build up within the earth adjacent to a fault, slippage of rocks along the fault will occur to relieve that stress. Re-activation of old faults is not uncommon. The unusually large cracks in the highway appeared to be caused by a low quality fill material that contained abundant clays and was used in the construction of I-80 at that location. The clays, in effect, amplified the small movements, creating large cracks. It had been a construction error, but one of little significance until the earthquake.

$$\leftrightharpoons$$

Liddy's shift began early that Sunday morning and her old sport-utility vehicle (SUV) had no trouble traveling through the deepening snow. But as the morning progressed, KWYN received several reports of closed roads. By noon the afternoon/evening shift personnel had all called in, either stuck somewhere, or to request that they be allowed to stay home because of travel difficulties. Liddy and two other co-workers, who were already at the station, would have to carry the workload for the duration of the storm. The forceful winds had piled snow into drifts over two feet deep and caused limited visibility for travelers. At least the station had a lounge with food, hot drinks, and two sofas that might allow for some periods of rest for Liddy and the others.

During the blizzard, KWYN's news coverage included public service announcements provided by the Wyoming Highway Department and local law enforcement and emergency management groups. Sunday morning's scheduled programming was mostly pre-taped or supplied from other sources, via satellite link. Liddy and one other technician had gotten the station up and running by six o'clock, with Liddy filling in on periodic news and weather summaries throughout the morning. Eric Larson arrived by mid-morning and asked Liddy to do the noon news broadcast. As it turned out, Liddy would actually have to fill in until two in the afternoon on the following day, when the regularly scheduled personnel would finally be able to return to work.

Liddy's first newscast was, for the most part, a prepared national summary that she presented with no additional commentary. As directed by Eric Larson, she eliminated comments and innuendos that were obviously opinions expressed by the news source. Eric was sensitive to the fact that many of the long-established national television networks continued to lose viewers to other sources of news because of consistently *left-leaning* political biases held by station owners, managers, and other personnel. In a subtle way, *conservative* social and political views were regularly shunned or distorted by the mainstream media. Eric required that *his* station give *equal* treatment to both political sides of issues; he refused to keep his listeners in the dark just to serve the gods of various *left-wing agendas* and *political correctness*.

As the station's owner/manager, Eric demanded that his staff report news objectively, that sources be checked for accuracy, and that *editorial commentary* be identified as such rather than passed off as *news*. His strict reporting standards had been tough to stick to at first when a local member of his preferred political party got caught in an impropriety and lost an election. However, truth has a way of transcending corruption, and his broadcasting efforts gathered more viewers and listeners than any other television or radio station in Wyoming. In fact, he was in the process of negotiating a satellite-based uplink that would make KWYN available nationwide.

During Liddy's national news summary, she reported that several formerly prominent U.S. Senators were being indicted on charges of conspiracy, called "treason" by some, for selling top-secret technology to several totalitarian governments known to oppose United States policies. The indictments were accentuated by the loss of several U.S. undercover agents and new revelations about a computer espionage network. Following the national update, Liddy read notes of local news interest along with the current weather summary and storm warnings.

For the noon news broadcast, Eric requested that Liddy include a few shots of Sam Westone and his CTC students examining the blockage of I-80, with the promise of a more complete report later in the week. The local storm was the story of the day, coupled with the current Wyoming Legislative budget session, and only a brief repeat of some of the national news. KWYN had received the written information release from the WOMG concerning the blockage of I-80, but did not air it immediately. It conformed to initial projections already made by Sam Westone, but according to Liddy, evidence obtained on the field trip with Sam indicated a volcanic origin for the I-80 blockage. A press release with erroneous information could embarrass the WOMG. Even if it might lead to interesting scientific conflict in the news, Eric decided to hold it until they had a final summary compiled from Sam's recent field examination results. It is easier to *not* state a conclusion on the air than to retract it later. Eric would check with the WOMG before airing their press release.

While coordinating pre-programmed material that afternoon, Liddy found time to begin compiling a half hour special of her field trip with Sam Westone and his students. Since Eric Larson couldn't get home, he assisted her and became quite intrigued with the story. The feature would focus on Sam and his CTC students learning geology and on their conclusions concerning the cause of the new dike. Liddy had some good footage with Sam's discussions of geology and field techniques, but she would have to visit with Sam and his classes in order to complete the program. Eric hoped that she could finish the project early this week. If she worked on her normal days off, he would allow her to take compensatory time the following weekend. He ordered Liddy to call Sam and make arrangements as soon as possible.

Late that afternoon, Sam answered his phone and was pleasantly surprised to hear Liddy's voice. "Hello, Liddy! I just finished work and was trying to make contact with a group of ham operators on Christmas Island, northwest of Australia."

"I didn't know you were a ham!" she exclaimed. "I have a

license too, but I've never been very active. My callsign is N7GED, but I haven't used it since I moved back to Casper. I guess I didn't see your antennas yesterday in the dark."

"Well, I like to chase DX. Station VK9XCZ is strong, but there's a pretty good pile-up on him. I'm running QRP with about two watts on voice peaks. I've been moderately active off and on since I was in high school…it's a good way to relax and keep in touch with friends."

"Yes, I suppose so. I should get back into it more." Liddy paused, then continued, "To change the subject Sam…would it be possible for me to videotape some conclusions from you and your students, concerning the I-80 dike eruption? I need to complete KWYN's video story."

"Sure, Liddy. That'd be no problem. I'd be glad to help," answered Sam.

There's more to it," she added. "We received a WOMG press release, but my boss was hesitant to air it until we checked with your conclusions. Their statements may be in error, and if so, we don't want to broadcast something that might cause them embarrassment." Liddy then read to him the WOMG news release they had received.

"Well," said Sam, "The WOMG will be shown to be wrong in their conclusions. The more spectacular possibility that the national news emphasized from my first interview appears to be correct. I'd rather not address the WOMG news release, but would prefer to ignore it and just stick to the facts that we've discovered. I think it can be presented as a learning exercise, rather than as an attack on their conclusions, however erroneous they may be."

"That would be great, Sam. Thanks," sighed Liddy. "I agree with your approach. You can preview the tape that I've compiled so far to make sure it portrays the information in the way you want. We'll just splice in footage of you and your classes, if that's okay? Is there a chance we could do it early this coming week?"

"The word is out that CTC classes will be cancelled on Monday," answered Sam. "The storm is projected to move out Monday afternoon, so if it's convenient, you could bring your camera and spend Tuesday accompanying me to my classes."

"Thanks a heap, Sam. Are you sure that won't be too

much trouble?" she asked.

"No trouble, Liddy...besides, that will give me a chance to demonstrate how geologic ideas can change as new data is acquired, and how my initial hypothesis was replaced by one that fits the new data."

"Thanks again, Sam. How about letting me buy you lunch, then after your last class you can review the final tape as I compile it?"

"I'll take you up on the whole deal for Tuesday," answered Sam quickly, "*if* you'll allow me to fix you a *real* dinner at my house after we finish with the video editing."

"That's a rather generous offer. How could I refuse?" she enthused. "Just don't put yourself out if you're too busy."

"Oh, no problem, Liddy," replied Sam. "I'll look for you Tuesday morning in my office, sometime before eight."

"I'll be there. I hope you're enjoying the snow," said Liddy, smiling as she hung up the phone. *What an assignment*, she mused. A good-looking guy who's not only interesting, but polite as well! I wonder if he's that way all the time, or if I just met him on a good day?

Liddy wasn't actively looking to build a meaningful relationship or to get tied down to anyone. She enjoyed her independence and was happy with her life the way it now stood. She had a satisfying job and several good friends. Not many women were certified TV broadcast engineers, and she was moving up into reporting and editing as well. That could lead to even better jobs! She didn't really want to change the direction her life was going.

However, it wouldn't hurt to check him out. *No harm in that*, she thought. *Sam...Sam Westone*...he just seemed to have something that attracted her. It was subtle, and it didn't have anything to do with his appearance. He was just a nice guy to be around. *Why am I even thinking like this*? It's probably just a passing fancy that will most likely drift away on the Wyoming wind. Liddy shut the door on her thoughts and returned to work.

⇆

On Tuesday morning, Liddy arrived at CTC well before

eight o'clock. She looked forward to spending the day with Sam and was glad to be out and about after her long confinement at the station. As Liddy approached Sam's office, her nostrils detected the pleasant and stimulating aroma of freshly ground coffee, flowing out through his half-open door. His "Good to see you!" was as warm as the cup of rich brew he handed her. They immediately talked of their experiences during the blizzard. Liddy had endured a wearisome shift, accentuated by her attempt to sleep on an unforgiving lumpy couch at the station.

"I prefer being trapped at home during a storm," related Liddy. "But at least I didn't have to worry about my kids. They were cared for by my next door neighbor."

Sam, taken aback by her mention of *kids*, hesitatingly replied, "Oh, you have children? I didn't know you'd been married."

Liddy paused in thought, realizing her poor choice of the word *kids*. "Oh, no, Sam! I've never been married, but I do have *dependants*. I have a dog and a horse. Grieg and Topo are their names. My neighbor Camile Brown boards my horse for me and she always helps out when I'm gone."

Sam's relief showed in his relaxing expression as he replied, "Animals really do become a part of the family. Remind me to tell you about a four-legged *brother* I once had. He then described his activities during the blizzard. Sam had been lucky. He had returned home just as the storm was causing roads to become seriously blocked and had spent his time writing and intermittently playing on his ham radio. He had managed to break through a gap in the pile-up of amateur radio stations calling and worked VK9XCZ. Sam thought it unfortunate that Liddy had to be trapped at the television station during the storm.

Returning to the main purpose of her visit to Sam's office, Liddy began to take notes as he explained most of what he had found out about the eruption and the mantle origin of the extruded material. He wanted to tell her about the possibility of diamonds and that he was convinced that he had found one. But he had only met her a few days before. He liked her but trust in a relationship is built up slowly. In the course of their conversations, she had seemed to express the same basic values of honesty and morality upon which he attempted to build his own life, with the underlying support of his faith in God. Looked at objectively, Sam was a religious man, and although far from perfect, he tried to live his life with constant consideration for others.

Sam was not one to rush into relationships at the drop of a hat, but deep down inside, he felt that Liddy was a very special person. There was a quality about her that he could not yet define. He decided that trust could only be built if one first *begins* to trust. He then made a quick decision that he would confide in Liddy. He would request that she keep this secret until he could take his classes out for a claim-staking exercise.

Sam asked Liddy to take no further notes for a moment and to keep what he was about to tell her in confidence. She agreed. Then he explained his analysis of what he believed to be a diamond. Her interest was intense, but not economic. She wanted to follow Sam's further analyses and perhaps accompany his class if they took a field trip to stake some claims. Liddy found geological sleuthing exciting.

"Could I look at your diamond later today?" she asked.

"Sure," answered Sam. "I'll show it to you after dinner."

Liddy positioned her camera in Sam's classroom. Then, using a small portable computer set up for video editing, she showed Sam what she had prepared from their Saturday field exam. He suggested that she might add some close-up shots and discussion of the samples he had taken, along with mineralogy comments accompanied by statements from his students. He would then add his own observations to those of his students' to complete their interpretation of the volcanic eruption. At the end of class, a relatively thorough understanding of what had happened would be compiled. Liddy could also videotape a similar exchange of ideas during the afternoon class. From both classes, she could splice together, with Sam's help, a developing analysis, which would culminate in a final summary by Sam. The special report was projected to air after Wednesday's early evening news program and would consist of twenty-eight minutes of uninterrupted video.

That same morning, Eric Larson phoned the Wyoming Office of Mines and Geology and asked to speak with Chief Gordon Aughey. Chief Aughey was not available. However, since his query dealt with the press release addressing the activity near Point of Rocks, his call was directed to Bill Burnhard. Bill answered the phone politely enough. But when Eric suggested that the WOMG might have made an error in their interpretation of the dike's origin, especially since their story conflicted with the findings of Casper's local expert, Sam Westone, Bill lost his temper. In no uncertain terms, Bill told Eric, "Our agency is the *final* word on geology in Wyoming! We have investigated the situation in the field and know exactly what we're dealing with! Our press release says *exactly* what we intend it to say. It's unfortunate that Mr. Westone is such a loose cannon spouting off hypotheses better left to…*space aliens.* He's crazy to think the dike has a mantle origin. Your TV station would maintain greater credibility if you didn't give so much time to *crackpots.* We expect our press releases to be taken as they are written, and if you have any further questions, I'll be available for comment."

Eric was shocked by Bill's attitude, but responded, "I was only attempting to verify your story before we release it in our news program. I would think you'd rather we check out such things, rather than carelessly put out *anything* that just happens to cross the news desk." But before Bill had a chance to reply, the rather irritated Eric simply and abruptly said, "*Goodbye!*" and hung up the phone. Eric was now strongly hoping that the WOMG press release would prove to be embarrassing for them. He immediately placed it in the pile of material to be read on the late morning news.

Liddy was very proficient at videotaping and editing. She had a knack for moving in on important points and maintaining optimum audio control to pick up key remarks, even from the softer voices of some female students. Similar ideas were brought out in both classes and she was able to combine them, editing in the clearest statements critical for understanding. Liddy bought Sam lunch at the college cafeteria. Their lunch was brief in order to allow as much time as possible for her to compile the video. At Sam's suggestion, she added a musical background to several of the panoramic sequences. After the final product was completed and reviewed by Eric, Liddy would make several copies of the tape for Sam and for CTC. If some of the students wanted to purchase copies, she could produce the required number at a later date. It had been a full day, but she had finished her tape, and it was now ready for Eric's review.

As Sam helped Liddy carry her equipment to her vehicle, he asked if she preferred going out to a restaurant, or if she would rather he made good on his promise to fix dinner for her. "Your choice," he offered.

Stowing her camera and computer in the back seat, she responded, "I'll take home cooking if that's all right? It's nice to sample someone else's cooking other than my own. Besides," she added with a small sigh and looking slightly tired, "I visit too many restaurants when I get lonesome and tired of fixing food for myself." She paused briefly, reflecting silently on what she had just said. *Do I ever really get lonesome*? Perhaps...I guess I never gave it much thought.

"That's fine," said Sam with an understanding smile. "I made some preliminary preparations, just in case you accepted my offer. I've eaten out too much also. It's easier to visit without those annoying restaurant background noises. Besides, I can also show you the diamond." Liddy perked up as they drove the few blocks to Sam's house.

When they pulled into the driveway, Liddy saw Sam's sixty-foot tower and amateur radio antennas. It reminded her of her father's setup in Buffalo, although Sam's HF yagi had four elements and covered five bands, instead of the three-element tribander her father had. Stepping out of the driver's door, she looked at his antennas and paused. "I got interested in ham radio when I was in high school, listening to my dad talk to stations around the world on voice and Morse code. His name is Warren, and his call is KA7HBS. Morse code, coming out of his radio shack, was the normal background music in our house as I was growing up. I was active briefly and talked with quite a few different countries, but I never applied for any awards. Later, I primarily used VHF to keep in touch with Dad when Mom and I fooled around in the mountains by ourselves."

"Do you ever get on the air? asked Sam.

Looking thoughtful, Liddy answered, "I haven't for quite a while. I don't have any gear and I can't even remember much of the code now."

As they walked to his front door, Sam remarked, "Small world, particularly on ham radio in Wyoming. I recognize your father's name and callsign. I've talked to him a number of times on eighty-meters. I've also talked to him on two-meters when I've driven through Buffalo. If you like, we can look at my station while supper's in the oven."

Sam liked to cook on occasion, as did Liddy. She offered to prepare the tossed salad as he put the final touches on his lemon curry chicken and brown rice. He would serve it with sourdough bread and a rosé wine.

Sam's home was quite modest in size and appearance, although it sat on a large lot with scattered cottonwoods, pines, and aspens. Sam kept things fairly neat, for a bachelor. The inside of his house was decorated with a western flavor, accentuated by pine trim and numerous slightly dusty bookshelves. A short hallway displayed several of Sam's photographs. While staring at the pictures, Liddy deduced that Sam was a backcountry skier, cave explorer, rock climber, and hunter. There was also was an obviously old picture of Sam posing in a karate uniform. He explained that he had earned a second-degree black belt in karate while he was in college, although he had not been active for several years.

Sam set dishes on his tiny, round oak table adjacent to the kitchen. He then added two candles for atmosphere. The chicken would take about forty minutes, so Sam gave Liddy a tour of his home, showing her his geological laboratory facilities and ham radio shack.

Sam's *shack* contained a modest high frequency (HF) transceiver, a two-meter FM transceiver, and a Collins S-Line transmitter and receiver combination that was more than a half century old. Liddy remarked that the S-Line seemed similar to the radio used by her father. Sam turned it on, letting it warm up as he switched the feed line from the ground position to his eighty-meter dipole, which was resonant at the frequency of the Wyoming Cowboy Net. The net was just starting, and the net control station was calling for check-ins from various towns, beginning in alphabetical order. Stations checked in as they were called, beginning with Afton, followed by Billings, Boulder, and then Buffalo.

From the speaker, they heard Liddy's father checking in, "KA7HBS, no traffic." Sam immediately keyed his microphone and said, "Contact."

The net control in Pinedale responded, "Go ahead contact."

Sam then asked, "KA7HBS...this is KC7QE. Warren, could you move up to 3.935 MHz for a short one?"

KA7HBS responded, "See ya there...you call."

Sam stated, "Thanks. KC7QE, QSY."

The net continued as Sam changed frequency to 3.935, listened to make sure that no other stations were occupying the frequency, and then asked, "This is KC7QE...is the frequency in use?"

After a pause, Warren answered with, "KC7QE...this is KA7HBS...go ahead."

Sam said, "Good evening, Warren. We haven't talked for a while. This is KC7QE, Sam, in Casper, and I have someone in the shack who would like to say *hello*." He then handed the microphone to Liddy.

Liddy surprised her father, saying, "Hi, Daddy...this is N7GED." She continued by explaining, "I've been working on a video of Sam and his geology classes, and he offered to fix dinner for me."

Sam let Liddy talk as he excused himself to run up and check on the chicken. When he returned, Liddy was telling her father about the blizzard and being snowed in at the television station.

Sam interrupted her, "The chicken is ready."

She then cleared with her father, saying, "Good talking with you, Dad. Say 'hello' to Mom. This is N7GED, clear."

Sam took the microphone, adding, "Have a good evening, Warren. I'll catch you farther down the log. 73, this is KC7QE, clear."

"Thanks Sam. 73, KA7HBS, clear."

Sam grounded his antenna, turned off the power to his station, and then led Liddy upstairs to dinner. They had an enjoyable meal, accompanied by classical music from his CD collection. The main course was followed up with ice cream and the last of the pie that Sam had served the previous Wednesday.

After dinner, Sam showed Liddy the stone that he believed to be a diamond and then explained the tests he had used to reach that determination. "*Wow!*" she exclaimed, turning it over carefully in her hand. "*I've never held a raw diamond before!*" Sam then placed the diamond under his microscope in a strong white light and described to her the trigons seen on the surface of the crystal. He also explained how diamonds are cut to bring out their most pleasing characteristics. Liddy was impressed, but she told him, with a thoughtful look in her eyes, "I understand what you're saying about cutting a diamond, but if I had one, I think I'd keep it as it is. It's already beautiful, and it's just so neat that you could find it in such an ugly rock…sort of like an ugly duckling or a frog prince in children's stories."

"I suppose you're right," he smiled. "It's actually quite nice for a rough diamond. I've seen a few much nicer, but most I've looked at were not gem quality. This is an exception." Sam explained the potential benefit to Wyoming's economy if his analysis was correct, providing that diamonds were relatively common in the new dike. More sampling would need to be done before the economics could actually be determined. However, Sam believed his present deductions were *interpretive projections* rather than *speculation*. He would let her know what he found out as he gained more information.

Before heading out the door to go home, Liddy asked Sam, "Would you like to go cross-country skiing on Saturday? The temperature is supposed to be back up in the mid-twenties by then, and I think the snow will be good."

"I'd love to go," responded Sam. "I haven't done enough skiing this winter!"

"Great! I'll give you a call Friday night to make final plans, but it will depend on any scheduling changes at the station. I earned a comp' time day off from my regular schedule, and," she paused with a twinkle in her eye, "it's my turn to fix you dinner!"

"How could I refuse?" beamed Sam. "But rather than you

calling me, why don't I just pick you up Friday evening, and we'll go to the *Wind In The Heather* concert at the Casper Arena? We could talk about the ski trip on the way."

"But you don't even know if I like Celtic music," teased Liddy.

"Ahhh…" stammered Sam.

After a pause and an impish smile, Liddy responded eagerly with, "Well, maybe a thousand out-of-pitch bagpipes might keep me away!

CHAPTER 4

Data Release and Fallout

▼

Miners put an end to darkness; they search the depths for ore far from light. They open shafts in valleys away from where men dwell; they are forgotten by others. - Job 28:3-4

The press release from the WOMG had the initial effect of impressing some of the state legislators who wished to keep the agency funded. There had been some past problems, but perhaps this was the beginning of a change. Compared to the first broadcast of events on KWYN, the WOMG release followed the rational geologic interpretation as first proposed, but did not get off on that *wild speculation* spouted by Mr. Westone on the national news. No wonder CTC was just a little college, considering the type of erratic people they employ! It was so refreshing to see such candid documentation from a state agency.

Some state legislators paid no more attention to details than did a large segment of the general population who were neither affected by nor interested in what had happened. Often the truth is in the details. These legislators did not hear, or chose not to hear, all of what Sam had said about his other possible interpretation of the dike's origin. Besides, in their eyes the WOMG was Wyoming's expert on geology.

⇌

A tired group of faculty members from the Wyoming State University Department of Geophysics and Geology returned to the campus late Tuesday afternoon. Dr. Chris Felsen, like all of the others whose return to Laramie had been delayed by the blizzard, had a flurry of paper work to catch up on and class notes to put in order for Wednesday. Chris was dedicated to his graduate students and often gave them priority in the scope of his busy schedule. After all, if their projects were successful, it reflected well on him as well as on the department, and his name accompanied theirs on publications. WSU not only required publishing from its faculty, but occasionally rewarded those who excelled at it.

Surya managed to get some of Chris's attention in order to explain the earthquakes, the dike, and the initial trial of his seismic analyses. Chris spent almost two hours with Surya on Tuesday afternoon, rechecking his conclusions. Surya was concerned that his interpretation conflicted with the WOMG news release. According to Surya's explanation, the dike began with a disturbance originating in the earth's mantle, and it greatly piqued Chris's interest. He had also seen Sam Westone's KWYN explanation and the WOMG press release. Chris always paid attention to details. Sam's rationale had been good all the way through, especially considering the small amount of facts that had been available for him to make his projections. Chris had noted Sam's comment about a possible lamproite eruption. Such a possibility warranted a quick investigation. Lamproites are not only rare, but if such material *had* erupted, the opportunity to study its physics and chemistry would put the DGG in a worldwide spotlight.

One of the points of contention between the DGG and the WOMG had been the WOMG's unwillingness to give any priority to the publishing of departmental papers. The WOMG wanted material of a more general interest, rather than those typical *esoteric tomes* that institutions of higher learning love. It also boiled down to a bit of *Ph D* academic arrogance vs. the *bureaucratic* arrogance of a well-established state agency. With a few excessive personalities added in on both sides to stir up their comrades, the associates in either organization would also follow their respective *company lines*. Other than subject matter and some professional jealousies, the disagreements were little different from those in most other groups who have developed a *"them versus us"* mentality. Missed opportunities often boil down to the acts of individual personalities. Both Gordon Aughey and his minion Bill Burnhard had irritated Chris Felsen on a number of occasions. Chris had also, with only a small effort on his part, been a pain in the posterior for both Gordon and Bill.

Although some political rivalry existed between WSU and CTC, it was nothing compared to that between the DGG and the WOMG. Chris and Surya made a conference call to Sam Westone at CTC on Wednesday morning, as soon as they could catch him in his office. Sam was surprised by the call, but also thought that increased coordination with WSU could be mutually beneficial. He was also thinking of one x-ray diffraction analysis in particular.

Chris led the discussion, "The new CTC seismograph is ready for calibration. Sam, would you be available part of the day on Thursday if Surya and I come to Casper?"

Having already been directed by the CTC Geoscience department head, Ralph Escobido, to oversee the new seismograph, Sam responded, "I'll be available between classes during the middle of the day."

"We're also interested in your interpretation of the new dike near Point of Rocks as possibly being a lamproite," continued Chris. "We noted the comment you made in your last television interview, and we have some data that might interest you. Surya Ganisalim, the student whose project funded the CTC seismograph, has analyzed data from last week's earthquakes. He projects a possible mantle origin for the disturbance that resulted in the dike. I'll let Surya explain it to you."

After Surya's five-minute explanation, Sam replied, "Bring the data with you when you come up tomorrow. I have some additional information that might interest you as well. I took my classes on a field trip to the dike and to the break in I-80 near Rawlins last Saturday, just before the storm. The dike contains mantle derived xenocrysts and xenoliths! We had a

KWYN reporter come along and videotape the field trip and some follow-up class sessions. That tape will be shown this evening as a human interest special on KWYN, just after the six o'clock news. I wish I'd had your seismic interpretations to include in that documentary. Perhaps we could work together on a publication, and maybe you and Surya might want to make some sort of press release?"

"That's a good thought," responded Chris. "We'll try to get something out tomorrow. If you saw the WOMG press release, I think you'll agree that they are way off base, particularly if they actually looked at the site."

"Yes," agreed Sam. "I think they just took my first crack at it before I had any real information and then went with that interpretation. The dike's vesicular material on the hill to the south is a dead give away as to its volcanic nature. I don't really see how they could have missed the mantle indicators either, unless they were in an awfully big hurry. Either of these would shoot down my first idea of an over-pressured shallow source. Olivine and peridotite nodules are also rather strong indications of a deep source for the dike material. I know I said *lamproite*, but it could be *kimberlite* or some other related rock type."

"We'll look forward to working with you, Sam, and we'll see you on Thursday. Thanks for your time."

As Sam hung up the phone, he reflected on how glad he was that he would now get his own conclusions independently verified.

Chris turned to Surya, relating a similar thought, "I believe your analysis has been confirmed. Write me a short paragraph, explaining in layman's terms your ideas for the mantle derivation of the dike. Then we'll send out our own press release on departmental letterhead."

Chris decided to wait until after he saw the special on KWYN before releasing Surya's note to the press. Better to be absolutely certain rather than make a *fau pax* like the WOMG had.

⇆

Sam Westone, Ralph Escobido, and a dozen students

gathered in the CTC Commons Room after six o'clock, Wednesday evening. They waited with anticipation for the KWYN special program on Sam and his students, along with their interpretation of the dike that had blocked I-80 six days earlier. The program was introduced by a somewhat self-satisfied Eric Larson explaining, "We cannot over-estimate the value of education and the contribution that Casper Technical College continues to make in the education of our young people…in this instance within the field of geology." Ralph was glad he had the foresight to tape the actual broadcast rather than rely on a copy of the program to be supplied by KWYN. The introduction alone would be extremely useful in advertising CTC Geosciences to prospective students.

The program began with some news footage of the dike blocking the highway, followed by audio recordings from some of the highway patrol and other emergency services. Liddy Hill provided the background monologue, explaining how Sam and his classes had taken the initiative to investigate current geologic happenings for the enhancement of the students' learning experiences. Her statements were then mingled with some of Sam's geological commentary enroute. Sam's on-site lecture about field techniques was mixed with student questions and close-ups of some of the features under discussion, followed by notes on the highway cracks near Rawlins, and then fading into classroom discussion and compilation of sample analyses. The program finished with questions leading into a summary presented by Sam, using maps and diagrams. After the special was over, Eric Larson threw in some brief comments about *"almost wishing he were a student again and taking geology at CTC."* Ralph, Sam, and the students thought that the presentation was well done. This was in fact the best advertising CTC had received in at least ten years.

⇌

To say that the WOMG did not fully appreciate the television special was an understatement. The whole program had carefully, methodically, and unintentionally discredited their press release of a few days before. Not only that, but it appeared that *mere college students* had done the discrediting, along with the gentle, guiding hand of their teacher, Sam Westone. The only thing that could have made it worse would have been a statement by one of the students, declaring, "*Elementary*, my dear WOMG...*elementary!*"

Gordon Aughey was furious! When Bill arrived at work Thursday morning, he was curtly ordered into Gordon's office. After the heavy wooden door slammed shut, Gordon's yelling, followed intermittently by return shouts from Bill, kept most of the other staff as far away from that scene of turmoil as possible. After twenty minutes, things quieted down and Gordon's door opened. Bill, flushed and shaking, stomped back to his office, and without saying anything to anyone, he grabbed his coat and left. As Gordon came out of his office, he harshly demanded, to no one in particular, that a few minor items be put in his vehicle. His lead secretary meekly obeyed, averting her eyes like a serf before the *lord of the realm*. Gordon then headed across town to his final defense of the WOMG's budget.

It wasn't pretty for Gordon. He had authorized the press release and his prize bureaucrat had let him down! *Bill hadn't even taken the time that a college student would to make sure he got it right*, he thought. The Governor's Select Committee on Budget had seen the KWYN special and had received several calls from interested politicians around the state. Two of the committee members had geologic backgrounds, having worked their way up through Wyoming's mineral industries to head companies and mineral development advocacy groups. Before the meeting, they had taken time to explain to the rest of the committee the errors of the WOMG and the importance of mineral economics to the state.

But to eliminate the WOMG would be a terrible mistake, due to the diversity of Wyoming's mineral industry. Wyoming's past economic boom and bust cycles, for the most part, closely followed the economics of mineral commodities. Coal, oil, gas, precious metals, copper, iron, bentonite, and trona had all contributed to the state's well being in the past, and no one could predict what the next important commodity would be. But everything from zeolites to gemstones and decorative stone had potential. Even diamonds had been found in the state, although there had been little activity in searching for them since the beginning of the twenty-first century.

The purpose of the WOMG was to not only provide in-depth geologic evaluations for environmentally sound economic development and evaluate geologic hazards, but to encourage diverse mineral exploration that could help smooth out the *bust* parts of Wyoming's economic cycles. They obviously needed better leadership to get them moving in the right direction.

The committee pretty much ate Gordon alive. He had no answers for their challenges of incompetence. He could only sit there and endure their criticism. Despite supportive arguments from the geologists on the committee, other members could see no reason to keep funding the WOMG. The tone of the session caused Gordon's mind to wander a few times to caricatures of the *Spanish Inquisition.* The meeting took less than an hour, and one member of the committee spouted out an insensitive final remark, suggesting that Gordon might do better to submit a resignation quietly, since only the Governor could fire him.

One week later, after conferring with the Governor, the Select Committee on Budget made their recommendation to the Wyoming State Legislature. They proposed that the WOMG be funded for the next two years at a fifteen percent reduction from the current level. Out of public view, the Governor was in the process of requesting Gordon's resignation. However, he had also told his committee to continue WOMG funding because he believed that no state government is complete without a department dedicated to mineral economics, geology, and related environmental concerns. This was particularly true for Wyoming, since the mineral industry, directly or indirectly, supplied the vast majority of the revenue available to fund the state.

Wyoming may be the least populous state in the union, but as long as he was Governor, it would not be diminished by not having all of the necessary agencies. The WOMG was valuable because mineral economics was of such extreme importance to Wyoming. A new agency head, capable of a bit more management oversight, should cure the problem. The Governor forgot that the WOMG already had an appointed Directory Board in place, which should have done its work to ensure effective agency management. But it, like many politically appointed bureaucratic groups, almost never criticized the political appointees that it was charged to oversee. Members of the board were mostly "*yes-men and -women*" who feared affecting their own replacement if they ever actually spoke up.

The Governor also had to satisfy certain members of the Wyoming House of Representatives who wanted to be rid of the WOMG in order to reroute funding to their own pet programs, hence the budget cut. These same representatives were also agitating for an increased budget for Casper Technical College. In light of the recent high profile activity at CTC (thanks to Eric Larson and KWYN), he would also bend slightly to that request. Satisfying both sides of a political issue is a delicate balance, and the Governor believed he had the correct mix, gauged to maintain his popularity through another election cycle. Once political power is acquired, the goal of many politicians is to maintain that power, even if a few deals must be cut and principles and ideas compromised.

⇌

Chris Felsen appreciated the thoroughness of the KWYN special presentation. Evidence reported for the mantle nature of the volcanic eruption was incontrovertible. Upon obtaining approval from his department head, Chris e-mailed Surya's press release to KWYN and to other news media, confirming Sam Westone's conclusions. KWYN aired that press release on Friday, with accompanying commentary by Eric Larson, reaffirming the capabilities of the local talent at CTC.

⇌

An elderly widow in Casper, whose husband had been a very successful geologist, had been following the story as presented by KWYN television. She had been a geology student many years past and had actually come to Wyoming because of the state's fine exposures of almost any type of geology that one would care to study. The television program featuring Sam and his students touched her emotionally. She reflected back on her younger days when she and her future husband had been enthusiastic students and was thrilled to see the same excitement in the current students at CTC. Having no heirs to her small fortune, she called the President of Casper Technical College and donated $1.3 million to CTC for an endowment to be used for the advancement of geologic studies and for scholarships. Finalization of the endowment would take another month. A resulting increase in laboratory facilities for the Geosciences Department appeared likely in the near future.

⇌

The current political and economic scandals that embroiled several United States senators had their origins in an administration at the end of the previous century. That administration had been shown to be one of the most corrupt in history. These long-time senators had, until just recently, escaped any implications of wrong doing, at least publicly. This was due to co-involvement by a few well-entrenched members of both the U.S. House of Representatives and the Senate, coupled with rather blatant, but un-fingerable blackmail that began in the early 1990s and continued through numerous election cycles. The scandal finally came to light when one of those involved suddenly died in the presence of his mistress, compelling his wife to release a safety deposit box full of evidence previously unknown to any of those involved. The evidence was given to an honest and zealous member of the U.S. Attorney General's staff. People were named, tapes of conversations were supplied, and over a dozen individuals had been arrested. The depth of the scandal was still unknown and was as intricate and sticky as a spider's web. One thing led to another, and when one person was touched, the tangled web stuck, extending to associates and associates of associates.

The senators involved were slowly being revealed, then indicted, beginning with those in several northeastern states and reaching out to Nevada and California. International involvement included both U.S. allies and those on *the other side*. The connections threaded through spying, technology transfers, money laundering, and also involved mineral deposits that included coal, petroleum, platinum, and diamonds. The tendrils of intrigue, accentuated by strong personalities, had slowly, beginning in the 1990s, eliminated the successful diamond exploration program that had existed in Wyoming.

Diamond exploration had at first been catalyzed through the efforts of the WOMG. But the potential economic boost to Wyoming slowly spiraled downward, fostered by the slow removal of the WOMG's leadership position in encouraging new development. First, funding was cut for WOMG personnel and their laboratory was eliminated. Then finally, through the weight of bureaucracy, the diamond exploration project at the WOMG had been eradicated. Even private exploration efforts ran into unexplained bureaucratic difficulties on both the state and federal levels. Improperly orchestrated environmental regulations had been used to stop projects that were determined to be *not environmentally sound*. But the application of that phrase often affected only certain mineral developments and not others, although most people would perceive them to be similar.

The Reef Group, a multinational resource consortium based in Jakarta, Indonesia, had been implicated in the recent investigations, but still seemed to operate autonomously. Closer looks at connections with the Reef Group always found dead ends, or occasional dead bodies. KWYN's special on CTC had attracted some attention in the Reef Group through Sam's mention of the dike with a probable mantle origin. The Reef Group had diamond interests in several parts of the world and did not want more competition. They often bought mining claims to eliminate competition and to maintain solid markets and favorable prices for their own production. They also supported environmental groups who actively tried to hinder mineral development, if such hindrance met Reef's agenda. Sam Westone had inadvertently rekindled the Reef Group's concerns about preventing certain potential mineral developments in Wyoming.

⇌

Andrew Merlott was a prospector and had been one most of his life. For more than forty years he had chased after the bounty, hidden by *Mother Nature*, under deserts, forests, and in streams. He had discovered numerous small deposits, worked them for a while, then sold them and moved on. *He had played the game rather well*, he thought. Andy, as his friends called him, had dealt with gold and other metals, as well as with decorative stones, gemstones, lapidary materials, uranium, oil, coal, and therapeutic mineral springs. His prospecting and mining activities covered much of the Rocky Mountain region from Mexico to Montana.

Now, at age sixty-three, he was starting to slow down just a little. He currently resided southeast of Atlantic City, Wyoming in an old camp trailer situated on several gold placer and lode claims. His home had once been rather unkindly described by a government bureaucrat, in his presence no less, as being *"dilapidated."* Andy preferred to think of it as *comfortably broken in*. The trailer was well insulated, had no leaks in the roof, and almost never had more than one mouse at a time in the cupboards. Andy had lived in that same home for almost twenty years. He had hauled it back and forth across the mountains to at least twelve different, but highly scenic, mining locations. He was very fond of his home!

Andy's claims sat astride an unnamed gulch that drained southward into Strawberry Creek. He had found the sheared apex of a steep-limbed antiform in 2.8 billion year old metagreywacke of the Miner's Delight Formation. The uniform black monotony of the thick sequence of metamorphosed dirty volcanic sandstone had kept the structure hidden from the inquisitive eyes of prospectors and geologists in the past. *But Andy had discovered it*! It was a structure analogous to an *anticline*, which is an upward bending of sedimentary rock strata. An *antiform* was different in that one could not identify for certain which side of the layering actually represented the top; it *looked* like an anticline. The tight fold of the antiform focused the stresses within the rock, causing faulting along the crest-line. The zone of shearing, broken by numerous small faults, then served as a conduit for auriferous fluids that more than once in the geologic past had left their golden treasure in pods and veins of quartz, then disseminated the remainder in the surrounding rock. Later, as the mountains wore away through the process of erosion, gold flakes and nuggets washed down the streams and gulches in the South Pass area.

Back in the 1800s, pioneers traveling west on the old

Oregon Trail would pick up a few nuggets and flakes in the area. When they stopped to refresh themselves at streams, they would occasionally pull out a pan to test for gold. They were successful in finding gold in the South Pass area as early as 1842. But animosity toward them, from indigenous inhabitants frequenting the locale, strongly limited any serious exploration activities until the 1860s. Before then, the possibilities of being murdered and scalped hindered exploration by small groups of prospectors.

But activity eventually increased as larger organized groups reduced the danger from tribes in the area. The mining district was worked heavily in the late 1860s and again around 1900. During the 1930s, gold miners in the district attempted to pull themselves out of the Great Depression through their prospecting efforts. Many succeeded, but activity stopped at the beginning of World War II. Random spurts of mining continued during the 1950s and through the 1980s, with only a trickle of activity since that time.

In spite of its intensive history of mining, Andy knew that large portions of this gold district, similar to a good many other mining districts, had never been fully explored. Both individuals and companies involved in mineral exploration, especially those that focused only on areas where others had already located gold, overlooked many prospective placer and lode deposits.

A year and a half earlier, Andy had wandered across much of the district that was open to claim staking, looking for places that might be of economic value for a small-scale miner like himself. He tested many streams, and several that he saw seemed to have good potential to reward him for his labors. But like most prospectors, Andy followed his *hunches*. Maybe to some that seemed akin to looking at which way his rabbit foot pointed, but Andy's hunches weren't based on luck or mysticism. They came from practiced eyes that held forty years of prospecting experience behind them. His hunches really meant that he recognized the proper indications for a valuable mineral deposit, even if he was not learned or articulate enough to translate those indications into a verbal or scientific description.

Andy found much coarser gold in his gulch than he had

seen in other locations around the district. He was also familiar with the amazing stories of the Burr and Hidden Hand mines and several others where prospectors had struck it rich, a few miles southeast of the gulch where he staked his claims. The Burr Mine had hosted several sporadic, but very rich ore pockets, containing as much as 250 ounces of gold per ton of ore, with one specimen grade sample running 1690 ounces of gold per ton of ore! The Hidden Hand had topped that with one rare sample assaying at 3100 ounces per ton! Granted, those were found in the late 1800s and early 1900s, but if one considered the past mining activity, compared to the overall size of the mining district, *most of the area had never been fully explored or even prospected*!

Andy found a 1.2 ounce gold nugget in his first test excavation at the lower end of his gulch. That nugget, combined with the character of the rock across the upper ends of two adjacent gullies, made up his mind for him. He had staked five placer claims for the loose debris that covered the surface and another five lode claims for the suspected vein deposits. So far, the claims were meeting his expectations, and his efforts were paying the bills. Andy found gold where no one had tried to mine previously. He had to work hard to recover it, *but he was getting gold*! However, if he could process just a bit more material or find a major vein that he believed lay hidden there, he might be able to save a little and get ahead, or maybe even retire.

His claims were just far enough from civilization that he had been able to fend off the U.S. Bureau of Land Management's attempts to prevent him from living on the claims while he worked them. Andy knew the BLM's mining claim regulations as well as the government's own experts. That knowledge had allowed him to survive, when overly enthusiastic government agents had put other prospectors out of business.

During the winter season, Andy would leave his antique Dodge pickup parked in Atlantic City near the café and ride a vintage snowmobile for transportation. Since his trailer was set up on his claims, Andy rode his snow machine to Atlantic City, and would then drive his truck into Lander once every week or two when he needed supplies. In early November, the snow had become too deep for his pickup, so his snowmobile had been his main transportation since then. This winter, however, he was wishing that he had staked claims in sunny Arizona rather than here under the deep snow of Wyoming. The snow and cold temperatures prevented any actual mining, thus temporarily halting his income. But he paid no housing rent beyond his claim rental fees to the government. His only utility bill was for an occasional refill of the small propane tank that fed his stove for cooking, along with a small heater. He had a couple of old solar panels on top of his trailer that kept an automotive battery charged for his reading light and his small twelve-volt television. The advantage of minimal bills allowed his survival until he could produce some more gold the next summer. He was, however, designing and building a set of sluices that he planned to feed with a small front-end loader after the spring thaw. Andy had also acquired a load of timbers suitable for shoring and cribbing. He was contemplating digging an adit where he found indications that a major vein might lay just beneath the surface.

Andy was able to watch KWYN on his six-inch black and white TV; it was the only station his antenna could receive. He never did get a satellite dish as the monthly fee was prohibitive. Lander and Riverton each had their own TV stations and were closer than Casper, but he lived just far enough below the ridge crest that his antenna could not receive their signals.

Andy saw the KWYN special on the blockage of Interstate-80 near Point of Rocks. He fully understood some of the unstated economic implications of a dike originating within the earth's mantle. He knew that diamonds and other precious gems were a possibility. Furthermore, Andy recognized the name of Sam Westone from articles and advertised books on prospecting that he had seen in the *Western Prospector's Journal*. He had been a subscriber to that monthly magazine since it first came out in the 1980s.

Andy decided that *he* would be the first to stake claims on this potential bonanza. He also knew that a mining claim could have economic benefits beyond the valuable minerals present, as long as the claimant played by the rules. The *nuisance value* of any claim, particularly if other activities are going on in the area, can be substantial, but it still must be a good claim. Andy didn't like to think of himself as a nuisance, but he had sold claims in the past, simply because he happened to stake where other development activities could not proceed until his claims had been removed from the ground in question. The weather had been a bit tough lately, but Saturday was supposed to be relatively mild, with no chance for snow and no strong winds predicted. Andy would head out at first light on Saturday to stake some new claims.

CHAPTER 5

Precursors

▼

You lift me up on the wind; you make me ride on it and toss me about on the tempest. - Job 30:22

Surya Ganisalim and Chris Felsen entered Sam's CTC office on Thursday morning, just after he had finished his morning class. After Sam's ritualistic offer of coffee, the three proceeded to the basement of the building where the new seismograph had been installed. Instrumentation was mounted on a freestanding pillar of concrete, isolated from the mass of the building, and set to a depth of thirty feet into bedrock. The seismograph was connected to a small computer with a large screen and printer. The computer was in turn joined with both fiber-optic and satellite links to other seismographs in Surya's array and to a dedicated WWV time standard link. Radio station WWV, in Ft. Collins, Colorado, broadcasts precise time and frequency information for the U.S. Department of Commerce, National Institute of Standards and Technology.

The seismograph site had been surveyed to the required accuracy when the concrete base was poured, and the steel anchors were set. Calibration was merely a series of self-checks and interconnection checks performed by the computer, with occasional specification data inputs by Surya. The entire calibration took only about twenty minutes, including giving

Sam instruction on the system's operation and local data output capabilities. Because of the interlinking, Sam would be able to execute the same analyses that Surya could in Laramie. The only difference was that Surya narrowed the adjustment range for his algorithms at all stations except at the DGG. He needed to make sure that these adjustments stayed relatively constant for his dissertation analyses.

After calibration, the three of them returned to Sam's office where he showed them some of the samples he had collected from the I-80 dike. Chris then gave Sam a copy of his department's news release. Their discussions centered on the new dike, the potential for new seismic analyses from Surya's methods and array, and the question as to why the mantle-derived material had erupted at the time it had. Clearly, the progression of eruptions in the Leucite Hills through time seemed to have some connection with this most recent eruption, even though its lithology and chemistry might differ from that of earlier eruptions. Surya and Chris both expressed hope that Surya's methods might offer a new view into the deeper circulation systems within the earth. Perhaps they might even be able to get some real data concerning the nature of Yellowstone and other hotspots around the world. The Leucite Hills exhibits a directional progression of eruptions from the mantle over time, but appeared to them to have no direct relationship to the Yellowstone hotspot. However, they all agreed that the causes of both might be related deep within the earth's mantle. The three men immersed themselves in a quick study and review of volcanism in and around Wyoming.

$$\rightleftharpoons$$

A *hotspot* is a place where the upper part of the earth's mantle is hotter than the ambient mantle temperature. This is expressed in a high geothermal gradient, which is a temperature increase with depth within the earth that is much greater than in other areas. A hotspot is hypothetically caused by a large heat plume, shaped like an elongate upside down raindrop, originating deep within the mantle. Such mantle plumes are relatively stationary over geologic time, and as crustal plates move across them, the heat melts parts of the earth's crust and supplies magma for volcanic activity. Episodic or continuous volcanism leaves a line of extinct volcanoes where the crust has passed over a hotspot. Active volcanoes are found above the hotspots where heat continues to melt the crust and/or mantle to supply magma. The processes within the mantle responsible for hotspots are unknown. Some speculate that deeper circulations within the earth's outer core might lead to the development of mantle plumes and their resulting hotspots.

Two of the best-known hotspots are Hawaii, beneath thin oceanic crust; and Yellowstone, beneath thick continental crust. Both areas are volcanic. The eastward progression through time of both hotspots is related to the movement of continental and oceanic plates within the crust, driven by deeper circulation within the earth. New crust is continually formed along mid-ocean ridges from where it moves outward, eventually to be subducted beneath the edges of continents. The continents are thicker and less dense, floating like icebergs on a sea of more dense rock, with the largest part of their mass hidden beneath the surface. The hotspots appear to be independent of the type or thickness of crustal material through which they are expressed. Their persistence and intensity of heat and volcanism must be based on very deep-seated activity.

Basaltic lava is characteristically associated with oceanic crust. But in several significant outpourings and in numerous minor ones, it has been extruded through cracks in continental crust also. Basalt is a dark extrusive igneous rock containing plagioclase and pyroxene and is rich in heavy dark minerals such as olivine, hematite, magnetite, and others. Basalt originates in the upper mantle and may mix with melted crust that contains less of the dark, heavy minerals and more of the lighter minerals, such as alkali feldspars and quartz. This mixing will yield volcanic materials of rhyolitic composition that are more characteristic of eruptions from the continental crust.

Hawaii erupts almost continuously, spewing out basaltic lava from a large shield volcano and related fissures. The eruptions in Hawaii are rather docile, with extensive lava flows and relatively smaller cinder cones. Violent eruptions, such as those associated with other volcanoes around the Pacific Rim, are absent in Hawaii. The line of the Hawaiian Islands traces volcanic activity and crustal plate movement through seventy million years of geologic time, with the oldest eruptions at the northwest end of the line and the current eruptions at the southeast end on the island of Hawaii. Oceanic hotspots such as Hawaii typically influence a large area as much as 500 miles across.

The Yellowstone hotspot similarly exhibits a record of past eruptions proceeding in a line from the oldest in the west to the youngest at the east end in Yellowstone National Park. An almost 500 mile long progression of volcanic eruptions began near the Oregon/Nevada border, about sixteen million years ago. However, here the similarity to Hawaii ends. These continental eruptions began with silicic magma, which is silica rich as opposed to Hawaii's basaltic eruptions. That lava erupted through continental crust, followed by extensive basalt flows on the Snake River Plain, as the hotspot and accompanying silicic volcanism moved northeastward. Some geologists also attribute the Columbia River flood basalts to activity of the Yellowstone hotspot. Those flood basalts, which are unimaginably huge outpourings of that material, totaled more than 42,000 cubic miles. Some individual flows produced as much as 312 cubic miles of lava in a very short span of time, estimated to be anywhere from as little as one week, to as long as ten years.

The time between major eruptions related to the Yellowstone hotspot has varied from about 500,000 years to as long as 3.8 million years, although 600,000 years seems to be the   general length of time between the last few. The direction of this progression is theorized, as a result of abundant evidence, to be caused by a stationary subcrustal hotspot over which the continental crustal plate is moving southwestward at a rate of about 1.8 inches per year. Each successive eruption was a little more recent and a little farther to the northeast than the preceding one.

The melted continental crust, which gave us more rhyolitic compositions for the volcanic materials, also contained more water trapped within the rock than is normally trapped within basalt. Perhaps this change in composition, combined with increasing crustal thickness, as the Yellowstone hotspot

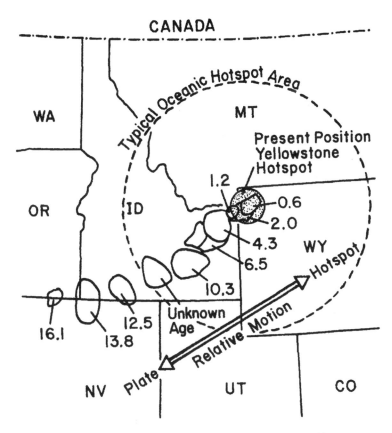

Past calderas associated with the Yellowstone hotspot. Ages in millions of years. Arrows show relative motion between continental plate and hotspot. Dashed circle represents the size of a typical area of influence for an oceanic hotspot. Adapted from Smith and Braile, 1993.

migrated toward the northeast, was responsible for the significant change noted in the type of eruptions. Whatever the cause, the eruptions changed about two million years ago from apparently localized silicic volcanism followed by outpourings of basaltic lavas, to violent explosive eruptions that stagger the imagination.

A *caldera* is a large basin-shaped depression caused by the collapse of a volcano's top into an underlying magma chamber, after an eruption. Three catastrophic caldera-forming eruptions tore Yellowstone apart in the recent geologic past. The first occurred about 2.0 million years ago, the second about 1.2 million years ago, and the last about 0.6 million years ago. Combined, these produced a total of more than 2040 cubic miles of eruptive volume. That amount of material could completely cover all of the states west of the Mississippi River to a depth of more than five feet! The last of those major eruptions, just over 600,000 years ago, produced the Lava Creek ash that blanketed almost the entire western United States, as far east as the Mississippi River and south into Mexico. If such an eruption happened today, the United States would be devastated far beyond any previous volcanic disaster in recorded history!

$$\rightleftharpoons$$

After their enlightening discussion, the three geologists visited a local Mexican restaurant for lunch. Sam queried the possibility of x-ray diffraction analyses on a couple of samples he was studying. Chris assured him that if he called first to make sure the x-ray diffractometer was not scheduled for that day, almost any time would be fine. Several professors or students could easily set him up for a few tests. The food was good, but Sam was not used to eating such a heavy meal at lunch. When they had finished, Chris and Surya headed back toward Laramie, while Sam returned to the campus. There he managed to squeeze in a bit of exercise in the gym prior to his afternoon class.

Late in the day and before he left for home, Sam retrieved a couple of books on the volcanic history of Yellowstone that included discussions of the Yellowstone hotspot. He thought he would delve further into that subject over the weekend so he placed the books in the jump seat of his small club-cab truck. This was the type of geological curiosity that caused his library materials to migrate back and forth between his home and office libraries, via his pickup. There were never fewer than six or seven books sitting in the jump seat of his truck.

⇋

Sam arrived at Liddy's home just after six-thirty Friday evening. He would have made it earlier, but the spread-out maze of rural subdivision roads, blocked in places by small fenced-off lots or by unplowed sections, limited his direct navigational approach to a place he had not previously visited. Liddy's dog, a neutered male Golden Retriever named Grieg, greeted Sam at the front gate attached to a woven wire fence. Liddy had named him after Norwegian Edvard Grieg who ranked near the top of her list of favorite composers. She had acquired the puppy while listening to *Peer Gynt*, so the name Grieg had seemed natural. Grieg loved people and voiced two happy barks at the new visitor. While excitedly wagging his tail, he ran to the front door to announce Sam's presence and then bounded back to elicit attention from the newcomer.

Liddy was enamored with Sam, but the real litmus test came from Grieg. Like many other animals, he could sense the character of the people he met. If Grieg liked someone, then Liddy generally liked that person also. But if he uttered a low growl or shied away from some person or situation, then Liddy knew also to be wary. If the dog showed extreme agitation, Liddy would either arm herself for protection or flee the situation confronting her. She always told her friends that Grieg was the best judge of humans, and she always listened to him.

Sam easily passed Grieg's character test. In fact, Liddy had never seen the dog give a warmer welcome to anyone. She opened the door before Sam had a chance to knock and invited him in, with Grieg close at his side. She then gave Sam a quick tour of her house before heading to the concert. Liddy's home was a small three-bedroom ranch, with traditional off-white plaster walls, decorated with a few western prints and landscape posters. A small piano sat in the living room, along with a sofa and two rocking chairs. An impressive stereo set-up and television/video entertainment system faced a tall bookshelf on the opposite wall. Her books covered a wide variety of subjects, and Sam noticed an introductory geology text sitting on the sofa. Liddy kept her professional technical references, computer, and a small electronics workbench, with various pieces of test equipment, in a separate room. That was her office when she needed to work at home. Another room was crammed with saddles and horse tack, camping gear, cross-country skis, bicycles, camera gear, and another bookshelf displaying a variety of novels and magazines.

The house, with an attached single-car garage, sat on a one-acre wind-swept lot. Liddy had planted a shelterbelt along the west side of the lot, but the trees were no more than two feet high and didn't protrude noticeably above the snow. In one corner of her yard, a board fence surrounded and gave wind protection to a small garden space. Her next-door neighbor to the west, an older widow named Camile Brown, owned a fifteen-acre lot with a small barn, corrals, and fenced pasture, where Liddy's horse mingled with two horses owned by Camile.

Liddy grabbed her coat, fleece headband, and mittens. She then tossed a rawhide chew to Grieg as she and Sam walked out the front door. The drive to the Casper Arena took only about ten minutes. All of the county roads and highways had been cleared of snow, but several of the private roads remained clogged with wind-packed snowdrifts.

"Sam, do you have any favorite places to cross-country ski?" inquired Liddy as they drove along.

"Oh, not particularly," responded Sam. "I've always liked to ski some of the more open meadow areas in the Medicine Bows or Bighorns. But with questionable road conditions, those might be a bit far for a day trip if you want to get much skiing in. There's always Casper Mountain, with its packed trails."

"I like the open areas too," echoed Liddy thoughtfully. "I prefer trailblazing rather than following a groomed trail. More freedom that way. And I can take Grieg along without worrying about him bothering other skiers. He loves to play in the snow.

About fifty miles west of here, there's a nice area where Grieg and I have gone skiing before and we haven't seen anyone."

"That sounds like my kind of place," commented Sam as they joined a growing stream of traffic headed for the Arena. "I'm always up for seeing new territory, especially if it's away from crowds."

"Great! We can take Poison Spider Road out; it should be plowed by now. Have you ever been to the Rattlesnake Hills? There's a small canyon going up Stinking Water Creek that we can ski in.

"I've worked in the Rattlesnake Hills before, but only on the south side. That's really wild country out there. What should we do for lunch?"

"How about just bringing munchies to trade," answered Liddy. Just don't bring anything weird like sardines, or I won't trade at all!"

"Don't worry," laughed Sam. "I've been known to eat a few of those, but they aren't my standard fare, particularly on a ski trip. Would you like cheese and bread, and maybe some salami?"

"Yeah, that would be much better. If you bring that, I'll find some other stuff to go along with it." Then she added, "You might want to bring your camera too. Some of the views are incredible, and we might see some wildlife."

"It should be a great trip! Do you want me to pick you up?"

"Why don't I drive so Grieg won't make a mess of your truck; besides, he's used to the back of my old SUV. Just stop by my place about eight in the morning, and you can leave your truck there. We can grab some fast food as we leave town."

"Sounds terrific, Liddy!" Sam smiled at her as they rolled into the parking lot amidst dozens of other vehicles.

⇌

After entering the doors to the huge building, they slowly pushed their way through the mingling throng. The crowd was larger than expected. The day had been calm and Saturday was expected to be windless and clear. In Wyoming, wind is *the* defining factor. Without wind, several inches of snow or very cold temperatures are not much of a problem. However, when accompanied by a strong blow, low temperatures or snow or both combined can mount up to life and death challenges.

Liddy encountered several friends from Casper and from Buffalo as well. She obviously knew a lot of people, and Sam would be lucky if he could remember any of their names. The conversations centered on Liddy's work or her old high school class from Buffalo. Sam wondered if her job at KWYN was the main driving force in her life, causing her to subvert all else to career goals? Or was this notion of his actually just a reflection of *his* life. He had been so wrapped up in his teaching job the last few years that he'd pretty much ignored his social life. Maybe *he* was the career fanatic. Did she actually have room in her life for other relationships? *Did he?* And why was he so attracted to her?

The brief sidetrack in Sam's train of thought moved back to the main line with the introduction of another of Liddy's acquaintances from Buffalo. The fine weather brought out quite a few people for a respite from the trapped feeling that winter storms can inflict. Sam was not usually a captive of such feelings, but he understood them. He also knew that northern Wyoming had been subjected to almost continuous sub-zero temperatures and harsh conditions, uninterrupted by the sunny, mild interludes, between storms, that Casper and southern Wyoming had experienced this winter. Liddy introduced Sam to several more old acquaintances as they made their way to their seats. A couple of Sam's students said, "Hello, Dr. Sam," as they passed, and Sam presented Liddy to some of his amateur radio friends in the crowd as well.

The band's leader began the concert with a few comments about Wyoming's weather, followed by an introduction of the band members. The *Wind In The Heather* had been in existence for more than thirty years, occasionally adding or losing members. However, their flair for exuberant performance and for whipping the audience into a Celtic frenzy never seemed to diminish. A recently formed local Scottish band, *Ceann na Drochaide Bige,* provided both backup and entertainment during the two short breaks. Sam and Liddy were both swept up in the excitement of the music and enthusiasm of the crowd.

The bagpipes, drums, pennywhistles, and other instruments beat a path of Scottish history and humor into the hearts and feet of the audience. Most of the crowd could not stay in their seats. The musicians fed on the excitement in a symbiotic relationship between the entertainers and the entertained, making an unforgettable experience for both.

During the intermission, Sam purchased CDs of each group and also cassette tapes for use in his truck. The dusty back-road nature of his driving was often intensive enough to rapidly disable a CD player. But he found that the cassette players and cassettes withstood the harsh environments better. He gave the CDs to Liddy and later stashed the tapes in his truck.

The collection from *Ceann na Drochaide Bige* contained a new piece called *"Templar's Cross"* which was composed by James Kirk Stuart, the group's lead piper. The piece had just been played before the break, and Sam and Liddy both really loved the words and music. It derived from the surge in Scottish patriotism over the preceding fifteen years. With a traditional fast beat and tune, it related in song part of the legend of the July 27, 1689 battle at the Pass of Killiecrankie that lasted little more than three minutes. The story, as told by J.K. Stuart, was that John Grahame of Claverhouse, Viscount Dundee, under the Jacobite/pro-Stuart banner of King James, was fatally shot through the left eye while galloping at the head of his victorious men, after over-running the Williamite line. The Williamites were under the leadership of Major-General Hugh Mackay. Suspicion ran loose that two of King William's men had infiltrated Dundee's ranks and had murdered John Grahame. His body, when retrieved, reportedly bore a gold Knights Templar Cross.

> *On the battlefield, God for lovin'*
> *Camerons, Macdonalds, and MacLeans*
> *Charged the line, six-hundred dyin'*
> *Save the golden cross for me.*
>
> *Through the eye by brigands runnin'*
> *Dundee's shot before we seen*
> *Under James' banner ridin'*

His soul in battle now set free.

Save the cross and save the nation
Templar's refuge and Stuart Line
Crushed the Williamite hoard a risin'
By the Pass of Killiecrankie.

J.K. Stuart had several other new but traditional sounding Celtic pieces, played by *Ceann na Drochaide Bige,* that were also gaining popularity in many quarters. The *Wind In The Heather* was even negotiating to use some of them—not bad for a small Wyoming group.

Although it was approaching eleven o'clock, the concert and encores ended way too soon for the excited audience. As Sam and Liddy drove out of the parking lot, they rehashed the concert highlights. Still energized by the music, Sam told Liddy, "It's easy to see why the bagpipes were banned as a weapon of war after the Jacobite rebellion. If the 'pipes had been calling me to battle, it would have been hard to resist! I could follow them anywhere."

Sam left Liddy at her front door before eleven-thirty. He briefly hugged her as he said, "I'll stop by around eight in the morning, or will that be too early?"

Smiling warmly, Liddy responded, "I'll see you at eight o'clock sharp! And if you're late, I'll send a piper!"

⇌

Liddy had to scramble to get ready for skiing. Although she had gone to bed later than usual, overdue slumber almost never delayed her awakenings. Her career at the station had trained her to be on time. But this morning she had slept unusually long and hard. Last night's concert had invigorated her to a high level, but the soft and sweet embrace from Sam had triggered in her a deep relaxation response. The fading into blissful sleep was like the soothing reward of a hot shower after a hard day's work outside. A well-earned rest can't be beat, but she certainly hadn't *physically* earned the right to sleep so soundly last night. If Grieg hadn't licked her face, she still would have been in bed when Sam arrived! As it was, she got up, completed her morning rituals, and just finished putting her pack together when he pulled up in front of her house.

The sky was free of clouds, and the cold air felt sharply fresh against Liddy's face. "It should be a great day for skiing," she relayed to Sam as her SUV was warming up. They fastened their skis to the rooftop carrier and placed their packs in the back seat. Grieg knew the signs of an outing and was excitedly running back and forth, making sure he wouldn't be forgotten. They were on the road ten minutes later, with Grieg contentedly peering out the back windows. A short stop for some fast food supplied them with egg biscuits and coffee for the road. This was Sam's second breakfast; he usually had a bowl of cereal along with orange juice as soon as he got up in the morning. But because of the physical effort of cross-country skiing, he figured he could easily handle a few more calories.

As they drove west on the partially snow-packed Poison Spider Road, Liddy explained to Sam, "We don't usually get enough snow for skiing at this lower altitude, but we've been lucky this year."

"You're right, Liddy," commented Sam as he watched the bright, silvery vista slide by to the repetitive tune of vehicle noise, combined with Grieg's occasional panting in the back seat. "When the weather provides a rare opportunity like this, its good to experience it as much as possible. I guess I've been too wrapped up in my teaching lately and haven't been getting out as much as I should."

"I haven't been out much either," replied Liddy. "In fact, if you hadn't decided to come with me today, I might have passed up the skiing and just took Grieg for a run around my neighborhood. Laziness, I guess. I really prefer to have company when I ski in remote areas like this."

Liddy was then quiet for a long time, and Sam began to wonder if she might be a bit moody. After all, he hardly knew her and couldn't begin to guess what many of her attitudes might be. Women think differently than men, and when they're silent, it's often hard to guess their feelings. Come to think of it, before he met Liddy, he hadn't been on a date for a couple of years. His last date had been with a CTC secretary, and they had only gone out together once. She had talked very little and their interests and attitudes diverged rapidly.

Sam had always been a bit shy around women, perhaps because they were too emotional at times and overly sensitive about so many things. He really hoped that he and Liddy shared similar attitudes and beliefs. They definitely shared some common interests, and he had very much enjoyed the small amount of time they had spent together.

After about an hour, Liddy slowed down and then pulled the vehicle around, facing east as she parked at the top of a low hill. The brilliant winter sun felt warm, with only a slight breeze curling down from the hills to the southwest. Grieg leapt from the vehicle into the deep snow as Sam and Liddy grabbed their gear. They stepped over a barbed wire fence and Liddy then led them southward up a small drainage.

The temperature was twenty degrees and the snow was powdery dry, with only intermittent stretches of wind crust. They were getting terrific glides between the short stretches of more deeply drifted snow. Sam skied on some rather ancient laminated wooden slats, while Liddy sailed along with some of the latest hi-tech composite materials fastened to her feet. Grieg followed them in an erratic meander, swinging back and forth across their trail while sniffing at each animal track he crossed. In the patches of soft, deep snow, Grieg bounded up and down in their ski tracks, not venturing to the side. Once in a while, Sam could see a faint trace of the old trail made by Liddy several weeks earlier.

Taking turns at breaking a fresh track, they followed the drainage as it wound gently upward to the southwest. Their route crossed expanses of nearly solid white snow, broken only by a dark shale embankment on the west side of the drainage and a few tips of tall sage brush just barely sticking up above the snow's surface. After the first mile the canyon deepened and Sam recognized a silver-gray ridge of the Mowry Shale, juxtaposing its fossil fish scales and bentonite, deposited beneath a warm Cretaceous sea, with the cold albino desert through which they now skied. After another quarter mile, the canyon narrowed as they passed through a resistant ridge formed by the relatively hard sandstone of the Cloverly Formation. Sam explained to Liddy their progression backward through geologic time as they skied southward across successively older rock layers. The Jurassic Morrison Formation, known for its dinosaur bones, displayed pink sand and silt through gaps in the snow below the Cloverly ridge. A quarter mile farther south, the deep rusty red of Triassic silts, sands, and shales peeked through the snow on steep slopes and cliffs, with the purple of the Alcova limestone just ahead of them framing a gateway to the steep north side of the Rattlesnake Range.

Both Liddy and Sam took photographs of the unique winter spectacle that surrounded and absorbed them. The dazzling sun showered their world, cutting diamonds from the snow that tumbled with the breeze and then vanished as the sparkling crystals touched warm red Triassic surfaces. Expressions of joy marked their faces and etched their memories with the wonder they beheld as they skied. The sky, a pale winter blue, caressed thin wind-blown streamers of white clouds toward the northern horizon in a canopy that was otherwise unbroken.

After two and a half miles, they stopped for a short break where the valley widened, and a side-drainage came in from the southeast. Here, the rusty red of the Triassic sedimentary rocks gave way to the orange-red of the Permian Goose Egg Formation sands and silts, cut by thin limestone and gypsum layers. Some scattered pines could be seen below higher ridges to the south, growing on what Sam guessed was an outcrop of the Tensleep Sandstone. As they approached the steeper slopes of the north side of the Rattlesnakes, the snow depth increased and only a scattering of stone outcrops interrupted the glistening white surface that beckoned them to the heights. Liddy suggested that they take a side drainage southeastward. It was steeper than the main arroyo, but it led about a mile up to a minor summit with a nice view from about 500 feet below the crest of the range. Cutting a path through the deeper snow, it took them almost thirty minutes to reach the top. Looking toward the north, they were rewarded with an incredible view of the Owl Creek and Bighorn Mountains.

After scanning the horizon, Liddy's gaze rested on Sam. With a friendly smirk, she asked, "What on earth are you carrying in that pack? It looks a bit on the heavy side. Did you bring your kitchen sink? Or maybe a few pet rocks?"

"Just my usual collection of gear, Liddy. Extra clothes, mylar blanket, munchies, camera, pistol, GPS, compass, first aid kit, matches, two-meter hand-held ham radio…and for this trip, I brought a thermos of hot chocolate, which probably takes up as much space as and weighs more than the rest of the gear combined. On a short day trip like this, I figure that a little extra weight will help to keep me in shape…would you like some hot cocoa?"

"Since you went to all that effort, how can I refuse? Chocolate is hard to pass up. Do you always carry a pistol and a GPS unit?"

"Usually," responded Sam as he poured a cup for each of them. "Unless I'm driving a college vehicle where the pistol isn't allowed. I have a concealed-carry permit, and the pistol weighs only about a pound loaded; it has a titanium frame. The GPS weighs only eight ounces, and it's useful if I go out without a topographic map, or if I'm working in flat country where it's hard to locate myself on the map. I'm always finding places that I might want to return to, generally because of some geological or historical interest. If I'm backpacking I usually leave the GPS at home and just carry a topo' sheet and compass, to save weight."

Sam and Liddy ate their lunches and then took a few photographs of each other and their surroundings. She used a very small digital camera from which she would later download images to her computer to make prints. Sam, on the other hand, carried a rather old-fashioned compact thirty-five millimeter camera, loaded with color slide film. He usually took slides so that he could show them in class. He would scan the pictures into his computer if he needed them for publications or formal presentations. Sam had used this almost archaic photographic system for years, but had recently been thinking about purchasing a digital camera.

"Maybe you could help me select some appropriate camera gear…to bring my operation into the modern world?" he asked Liddy.

"Sure, I can show you my system when we get back to town," she replied. "It's expensive, but you could improve your results with some of the newer gear and probably reduce the weight in your pack as well. Maybe then you could tell me about your titanium pistol. My father gave me a stainless nine-millimeter when I left home. It has sentimental value, but it's always seemed to be a bit heavy to just toss in a pack, so I usually leave it behind."

"Lightweight pack guns are pretty common. You can educate me on the hi-tech cameras Liddy, and I'll fill you in on hi-tech shootin' irons. I do a lot of target shooting, and I often plink when I'm out skiing or hiking. The new lightweight materials are really good for that, but most of my shooting is of the *cowboy action* type. That's where you dress western and use arms of the late nineteenth century in rapid-fire competition."

"I know what that is. I helped put together a news short on cowboy shooting several years ago," she commented. "But I never really did have a chance to study what was happening. What I did see was entertaining though."

"Well, maybe I can drag you out to one of the shoots when the weather gets nice," said Sam. Looking around them, he added, "This really is a pretty place to ski. Have you been here often?"

"This is my third time here," answered Liddy. "Grieg and I found it in November when we were roaming around the country. I actually got stuck turning around about a mile up the road, and a rancher helped me get out. He told me about this area. It used to be private land 'til the Game and Fish bought it a year ago. Oh! Look over there!" she exclaimed, pointing to a bunch of elk standing on a distant slope to the west. "I've seen elk every time I've come here!"

The elk were too far away for good photographs, but Sam and Liddy enjoyed just watching them until the last one ambled out of sight behind a distant ridge. The two skiers continued to absorb the openness of the surroundings during their leisurely lunch break. Pointing out familiar mountains and drainages to each other conveyed their mutual appreciation for the open country that they now enjoyed.

As they prepared to leave the area, Grieg cocked his head nervously and whimpered, then ran over to Liddy. Sam and Liddy stood up, but then faltered when they felt a rolling motion and heard an ominous, almost imperceptible low rumble. The time was 11:45 a.m. Southwest of where they stood and below the high ridge, a cornice broke loose, tumbling several hundred yards down the slope in an avalanche. A second small avalanche in wind-crusted snow slid about fifty feet from the side of the drainage up which they had skied. The rolling motion lasted for about five seconds. It then became very quiet.

Liddy nervously looked at Sam and whispered, "Earthquake?"

"*Earthquake!*" answered Sam. Then after a pause, he added, "I'm glad we weren't in the gully when that snow broke loose. It was small, but even a small slide can be dangerous, especially a slab like that."

"Lets wait a few minutes before we ski down, just to make sure it's over," said Liddy, shakily.

⇌

That same beautiful Saturday, Andrew Merlott left his trailer at first light and headed down the highway toward Farson and Rock Springs. The back of his pickup contained numerous six-foot long pieces of three-inch diameter PVC pipe, pipe caps, a bundle of three-foot long pieces of half-inch rebar, several cans of orange spray paint, a sledge hammer, and a shovel. All of this was in addition to his normal pile of sleeping bag, camp stove, tire chains, and related equipment that, for want of other facilities, was perpetually stored in his truck under the camper shell. He also brought some food and water, his compass, 300-foot measuring tape, partially blank mining claim notices, and small plastic bottles in which to stuff the claim notices. In addition, he carried sample bags, USGS 1:24,000 scale topographic maps for the Bitter Creek NW and Black Buttes quadrangles, a USBLM 1:100,000 scale Red Desert Basin mineral ownership map, and a belt-mounted string measuring instrument.

This last device he had used for more than twenty-five years; it allowed him to rapidly measure out claim dimensions by himself. Thread from the device was tied to a starting point and then pulled out through a meter as he walked. When the large meter indicated the desired distance, he would mark another point or claim corner. As long as he walked in a relatively straight line, his measurements were well within acceptable accuracy limits for laying out claims. "Better equipment makes light work," he spoke out loud to himself as he mentally inventoried his gear while waiting for his truck to warm up.

Andy reached the dike after two hours, driving south to Rock Springs and then east along I-80. Construction efforts to clear the blocked interstate were still underway, and as a result, most of the small back roads near the site had been cleared of snow to allow vehicles access around it. Andy parked his pickup on public land about two miles south of the interstate, next to the new dike. He then went to work. Here the land and mineral ownership pattern was part of what was called the "Union Pacific checkerboard."

During the 1860s, part of the incentive for construction of the transcontinental railroad was the deeding of every other section of land, twenty miles on either side of the right-of way, to the railroad. One section covers approximately one square mile (640 acres) in area. The railroad would supposedly sell off land, as necessary, to finance railroad operations and for maintenance to keep the transcontinental route open for the good of the country. However, it never really worked out that way. In the 1860s, power and money in the U.S. Congress orchestrated the give-away. Then later, the Union Pacific created a *lands and minerals division* as a separate subsidiary. With the appropriate corporate setup in the late 1900s, they again begged the federal government for money to support their passenger train service, hoping that most congressmen and others would have forgotten their 120 year-old deal. When the new subsidies ran out, they dropped much of the passenger service like a hot potato and let passengers fight for busses or airplanes. Unfortunately, no politician had the guts to hold the U.P. to a contract that old, and Congress appropriated new subsidies every five or ten years.

For Andy, this meant that he could only stake claims on the lands managed by the U.S. Bureau of Land Management (BLM). The Union Pacific owned the minerals under the other part of the checkerboard, which amounted to a bit less than half of the length of the dike. Andy found a section corner to begin from just off of the gravel road and about one-quarter mile from the dike. This section corner, and several others, had been located and uncovered by work crews trying to assess damages to various power lines and pipelines. On the section line between the public land to the north and the Union Pacific land to the south, Andy measured the bearing and distance to the dike's center. Here he used his sledge to pound a three-foot piece of rebar half-way into the ground and sprayed orange paint on the part left sticking out. He then placed a six-foot length of PVC pipe over the rebar and shoveled in some fine dirt and sand to hold it in place. He piled several of the soft dike rocks up around the pipe to give it more stability. The orange paint would help him find the rebar in case the PVC pipe got knocked over by range cattle or through other causes.

Andy filled out his notice for a lode claim that he named "Diamond Lil #1." Not a very original name, but he liked the sound of it. He then filled out a second copy for his records. This he would feed through a copy machine later in order to file the claims with the Sweetwater County Courthouse in Green River and with the BLM in Cheyenne. Andy then placed the claim notice in a plastic bottle and attached it to his claim post with a piece of bailing wire. He took a compass bearing on the direction of the dike. He then measured 300 feet along the section line on both sides of the dike away from his claim post, roughly perpendicular to the dike bearing. At those points he pounded pieces of rebar into the ground, leaving about a foot of each sticking out. He painted the exposed rebar orange.

Tying one end of his string to the rebar on the west side of the dike, and using his compass to direct him in a straight line parallel to the dike, he measured out 1500 feet. He tapped a piece of rebar into the ground at this point, but not deeply yet. He then turned a ninety-degree corner to the east and measured 300 feet to what he hoped would be the center of the dike. He then set another claim post the same as his first, only this time with the claim name "Diamond Lil #2." Andy measured another 300 feet east of the claim post on the same bearing he had set at the rebar where he had turned. He pounded in another rebar and painted the top orange, then crossed back over the dike to the rebar where he made the turn, setting it deeply, and again painting the top orange.

Andy now had one claim staked and had started a second

claim. It would have been faster to walk the length of the dike on its top, if it had been less rugged and more stable, but offsetting 300 feet to the side of the claim wasn't much of a problem. Lode claims measure 1500 feet long and 300 feet each side of the centerline in maximum dimensions. Under ideal conditions these claims are rectangular, but because of the dike's angle to the section lines, Andy's claims were parallelograms. His second claim actually overlapped the Union Pacific land slightly on its northwest corner, but he didn't really worry about it. The section was odd-shaped, and a mineral survey would only give him access to the federal minerals. Minor adjustments like that can happen. He would be certain to have the minerals claimed right up to the Union Pacific boundary line. At least that was how his written description of the claim would read. A small triangular-shaped piece of public land, hosting 400 feet of the dike, remained to be staked to complete this section of the dike.

As Andy finished the last corner on his second claim, he felt the ground move beneath his feet and heard a low rumbling noise. Andy recognized this as an earthquake. Several rocks tumbled down from the dike toward him, and a small rock struck his lower left leg. A larger one could have fractured the bone! It was bad enough, however, as he had procured a very painful bruise. Andy limped back to his truck and sat in the cab. He then poured himself a cup of coffee from his thermos and ate a sandwich. At least it wasn't windy or terribly cold. But his leg hurt! Wrapped in pain and agitation, he forgot about the small triangular section of dike at the north end of Diamond Lil #2. He drove south on the gravel road, then northwest, then back southeast for a total of nearly four miles to a point on the dike northwest of where he had ended Diamond Lil #2.

He was again on public land and he hobbled uncomfortably around to a marked section quarter-corner. There he could survey to the center of the dike on the section line and start laying out another claim. Because of his sore leg, he moved much more slowly. But he thought that if he didn't finish the job now, some one else might get the jump on staking claims here. By late afternoon he had staked three more claims. Climbing back and forth across the dike was difficult and probably hazardous as well. The last two claims were not quite

1500 feet long because of irregularities on the dike that made some points impossible for him to reach. There was still a strip of public land north of Diamond Lil #5, but he was just too tired and sore to continue staking that day. If he'd been younger, if it had been warmer, if his leg didn't hurt, if…then he might have camped out and finished the job in the morning. But Andy was beat and just wanted to get back home.

Before leaving, Andy loaded several large chunks of the dike material into the back of his truck, carefully labeling them and those from the other claims he had staked. It was almost dark before he drove west on I-80 toward Rock Springs. There he filled his truck with gasoline and grabbed some fast food, before heading north out of town. Andy reached Atlantic City about eight o'clock and was back in his trailer forty minutes later. He had carried a few samples with him on the back of his snowmobile, but had left most of them in his truck to pick up later. Andrew Merlott felt worn-out when he went to bed, but he felt like he had accomplished something significant, at least in the possibility of future income. Andy felt good about his new claims. Too bad he hadn't had the time or endurance to finish staking the entire dike near Point of Rocks. A complete mining property holds the strongest marketing position possible, while a partial property allows other *unknowns* to control operations or set prices.

⇌

After waiting an endless five minutes, Liddy, followed by Sam and Grieg, cautiously skied back down their track. It was a nice run, but they appreciated it more after they perceived that no further danger existed to them. Only then did Liddy and Sam take pictures of the avalanches. When they reached the main drainage, they decided to return to their vehicle and then to Casper rather than ski farther that day. They both were concerned about unstable snow conditions, and Liddy proposed that they spend what remained of the afternoon just visiting at her house. Besides, Sam could meet her horse, *Topo*.

Their ski back to Liddy's vehicle was smooth and fast. The inevitable Wyoming wind, now at their backs, was beginning to spin drifting snow across the white ridges, swirling sparkling crystals in plumes off the north and east sides of any high ground. As the wind picked up, a rolling tumbleweed latched onto Sam's legs and then freed itself, only to be grabbed again by the wind. The skeletal sphere, surrounded by flying ice crystals, rolled and bounced rapidly out of sight toward the horizon. Following their tracks carefully, with his tail low to the ground, Grieg slogged through the deeper snow behind them. He would bound forward and keep up with them where hard drifts kept him from sinking in. They stopped several times in the longer deep stretches to let him catch up, while the ground-drift slowly buried their skis, only to be broken and scattered when they began moving again.

The gusts and blowing snow rattling on their windbreakers made conversation difficult, so no words were spoken on the return trip. Their thoughts were active with the winter beauty that they had experienced and the avalanche they had escaped. The sounds of the wind and drifting snow, accompanied by the rhythmic swish of their skis, seemed to hypnotically propel them forward with great speed. It was as if they sailed effortlessly on the wind, only forcing a stop occasionally to wait for Grieg. He would be tired when they reached Liddy's vehicle. The only ragged disruptions to the smooth pleasantness of their thoughts were questions about the earthquake.

Liddy's vehicle, having been warmed by the sun, was a welcome haven after they had taken the packs off of their sweaty backs and had stowed the skis on the roof rack. Snowdrifts had formed next to the vehicle's wheels, but they had no trouble pulling back onto the road. As she drove toward town, Liddy broke the lingering silence, "Do you suppose that today's earthquake was related to the ones last week?"

"I don't know for sure, Liddy. It's possible, but not likely. Repetitive related quakes can happen along major geologic structures or in volcanic areas, but we just don't have any known active major faults in most parts of Wyoming."

"You say *most* parts of Wyoming?" asked Liddy with curiosity. "What parts have known active faults?"

Sam continued his verbal consideration of the recent events, "The western Wyoming ranges, the Tetons, and

Yellowstone exhibit the most energetic large faults in the state. And other than the new dike, Yellowstone is the only active volcanic area in Wyoming. It could be some other small fault we haven't noticed before that caused the quake. I'll check the seismograph on Monday and talk to a grad' student in Laramie who's studying seismology and earthquakes."

"Where do you think the quake was centered?" questioned Liddy with interest as the Rattlesnake Hills receded from view behind them.

"Unless we hear about it on the news, or check the USGS website, we won't know until I look at the college seismograph."

"I wonder how strong it was. Earthquakes aren't *that* common in Wyoming, are they?" inquired Liddy, the subject drawing her increased attention.

"Hard to tell how powerful it was without instruments or observable structural damage to buildings," said Sam thoughtfully.

Liddy remembered hearing about earthquakes in Wyoming in the past, but she had never really paid attention to them in a connected manner. Now, as she drove, she continued to question Sam with an unfulfilled curiosity. His answers begged for more questions from her. It reminded her of listening to AM talk radio, when she didn't want to shut it off until the program was finished.

Sam continued, "Earthquakes are generally uncommon in Wyoming outside of the western Wyoming ranges near the borders with Idaho, Montana, and Utah, and those places are too far away for us to feel anything, other than really big events. One or two small quakes will happen randomly around the state every few years. The northern Laramie Range, southeast of Casper, has a record of a few moderately strong quakes spread over the last one hundred and fifty years. However, more than two or three earthquakes outside of Yellowstone or western Wyoming, in a short span of time, is *highly unusual*."

"How often does Yellowstone experience earthquakes?"

After offering Liddy a fruit bar, Sam explained, "Yellowstone gets small quakes quite often. Sometimes weekly, sometimes daily. Yellowstone contains one of the world's biggest calderas, which is a collapsed volcano. It's considered to have high potential for a new, very large eruption. Magma, which is melted rock, is known to exist at a shallow depth of only about three to five miles beneath Yellowstone. Many small quakes at Yellowstone are related to movement of melted rock within the magma chamber beneath the park."

As Liddy steered around a newly formed snowdrift in the right lane of the highway, she quizzed Sam, "How do people know that?" She hoped to learn as much as possible before they got back to Casper, where this particular line of discussion might get sidetracked.

"Seismic studies…heat flow studies…geologic history of past eruptions," answered Sam. He continued his explanations and descriptions of earthquakes, volcanoes, and Yellowstone all the way back to Liddy's home. She was fascinated. She had known a little bit about Yellowstone's geology from trips there with her family when she was growing up. But now Sam's explanations brought it to life, just like his descriptions had brought geologic history to life for her on the field trip the previous Saturday. It was awe-inspiring and remotely scary for her to think that Yellowstone actually had the potential to become an active volcano, and a dangerous one at that!

CHAPTER 6

Yellowstone

▼

O Lord, how manifold are your works! In wisdom you have made them all; the earth is full of your riches. - Psalm 104:24

The two fatigued skiers arrived in Casper by mid-afternoon. Sam stashed his skis and backpack into his truck and then carried Liddy's gear into her house. The succulent aroma of simmering meat captured Sam's attention.

"That sure smells good. What's cooking?" inquired Sam.

"Elk roast," answered Liddy as she dumped her coat on the sofa and then continued into the kitchen to check on it. "I put it in the crock pot just before we left this morning. I figured it would be done by late afternoon."

"Can't wait to taste it! I use a slow cooker fairly often myself," noted Sam as he followed her. "It's pretty handy when you're on the go."

Opening the lid and checking to make sure the meat was still moist, she continued, "My dad shot it last fall when he was hunting in the Bighorns." A cloud of steam rolled outward from the pot, releasing an intense savory aroma that stimulated Sam's mouth to water and brought Grieg to attention. Engulfed in the vapor, she added, "I hope you like elk?"

"I love wild game, and I enjoy hunting too," offered Sam with a grin like that of an over-worked cowboy as he nears the end of a chow line. "Since elk are such large critters, I can usually make one last at least two seasons in the freezer. I only go after them every couple of years or so. I hunted last fall, but didn't get one."

"Good! Oh, not that you didn't get one," Liddy flushed slightly at stumbling on her words..."but that you can help me eat some of the meat my dad gave me." She was glad to have his company, but felt that maybe she was struggling just a bit too hard to please him. Liddy noticed that her generally prevailing self-confidence around people seemed to disintegrate in Sam's presence. *Why this sudden need to be so perfect?*

Liddy continued, "I need to throw some vegetables in with the roast...they should be done by about five...I hope you don't mind the wait. I also made an apple salad to go with it. And," she paused, "don't let me forget to put the rolls in the oven around four-thirty."

"Sounds good to me, Liddy! I'll try to remember to look at my watch, but you'd better be careful not to distract me, lest I forget," smiled Sam. He perceived she was slightly nervous and trying to impress him. He also deduced that she was much more relaxed in activities other than putting on a show of homemaking skills. Perhaps his attempt at subtle humor would put her more at ease.

"I also made a chocolate cake for dessert," she added, with a hint of awkwardness reminiscent of a timid child seeking approval from a fastidious teacher.

"I can't resist anything chocolate!" said Sam with a huge smile. "You really went all out. I'm starving, but I'll wait 'til you say it's done." His stomach growled audibly and he hoped that she hadn't heard it.

"While it's still daylight, let's go outside to see Topo...and Camile, if she's home," invited Liddy.

Camile wasn't around, but Liddy's horse was glad to see her. Topo was a striking, loud-colored Appaloosa gelding of about fifteen hands. A handsome buckskin with a large spotted blanket over his hips, he had an irregular marking on his left side that looked almost like two concentric lines around a hill on a topographic map. The lines joined at the lower edge of the pattern, and the appearance was such that anyone familiar with topo' maps could easily see where the horse got his name. He was calm and friendly, and Liddy said he handled very responsively with nice smooth gaits. Camile's large corral also held two other geldings: a dark, smoky gray Arab named *Sizzler*, and a chestnut overo paint named *Fritz*. Sam had never seen such colorful horses together in one spot.

Occupying the top of the pecking order in the confines of Camile's corral, Topo was first in line for Sam and Liddy's attention, while the other horses watched from a distance. Liddy occasionally rode Sizzler or Fritz when she went riding with Camile. All three horses were well trained, and since Sam wasn't used to horses, Liddy assured him that he would have no trouble handling any of them if they were to ride together sometime. They stood for a few minutes by the fence while Liddy, out of habit, visually inspected the condition of the horses.

As they leaned against the corral poles, Liddy probed Sam, "The other day you told me to ask you about a four-legged 'brother' you'd had. Tell me about it."

"When I was less than four years old, my parents brought a little mongrel puppy home. He was a tan-colored shaggy mutt, named Teddy. I guess you can say that we grew up together, and he was almost as dear to me as my *real* brother Ben. Teddy went everywhere with our family; we never had the heart to leave him behind. He was an important member of the *pack*. Liddy, it's hard to find a more loyal friend than a dog. I wish their life spans equaled our own; their lives are way too short! Teddy was sixteen years old when I left home to continue my education. He was hard of hearing by then, and stiff with arthritis, but generally healthy."

Sam continued, "The strange thing was that after I'd been gone about five months, Teddy disappeared. My parents searched for him for days. They finally found his body in an old gravel pit on the edge of town. It was a place where Teddy and I had played together countless times when I was in grade school. What was really unusual was what they found next to Teddy's body…a frazzled, old piece of yellow rope…the same rope that Teddy and I used to play *Tug-of-War* with through the years, often at the gravel pit. Whether Teddy had found it in the pit or dragged it from home before he went off to die, know one knows. I hadn't seen the rope in years…Teddy must have had it stashed away somewhere. He probably thought of the rope as a little piece of *me*."

"Gosh, Sam, that's a real sad story," began Liddy as she groped in a jacket pocket for a tissue to wipe her eyes. "Animals are something else, aren't they? If people can't get the love and loyalty they need from other humans, at least the animals will gladly oblige!"

The wind picked up slightly, and a few thin clouds diminished the strength of the sun, bringing a chill to the air. Liddy shivered as a sensation of fatigue overcame her, no doubt from the previous hours of breaking trail through the snow. They walked back to her yard where Grieg was impatiently waiting for their return. Sam and Liddy chased him around the yard a few times before going indoors to warm themselves with large mugs of gourmet coffee. Liddy talked of her experiences riding the trails of the Bighorns. She had taken quite a few pack trips with her parents when she had lived in Buffalo. But school and work had bogged her down in recent years, and she'd managed only one horse trip, with Camile, into the Wind Rivers. The conversation migrated from riding to hunting and then to their mutual desires to explore some of the wilder and more remote parts of Wyoming, including the backcountry of Yellowstone and the adjacent Absaroka Mountains. Liddy dug out one of her books on Yellowstone, and together they looked it over.

Yellowstone was the *first* national park, not just in the United States, but also in the entire world. It was set aside by law enacted by the Senate and House of Representatives of the United States of America in Congress Assembled, "...*that the tract of land in the territories of Montana and Wyoming lying near the headwaters of the Yellowstone River is hereby reserved and withdrawn from settlement, occupancy, or sale under the laws of the United States, and dedicated and set apart as a public park or pleasure ground for the benefit and enjoyment of the people.*" This act of Congress was signed by James G. Blain, Speaker of the House; Schuyler Colfax, Vice-President of the United States and President of the Senate; and Ulysses S. Grant, President of the United States, on March 1, 1872.

In the early 1800s, reports from trappers and explorers told of smoking rivers, intense sulfur smells, and geysers in the area. But trappers such as John Colter and others had reputations for telling *tall tales* that most people assumed were fabrication. Stories, such as *Colter's Hell* and similar tales, were often repeated or embellished by those who passed through the Yellowstone region. An expedition sent out by the Geological and Geographical Survey of the Territories (the predecessor of the United States Geological Survey), under the leadership of geologist Ferdinand V. Hayden, visited the Yellowstone area during the summer of 1871. They brought along photographer William H. Jackson and artist Thomas Moran. This expedition made a geological reconnaissance study and provided pictorial documentation of the fabulous wonders reported a year earlier by the Washburn-Doane Expedition. It was this documentation that convinced Congress to set aside Yellowstone as a national park.

Both Sam and Liddy had traveled by car through Yellowstone, and Sam had done some geological work in both the Absaroka and Beartooth Mountains, just outside of the park's boundaries. Portions of *Colter's Hell* may actually have been seen on the Shoshone River above Cody, under what is now Buffalo Bill Reservoir. Inactive hot springs accompanied by tuffa deposits, fluorite, sulfur, and several trace metals are found west of Cody.

"I just remembered that I've got some Yellowstone reference material behind the seat in my pickup. Would you like me to get it?" asked Sam.

"Sure," answered Liddy. "This is interesting. Maybe we should think about taking a horse trip into the area next summer? I'll bet Camile and maybe my parents would like to go too."

"I'd be game," responded Sam, "although I think I'd like a bit of instruction and experience on a horse before taking a long trip like that. I'll be right back in with the books," he said as he headed for the door.

Sam returned a few minutes later with the references that he had pulled from his office library on Thursday. Liddy, while Sam was out, had fixed them each another mug of coffee. They began looking over his books, with Sam explaining and simplifying some of the more complex geological ideas in order to help her understand. Liddy was learning a lot through this private geology lesson!

Yellowstone National Park is a seismically active area that has, for many years, averaged about five earth tremors or small earthquakes daily. Sometimes as many as one hundred or more tremors are recorded in the park by seismographs over the course of a single day. However, most of these are too small to be felt, but occasionally, stronger quakes do occur. The strongest recorded quake was around magnitude 7.5 on the Richter scale, on August 17, 1959. During that quake an area of about 200 square miles, including Hegben Lake, subsided a foot or more and in some places as much as twenty feet. That quake was actually felt over an area of 600,000 square miles.

Most of the earthquakes in Yellowstone seem to be centered at depths ranging from about two to six miles and are usually less than magnitude 4.5. Historical records compiled by the USGS and the University of Utah show that Yellowstone quakes have occurred in swarms that may last for several months. These swarms often correspond to changes in geothermal features such as hot springs and geysers. Such swarms occur at irregular intervals and seem to be related to magma movement at depth. Most of the quakes correspond to faults and fractures that either form a rough ring around, are adjacent to, or radiate outward from the Yellowstone caldera. The caldera takes up almost one third of Yellowstone National Park and covers about 1000 square miles.

Sam related to Liddy much of his discussion with Chris and Surya about Surya's seismic project and the history of violent volcanic eruptions from the Yellowstone hotspot. Liddy had never realized that the eruptions had been so large, that ash had been spread so widely, or that most geologists consider Yellowstone to have the potential for renewed violent eruption with little or no warning. Sam had told her some of this on the drive back from skiing, but seeing the extent of ashfalls on a map, representing past eruptions of Yellowstone, allowed the information to take on a serious new meaning.

The violent eruptive progression in what is now Yellowstone National Park temporarily ceased about 600,000 years ago in a caldera that now occupies a large area of the park. Immediately after the collapse of the caldera, magma rose beneath it causing the rocks to bow upward in its northeastern

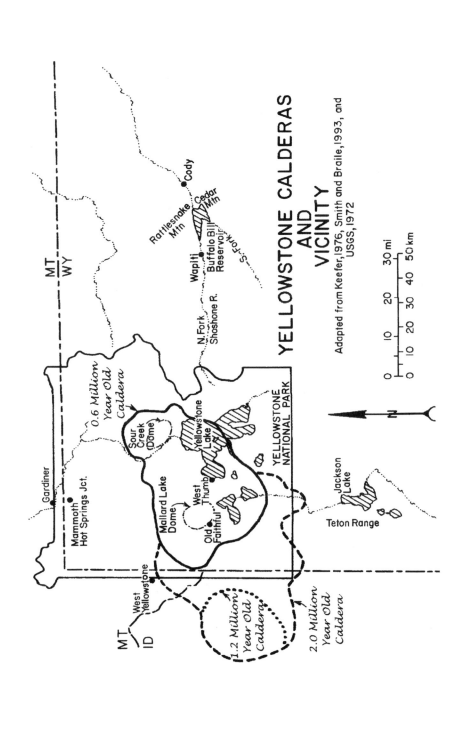

YELLOWSTONE CALDERAS
AND
VICINITY

Adapted from Keefer,1976, Smith and Braile,1993, and
USGS, 1972

portion, forming what is called Sour Creek Dome. About 150,000 years ago, magma again pushed upward in the southwestern part of the caldera, forming Mallard Lake Dome. Between 150,000 and 70,000 years ago, forty or more small silicic volcanic eruptions took place on the Yellowstone Plateau, and several small basaltic eruptions penetrated the margins of the plateau. Today, hot geysers and springs hint at what exists beneath the surface.

Sam's references emphasized the significance of past volcanic activity and the potential for future Yellowstone eruptions to dramatically affect North America and the world climate. The Lava Creek ash deposit of 600,000 years ago is estimated to represent approximately 240 cubic miles or more of molten rock, blasted into fine particles and spread across the western United States. This can be compared with the *puny* one-quarter to one-half cubic mile of material vented by Mount St. Helens in Washington on May 18, 1980. Mount St. Helens was considered a catastrophe and fine ash from that eruption had fallen as far east as Wyoming.

Sam's copy of the *Encyclopedia of Volcanoes*, published around the turn of the twenty-first century, described several volcanoes and provided useful comparisons to put Yellowstone in perspective. Krakatau, located between Sumatra and Java in Indonesia, about 100 miles west of Jakarta, vented *4.4 cubic miles* of ash and debris on August 27, 1883. Dust blotted out the sun, bringing on darkness in Jakarta, and reddened sunsets were observed in the United States and in Europe after that eruption.

The volcano Tambora, on the island of Sumbawa in Indonesia, erupted an estimated thirty-six cubic miles of material on April 10, 1815, resulting in what was known as the "year with no summer." In the year following that eruption, snow fell on New England in June and cold temperatures were recorded all along the east coast of the United States, accompanied by severe crop failures. From other historical sources, they learned that daytime skies over Europe were darkened substantially. Crop failures due to frost plagued both Asia and Europe during 1816 and 1817. In London, record high prices for grain reflected the agricultural catastrophe resulting from Tambora.

However, all of these volcanoes were *dwarfed* by the large

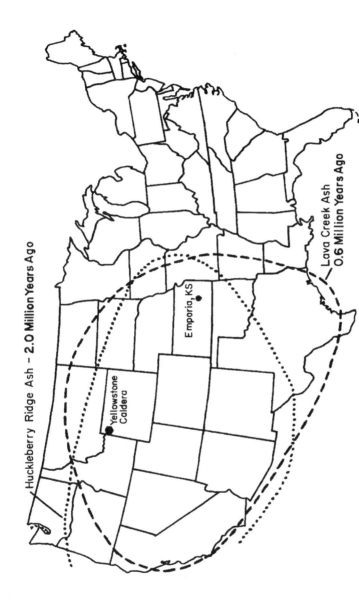

APPROXIMATE EXTENT OF ASHFALL DEPOSITS FROM PAST ERUPTIONS
OF YELLOWSTONE
Adapted from Sarna-Wojcicki and Davis, 1991.

violent eruption from Yellowstone about two million years ago. That cataclysm, more than sixteen times the size of Tambora, vented an estimated eruptive volume of *600 cubic miles of ash*! That ash is now represented in a thick deposit known as the *Huckleberry Ridge tuff* that was spread throughout the western United States. The climatic consequences of that eruption can only be guessed at, although speculation suggest possible correlations between major volcanic eruptions and some Pleistocene glacial advances. Sam summed up his thoughts with a long contemplative sigh, "Mount St. Helens was just a small popgun in comparison to Yellowstone. *Truly, Yellowstone is a geologic force worthy of serious consideration!*"

Liddy suddenly jumped off the couch when she noticed the time. After teasingly chastising Sam for forgetting to look at his watch, they set Sam's books aside and she put homemade whole-wheat rolls into the oven. "They should be ready in about twenty minutes," she told him. "Everything else is done. Could I get you a small glass of wine?"

"Yes, thanks," replied Sam. "That is unless you think it will further limit my ability to keep track of the time. But if you aren't keeping track, I won't either."

Liddy brought two glasses of wine from the kitchen and handed one to Sam, who responded with "Mange takk!"

"What was *that*?" asked Liddy curiously.

"Norwegian. My mother's maiden name was *Haaland*, and her Norwegian expressions became a part of my vocabulary when I was growing up. I only know a few. *Mange takk* means *many thanks.*"

"Well, my knowledge of foreign languages is pretty limited, but I do know a few Spanish words and phrases." As she walked toward her stereo system, Liddy asked, "What type of dinner music would you like?"

"How about *Grieg*?" suggested Sam. The dog lifted his head and cocked his ear in recognition of his name.

"Grieg it is," she said as she picked up a CD and inserted it into the player. Grieg, wagging his tail, focused his gaze on Liddy as his name was spoken again.

Liddy showed Sam the details of her electronic entertainment center as music softly filled the house. The bulk of her CD collection was mostly rock and classical, but included an assortment of Celtic, folk, and western swing scattered throughout the shelf. Liddy loaded several CDs into the changer before they walked into the kitchen for dinner.

When they had finished eating, Sam complemented Liddy, "You are definitely a woman of many talents. Did you attend a school of culinary arts too? I haven't had a meal like this in ages. My mother used to cook like this." It occurred to Sam that whatever Liddy Hill fixed would probably taste good to him. But it was her company that pleased him the most.

Sam helped her clean off the table, and they piled the dishes by the sink, to wash later. They then relaxed in the living room for the short remainder of the evening, until Liddy decided to call it a day, knowing that she would have to be at work by five in the morning. She now had Monday and Tuesday as her regular days off until the following Sunday, when her March schedule would begin. She would then have regular weekends off for at least four months.

"Perhaps we could get together again on Monday or Tuesday?" she queried softly, hoping not to seem too forward.

"I think I'll be free Monday evening. Could I take you out for supper after I get off work?" ventured Sam while rounding up his coat. "Why don't I pick you up, and we'll figure out a place to eat at that time."

"That sounds good...I'll be waiting for you," answered Liddy with a broad smile.

Sam continued, "On Tuesday, I'm hoping to go to Laramie after my morning class to x-ray those samples I showed you. If you'd like to come along for the ride, I'd enjoy the company. I've got a meeting that evening that I need to attend, so I plan on getting back here around seven at the latest."

Liddy replied, "Actually, I could use a change of scenery for a day. Should I just meet you at your office?"

"That'd work out fine. And I'll stop by here late Monday afternoon. Thanks again for the great ski trip and fabulous dinner!"

"The pleasure was all mine," Liddy murmured as Sam gently embraced her. Liddy relaxed as they held each other for several seconds until Grieg pushed his wet nose between them, jealously feeling left out. Liddy massaged the dog's neck and regretfully said, "Tomorrow morning will come early. I really must call it a day."

Gently squeezing her hand, Sam spoke softly, "See you Monday evening." Hesitatingly, he loosened his grip on Liddy's hand, then rubbed Grieg's head and left for home.

⇌

The local Sunday morning newspaper mentioned Saturday morning's 11:45 earthquake. According to the United States Geological Survey, the magnitude 5.3 quake was centered just south of Sweetwater Station in central Wyoming. The USGS had also mentioned four other small to moderate earthquakes, occurring in northwestern Wyoming and neighboring Montana. Liddy reported these quakes on KWYN's early newscast, noting that dishes in cupboards were rattled in Casper, Rawlins, Thermopolis, and several other cities before noon on Saturday.

Sam was occupied with various commitments on Sunday; he didn't have time to go by the college to check Saturday's seismic data. After attending a morning church service, he met with several amateur radio friends for lunch, and then he spent the afternoon servicing and cleaning his pickup. Actually, he would have preferred to put off the service work, but it needed to be done before driving any distance away from Casper. He probably could have rearranged the day's schedule to get even more things done, but he was just a little tired from the ski trip. Although Sam was in decent physical shape, he hadn't done much cross-country skiing this winter and had stretched a few muscles that were used less during his normal activities.

⇌

Sam arrived at his CTC office early on Monday morning. He then headed directly for the basement to check on the seismic data that had been collected over the weekend. Sam loaded the data from the LSU to the main memory on the computer. The LSU (*large storage unit*) was a dense block of memory internally coupled to the computer and designed for storage of extraordinarily large amounts of sequential data. The unit was capable of storing all data acquired by Surya's seismic network, collected over a three-month period. Before this unit reached memory saturation, it would be necessary, on a routine basis, to archive the data to long-term laser disk storage units. But that could occur some time in the future. For now, Sam just looked at the seismograph trace and interpretations that were synthesized, using Surya's algorithms.

The results showed an astonishingly clear depiction of Saturday's 5.3 magnitude earthquake that was centered about two miles south of Sweetwater Station, at a depth of eighteen miles. The quake was focused on a fault trending northeastward from the north edge of the Red Desert and into the Granite Mountains where it faded out. The three-dimensional view of the fault, along which the quake had occurred, was fascinating. On Friday, Surya and Chris had added the seismograph installation at Salt Lake City to the network, bringing on-line five out of the proposed seven stations in his array.

A further look at the data showed that five earthquakes had occurred within half an hour of each other: Cody was first at 11:32 a.m., centered on a northwest trending fault at a depth of 9.3 miles; the second quake at 11:36 was near Gardiner, Montana at 6.2 miles depth along a north-northwest trending fault; and a quake at Thermopolis occurred only a minute later at 11:37, centered at a depth of 13.7 miles along an east-west fault. An 11:58 a.m. Geyser, Montana quake at 5.0 miles depth appeared to be along a northwest trending fault, although its location outside of Surya's network of stations made details sketchy.

But what appeared to be even more interesting to Sam was a series of small, almost continuous quakes at depths of less than 7.5 miles, ranging from magnitudes of about 2.1 to 3.4, scattered in and around Yellowstone National Park. These very tiny quakes had not been mentioned in the USGS news release, probably because they would for the most part be too insignificant to be felt. These began at 11:24 a.m., shortly before the Cody quake. The swarm of quakes continued for about two hours before gradually dying out. A map, constructed to depict locational data, showed these quakes to roughly outline part of the Yellowstone caldera and to highlight linear structures that were most likely faults radiating outward from, or tangential to, the caldera.

This was all neat stuff and of great interest to Sam, but he needed to get to work. He had spent almost an hour looking at seismic interpretations and had yet to complete his class preparations for the day. Sam went back to his office, poured himself some coffee, and began to rearrange his class notes to include new bits of information that he had recently acquired. His lecture would cover geologic structures, but focus on faults in particular. Some of the seismic data he had just looked at would be useful to fuel the curiosity of his students.

The first questions asked by Sam's students addressed the earthquakes reported on Saturday. Several of the students had felt the 11:45 a.m. tremor in Casper and queried, "Where were the earthquakes centered?"

Sam explained the epicenters for the five earthquakes, but did not address the small swarm of quakes at Yellowstone. He wanted to talk to Chris and Surya to confirm that analysis; he needed to make sure that it wasn't some sort of noise in the system before he cited it as fact.

Another student asked, "Were all of the recent earthquakes related, maybe resulting from current regional uplifting within the North American crustal plate?"

Sam explained, "Although that is a possibility, we don't want to get involved in a geological witch hunt for mega-causes before we have sufficient data to support such an hypothesis. We should wait until we have more information before tying ourselves to a particular idea. Some faulting and related earthquakes might be expected to accompany regional uplift. However, we would also have to have supporting data to show a regional rise in elevation. We have nothing to support such a conclusion at the present time."

Sam urged his students to ask lots of questions. He did not want them to be satisfied with doing things just because they had always been done in a certain way. He encouraged students not to accept statements as facts until they had actually researched them by examining several sources. Sam thought that too many people were overly complacent and accepting of just about anything that was fed to them—if some *expert* on television makes a statement, people often believe it as a fact, without ever questioning the veracity of the statement or the credentials of the person making the claims. Reports on many aspects of current events and natural phenomena, no matter how distorted, are believed simply because they are seen on television shows and documentaries. Sam was genuinely concerned that many aspects of United States history, as well as environmental studies, were being taught in a severely altered form in order to promote various political agendas, even at CTC. Sam had, unbelievably, talked to students who now thought that the United States had been an aggressor nation during World War II. *Thought control* had become quite common in many of the nation's classrooms. "How can I make these kids think for themselves?" was a question that Sam often posed to anyone who would listen.

Sam encouraged his students to use the scientific method to test their hypotheses, to research problems in detail, and not be afraid to change their ideas when new data comes along. He told his students, "If you learn to use sound investigative methods in geology, then you will see that the same methods of research can be applied to solve problems in society as well. These same techniques can be used to decipher *truth* from the tangle of political babble and obfuscation so prevalent in today's left-wing mass media dominated culture."

After his morning class, Sam phoned Chris Felsen in Laramie. Chris was not available so Sam left a message for him to call back. He then asked for Surya Ganisalim. When Surya answered, Sam asked him about the recent earthquakes and whether there was in fact a swarm of small quakes in Yellowstone. "Yes," responded Surya, "there *was* a swarm in Yellowstone." Sam's replication of Surya's interpretations with the CTC seismograph was a valuable confirmation of Surya's technique. Through a university in Utah, Surya had also been able to tap into a seismic network at Yellowstone. It was useful to have the Yellowstone network available, but for a number of complex technical reasons that included software, hardware, machine language, and surveying, the Yellowstone seismic network could not be directly tied into Surya's own array at the present time. However, he hoped that it could be done in the near future.

Sam continued with his class work and then put finishing touches on one article he was writing for an August geological conference, when he received the return call from Chris Felsen.

Sam inquired about the possibility of doing some x-ray diffraction analyses the following day. Chris checked the lab schedules and replied that Tuesday would work out fine. Sam planned on getting to Laramie during the noon hour. Chris said he would have the x-ray diffractometer ready at that time with some crystal mounts rather than the powder mounts. Most x-ray diffraction analyses make use of a mineral crushed to powder. Special mounts are needed for whole crystals to be examined. Sam could have used an electron microprobe for a micro-chemical analysis. However, the sample preparation time was much longer. He hoped to complete the analyses for two crystals in one afternoon; he had one other crystal to check in addition to the suspected diamond. After confirmation with Chris, Sam cleared his absence with Ralph and arranged for another instructor to take his Tuesday afternoon class.

$$\rightleftharpoons$$

Sam finished work a bit before five o'clock and walked home. After freshening up and changing his clothes, he drove north across town, arriving at Liddy's front gate to receive an enthusiastic doggy "hello" from Grieg. Liddy was ready to go. She and Sam smiled at each other as they got into his truck and drove off.

Sam would rather have greeted her with a meaningful embrace, but he didn't want to seem too forward. Such behavior might be interpreted as overbearing. He hoped that she was attracted to him as much as he was to her. But, after all, he had only known her for less than two weeks. Maybe it was his shyness getting in the way, but he preferred to think of himself as being considerate.

"Where would you like to eat?" he asked.

"Whatever you suggest will be fine," she replied.

"Have you ever been to the Mountain Steak House?"

"No, but if you're recommending it, I'll give it a try."

"It's a great place," he said, as he headed east on a four-lane highway that skirted the northern edge of town. "I've been there several times and haven't had a bad meal yet."

Driving toward the downtown area, Sam pointed out a

new restaurant on their left called *"The Cave,"* which was scheduled to open early in the spring. "I know the people who own that place. They're members of the college caving club, and I've gone on several cave trips with them. We'll have to check it out when they open!"

"When I ate supper with you after our videotaping," Liddy commented, "you mentioned that you had explored caves, and I also saw some cave pictures on your wall. Are those caves around here?"

"There *are* a few caves in the area, but the pictures you saw at my house are of some of the largest caves in the northern part of the state. Have you ever gone caving, Liddy?"

"No, I've never explored caves. But when I was in Huntsville, I knew a person who did. I guess there were tons to explore in Alabama and the surrounding states. I did go to a couple of really pretty caves down there that were tourist attractions. And when I was in junior high, my folks took me to see Jewel Cave in South Dakota. I knew there were some caves in the Bighorns, but we never gave them much thought."

"There's quite a few caves in the Bighorns. Some are large dolomite caves that are very cold and prone to severe flooding. Others are dry and dusty and full of tight crawlways that can tear your clothing apart as you squeeze through. Short, skinny people usually have an advantage over big guys like me. I once had to take my shirt off just to get through one particularly narrow crack. Exploring caves requires stamina and the willingness to contort your body into every imaginable position, while plastering it with mud or dirt to boot! I'm the advisor to the college caving club now and actually started caving with that group just after I began teaching. Would you like to give caving a try this summer?"

"Well, maybe," began Liddy. "I'd have no trouble crawling in the dirt and mud. But I'm not sure I could handle the really tight places. I remember feeling a bit claustrophobic in those tourist caves, but that could be just because I'm not used to them. I'd consider it, but I'd want to be able to turn around and get outside quickly. Ask me again some other time," she added as Sam pulled into the restaurant parking lot.

The Mountain Steak House was a bit pricey compared to some other restaurants, but the food was excellent. As they ate,

Sam related to Liddy what Surya's seismic analyses had shown, and also that a two-hour swarm of small, but continuous earth movements was evident beneath Yellowstone.

"Are those small quakes related to the larger quakes?" she asked.

"Possibly, but there's no way to tell at the present time," he answered. "We need a lot more data to show a relationship beyond just the time of occurrence. However, I'm beginning to wonder just a bit," he said with a look of thoughtful puzzlement. "We've had more earthquakes in Wyoming in the last two weeks than we've had in the previous six years, at least that I'm aware of."

Their dinner conversation, as had their earlier discussions, ranged widely in content, from caves and earthquakes, to weather and jobs. After ordering dessert, Sam inquired, "Will you be able to come with me to Laramie tomorrow?"

"Yes. Do you still want me to meet you at your office?"

"That would work out best. Then we can leave right away when my first class is over at ten."

After they finished eating, they drove back to Liddy's and spent the rest of the evening in her living room, talking about geology and traveling.

On his way home, Sam reflected on his obviously growing feelings of affection for this woman who had so recently come into his life. He had never before enjoyed anyone's company as he now enjoyed being with Liddy. He hoped that he could overcome his timidity and allow a solid relationship to develop between them. Sam's dedication to his work had occupied too much of his time, particularly during the last several years. He had never met anyone like Liddy before and was now anxious to press forward into this new chapter of his life.

$$\leftrightarrows$$

Liddy walked into Sam's office on Tuesday morning and waited for him to finish his class. She brought with her a duffel bag containing an extra jacket and insulated snow pants, in addition to food and water. As a result of growing up in Wyoming, she knew how fast and unexpectedly the winter weather could shift from balmy to violent, and common sense required sensible preparations for out-of-town travel. It was now March and wild fluctuations in weather conditions were especially common this time of the year. Sunny and mild spring days can easily transform into furious blizzards, and Liddy had seen it happen many times. Those storms would sometimes pass by in less than an hour, but at other times they could last for days. Roads that became clogged with drifting snow could be closed for a few hours or sometimes for a week. People in cars that became caught in snowdrifts were wise to stay with the vehicle. Liddy had heard quite a few stories about people who left their stuck vehicles to try to walk to safety. It would seem like an easy task, but many had died in such attempts.

Liddy had once been a foolish, infallible teenager who had spent a miserable night alone, stuck in a highway ditch, with only a thin fleece jacket to warm her. An unexpected spring storm had blown across Wyoming like a long-confined stallion, suddenly released from his stall. Her view of the road had been immediately and completely wiped out. She would never forget the hours of painful shivering, and she was determined not to let that happen again!

Liddy also remembered one bitterly cold winter, several years past, when she was driving between Casper and Medicine Bow. Through a gap in the blowing snow just past the side of the road, a haunting and distorted figure of an antelope had stood upright, frozen in place, with its head cocked skyward. That antelope had stood there for more than a month, until the spring thaw toppled it into oblivion.

"Hey, Liddy!" Her retrospection was jarred by the sound of Sam's voice. "What were you thinking just now? You seemed off in a distant place."

"Oh, sorry...I was just thinking about winter weather, Sam."

"Are you ready to go?" he asked as he grabbed his hat, coat, and briefcase that contained the samples for x-ray analyses. "Don't worry too much about the weather. I always carry a ton of survival gear in my pickup...shovels, tire chains, stove and matches, sleeping bag, down jackets, food, water...you name it, it's in there."

As they drove towards Laramie, Sam explained to Liddy

some of the roadside geology along the 150-mile route. He pointed to the Shirley Mountains, a Laramide uplift; Como Bluff, one of the most famous early dinosaur quarries; and explained some of the Quaternary erosional history of the Laramie Basin. Liddy remembered the spot along the highway where she had seen the frozen antelope. She mentioned it to Sam, who commented that he'd once seen a frozen sheep in North Dakota that had managed to get stranded in deep snow, where it too froze in place while standing on all fours. The images brought to mind by their discussion made her shiver.

Sam and Liddy arrived at Chris Felsen's office before one o'clock. After brief introductions, Chris led them to the x-ray diffraction laboratory where mineralogy graduate student Ivan Boswell had the x-ray diffractometer warmed up and ready. He would actually run the analyses for Sam. This was a pleasant surprise! Sam had done x-ray diffraction by himself before, but it would go a lot quicker with someone who was familiar with the newer equipment at the DGG. Like many institutions, they rarely used equipment that was more than ten years old, and this lab was less than two years old.

After a brief discussion, Chris left for class, stating that Surya would come to the x-ray lab a bit later to talk with Sam about his seismic array. Sam handed his two crystals to Ivan and watched as he quickly set the larger crystal in a precision mount and checked its initial orientation. He then asked if Sam had any guesses as to what mineral the crystal might be. An educated guess often helped to reduce x-ray diffractometer time by rotating the crystal only through the range of angles diagnostic of a specific mineral, along with those minerals with which it could be confused. The first test crystal was what Sam believed to be a diamond. Ivan checked his references, set the diffractometer to run through the proper angles, closed the cover on the machine, and then selected "start" on the computer control screen.

While the machine was running, Ivan put the second crystal in a mount. Contrasted with the first crystal, this one was about 1/8 inch long, black, and opaque. It somewhat resembled ilmenite, but under Sam's microscope it had seemed to exhibit a cubic crystal habit. Sam suspected it might be spinel, but his optical examination was not sufficient to make the identification. Ivan checked his references for spinel and noted the settings he would use after the first crystal analysis was completed. Liddy observed the process while Sam and Ivan chatted about the operation of the diffractometer. Sam could probably now operate the diffractometer, if need be, in the future. The instructions were simple, and the whole setup was computer controlled, with prompts for the operator. The only difficult part was either mounting a crystal or preparing a powdered sample, both of which Sam had done before.

After twenty minutes, the x-ray run for the first crystal was completed. A few keystrokes on the computer control brought up the crystal's diffraction pattern, compared to the nearest match in the pattern library. The crystal's peaks were almost identical to those of diamond, shown in the library. The computer match identified it as a *diamond*. Sam hoped that Ivan wouldn't ask where the diamond had come from, so he immediately asked if he could operate the machine for the second crystal. Ivan was happy to coach Sam through the diffractometer operation.

The second crystal, after another twenty-minute analysis, was computer identified tentatively as *spinel*, although there were a few other patterns that were close. For many minerals, x-ray identification is not diagnostic, but rather is supplementary information to be used in conjunction with other physical and optical tests. Ivan printed out the results of both runs and then excused himself to head for a class.

Surya had not yet come to the x-ray lab, so Sam and Liddy went looking for him. The secretary at the main desk directed them to his office. Surya was in and explained to them some aspects of his seismic analysis programs. He also noted that the last two seismographs in his array, at Rock Springs and Sheridan, would be operational by the end of the week. The information he had already obtained gave him some rather spectacular three-dimensional views of faults, fractures, and the new dike near Point of Rocks. However, once the last two seismographs were operating, he hoped to filter data such that he could compile a more detailed view of parts of the earth's mantle than had ever before been described.

Perhaps, Surya speculated, he might even get some insight into deep circulation systems beneath the mantle. One thing, however, seemed a bit troubling to him—the recent earthquakes across the region. Although they appeared unrelated, except for their times of occurrence, Surya told Sam and Liddy that he had the uncomfortable feeling that they *were* all related. He just couldn't figure out what sort of activity could possibly connect them.

Chris had not yet returned before Sam and Liddy prepared to leave, so Sam asked Surya to thank him and Ivan for their help. Then the couple hit the road by mid-afternoon, discussing diamonds and other gemstones for most of the return trip to Casper. Sam let Liddy off at her vehicle and asked her, "Would you care to join me for dinner on Thursday? I'll be sure not to keep you out too late since I know you have to work early Friday."

"Oh, thanks. I'd love to, but Camile and I already have plans," she answered with some disappointment in her voice.

"Would Friday be a possibility instead?" offered Sam.

"That'd be great!" she enthused with a smile.

Sam squeezed her hand, stating, "I'll call you tomorrow evening so we can set something up."

"Better call me at the studio during the day instead," she replied. "We've got stuff going on Wednesday evening as well, and I won't be home. Thanks for taking me along."

Sam waved goodbye and then hurried for his meeting. His thoughts turned toward staking mining claims on the dike near Point of Rocks and to Surya's parting comment about a possible connection between all of the recent earthquakes. By implication, that meant that the emplacement of the new dike was tied into the earthquakes and to some unknown underlying cause as well. It's easy to arm-wave about mega-causes in geology, but proving such things is usually next to impossible. Final results in such efforts are often hypotheses that are well presented, but shine in the public eye only briefly before being swept aside by new data and newer hypotheses.

Will a plausible answer connecting these recent events ever be found? Sam wondered.

CHAPTER 7

Divergent Connections

▼

...Whom have I cheated? Whom have I oppressed? Or from whose hand have I accepted a bribe to blind my eyes to it? - 1 Samuel 12:3

Wednesday morning was the first time since his claim staking that Andrew Merlott felt like moving around very much. The bruise on his leg had disabled him much more than he thought it should have. As soon as Andy arrived home on Saturday night, he had swallowed some aspirin and applied cold packs to his leg, but the soreness remained. On Sunday, he soaked it in hot water laden with Epsom salts and repeated the procedure twice a day thereafter. When he was younger, such a bruise would have been ignored. He thought about seeing a doctor, but he didn't have any health insurance. By Wednesday he actually felt a bit better, although his leg was still stiff. Perhaps moving around would help the circulation; hence, he decided to drive to Green River in order to file his claims in the Sweetwater County Courthouse. He had already filled out the paperwork for submission of his claims to the Cheyenne BLM office. But first he would make copies of everything, and then he would mail off the forms.

Andy got a late start that morning, and it seemed to take forever to snowmobile into Atlantic City to get his truck. The day was overcast with scattered snow showers, but for the most part, the roads to Green River were in good shape. Andy stopped in Rock Springs at a photocopy center and made the necessary duplicates of his paperwork. He then mailed the package, along with a check to cover the filing fees, to the BLM in Cheyenne. If his leg had felt better, he would have taken the time to stake a few more claims. However, he probably would not be up to the task for at least a couple of weeks. "*Getting old is tough,*" he said. Then he realized he had been talking out loud. Hopefully no one in the post office had heard him. Living alone as he had for years, it was only natural to talk to himself. "*I guess so,*" he answered out loud as he got back into his truck and drove off.

Andy's claims were filed in the Sweetwater County Recorder's office that same day. He was glad to get the paperwork out of the way so he could leave for home early in the afternoon. The claim notices and ground stakes are the final word if someone decides to argue about claims, but the filed paperwork is what the Feds rely on if they decide to go after the claims. Andy was timely in his filings and paid the appropriate fees. Now if he could just find some interesting minerals in his samples, he would have something he could market, hopefully for a tidy profit.

Upon returning to Atlantic City, Andy stopped to order a hamburger at the Miner's Haven Café. Three other local patrons, two of whom he knew, were there sipping coffee. Andy was not always tight-lipped about his activities, and this situation was no different. When pressed with questions about where he had been, Andy told them, "*I think I might have got myself a diamond mine*! I staked five claims on that new dike near Point of Rocks, south of the interstate." When asked why he thought there might be diamonds, he explained, "When I seen that feller Sam on TV talkin' 'bout volcanic stuff comin' up from the earth's mantle, kinda like in the Leucite Hills, I figured there was a good chance. After all, didn't ol' Bert say he'd worked with some guys who found some diamonds out thata way several years ago?"

His audience nodded in agreement that maybe diamonds were a possibility. Andy then informed his listeners about his staking activity, the small earthquake, and getting hit on the leg with a rock. Now he needed to analyze his samples, and he would let them know what he found. When Andy finished eating, he loaded the rest of the samples from his truck onto his snowmobile and headed for home.

Often repeated stories can be the source of rumors, and Andy's disclosure in the café became just that. When cold weather keeps people inside, tales and gossip spread easily over coffee or stronger drinks. The story about a prospector who had found diamonds near Point of Rocks was the natural evolution of Andy's conversation with his Atlantic City associates. If the story is told in a certain way, facts become irrelevant.

⇌

On Wednesday morning, Sam's mind was full of divergent thoughts. He had discovered *diamonds* in the new dike! That secret would not stay hidden for long, particularly if anyone else took the trouble to investigate, and he was sure that others would. The recent earthquakes seemed to represent something more than just a few quakes beyond the historical average numbers. Perhaps they *did* relate to Yellowstone, or was that idea just coincident with his and Liddy's interest in the park? *Liddy!* Liddy was on his mind most of the time, overriding his other thoughts. *He had fallen in love with her*; that he did not question. He had never been in love before. Was Liddy the one person he could spend the rest of his life with? They shared many interests, and their personal values and beliefs seemed to be quite similar.

Looking deep into some invisible mirror, Sam considered, *Get real! You hardly know her!* Are you really considering marriage? Think of how that would change your life! You certainly need to spend more time to get to know her better. She must have some hidden annoying habits. Do you have the patience to overlook the little irritations in life? Are you willing to give more than take? That is what marriage would require from each partner. You've been living pretty free and easy, except for your commitments to teaching. A lot of that would have to change. *Or would it?* Think about it later. *Now you need to prepare for your 8:30 class!* His silent introspection ended when he realized that he had been sitting at his desk staring blankly at his class materials for close to an hour and had yet to make any progress.

The day seemed to pass more slowly than normal for Sam. He would talk to Liddy this evening on the phone, *but he felt like seeing her again now*! His self-reflection hit him like a sudden awakening from a sound sleep. He knew his situation was serious, but he needed to be patient. *Love is not like science; you cannot analyze the details. You can only give and accept completely without conditions.* He then immersed himself in his classes, while also considering what to do about the newly found diamonds. He must stake some claims and also do more extensive research on Yellowstone.

⇌

After his first class of the day was over, Sam thought more seriously about the diamond and peridot he had found in the dike. The peridot alone might be economic, and the dike rock, although still not formally identified, was relatively soft and would be easy to mine and to beneficiate. The fact that he had found one diamond of about one-quarter carat did not tell him the overall grade of the deposit; an isolated diamond can be a unique find. Much larger samples would need to be obtained before diamond economics could even be guessed at. However, the presence of abundant peridot could be used to make a rough projection of the value of that gemstone in the deposit—assuming that Sam's spread of samples was representative of the dike as a whole. Indeed, it was his first impression that they *were*. Since initial indications were good, it would probably be best to stake some claims and then take detailed samples to determine if the project should be pursued further.

Any person or company with knowledge of diamond exploration in Wyoming, and who had noted in the news reports that the new dike near Point of Rocks was of mantle origin, would probably be beating a path to the dike at the first opportunity. The weather had been reasonable, but not ideal, for staking mining claims. Even so, Sam thought that the dike might have already been staked. But that was not likely, since most companies involved in diamond exploration have their own bureaucracies that slow them down significantly. On the other hand, individual prospectors can often move rapidly on a whim. Perhaps he should try staking claims now rather than wait for nicer weather to work it into a class exercise. He decided that if the weekend weather looked good, he would do his claim staking on Saturday. Liddy had to work then, so he would go alone. He planned to leave early and return early, thereby to meet with her again Saturday evening. With that plan settled, Sam turned his thoughts to Yellowstone.

A rather large amount of information exists on Yellowstone. Sam's biggest problem would be to sort through it to get an overall geological picture in his mind. This was the way he approached most problems. After acquiring a general mental picture, he would then move in on the details that would clarify whatever problem he was addressing. In this case, he decided that the questions of greatest interest addressed whether the recent earthquakes and the dike near Point of Rocks all relate to the same, as yet unknown underlying cause, and was this same activity related to Yellowstone or not? If it was related to the Yellowstone hotspot, did it have anything to do with Yellowstone's eruptive potential? Then, thinking further, what would the precursors for a Yellowstone eruption be? Coupled with that, are such precursors present?

Sam was neither a seismologist nor a volcanologist, but he understood some concepts of both fields and had studied volcanology. Perhaps he should investigate these problems by trying to interpret the data that he and Surya had acquired and by learning more about hotspots in general, along with specifics about the Yellowstone hotspot. Relating all of that to what he already knew about mantle-derived materials might pose some complex, but possible answers. Above all, he wanted to avoid jumping to any conclusions that were not supported by the information already collected.

Sam began his research into the problem by reviewing sources of heat within the earth and what is known about the earth's internal circulatory system. Radioactivity and the conversion of gravitational energy to thermal energy are believed to be the major sources of the earth's internal heat. When the earth began forming more than 4.5 billion years ago, planetary accretion and compression, due to gravity, slowly heated the earth's interior. Additional heat derived from radioactive decay of elements such as uranium, thorium, and radioactive potassium. That led to subsurface temperatures higher than the melting point of iron and other rock materials. Extensive melting allowed the segregation of many elements, with an abundance of iron sinking in the melt and many lighter elements rising. This resulted in the earth being differentiated into zones of materials making up the core, the mantle, and the crust.

Sam further noted that chemical affinities also influenced the separation of elements within the earth. Some heavier elements, such as uranium, formed compounds with oxygen and became concentrated in the crust rather than in the core. Concentrations of radioactive uranium, thorium, and potassium are distributed in granitic rocks to a much greater degree than in basalts or peridotites. The radioactive decay produces small but measurable amounts of heat that, in the large mass of the earth's crust, is substantial. All of this leads to increased temperatures as depth beneath the surface increases. Temperature variations and related density imbalances in any system, as Sam knew, lead to movement and circulation of materials within that system.

General ideas concerning circulation of materials within the earth's crust are well known. Basaltic material is added to the crust at *mid-ocean ridges*. These are areas where new crust, in the form of oceanic plates, spreads outward. At the edges of continents, the heavier oceanic crust is subducted beneath the edges of the lighter granitic material of the continental crustal plates, as the oceanic and continental plates converge. This material heats up as it is forced downward, leading to melting and volcanic activity near the edges of continents along *subduction zones*.

The thick, lightweight continental plates and the thin, but heavier oceanic plates move around over geologic time, bumping into each other, breaking apart, and recombining. As

Sam had explained to his students, in lectures on the history of geology as a science, Alfred Wegner had first aggressively advocated the movement of large plates within the crust in 1910, under a theory called *continental drift*. However, the idea probably originated with Sir Francis Bacon who, in 1620, noted parallelism in the shorelines bounding the Atlantic Ocean. This idea was slowly refined, and then in the later part of the twentieth century it was universally accepted as the theory of *plate tectonics*. *Plate tectonic theory* refers to the mountain building actions caused by the plate movements. The exact mechanism causing these movements has never been completely defined, although heat and material flow within the earth most certainly are root causes.

Beneath the crustal plates are hotspots in the earth's upper mantle that seem to be relatively stable over long periods of time. Plots of plate movements over time seem to show that the hotspots are *fixed in place* and that the plates move across them with different types of interactions, depending on whether the plate is oceanic (thin basalt) or continental (thick granitic material). The hotspots are expressed through very high heat flow measurements and by volcanic activity that penetrates the plates. Hotspots beneath oceanic crust generally produce outpourings of basaltic lavas in relatively *placid* volcanic eruptions, such as in the Hawaiian Islands. On the other hand, beneath continental crust such as at Yellowstone, a hotspot can result in *violent* eruptions of lighter silicic materials such as rhyolite. Speculation about the causes of hotspots wanders around vague relationships to very deep, but unknown circulations within the Earth.

A large hotspot lies beneath Yellowstone National Park and is characterized by extremely high heat flow of about 2000 milliwatts per square meter (mWm^{-2}). That is about thirty times the average for the North American continent. This is a total continuous energy release of approximately 2000 megawatts from the area of the Yellowstone caldera. It is analogous to the output of a moderately sized power plant. In North America, only Long Valley, California (which is also a caldera) and Valles Caldera in New Mexico, with one quarter to one third of the heat flow of Yellowstone, show anything that might be comparable at 630 mWm^{-2}, and 500 mWm^{-2}, respectively.

Neither Long Valley nor Valles Caldera is a hotspot; both have heat attributable to crustal rather than mantle sources.

The Yellowstone hotspot, generally centered beneath the Yellowstone caldera, appears to host melted or partially melted rock at shallow depths of as little as three miles, based on seismic studies done during the twentieth century. At that depth, temperatures are estimated to range from a minimum of 650 degrees Fahrenheit to greater than 850 degrees, hotter than the temperature needed to melt the lead used in fishing sinkers and bullets. During the late 1900s, direct temperature measurements, from a few shallow drill holes within Yellowstone, showed temperatures exceeding 460 degrees at depths of less than 1000 feet.

While the information on temperatures and heat flow in Yellowstone was interesting, Sam's attention was quickly focused when he found material, apparently more applicable to his problem, in records of recent geologic activity in Yellowstone National Park. The Yellowstone Plateau, which includes most of the park, has been the site of one of the most notable measured deformations of the earth's crust in historic time. Various detailed surveys showed that benchmarks, placed across the Yellowstone caldera in 1923, had risen in elevation as much as thirty inches by 1977, and another 9.8 inches by 1984! In 1985 this uplift reversed, with subsidence of as much as 4.7 inches by 1991. Geologists working in the area at that time believed that both uplift and subsidence were the result of magma movement in the upper part of the earth's crust.

For as much as 250 miles in all directions, the area surrounding the hotspot appears to be domed slightly upward, compared to the rest of the continent. Early studies of the overall shape of the earth, based on satellite observations, first noted a slight bulge or doming across a part of the North American continent generally centered on the Yellowstone area. The height of the bulge is slight; it is only on the order of about thirty-three feet across 500 miles. However, this wide regional doming, most likely related directly to the existence of the Yellowstone hotspot, has not been measured as an active historical event.

More recently, rapid uplift was noted again beginning in the middle of the 1990s. However, toward the end of the twentieth century, funding was diverted from Yellowstone's monitoring stations and surveys to areas of perceived greater concern, such as Washington, Oregon, and California. In that region, large populations are concentrated near potentially violent volcanoes and along faults known to produce devastating earthquakes. This transferal of funds and prioritization of projects was again reinforced around 2002, when USGS studies showed that the Three Sisters Peaks in central Oregon were rising at a rate of about one inch per year. Two other mountains along the heavily populated west coast of the country also showed similar activity. As a result, much of the USGS budget and other federal funds were further diverted from Yellowstone to situations that appeared to be much more threatening to large population centers.

Prior to those budgetary changes and even cuts in several federal programs, the renewed uplift in Yellowstone had amounted to *almost four feet*! That wasn't much different from historical measurements, but Sam was unsettled by the thought that the measurements ceased before a stable condition existed. *Yellowstone could still be rising for all anyone knew*! Laser leveling equipment was installed near Yellowstone Lake in the late 1990s because of concern that trees along the south shore of the lake were drowning. The laser leveling confirmed a suspected twenty or more years of relatively rapid local uplift north of the lake. However, that situation appeared to stabilize within a few years of the end of the twentieth century. Federal budgets for the USGS and the National Park Service have remained tight since the beginning of the twenty-first century, and no extra funds have been allocated to continue with monitoring and measurements in Yellowstone.

Sam knew that upward doming of the Earth's surface often precedes volcanic eruptions. The area of doming is sometimes obvious in smaller volcanoes, such as in the well-documented 1980 eruption of Mount St. Helens in Washington. A gradually increasing bulge on the north flank of the mountain developed over a period of a few months or so before it collapsed in the landslide that triggered the eruption. However, in many volcanoes, doming is not noticeable prior to an eruption.

Sam realized that volcanoes and earthquakes can behave

in unpredictable ways. Earthquake swarms often occur beneath a volcano prior to its eruption, but not always. The earthquakes occur where stresses within the earth are concentrated, but not necessarily where the magma is located. Stresses inside the earth may be concentrated many miles away from where an eruption occurs, and yet the earthquakes are still related to the eruption. Large calderas such as Yellowstone normally show frequent signs of seismic unrest, making it difficult to determine if an earthquake swarm is a precursor to an eruption, or if it is just another false alarm. A lack of historical large caldera eruptions, also known as *super volcanoes*, precludes any first-hand knowledge of their precursors.

⇌

Sam applied himself vigorously to his questions about Yellowstone and compiled his teaching notes for the following day, before his afternoon class began. He was throwing himself into his work and his afternoon class seemed more responsive to his leading questions than usual. He was over-compensating successfully in applying the logical portion of his brain to the exclusion of his emotions. Toward the end of his class, he suddenly realized this and made an unusual pause in his summary remarks to the class, before finishing the sentence that he had started. When the class was finished, Brent McKay asked, "Is somethin' troubling you Sam? You seemed to be in *la-la-land* for about ten seconds near the end of class."

"Nothing troubling," Sam replied. "Just thinking about too many different things at once."

Brent was an older student and was in fact twenty years Sam's senior. "I thought so," he volunteered. "You got hooked on that gal from the TV station the day of our field trip. I've seen it before, and it happened to me just before I got married."

"Well...I..." started Sam as his face reddened slightly.

Tossing a knowing grin Sam's way, Brent interrupted, "That's okay, Dr. Sam. We all get caught eventually. If my wife and I can help you out, give us a call. But if you want my advice, relax and don't fight it. Just give it some time before you make any decisions. See ya tomorrow."

Sam flushed a bit more and then smiled inwardly as he returned to his office to wrap things up and call it a day. An enjoyable short walk in the fresh, cold air brought him home by five o'clock. As he entered his house, he suddenly realized that he had forgotten to call Liddy. He thought she might be home now, so he immediately dialed her number.

"Hello, Sam," she answered. "Good timing on the call. Camile had a change of plans for this evening, and we aren't going out after all. She and I are just getting some things together for dinner here. Would you like to join us?"

"Why, yes. I'd love to!" Sam answered with surprise. "When?"

"Oh, whenever you can get here. I'd like you to meet Camile."

"I'll leave here in a short while," finished Sam. His brain had been working overtime today, and he looked forward to an evening of rest, absent of fervent geologic thoughts.

⇋

Sam arrived at Liddy's home forty minutes later and was introduced to Camile Brown, her neighbor and close friend. Camile was of average height and medium frame. She had short, dark hair, sparkling brown eyes, and appeared to be an energetic sixty-four-year-old. Her husband had died in an industrial accident eight years previously, and since then she had lived alone. Her only son, Eduardo, resided in Cody with his family and occasionally came down on weekends to visit, or Camile would often drive up to see them. She was lively and more talkative than Liddy and sported a mischievous smile that seemed to speak of likeable pranks behind the scenes.

"Pleased to meet you, Sam. Liddy has talked about you a lot," she said as Liddy blushed slightly.

"Glad to meet you as well," replied Sam. "After our ski trip on Saturday, we stopped by your place and pestered your horses for a while. Liddy said you were a good horse handler."

"I've been riding more years than I care to count," answered Camile. "My late husband and I used to take pack trips into the Bighorns and Wind Rivers years ago. Are you

hungry? Liddy made some soup, and I made salad and bread."
Taking control of the situation, Camile continued, "It's ready,
so let's eat right now!"

As the three of them sat down to dinner, Grieg snuck
under the table in hopes of catching some stray morsels. Liddy's
soup contained blue grouse and vegetables. It was delicious, as
was Camile's tomato salad and whole-wheat rolls. Camile had
insisted that they eat by candlelight. Liddy was her best friend
and she knew how Liddy felt about Sam. Camile was doing her
best to be a matchmaker and set the mood for the evening.

Over dinner, they talked about backcountry riding and
hiking. Then the idea of taking a horse trip into the Yellowstone
wilderness came up.

"It might be an interesting goal to work toward," said
Camile, "but I'm not so sure about packing in grizzly country.
Back when I was a kid, bears were seen everywhere in
Yellowstone...along the highways looking for handouts from
tourists and pillaging the campground garbage cans. Close
encounters, with black bears especially, were common. I
remember one crazy incident when a mama and two cubs
chased our family away from a picnic table...they sat down at
our table, just like humans would, and devoured all our food!
Then one other time, a cute, sociable bear peeked in the open
back window of our car, and when I proceeded to reach over to
pet the friendly creature, he swiped me across my face, leaving
a ghastly, bloody wound right between my eyes!" Camile no
longer appreciated bears in close company, and she emphasized,
"Once is enough for this ol' gal!" She suggested that perhaps
the Bighorns might be a better destination.

"I never heard you tell that story before, Camile," said
Liddy. "Did the bear leave a scar on your face?"

"For a while...kids heal up in no time! Of course, those
tourist/bear encounters are pretty rare these days...at least in the
public areas. Yellowstone has had much more sensible bear
management policies in the past few decades. Bears are more
leery of humans now, and that's as it should be!"

The discussion then shifted to the geology of Yellowstone
and its potential for eventual volcanic activity. Slipping his
brain back into high gear, Sam related to them some of what he
had read that day and talked about the potential for an eruption.

"Yellowstone will definitely erupt some day, and there will probably be some kind of warning beforehand. But the type of warning signs and the timing of such an eruption are at the present speculative. It could erupt a hundred thousand years in the future or next week."

Camile seemed a bit concerned by the discussion, possibly because her son and his family lived in Cody. Sam then assured her that there would most likely be definite indications before that happened, and she shouldn't worry. As Camile relaxed, he changed the subject to things that might be less troubling for her. He asked her about gardening, a subject that she was only too happy to talk about.

Sam and Liddy each had their own little vegetable gardens, but they were nothing compared to Camile's. "When spring arrives," she said, "I'll show the both of you how a garden should be handled."

Camile's cherry pie topped off the meal, after which she thanked Liddy and Sam for the enjoyable get-together. Camile then mentioned that there were several things she needed to take care of and politely excused herself before walking out the door. Sam helped Liddy clear the table and asked where she kept the dishwasher. It wasn't in the usual position next to the sink. Liddy commented, "Oh, I don't have one. I always wash them by hand in the sink. I think dishwashers are more trouble than they're worth. Besides, without one, I have more storage space in this tiny kitchen."

Sam had found Camile to be an amusing woman, as Liddy had said he would. However, he did apologize to Liddy for saying anything that could cause Camile to worry. He also told her of his plan to stake a few mining claims on Saturday if the roads were in good shape. She wished she could go along, but after his explanation, she understood his eagerness to stake claims right away. Perhaps he could have some leftover soup at her house when he returned to Casper. Sam lent Liddy his two-meter handheld radio and would give her a call on the Casper Mountain repeater when he was about an hour from town. He enjoyed using amateur radio and hoped to rekindle a similar interest in Liddy.

Not wishing to forget their plans for Friday evening, Sam arranged to pick Liddy up around five. He would cook dinner at his house, and she was welcome to invite Camile along also. He thanked her for the great evening, but due to sudden, almost overwhelming feelings of fatigue, he decided to hit the trail for home earlier than he would have liked. Sam had been throwing himself into his work with more intensity than normal. Mentally, it had been a very tiring day.

⇋

Thursday morning, upon arrival at CTC, Sam decided to check the seismograph records, as he had not done so since Monday morning. Learning that three minor quakes had occurred, he was happy to have new data to look at, although he had misgivings about wishing for more earthquakes. He noted that a three-hour long swarm of almost continuous minor quakes took place on Wednesday morning in the Yellowstone area. Similar to some previous quakes, they were small, with magnitudes not exceeding 2.9, and they were centered near the northwestern edge of the caldera at depths ranging from three to five miles. There was also a 3.8 tremor near Elkhorn Hot Springs, northwest of Dillon, Montana; and a 3.9 quake near Arco, Idaho, west of Idaho Falls. These were centered at depths of 5.5 miles and 7.5 miles, respectively.

Sam phoned Surya to see how this compared with his observations. Sam's call was routed to the main secretary at the department who stated that Surya was out until next Monday. Apparently, Surya was completing the calibration of the last two stations in his seismic array. Sam appreciated the information. He also liked the Geophysics and Geology Department's new phone system. They had done away with the old voice mail and substituted a real operator when someone did not answer their extension. This gave a more personal touch, although the option of leaving voice messages was still present. One of the companies that had given the DGG a large grant had specified that this phone system be one of the conditions for the grant. The owner of that company did not like answering machines.

After leaving work, Sam loaded everything he would need for claim staking into his truck, adding to the ever-present stash of winter survival gear. Saturday was predicted to be dry and sunny, but very cold. After a late supper, Sam hurried off to attend a weekly discussion group at his church. He tried to make it to these meetings as often as he could, not only to take part in the lively discourses, but also to socialize. The group usually consisted of five to a dozen people ranging in age from eighteen to eighty. He wondered if Liddy would want to join the group. He hadn't really discussed things like religion or politics with her. Come to think of it, there were countless things he hadn't yet shared with Liddy and so much that he wanted to know about her.

As Sam walked up the stairs and through the back door to the church, he realized that he was a few minutes late as the discussion was already in progress. Quietly, he slipped into the room and claimed a spot on the carpeted floor. No one liked sitting in the small rigid, upright chairs; the group preferred comfort and informality. Topics varied from week to week, and sometimes, impromptu subjects of anyone's choosing were batted around the room.

Tonight the conversation centered on the book of Ezekiel. Participants took turns reading the baffling verses…"As I looked, a stormy wind came out of the north; a great cloud with brightness surrounding it and fire flashing forth continually, and in the midst of the fire…glowing metal or amber…" Sam's thoughts turned again to volcanoes, no doubt triggered by the words he was hearing. *He couldn't seem to clear his mind of the subject*! The rest of Ezekiel's experience and his prophecies seemed to fade as Sam wondered about whether Ezekiel might have seen a volcano that inspired his vision. A sudden question brought him back into the discussion, and the conversation continued in lively exchanges until the end of the session.

⇌

That same Thursday afternoon, only two weeks after the eruption of the new dike near Point of Rocks, the Governor of Wyoming retrieved a pre-signed letter of resignation from Chief Gordon Aughey of the Wyoming Office of Mines and Geology. The Governor kept such pre-signed letters for the heads of all state agencies in a locked file. As a matter of course, they were required of individuals appointed to those positions. If the department head either screwed up badly, or for other reasons fell out of favor, a resignation letter could be retrieved and dated. This was much less messy than having to fire someone.

Gordon was notified that his resignation would be accepted, effective the following day. However, as was the established procedure, he would be asked to stay on a little while longer until a replacement was hired. Gordon had been expecting this ever since his last budget presentation. The search committee, including a special Governor's appointee in the Human Resources Department and the WOMG Directory Board, would begin looking for a replacement in early April. It would most likely take two to six months to find a new WOMG Chief.

⇌

On Friday, a federal employee, working in the Mining Claims Recordation section of the Wyoming State BLM Office, noticed a new filing for diamonds and other valuable minerals on five claims staked by a Mr. Andrew Merlott. She made copies of the filings, folded them carefully, and then placed them in an envelope addressed to a post office box in Denver, Colorado. She then dialed a number in Denver and asked for a Mr. Sawyer. When a male voice answered, she said, "The information you requested has been mailed." The voice said, "Thank you." She then hung up her phone. That information would be publicly available within two weeks, but for eight of her ten years in the Wyoming State Office, the early notification of any new mining claims for minerals, on a list specified by Mr. Sawyer, was worth a cash payment to her for each notification, unbeknownst to the BLM.

She had met a man once who just had to have information right away. When she expeditiously met his request, he rewarded her with a handsome tip that she had not reported. After three such tips in one year, he had asked her to just mail the information and then call Mr. Sawyer. Shortly afterwards, the predictable tip (in cash) arrived from Denver in an envelope with no return address. She averaged three or four such tips per year, and in the odd years when no claims were staked for those minerals specified by Mr. Sawyer, she received one envelope at Christmas. No one needed to know. The cash *gift* never made it into her IRS Form 1040; after all, the material she mailed out was public information anyway.

Mr. Sawyer, although that was not his real name, received the envelope with the information the next day and then faxed the same to a toll free number. He did not know where that number was located (it was in Jakarta, Indonesia), and it did not matter to him. This was just part of his job.

⇌

Some environmentalists saw the *Greater Yellowstone Ecosystem* as encompassing too small of an area. A few even held the view that a much greater area of land should be treated as a wilderness park; from Cody on the east; to Rexburg, Idaho and Dillon, Montana on the west; from Bozeman, Montana on the north; and to Interstate-80, across southern Wyoming, on the south. This rather extreme view has been ascribed to "*environmentalists*." However, like other words in the English language, to attribute this outlook to environmentalists is like applying the term *greedy* to any persons employed by a financial institution.

This radical persuasion, played out with exaggerated emotionalism and distortion of facts, and enthusiastically aided by a predominantly socialist news media, easily swayed a left-of-center President and administration into shutting down gold mining activities northeast of Yellowstone in the late 1900s. The general story was that the mining might pollute the stream below the mine and ruin Yellowstone National Park. Yellowstone is a public icon that *all* citizens can relate to and *no one* wanted to see anything happen to it. In actuality, the mining would have cleaned up and stabilized hazardous one-hundred-year-old tailings. Few people troubled themselves enough to become familiar with the actual facts. The politics of this decision not only left century-old tailings as they were, but also left millions of dollars worth of gold in the ground. It further had the effect of keeping the local economy suppressed through a lack of jobs.

However, like many things, this is an over-simplification. The complexities involved activities by the *Reef Group*, which actually began developing its influence in the United States during the 1970s. Slowly at first, they bought, blackmailed, and bribed politicians, political appointees, government employees, members of the news media, owners of businesses, and political activists. It was, at first, very subtle. It is easy for a person to accept money from someone else to do something that he was maybe going to do anyway, particularly if whatever it was seemed to make good sense.

Once that person has accepted the money, he or she has been bought. Personal values, actions, and eventually beliefs become prostituted for a specified fee. Successive favors for a fee become a habit. Then, maybe sometime, a favor isn't quite to the person's liking, but that extra money seems to be needed. Eventually the person cannot escape from doing the favors for the fear that exposure of such past activities might not be acceptable, either socially or legally. Then later, in small instances, an example has to be made of someone who received favors, but decided they wanted out of the game. That type of example served as a warning to others who might have a change of heart. In the modern *enlightened* society, the Reef Group found that such warnings were not often necessary.

The Reef Group's game of influence was like a cancer; once it gained a hold, it did not let go, and it continued to send its tendrils deeper into organizations. Requests by the Reef Group, or more correctly by their representatives, with no apparent connections to the parent, seemed innocuous at first. They sometimes even appeared to make sense—for saving the environment or for other benevolent purposes. But the overall picture of their activities remained hidden and was never noticed by anyone outside of their organization. By the late twentieth century, an easily influenced administration in Washington had been emplaced, in part through the finances and efforts of the Reef Group. This secured for them people in high positions and a resulting hidden control for many of their interests in the United States. This, at least for a while, also ensured that an overall picture of Reef's activities would not be compiled.

The mining of gold near Yellowstone actually competed with Reef Group holdings in other parts of the world. Environmental concerns were merely a convenient excuse. In fact, that excuse played well in the news media and served to limit many mining and other industrious activities in the United States. Over time, the reliance by the United States on strategic minerals such as platinum group metals, diamonds, and other commodities, including petroleum and timber from sources controlled by the Reef Group and its associates, would increase. Influence is power, and money is power. The beauty of the Reef Group's methods was that they had one of the wealthiest nations on earth eating out of their hand, and most of that nation did not even know it. It is not the product that you sell that is important; it is how you package it.

⇄

Sam Westone was neither aware of the Reef Group, nor of its activities. However, he would eventually, but unknowingly, do business with them. He would also learn that packaging is important, more so for ideas than for merchandise.

CHAPTER 8

Food for Thought

▼

This is a hard lesson; who can accept it? - John 6:60

Friday morning at 2:33 a.m., a magnitude 5.2 earthquake shook northern Yellowstone and awakened people in Cody, Wyoming and Gardiner, Big Sky, and Ennis, Montana. People in other nearby towns felt the shake as well. Sam first heard about it on television during Liddy's early morning weather and news summary. He was usually an early riser and had quite recently begun to schedule his breakfasts to coincide with her broadcasts.

Apparently the quake did little harm and merited only a "no damage" statement from the National Park Service. Sam was intensely curious and hurried to CTC to check Surya's seismic network and computer interpretation. He headed straight down to the basement seismograph, not even taking the time to start his morning coffee on the way. There he learned that the quake was centered along a west-northwest trending fault north of West Yellowstone, Montana. This town had not been mentioned in the news, probably because no one there felt like getting agitated over yet another earthquake. The focus of the quake was at a depth of 6.2 miles. However, of greatest interest to Sam was a swarm of small quakes that began at the same time, but rather than ending after eight seconds as did the larger quake, the swarm continued to the present time of 7:46 a.m. Locations seemed to vary around Yellowstone's northern caldera rim and northward for almost twenty miles. Magnitudes ranged downward from 3.2. The shallowest quakes were in the caldera about three miles below the surface, but they gradually increased with depth northward to greater than eleven miles.

Sam suspected that these small, continuous tremors were related to magma movement. He would check the seismograph again after his morning class. Not one to miss opportunities for higher learning, Sam rearranged his class notes for about the third time since the semester had started in early January. A portion of his section on seismology and volcanism was now moved in to switch places with part of his geologic structures unit. It was a good move and caught the students' interest. The entire class visited the seismograph during the last fifteen minutes of the session. Students were able to watch the seismograph tracing an active swarm of small quakes in the Yellowstone area, followed by the map and cross-sectional graphics produced by Surya's algorithms and program. The swarm appeared as it had earlier, continuing with no noticeable change.

Around noon, Liddy called Sam's office while he was eating lunch. "I'll be running some errands after work with Camile. Would it be okay if we just drive by your house around five, rather than you having to make a trip across town to pick us up? By the way, Camile will be coming for supper. She wants to see where you live."

"That'll be fine, Liddy," replied Sam. He also started to tell her about the swarm of small quakes in the northern part of Yellowstone.

But Liddy could only talk briefly at the moment, hurriedly saying, "Fill me in later. Gotta run, Sam! See you around five."

KWYN had not yet hired extra help after Vance's death, so Liddy was much busier at work than she liked to be. Despite the longer hours, her job was usually enjoyable and was a source of pride for her. In addition to the technical requirements of a television broadcast engineer, a certain amount of artistic talent was necessary to capture and edit video footage in a timely manner, with results that were aesthetically pleasing. She maintained the station's video equipment and could, if necessary, service the transmitters as well. KWYN was slowly expanding, but it was still a small station, and many jobs there included duties that, at larger stations, would have been distributed among several employees. Liddy had now become a host for the early morning news and weather show, and she randomly substituted as a host to fill other gaps in the station's scheduled programming. This was in addition to her former regular duties.

Liddy found that, due to her appearances on television, she was being recognized more and more while out in public areas. Such recognition was new to her, and she found the comments and complements from strangers to be generally positive. However, her extended work hours tended to drag out a work schedule that was already too full. She was beginning to feel the need for other activities to guide her life, beyond the slowly expanding and overriding control exerted by her job. It just seemed that the more she did, the more she was asked to do. With every little change in her work schedule, she gave up more leisure-time activities. Often this was because she would feel beat at the end of her shift.

Off-setting the downside of work, she was enjoying her budding relationship with Sam and wanted to know him better. But her job threatened to constrain her available time with him. Liddy admitted that she was developing strong feelings toward Sam, but her job, in which she took so much pride, might get in the way of this new relationship. This introspection seemed odd to her. How was it that Camile had put it? *"Independent Liddy! Well, you've been actin' weird ever since you met him. This is the first time I've seen you that interested in any creature other than a good horse. I think that fisherman accidentally hooked you, and you're about to get yourself reeled in."* Liddy wasn't sure about that, but she had to admit it was a possibility. It was scary and exciting all at once, but she needed to apply a bit of logic to her emotions. Keep up with the job now, and when Vance's replacement is hired, the workload will slack off.

$$\leftrightharpoons$$

When Sam brought his afternoon class down to the

seismograph, the swarm, having lasted almost twelve hours, had gradually ended. Using the computer, Sam was able to call up the replay as seen by the morning class. The students were impressed and generally quite attentive. Students were often more interested in geological phenomena that could be visually observed in *real time*. Abundant video materials on floods, landslides, volcanoes, and earthquakes always commanded more attention than discussions concerning slow uplift and other changes that are spread out over eons of time. The new seismograph brought small earthquakes to life in real time. However, it seemed to Sam that this semester's students were more alert as a group than any previous classes he could remember. Or perhaps it was *his* greater enthusiasm that was simply contagious.

When the session had ended, Brent apparently answered that question when he said, "Dr. Sam, you sure have been wired in class ever since our field trip. Even the kids noticed; they're saying it's 'cause of that gal from the TV station. Now don't get me wrong…they all like her and think it's great. I just wanted to tell you…like I said before…you ain't hidin' nothin', and if you're thinkin' about maybe gettin' hitched, don't rush it."

"Well, Brent, thanks for the advice," answered Sam. "I appreciate your concern. And yes, the thought *has* crossed my mind. I won't rush anything. But just keep it under your hat for a while, okay?"

"You bet, Sam. I understand. Just enjoy it. Savor every change, every feeling, and every moment. Those will be your most treasured memories in the future. My wife and I are rootin' for ya."

"Thanks again, Brent."

"Any time. See ya Monday, Dr. Sam."

Sam headed back to his office and wrapped up loose ends for the week. He put off the grading of papers until the following week and prioritized the piles of paper neatly arranged on his desk. He also checked his calendar and noted that his only scheduled appointment was a Geoscience departmental staff meeting at noon on Monday. Ralph usually held meetings about once a month. Feeling organized and with no students presently needing help, Sam was able to leave for home by four o'clock.

Sam's short walk to his house always seemed to refresh him, and he realized that it was one of those comfortable little habits that he enjoyed. *People are creatures of habit*, he thought as he walked along. Habits develop to fit situations and then fluctuate with changing circumstances. But habits do give people an unconscious feeling of stability, and that is probably why they develop in the first place. As he reached his house, he realized that his present thoughts about *habits* came from his consideration of the direction his life was heading. This would lead to changes and to new and different habits. *Probably for the better*, he thought. But as Brent had said, *"Don't rush it; savor it."*

Sam quickly cleaned his house and started the gas grill in the back yard. He would grill hamburgers and serve them with onions, tomatoes, lettuce, and barbeque sauce. He had frozen french fries to bake in the oven and a store-bought bean salad for accompaniment. For dessert he would serve pecan pie, purchased at a Christmas bake sale. Sam routinely visited holiday bake sales, and he actually had a nice supply of goodies stashed in the freezer for occasions when he didn't have time to fix something himself. Sam figured that his high metabolism, combined with plenty of exercise, kept him thin. It certainly wasn't a conscious rationing of desserts.

Liddy and Camile arrived just as Sam was loading a stack of CDs into his stereo system. He had selected an assortment of western songs. Sam's taste in music varied over a wide range, but leaned toward western, folk, and Celtic. Camile especially approved of the evening's selection, commenting about how rarely genuine cowboy music is played on the radio. Sam gave Camile a tour of his home, during which he felt like Camile was acting the part of a scrutinizing *mother hen*, making sure that he was *acceptable* for Liddy. After their Wednesday dinner Sam expected this and it didn't bother him. He understood why Camile would be somewhat protective of her neighbor and best friend. Sam was not overly concerned about measuring up to Camile's standards, but just the same, he hoped that she would totally approve of him.

The relaxing evening passed by too quickly and before the two women went out the door, Sam handed Liddy his two-meter handheld radio, saying he would call her tomorrow afternoon on his way back into town. Sam gave them each a quick hug as they left, and Liddy parted with, "Thanks again for supper, Sam. See you tomorrow."

Camile echoed Liddy with an approving, "Thanks for inviting me along, Sam. I'm sure we'll be seeing more of each other."

⇋

The next morning Sam motored down the road well before sunrise. He wanted to get the work done early enough so that he could return to Casper in time to share supper with Liddy. Yes, his priorities *had* changed. And from what he gathered through conversations with Liddy and Camile, particularly with Camile, Liddy's priorities had changed as well. He wondered how their relationship would develop over time.

As he drove along, Sam's thoughts shifted to the task at hand. He mentally re-inventoried the supplies he'd brought along to stake claims, including mineral ownership maps. Sam didn't use a string measure like Andrew Merlott did. Instead, he used his GPS, compass, and 300-foot cloth tape. Sam also used four-inch square by six-foot wooden claim posts rather than PVC pipes. They cost a bit more and were heavier to lug around, but they were not as subject to breakage and removal as were the PVC pipes. He preferred using heavy solid markers for his claims.

Sam stopped in Rawlins to grab some fresh coffee and then later exited the I-80 ramp toward Bitter Creek. Just south of the interstate he took a frontage road westward for nearly four miles, before turning left on a now well-used side road for another three and a half miles. This brought him to where the dike cut across the old gravel road. A recently constructed bypass route now looped around the south end of the dike, replacing the severed road. He stepped out of his truck before nine o'clock and noticed that an overhead power line, cut by the eruption, had been replaced. He also saw what appeared to be a white post on the crest of the south end of the dike about a quarter mile away, then another one closer on the dike crest just north of the severed road. Sam put on his pack and headed for the nearest post. He hoped it was some kind of survey effort, rather than a claim post, but he guessed that someone had beaten him to the stake.

It was a clear, frigid day with a moderate westerly wind. Mittens, stocking cap, and a windbreaker over his sweater felt just right as he hiked along through the deep snow that covered sagebrush and the scattered debris from the dike. The wind had not yet launched the snow into its inevitable drifting for the day. Sam felt invigorated and stepped lively as he moved along. He enjoyed being outside and his senses seemed keen, like that of a wild animal. His eyes picked out distant details on the dike and more white posts to the north.

When he reached the first white PVC pipe, there was no question that someone had beaten him at staking claims. Before he had even reached it, he encountered the thread from Andy's measuring device and recognized it for what it was. He remembered once meeting a character named "Andy" who used this type of arrangement, and he wondered if it might be the same prospector who had now beaten him. A few minutes later he was reading the claim notice and recognized Andrew Merlott's name. In his field notebook, Sam copied the information and address from the claim notice. He then decided to walk the claims to see if there were any gaps between them and to see if the entire length of the dike had been staked. He also collected a few more rock samples and wrote notes to describe anything that he might have missed on his first field trip.

Sam followed the dike north and noticed the small, unstaked triangular area at the end of Diamond Lil #2. However, he continued north until he reached the end of Andy's Diamond Lil #5 claim. By now the wind had picked up and dry, powdery snow was drifting in shifting patterns across the ground. There appeared to be an unstaked stretch of dike between that point and the edge of the Union Pacific section. The U.P. section hosted privately owned minerals that could not be claimed, and that section was almost bisected by Interstate-80. Sam, using small piles of rocks as markers, laid out a lode claim centered on the dike. This claim measured 940 feet long by 600 feet wide, actually overlapping the U.P. land by about two feet on one corner. Sam verbally described the claim as ending at the edge of the U.P. section. It was not exactly what he had hoped for, but it was still of reasonable size, and Sam's record of his earlier samples showed that *this* claim had produced the sample that contained his diamond. The radiant sunshine felt warm to Sam, but the wind had a bite to it; he could write only briefly in his notebook before he needed to put his gloves back on. If there were more diamonds here, most likely they were spread uniformly throughout the whole dike. But just the same, it was nice to have some *known* pay dirt from *his* section of the dike.

After laying out the claim, Sam returned to his truck. He was able to drive around the end of the dike and to within 800 feet of the south end of his claim. From his truck he carried a four-by-four post for his discovery point, five pieces of rebar for the corners and centerline, a small hand sledge, and a claim notice that was also recorded in his field notebook. Sam collected a large sample from the west side of the dike where the wind had blown the snow clear. It made his pack extremely heavy, but it was only a short walk back to the truck. By eleven-thirty he was back in the driver's seat and sipping lukewarm coffee from his thermos, having completed his work on the claim, "Little Gem #1." Hot coffee would have been preferred, but warm was tolerable.

Sam finished the coffee as he looked over his mineral ownership map. He then drove back to the frontage road and turned west, then north under I-80 to try staking the north end of the dike. A little more than two miles from the underpass, the dike had been excavated to clear the blockage of the frontage road that was, in fact, used as a haul road to move coal to the power plant. The coal company had *their road* back in operation in less than two weeks. They had the equipment, the know-how, and the incentive to do so. It would take yet another two weeks for the interstate to re-open and three months before it would be repaved across the construction area.

The dike, where it crossed the frontage road, was massive, and debris had been scattered for quite some distance when it collapsed. Sam set one claim just off the road's right-of-way to the north and one to the south. He managed to stake a total of three claims that day. They were called "Little Gem #s 1, 2, & 3." The easy access to #s 2 and 3 allowed him to stake two

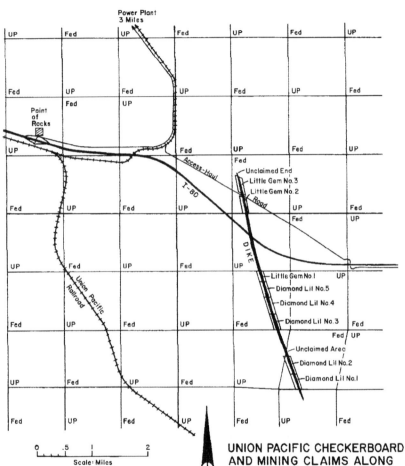

UP	Fed	UP	Fed	UP	Fed	UP

Power Plant
3 Miles

Fed	UP	Fed	UP	Fed	UP	Fed

Fed | UP

Point
of
Rocks

UP | Access-Haul | Fed | UP | Fed | UP

I-80

Fed

Unclaimed End
Little Gem No. 3
Little Gem No. 2

Road

Fed	UP	Fed	UP	UP	Fed

Fed | UP

DIKE

UP	Fed	UP	Fed	UP	UP

Little Gem No. I
Diamond Lil No. 5
Diamond Lil No. 4

Union Pacific Railroad

Fed	UP	Fed	UP	Fed	Diamond Lil No. 3	Fed

Fed | UP

Unclaimed Area
Diamond Lil No. 2
Diamond Lil No. I

UP	Fed	UP	Fed	UP

Fed	UP	Fed	UP	Fed	UP	Fed

0   .5   2
Scale: Miles

Fed = Federal minerals, open to claim staking
UP = Union Pacific or other privately owned minerals

N

UNION PACIFIC CHECKERBOARD
AND MINING CLAIMS ALONG
NEW POINT OF ROCKS DIKE

claims in less than an hour and a half, finishing up by early afternoon. He was even able to load some rather large rock samples directly into his truck, without having to pack them on his back. The southern claim ended almost on the north edge of the U.P. section. The north claim ended fifty feet short of the north end of the dike that rather abruptly tapered down to only five feet wide, near the end of his claim. Sam decided that he would leave that last narrow fifty-foot slice for someone else.

He really didn't think he needed to stake it all. His plan was to process the samples and then sell the claims to a company who might want to develop them. Sam was into prospecting and the excitement of discovery, but he had no desire to actually set up a mine himself. Also, it was getting late enough that he wanted to head back to Casper for his dinner date. He felt that dinner with Liddy would be much more desirable to him than ownership of one more claim on the thin end of the dike. It was mid-afternoon when Sam turned east toward Rawlins.

As he later approached Casper from the west, he contacted Liddy on his two-meter ham radio, via the Casper Mountain repeater. Their exchange was initially brief as he related to her the weather conditions near Point of Rocks and told her that he had staked three claims. Sam was about an hour from town, and Liddy's soup would be ready when he arrived. As they both signed off, two other stations came on-air, saying "hello" to Sam, but calling Liddy. They both wanted to introduce themselves to the *new voice* that they had not previously heard on the repeater. They offered her a warm welcome from the local amateur radio club and expressed the hope that she would get on the air regularly. They also invited her to attend their scheduled meetings and random get-togethers. A four-way discussion continued until Sam and Liddy both signed off as he pulled up in front of her home.

$\Longleftrightarrow$

Sam was joyfully greeted by Grieg at the gate and then given an affectionate hug by Liddy as he entered her door. The soup was ready, along with crusty rye bread and salad. While they ate,

Sam related his experiences staking claims. It had been a tiresome day for both of them, so after supper they spent the evening listening to music on Liddy's impressive sound system, which Sam found to be incredible in its clarity. She played the CDs that he had given to her of the *Wind In The Heather* and *Ceann na Drochaide Bige,* along with several others.

Liddy took the initiative to sit close to Sam on her sofa, and his shyness gradually melted. With a trace of hesitation, Sam wrapped an arm around her as she edged closer to him. Grieg dropped down next to them with his head resting on Sam's boot. The evening floated by in small talk as a heady dreaminess enveloped them both. Drifting in and out of wakefulness, they could neither tell when the dreams began, nor later remember what they had discussed. But when Grieg stirred, they realized that it was late, and the music was no longer playing.

Sam and Liddy reluctantly stood up as an unseen artist's paintbrush washed across them an enduring image of fondness for each other, such as they had never before perceived. Time hung on the warmth of that moment until Sam spoke softly, "It's getting late, Liddy." He kissed her gently and embraced her for several seconds, slowly releasing her.

As Sam retrieved his coat, he asked Liddy, "Since you have tomorrow off, would you like to attend church with me in the morning? We're having a classy folk music group in from Cheyenne. They'll be playing acoustical instruments, and we'll get to sing along. I think you'll enjoy the music, as long as you don't listen too closely to my voice."

"Oh, I'd love to go!" she enthused. "And I *would* like to hear you sing!"

⇌

Sunday turned out to be an amplification of many of Sam's and Liddy's thoughts and feelings from the previous evening. They attended Sam's church, sharing moments of peaceful meditation and prayer, while shedding thoughts of work schedules, deadlines, earthquakes, and newscasts from their cluttered minds. In the last several years Sam's church had incorporated a variety of styles of music into its worship services, following a general trend throughout the country. Traditional classical hymns were often intermingled with very creative and original contemporary songs. Sam saw that Liddy was thoroughly enjoying the music. The voices of the worshipers synchronized beautifully with the guitars, fiddles and mandolin. Even Sam felt like he contributed something. He noticed that Liddy was blessed with a beautiful alto voice, and he imagined her standing alone, singing among lodgepole pines in a quiet, dimly lit forest.

Sam's attention then turned from thoughts of Liddy's golden voice to the meaning of the words they were singing. The contemporary piece focused on love...love of Christ for all mankind, love as a gift from God, the power of love to bring new life, and the gift of love between a man and a woman. It seemed to Sam as if the song was a manifestation of his growing attachment to Liddy. As he turned his head toward hers, their eyes locked and held in a penetrating gaze into each other's souls. A flash of eternity shimmered in the space between them. *Was this real, or was it a dream?* The beautiful moment passed as the song ended, but the memory lingered with him as the smell of freshness lingers in the air after a summer rain.

At the end of the service, Liddy was introduced to the pastor and several members of the congregation. Sam thanked the singers and players from Cheyenne, urging them to return again. It was late in the morning when the sun's rays, until then shielded by a cloudbank, suddenly burst through the south stained glass window, bathing the sanctuary with scattered pinpoints of colored light. Mesmerized by the unexpected light show, Sam and Liddy were reluctant to leave. When they finally exited the church, the sun seemed unusually brilliant, casting sharp shadows on the snow and accentuating the colors and shapes of the buildings and trees around them.

As they walked to Sam's truck he asked, "Where did you learn to sing so well, Liddy?"

"Oh, I'm not so great," she laughed, "but I *do* love to sing."

Sam noticed that her beautiful green eyes sparkled surreally in the bright winter sun. It seemed as though a cup of utmost joy had been spilled over both of them. They grinned at each other with mutual affection as they climbed into his pickup. Liddy's thoughts reflected back on Sam's singing. He had not sung very loudly, and it was a real contrast to his normally strong speech. She guessed that it was due to his recognition of his own musical limitations. He'd had trouble finding the right pitch, and in fact, he couldn't even maintain a basic rhythm. But he truly enjoyed music and could recognize musical talent—a talent that, unfortunately, was absent in him. She felt like giving him a big hug, but being restrained by her seatbelt and not wanting to seem too bold, she reached out and gently touched his hand saying, "Church is a great place to stretch the vocal chords, Sam. You can't imagine how much I enjoyed the music and the service. Thanks for taking me with you!"

"My pleasure!" responded Sam with an even wider smile than before. He could visualize her going with him to church often and sharing other important things with him. To him, the future appeared as bright as the permeating sunshine, and his soul savored the happiness of the moment.

As he guided his vehicle out of the parking lot, Liddy inquired, "Are you hungry, Sam? Why don't I buy you lunch?"

"Thanks," he answered. "That'd be great. Do you have some place in mind?"

"Yeah," she smiled. "Let me surprise you. You drive; I'll direct."

Following Liddy's directions, Sam drove to a small café out on the extreme east end of town. It was one of her favorite spots for homemade soup. They enjoyed a long and lazy lunch hour, engaged in light-hearted trivial conversation.

As the afternoon waned, they returned to Liddy's house to take Grieg on a long walk through the snow. They bundled up in heavy jackets and slowly walked a couple of miles north and back again, while Grieg chased rabbits and drifting snow. The westward advancing sun cast pale blue shadows behind sage and grass, tinged yellow and pink in the weakening light. Their faces felt an invigorating chill from the wind, but their winter coats and full hearts provided inner warmth that sealed mutual smiles in memories that could be relived again and again. They didn't speak, while hand in hand they returned to the house, just as the sun touched the western horizon. Liddy set the table and prepared leftovers to share with Sam.

The evening passed quickly while they watched a classic old Humphrey Bogart movie, *The African Queen*, and considered what it might really mean to travel under difficult conditions. Neither Sam nor Liddy could think of any perilous traveling that either of them had done beyond battling a few blizzards. And if one was prepared for them, the danger could be overcome.

After the movie, Liddy entertained Sam with several short videos that she had compiled either for work or for fun. The shorts included an assortment of sporting events, flying, elk hunting with her father, and several outdoor documentaries. Also included was an artistic twenty-minute piece on nature and weather in the Bighorn Mountains that Liddy had made for her parents as a gift. Sam expressed to her his admiration of her obvious video talent.

Sam's favorite was a short video titled, "Urban Iron Man Competition." The competition began four years earlier when the owner of a local store, *Platte Hardware and Builders Supply*, came up with the idea to promote its merchandise. The annual competition included a wide variety of competitive events and gained ever-increasing popularity and crowds. Last year, the crowd of about 1500 people consisted of more spectators than participants in the timed and graded events. The events ranged from individual and team lawn mowing to garden weeding, hoeing, and bathroom plumbing. Stud wall framing and construction of a standardized section of foundation required both speed and skill, coupled with stamina. Professionals did not compete with amateurs and there were enough categories of entry for most participants to have a good time, even if they did not win.

Although a simple description of the competition sounded a bit mundane, its oddity and its location in the center of Wyoming attracted visitors in a manner similar to well-known logging skills competitions. Platte Hardware and Builders Supply had secured a name for itself along with television coverage. In the tough competitive world of hardware and home improvements retailing, and with many local stores being shoved out of business by mega-national chain stores, Platte had acquired a dedicated following of customers and competitors. With the addition of some hired entertainment and catered refreshments, *Platte* was making tidy profits from the event each year and drawing some regional notice to Casper as well.

"We could go together on an entry this coming July if you'd like," suggested Liddy. "Entries don't have to be in until around the first of July."

"That'd be something different," answered Sam. "I'll bet that we'll both be in shape by then from our gardening and lawn chores to make a reasonable showing. Any ideas on which category we should enter?"

"No, not really. We'll have to wait for the official listings to come out before we decide."

"Okay, we'll let the idea float and choose what seems best at the time. What do you suppose makes such an unusual competition like this become so popular?" asked Sam.

"I'd guess," answered Liddy, "that Platte offers participatory entertainment while providing customer service, rather than trying to *coerce* customers with guilt if they fail to support the local store. No one likes coercion. Retail businesses are different than things like politics, where so many just push to get ahead, no matter what principles they run over. I've done a few stories on business failures, and there have been quite a few of them. One common factor, beyond a lack of knowledge, seems to be an attitude by the owners that the community *owes* loyalty to the business, no matter how expensive their merchandise, or how poorly they treat their customers. They try to use *coercive advertising*, rather than cater to their customers' real needs. Platte is successful because they cater so well to customers."

"I guess I don't have much experience with business beyond my limited consulting work," explained Sam. "However, I usually buy hardware at Platte because they're friendly, their prices are reasonable, and if they don't have what I'm looking for, they'll have it for me in a day or two at the most. And," he added, "I know what you mean about politics. Sometimes it's hard to tell who pushes harder to get to the head of a line...children in grade school, or adults in congress."

"Oh, I think you understand quite well, Sam," laughed Liddy. "Your political analogy is humorous, but unfortunately it has too much truth in it."

⇌

Monday morning was hectic for Sam. He arrived at his office at seven-thirty and spent an hour organizing class notes and laying out lesson plans for the week. This helped to keep his classes running smoothly and also made it easier to make unexpected adjustments in his schedules.

After his morning class, Sam called Surya at Wyoming State University, who answered, "Good morning, Dr. Westone. Did you get a chance to see the data and interpretations from last Friday's series of quakes in Yellowstone?"

"I sure did...I studied them, but I wanted your personal take on what was happening. I think those longer duration swarms are magma movement. What do you think? By the way, you don't need to call me *Dr*. I don't have a doctorate, and I prefer *Sam*."

"All right...Sam it is!" replied Surya. "There is no question about it, Sam. We're seeing quite a bit of magma movement under Yellowstone. Those low magnitude, long duration quake swarms are pretty characteristic. However, I just can't explain the scattered larger quakes that are more numerous for this region than historical records suggest they should be. There doesn't seem to be any connection between them and the magma movement, except that in directly preceding the magma movement, some of the quakes appear to be triggering it. But...that can only be demonstrated after multiple correlations of numerous events that we don't have a record of."

"Surya, your assessment matches mine, and I've been spending some extra time researching Yellowstone's past activity. Because of the recent magma movement, I'm trying to get an idea as to what precursors might precede an eruption and whether those precursors are present."

"Are you actually thinking that Yellowstone could erupt?"

"Well, Surya, while I think it's conceivable, I don't feel that this recent magma movement by itself has demonstrated such a thing. We have to remember that seismic identification of magma movement in Yellowstone is not new. Motion of magma under that area was shown to be taking place back in the 1950s. I believe that your seismic network, particularly your computer derived three-dimensional representations, may have the capability to help demonstrate such a possibility...if it currently exists. I'll let you know if I figure out something specific to look for that could shed some light on the possibility of a future eruption."

"Okay, Sam. Thanks for calling. I'll talk to you later."

After Surya hung up, Sam continued his research into Yellowstone, working until almost noon. He then packed a few papers into his briefcase and hurried off to the monthly departmental meeting.

⇌

The noontime March staff meeting at the CTC Geosciences Department began with the department head, Ralph Escobido, presiding. Ralph liked to keep meetings brief and informative. This meeting was no different, and all technical staff, instructors, and secretarial staff were present. Ralph started with comments about the recent favorable public exposure they had received on KWYN television, courtesy of the efforts of Sam Westone. Ralph praised Sam and his students for their fine job.

Then Ralph threw in the *surprise*..."A large endowment has been given to CTC for use by the Geosciences Department, as a direct result of the television coverage of Sam's field trip and class activities. One of our local television station's viewers was apparently very impressed with your performance, Sam. Congratulations!" *Sam was speechless*! Ralph continued, "Improvements that instructors may have been wishing for, particularly laboratory facilities and equipment, should now be evaluated and submitted as proposals to me by the middle of the spring semester. There is also the possibility for some minor pay raises next fall." Sam would happily accept a raise, but at the moment he was making a mental list of lab equipment that he thought would help in his classes.

The meeting continued with some five- and ten-year service certificates being handed out. Ralph, after asking for comments and suggestions, concluded the meeting in only twenty minutes. He then announced, "I brought doughnuts for all," and he placed two large boxes on the conference table. "Keep up the good work."

⇆

Following the staff meeting, Sam continued to ferret out information on Yellowstone. He learned that the Lava Creek ash, deposited from Yellowstone's most recent large eruption of slightly more than 600,000 years ago, had accumulated to at least one meter deep near Emporia, Kansas. As the crow flies, Emporia is more than 800 miles southeast of Yellowstone! He also learned that the compacted ash thickness from the Yellowstone eruption of two million years ago had been found to be over seven inches thick at a distance of 930 miles from its source in Yellowstone. Sam figured that such an incredible amount of ash would play havoc with transportation, clog rivers, and probably collapse numerous buildings. Wind patterns, most certainly, have a lot to do with the ash distribution, and they, of course, are unpredictable.

The mind boggling portion of Sam's new information was that he didn't know how deep the ash might have been closer to its source, but it undoubtedly did get deeper at sites closer to the actual eruption. Sam was determined to find out just how deep the ash from Yellowstone had actually piled up, particularly close to home. He thought it was a definite possibility that geologic history could repeat itself—he just *might* end up shoveling ash in Casper.

CHAPTER 9

Character

Better is a little with righteousness than great revenues without right. - Proverbs 16:8

In the middle days of March, the white winds of winter suddenly softened their grasp on central Wyoming. A series of unusually warm and vigorous chinook winds claimed the skies as they roared across the plains, swiftly exposing the rocky south slopes of hills, and burning paths through the ridges of deeply piled-up snow along the streets and sidewalks of Casper. The snow could linger in the forests and alpine regions of the higher elevations until June or even August, but by the end of March, Casper's streets and lawns would be dry, and the gray wintry moods of its residents would be melted away.

Sam and Liddy either saw each other or talked on the phone almost every day during March and April. Liddy had weekends off for the entire two months, and they made the most of their time together. They skied cross-country until the snow crusted over and vanished. Then the friendly, warming winds beckoned them to explore the drying gullies and washes that ripped through the basins and mountain slopes of central Wyoming. They searched for agates and jasper, plucked from the freshly eroded soil by rivulets of running water, and shining for the first time in the sunlight. Sam taught Liddy a great deal about rocks on these excursions, and together they packed out several specimens that would be worth the efforts of polishing.

Sam's horizons and circle of friends also expanded as Liddy instructed him in horse care and riding and took him along to several *Windy Trails Horsemen* spring rides and social gatherings. Sam came to really enjoy riding after his newly discovered muscles got used to the saddle, and his balance and confidence increased. Liddy taught Sam to "think like a horse" and to anticipate the horse's reaction to its surroundings. Sam discovered that he could often spot interesting rocks and details of geology better from the back of a horse than on foot because of his increased height above ground. Perhaps he could do some geology fieldwork, in open country, from horseback with Liddy assisting him.

Sam's appreciation for Liddy, her talent, and her perspectives grew with each passing day. She would see things in situations or in the landscape that he hadn't noticed. Her comments seemed to amplify or blend with his to the benefit of both. It was like having poor vision and then putting on eyeglasses, or having someone explain the deep, hidden meaning of an already entertaining novel. Sam never dreamed that life could be so full and varied—and all because of Liddy.

On Sundays, Liddy attended church with Sam. She got to know the people there and even helped out with the services by singing and playing the piano on a few occasions. Liddy was enjoying life! She appreciated the regular weekends off work, the new social activities, and most of all Sam's company.

Liddy had never known such a downright well mannered gentleman as Sam. He was a throwback to a more chivalrous time. He treated her like a real lady and had never made untimely or inappropriate physical advances toward her. Liddy had resisted her share of shallow come-ons by other men in her past. She hadn't wanted to mess with them. She had been saving her affections for some future, unknown, special guy who might one day enter into her life. That day had now arrived, and Liddy knew for certain that she was totally under the spell of Sam Westone.

On weekday evenings, Liddy and Sam would often dine together and occasionally attend cultural events at the college. Their favorite was a comic play written and produced by CTC theater students. It was a spoof on Shakespeare's *Mac Beth*, and was called *"Mac Chocolate."* The short, tragic farce was hilarious, keeping the audience in stitches, and feeding on many people's weaknesses for chocolate. Sam and Liddy particularly liked a passage from the second act:

> *"Is that a chocolate that I see before me,*
> *The wrapper toward my hand? Come let me clutch thee.*
> *I have thee not, and yet I see thee still.*
> *Art thou not, cocoa vision, sensible*
> *To tasting as to sight? Or art thou but*
> *A chocolate of the mind, a false confection,*
> *Proceeding from the chocolate-starved brain?"*

The final scene left people hungering for more, and chocolate candy was handed out as attendees left the theater.

Liddy speculated on the parallels between *Mac Chocolate* and its Shakespearean inspiration, *Mac Beth*. "When Mac Beth contemplated murder to achieve his desire for power, he saw a vision of a dagger, but Mac Chocolate, contemplating gluttony to feed his desire for a taste sensation, visualized a chocolate bar. Does this," she questioned Sam, "show that dreams of over-indulgence in one's desires can lead to actions counter to one's sense of right and wrong? Or are the visions a result of decisions already made to act counter to one's inhibitions?"

"I think either one is a possibility," answered Sam. "However, I think the characters in both plays share a lack of moral convictions."

"Probably true, Sam," said Liddy, licking her lips. "But *my* vision suggests to me a chocolate shake. How about it?"

"Thou hast caught me in a *similar* vision, my Lady. But fear not...although my mind conjureth up a tray full of shakes, I think I shall limit my intake to *one*. You shall not find *me* succumbed in a pool of melted chocolate!"

⇋

During several evenings in mid-March, Liddy helped Sam process the rest of his samples from the Point of Rocks dike where he had staked his claims. They spent a grueling time crushing, washing, sifting, and doing gravity separations in Sam's basement. Liddy learned the nitty gritty of sample processing, and she took pictures of the procedure for an article Sam was writing on prospecting for diamonds. They carefully picked through the sample concentrates, looking for anything that might resemble diamonds. When they had finished, they possessed a small container of possible diamonds.

On the forth evening, Sam showed Liddy how to identify which ones were truly diamonds. Out of fifteen small stones they had set aside and tested, they confirmed two as diamonds. Liddy was particularly ecstatic since she had picked out both of them herself. They weighed 0.22 and 0.137 carats. Both diamonds were quite clear, but had slightly brownish to amber casts. Sam later took these to a local jeweler he had met at one of Liddy's horse club gatherings. He had the jeweler mount them in a pin that was shaped like a horse. The rough diamonds represented large spots on the small, silver Appaloosa pin that Sam gave to Liddy.

When he handed her the pin, tears filled her eyes. "It's so beautiful, Sam…it was so thoughtful of you!" The diamonds were rough so they didn't sparkle like cut gems would have. But they were perfect in the setting for the pin. Liddy loved the little things that Sam did for her, such as giving her this wonderful gift, but even though she realized he was shy, she wished that he would *verbally* and *physically* express his feelings more. Liddy showed Camile her pin at the very first opportunity. Camile commented to the beaming Liddy, "You look like a Cheshire cat with that grin! I'll bet that it won't even rub off with sandpaper!" Liddy wore her treasured pin almost constantly.

⇌

Seismically, most of March was rather quiet. It wasn't until several small earthquakes occurred on a Sunday and Monday, toward the end of the month, that Surya's network had anything significant to look at. The quakes in themselves were of brief duration, but nearly continuous, small magnitude earth tremor swarms accompanied them. The swarms appeared similar to the ones noted by Sam and his students early in the month. But these more recent swarms were of a much longer duration, lasting almost one week, with a few intermittent stops and starts. Both Sam and Surya agreed that this was definitely due to movement of magma beneath Yellowstone, but they still could not tie down any *cause and effect* relationships. However, Surya's computerized interpretations were beginning to show some details related to magma transport beneath Yellowstone. These depictions seemed to be but isolated pieces of a much larger puzzle. It would take many more interpretations, scattered over a much wider area, to bring clarity to the, as yet, unknown picture.

Four more small earthquakes rattled various parts of Wyoming, Montana, Idaho, and northeastern Utah during March and April. They were widely scattered and seemed to be quite random in their distribution. As before, the only thing that appeared unusual was the fact that this region had seen so many earthquakes since February. Across Wyoming, *more small quakes had been felt in the past few months than in the previous fifteen years*! Sam thought that their occurrences might account for something in deciphering the Yellowstone puzzle, although he, at the moment, did not know what. He was beginning to believe that maybe the whole northern Rocky Mountain region was acting up, but he would have to acquire more details before meaningful conclusions could be reached.

Andrew Merlott almost never had any visitors during the winter and early spring, particularly at his present remote location. The exceptions included lost snowmobilers or government agents who had nothing better to do with their time. On a Tuesday morning during the third week of March, Andy was slightly startled when someone knocked on his trailer door. Andy was always hospitable to visitors, but just the same, he usually kept a small revolver in his pocket, or his rifle nearby. When he opened the door, a man who was probably in his thirties and dressed in a snowmobile suit asked, "Are you Andrew

Merlott?"

This took Andy by surprise. The man did not appear to be a government agent, and Andy wondered what the man's business with him was.

"Good morning, Andrew," began the man, extending his hand.

"Just *Andy*, if you don't mind," interrupted the prospector as they shook hands.

"Fine, Andy, my name is Wolf Penstock, and I'm working for a company that might be interested in some mining claims that were recently staked by you."

"Come on in and have a seat. I've got some time today. Would you like some coffee?" Andy had only one empty guest chair and two clean mugs.

"Certainly," replied Wolf as he set down his helmet and gloves on the floor and removed his outer coat.

Wolf was hired by a representative from the Reef Group to investigate and acquire Andy's claims. It was an easy task for Wolf, who hired himself out as a permit man for mineral development companies. The Reef Group representative supplied Wolf with the name of a small mining company, Arcturus Mines, Inc., that would like to purchase the claims. They paid Wolf a $1000 service fee in advance to acquire the claims for them. The Reef Group's representative informed Wolf that they had already made arrangements with the Union Pacific Mining Division for the controlling rights on the U.P. part of the checkerboard land pattern. In fact, they had already bought out much of U.P.'s mineral holdings several years earlier, using a front company called *"American Golconda Mining and Land Enterprises"* in order to hide their true identity. Others involved in diamond exploration in Wyoming had always wondered why the Union Pacific had no interest in mining diamonds, especially after a diamond mine accidentally edged onto their property in the Wyoming/Colorado state-line kimberlite district in the 1990s. Most people had just assumed that the reason was management incompetence, typical of many financially troubled businesses that have put personal egos and politics above profit. That secret was not in any danger now of being exposed.

Sitting at Andy's small table, Wolf explained that

Arcturus Mines believed that Andy's claims were well positioned. Arcturus wished to tie up the area for exploration, and hopefully for eventual development, providing their exploration and sampling went well. Wolf offered, "Arcturus, in the unproven hope that they will find diamonds, is prepared to offer you $7,500 and a five percent royalty on any future production, plus reimbursement for your staking expenses, in exchange for a quitclaim deed to your claims."

Andy casually argued, "Well, that sounds like a reasonable start, but I think I can do a lot better than that if I mine the claims myself. I've already taken some samples and was just fixin' to start processin' them. Would you like to try again?"

"Andy, if you have actually *found* diamonds in your samples, I might be able to come up a little bit," responded Wolf. "But if we are only dealing with hopes and possibilities, it would be difficult to offer more."

"Well, no, I don't have diamonds *yet*," admitted Andy, pausing to sip his coffee. "But if I was to find even one diamond in these here samples, I'd shore sell my claims for twice that."

"But Andy, you haven't even processed your samples yet, and I'd bet you might have some trouble even identifying diamonds. You *will* need some special processing equipment to find diamonds in your samples, let alone actually mine them," countered Wolf as he leaned forward with the intensity of a used car salesman. "I think your initial expenses in that direction will easily exceed the price I'm now offering you."

"True in part," said Andy, leaning back in his chair away from Wolf. "But I can easily crush the samples and do a gravity separation myself 'fore summer arrives."

"That's a lot of work, Andy. You might profit better by selling those claims and sticking to your gold placer. I hear you made pretty good wages on that last year."

Andy was thinking hard about the offer, aware that the stiffness had not yet left him. He now managed to think to himself rather than out loud. This guy may be right. Maybe I should take the money and stick to my placers. That would be one of the quickest and easiest $7,500 dollars I've ever made. Then out loud he said, "Tell you what, Mr. Penstock. If you made that $15,000 along with the royalty, you'd have yerself a deal."

"Andy, Andy," sighed Wolf as he settled back in his chair and took another swallow of coffee. "Arcturus wanted me to buy the claims for a fair price, not spend their exploration budget before they've even had a chance to look at any samples. I know that would be good for you, but I really have to consider their interests as well. If you really think you want to mine those claims yourself, I guess I'd better tell them that you drove too hard of a bargain."

Then Wolf stood up as if to leave.

Detecting a slight hesitation in Wolf's actions, Andy slowly stood up and sighed, "I suppose you're right, Mr. Penstock. Thanks for stopping by, but I'm sure I can do better than that if I do my own mining. And I suspect you won't be the last character to try buying my claims."

Wolf picked up his winter gear and helmet and walked toward the door, then paused and turned. Andy had seen this maneuver before and was anticipating Wolf's final offer, when Wolf, looking somewhat pained as if he had just spent his last nickel, said, "I'll tell you what, Andy. My final offer, *and I'll probably catch some trouble for it*, is $10,000 with five percent royalty on production. I'll take the samples you've already collected, and you sign a confidentiality agreement and the quit claim deed to your *Diamond Lil #s 1 through 5* claims."

"Well," drawled Andy slowly, "Yer prob'ly cheatin' me out of my retirement, but I'll go along with that, as long as you make it a bank or certified check."

"I'll do that, Andy. And if you like, we can go to your bank today to finish the deal."

"Sounds good to me!" sparked Andy. "My bank is in Lander. Give me a minute to crank up my snowmobile and I'll follow you. I think we can get all the samples on both machines."

Andy was smiling when he followed Wolf toward town, and again later when he and Wolf left Andy's bank in Lander. Then, thinking out loud again, Andy declared with a broad grin, "And who says that prospectin' don't pay?"

⇌

The Reef Group had also been notified of Sam's claims on the Point of Rocks dike, but it wasn't until the last Friday in March that Wolf Penstock paid a visit to Sam with an offer to buy his claims. Wolf called on Sam at home, just as he and Liddy were fixing supper.

"Good evening, Mr. and Mrs. Westone," he began, "My name is Wolf Penstock." Liddy blushed slightly, and Sam didn't bother to correct him. The man apparently was not from the Casper area, since he mispronounced Sam's last name as "*wee-stone*." He also did not mention having heard about Sam's television special, concerning the geologic conditions responsible for the dike to which he referred. "The company I represent, *Arcturus Mines*, has learned that you have staked three mining claims along a dike near Point of Rocks. Arcturus Mines would like to purchase your claims as part of an exploration effort on a larger property that they believe may have potential for development. Arcturus, in their unproven hope that they will find diamonds, is prepared to offer you $4,500 plus a five percent royalty on any future production, along with reimbursement for your staking expenses, in exchange for a quitclaim deed to your claims."

"I appreciate your interest and your offer," replied Sam with a sigh. "However, I may not be ready to sell, because the claims that I hold have been proven to host diamonds."

"How can you know that?" responded Wolf incredulously. "Arcturus was not aware of any sampling program being conducted."

"I'm not familiar with Arcturus Mines," said Sam with pedagogic authority. "But, in their all-knowing wisdom, they should surely be aware that any self-respecting prospector takes representative samples both before and after staking. In fact, sampling on diamond development properties is a continuously expanding process until you are really mining rather than sampling."

"Well, Mr. Westone," said Wolf defensively. He usually had the upper hand, but became a bit flustered when the tables were turned. "I merely work for the Arcturus land acquisition and permitting branch, and I'm not that well versed on geology and mining." Then, trying to recover his composure, he added, "Are you sure you actually have diamonds? They are, *in fact*, easily confused with other minerals."

"Mr. Penstock," continued Sam with a business-like air, "I have worked in diamond exploration for a number of years and am well aware of the problems associated with identification of diamonds, as well as with their mining. We've already found three diamonds *and* gem quality peridot in just a few relatively small samples. If Arcturus is seriously interested in the purchase of these claims, at a figure that reflects the already known recovery of diamonds from them, I'll entertain their offer. I can supply Arcturus with documentation of the authenticity of the diamonds and with samples of the peridot. The diamonds already found are not for sale. If they wish, your company may purchase exploration rights to my claims, to verify for themselves the existence of diamonds, prior to the actual acquisition of the claims."

"Mr. Westone, what sort of exploration rights agreement or sales price did you have in mind?"

"First off, and in either case, I would supply all information that I have currently compiled and allow examination of one of the diamonds."

Liddy added, "Sam, they can look at these two also, but they can't take them anywhere."

Wolf's eyes seemed to open a bit wider when he saw Liddy's pin with the two mounted gems.

"Okay, they can examine all three diamonds here," continued Sam. "Exploration on the three claims for one year will cost $6000, plus twenty-five percent of all gemstones found...*or*, we could work out a long term lease. We can discuss details later. If Arcturus would like to purchase outright within a month, the asking price is $20,000 per claim, or $60,000 for all three claims. After that time, the price cannot be guaranteed to be as low."

"Gosh! That's a pretty stiff deal!" exclaimed Wolf. "Do you really think that's reasonable?"

"If I didn't think it reasonable, I wouldn't have said it, Mr. Penstock. Now if you will excuse us, we have dinner waiting. If you want to entertain further discussion, I'd prefer to be called first for an appointment," finished Sam. Smiling, he handed Wolf a business card and escorted him to the door.

After Wolf had left, Liddy asked, "Sam, was that really a reasonable price? It seemed like a lot to me!"

"Yes, it was very reasonable," replied Sam, "but only because we *do* have diamonds. I think he'll be back to dicker if they're serious. Anything we get will be good, but if we don't start out high enough, we can't raise the price later…$45,000 plus a production royalty is actually what I *wanted* to shoot for over all. If we hadn't found the diamonds, I would have tried for $9000, but could have been argued lower."

⇌

Wolf Penstock phoned Sam on a Wednesday in early April, making arrangements to meet with him on Thursday morning. Wolf brought a diamond "expert" with him. They met at ten-thirty at Sam's house and dickered for the better part of an hour. Sam's diamond and his documentation convinced Wolf and his associate of the veracity of the claims. Liddy's diamonds did not need to be examined. It also helped that the *expert* had read several articles by Sam, and was familiar with his reputation. The final result that all three felt to be reasonable was $45,000 for Sam, plus a seven percent royalty on any future production from the claims. The deal also included a *confidentiality statement*, signed by Sam, eliminating the release of any information about the property. That confidentiality agreement also pre-empted the article about diamond exploration that Sam had been working on.

Before signing, Sam had to check with Liddy because Arcturus also wanted the pictures she had taken documenting their sample processing. He phoned Liddy at work and was able to connect with her right away. She agreed, and the deal was done.

That evening, Sam and Liddy went out to dinner and discussed his claims deal. Sam wanted to give Liddy half, but she insisted that her part in the work had been minimal. Sam emphasized that without her help, he might not have gotten around to processing the samples for some time and would therefore not have been in such a strong bargaining position. The two additional diamonds, found by Liddy, had conclusively confirmed the diamond-bearing characteristics of the dike.

After much discussion, she finally agreed to accept $15,000, but told Sam to keep the production percentage. Liddy said thoughtfully, "Perhaps this summer I'll look for something newer and with a lot less miles on it than my old SUV."

"Since I did so well on the deal," stated Sam, "I think I'll put some of it into a few worthy causes. Would you like to help me out in the selection?"

"Oh, of course I would," chimed Liddy. "Giving gifts is always fun. We could put some of my share in as well."

"I consider half of another $15,000 a part of your share anyway. We can always find a way to spend money on ourselves, but we don't really need to."

Over the course of the next few days, Liddy and Sam anonymously sent out contributions totaling $15,000. They split it between various charities, youth organizations, and Sam's church.

Neither Sam nor Liddy ever suspected the link between the sale of his claims and the political shenanigans reported almost daily in the national news. Despite some of the nefarious methods and questionable business practices of the Reef Group, financial resources of that organization, filtered through the hands of Sam and Liddy, found their way to noble purpose. The *scoundrel* may sometimes serve the greater good through the unwitting hand of the *innocent*.

CHAPTER 10

Rising Concerns

▼

The time is come, the day of tumult is near... - Ezekiel 7:7

On a Monday morning in mid-April, two of Sam's students, Ginny Pryor and Mike Hulett, stopped into his office before class. They were members of the college caving club and had been actively involved in cave exploration and mapping for the past two years. As the club's faculty sponsor, Sam was aware of their activities. He had been helping the club to gain recognition as a student chapter of the *National Speleological Society*. The *NSS* is a national organization dedicated to the exploration, conservation, and scientific study of caves. The new chapter, known as a *grotto*, was named the *CTC Student Grotto*.

Over the previous weekend, Ginny and Mike had visited a cave on the west side of Rattlesnake Mountain, just west of Cody, Wyoming. Members of the grotto had named it "Grizzly Cave" upon discovering it the previous summer. They had made several trips to the cave to survey and study its contents. Grizzly Cave had apparently developed along joints in the Mississippian age Madison Limestone by sulfurous waters related to paleo-hot springs. It had already been surveyed to a length of 4900 feet. The previous fall, Ginny had begun to study some cold-water bacteria that derived nourishment from sulfur. Similar unique bacteria were already known to exist in hot springs in

Yellowstone National Park, but had not been previously identified in such a cold habitat as existed in Grizzly Cave.

In the process of her studies, she and Mike had done a detailed laser instrument survey of a long, narrow, three to six-foot deep pool of water that hosted the bacteria. Over the preceding weekend they noted something very unusual—the cave passage that contains the pool runs west to east, and it seemed to have been *tilted* upward to the west by about one-half inch over a distance of 1300 feet.

Ginny explained, "Last fall we drilled small holes in the rock at the water's edge, on both the sides and at the ends of the pool. Then we set permanent plastic markers. The plastic doesn't react with the water, and the markers serve as stable survey references for several types of studies, including water level measurements. On Saturday, when we checked the water level, the eastern-most marker was slightly *below* the water, and the western one was slightly *above* the water. Dr. Sam, this is a narrow, two-foot wide pool with no apparent water flow. We used some of the latest laser surveying equipment, both last fall and this weekend. We also double-checked our surveys on both occasions. Our accuracy should be to less than a sixteenth of an inch! *What would cause tilting of the pool in Rattlesnake Mountain*? Or is there some other explanation that we're missing?"

"That certainly is a curious observation," noted Sam. "Did you recheck the calibration of your instruments?"

"We rechecked both the survey and the instrument calibration at least six times," offered Mike.

"Is there any chance that the initial positioning of your markers was off last fall?" queried Sam.

Ginny responded, "We've thought about that. It had me worried until Mike reminded me that he photographed each marker for a starting record after it was placed. The photos show the markers exactly at the water-line." She handed Sam copies of the prints, and then continued, "These are the photos from Saturday and Sunday."

Sam asked, "Did you check to see if any of the markers had come loose, perhaps forced upward by frost action or expanding clay beneath a marker? Because of the reflection in the second set of photos, you can't see below the water-line to tell if the tops of the markers are still in the same positions, relative to the rock surface, as in the first photos."

"Gosh, that would be *my* error on the photos," Mike admitted. "I guess I should have noted the rock surfaces as well as the water surface in the pictures. We also didn't think to check the markers for looseness."

Ginny added, "The cave is too warm to freeze, and it's at a very stable temperature of about forty-four degrees F. We haven't observed any clay near the pool, although there is some on the pool bottom."

"You've built an interesting puzzle," agreed Sam. "However, you're dealing with rather small measurements. You'll have to recheck your markers for looseness and then photograph the markers' positions, relative to the rock surface, before you have a solid case for *regional tilting*. You also might discuss it at the next grotto meeting. Maybe someone else will come up with an idea. When you have a chance to recheck things, let me know what you find. *It might relate to another problem that I'm working on.*"

Ginny and Mike thanked Sam for his help and then rushed off to class.

Sam's students presented an interesting question, with equally interesting implications. In his consideration of Yellowstone, Sam had addressed local uplift due to magma emplacement that was, he believed, happening. But what about regional effects of the Yellowstone hotspot? Sam had learned earlier that the hotspot was interpreted to give rise to regional uplift, *but only over the course of geologic time*. None of the hypothesized regional uplift had any *historically measurable* evidence.

Sam decided to phone Dave Clement, a professional surveyor whom he had met while consulting. Dave and Sam had become good friends over the years, while participating in numerous activities of mutual interest. Sam asked Dave, "Where could I find out about surveys that would show minor elevation changes, over time, across parts of Wyoming, Idaho, and Montana?"

Dave responded, "Can I call you back in about an hour? I remember reading about some surveys and information that may address some of what you're asking. Most of it is in electronic formats, so I can easily e-mail it to you if you'd like."

"Terrific, Dave. I'll look forward to hearing from you. Thanks."

After hanging up the phone, Sam remembered reading about something related to the mid-1990s trona mine collapse near Green River. After a brief search of his files, he found the report he was looking for. Prior to the mine collapse, a survey along I-80 in southern Wyoming had shown a slight doming across the area between Little America and the intersection with U.S. Highway 189 east of Evanston. The rise amounted to almost eight inches higher than what was surveyed twenty years earlier. The 1990s survey was compared to an earlier and admittedly much more crude measurement that covered a distance of about fifty miles. However, in Sam's mind, the age of the earlier survey, because of the less precise technology used then, made any uplift or deep regional stress conclusions only suggestive rather than definitive.

This might be a real stretch, thought Sam, but it *could* relate to the projected southern limits of influence of the Yellowstone hotspot. The same stress that caused the uplift might have also provided a deep-seated fracture to assist whatever conditions led to the Point of Rocks dike. The two different types of volcanism, in Yellowstone and at Point of Rocks, could not possibly be related. But wide-area stresses induced within the earth by the hotspot could have resulted in broad uplift. Such uplift could certainly *cause*, or perhaps *aid*, incipient fracturing that may have been close to actively rupturing. Come to think of it, if uplift was *that* broad, it might even explain all of the recent regional earthquakes *if* they occurred within the area under uplift tension. But that would take a lot of good data and good luck to prove.

As Sam finished this bit of research and speculation, his phone rang, with Dave calling him back..."I've found only three surveys that might be of interest to you. Odd bits of information such as these turn up occasionally, but usually they never leave the offices where they're noted. You might ask someone at the USGS, but the way their budget has been, I don't expect you'll find too much. Most of their detailed survey efforts have been concentrating on volcanic and earthquake hazard recognition near highly populated areas on the west coast. I noticed that they have quite a bit of information on volcanic mountains in Washington, Oregon, and California. They've also been doing a bunch of work around San Francisco and Los Angeles. Check your e-mail; you should have the information now."

"Thanks for all the help, Dave. I'll let you know if I find anything interesting. I'll probably see you sometime next week anyway."

Sam hung up the phone and opened his e-mail. He found the reference to the survey he had just looked at (west of Little America), which was identical to the one in his files. The other two references were new to him. About two years earlier, a Montana surveying contractor reported that new measurements along Interstate-94, between Laurel and Whitehall, showed an upward bowing of the land, compared to a survey made back at the end of the twentieth century. This recently obtained data was probably reliable. Maximum upward bowing of four inches was centered between Bozeman and Three Forks, tapering to nothing at both ends, near Whitehall on the west and Laurel on the east.

The third report was a miscellaneous note from a surveyor's conference in Billings, from November of last year, by the owner of a small surveying outfit out of Worland, Wyoming. He and his only employee were outdoor enthusiasts. They had surveyed the summit elevation of Franc's Peak, the highest point in the Absaroka Mountains east of Yellowstone, when they had climbed it in July of that year. Their figures showed the peak to be just over four inches higher than its previous measurement, obtained during August, six years earlier. The surveyors used the latest equipment and were proud of their work. An individual employed by the USGS, who also had outdoor interests, had completed the earlier survey. That survey had been made in his own spare time and was not part of a regular USGS project. However, that elevation was shown to be one-half inch higher than the previous official USGS survey done during the mid-1970s.

It appeared to Sam that there could very well be some regional uplift, and that it *could* possibly be related to the Yellowstone hotspot. However, the connection to the hotspot had yet to be proven. When compared with the possible tilting observed by Ginny and Mike, the problem was certainly crying out for an answer, but Sam's supporting information was still tenuous.

⇌

After finishing up his Tuesday morning class, Sam received a message that Surya had called and wanted Sam to contact him. Returning the call, he found that Surya had stumbled on to some very intriguing data while attending a graduate students' barbeque on Saturday.

Surya began his explanation immediately, "I was talking to some friends about my dissertation and speculating about possible changes in Yellowstone, when one of the other geology student's girlfriend mentioned that she had seen some satellite imagery suggesting that this year's snow pack was melting *unusually early* in Yellowstone. She is a student in forestry management. I asked if I could look at her data and was able to study it on Monday morning. I don't have exact temperatures, but her studies of trees suggest unusually warm growth conditions over the last two to three years. And although this looks like a normal snow melt year all across the northern part of the Rockies, *there is a roughly circular area centered around the Yellowstone caldera that appears to be melting out much earlier than in previous years.*"

Surya continued, "Sam, I was able to get the address and then access satellite images for the last fifteen years. I have attached selected images in an e-mail to you. They show bare ground appearing around the caldera earlier each year for the last three, and possibly for the last four years, although that first year is not certain. Ground temperatures definitely are rising in and adjacent to the caldera. I showed this to Dr. Felsen, and he thinks that we should talk to the Central Emergency Management Group, *especially* if we can find any further changes or definite markers suggestive of a future eruption there."

"Thanks for your efforts, Surya. I've just encountered some evidence that there may be active uplift or ground swelling over a wide area around Yellowstone, but it needs to be tied down more tightly before it can be accepted as fact. And I agree with Chris that if any conclusive data comes to light pointing to an impending eruption, we should make it known immediately. Is Chris willing to put his name *out in public* if such an announcement becomes necessary?"

"Yes he is, Sam. In fact, he has been researching gravitational and geomagnetic changes in the Yellowstone area over the course of the limited historical record. So far, Yellowstone shows up as an anomaly gravitationally and in geomagnetics, but there have been no noticeable changes over the course of the records. The area beneath Yellowstone has always been somewhat of a low velocity seismic zone, and other than a possible hint of that zone increasing in size, no changes are noted *there* either."

"That's interesting," mused Sam. "I would have thought that those geophysical methods might have indicated at least a few changes within the caldera. Have you found any other possible sources of information?"

Surya continued, "We checked with a university in Utah that has, in cooperation with the USGS, operated a twenty-two-station seismograph network in Yellowstone for many years. They confirm our interpretation of magma movement, but they have not really looked at their data for some time. Apparently, their data acquisition is continuing, but their efforts are grant-funded and their present deadlines emphasize west coast volcano studies. They recently received a small grant to analyze their data from Yellowstone, but their funding and hence their study cannot begin until the first of August. I have been trying to connect their Yellowstone seismic network to mine, but differences in software are a problem. Also, they have been continuously collecting GPS data from three wide-spread stations in Yellowstone, but interpretations of that raw data won't be available until after their new grant kicks in during August."

"Is there any way to acquire that raw data out of Utah…so we can analyze it ourselves?" asked Sam.

"No, Sam. Unfortunately, their complex archival system requires a fair amount of effort, and they seem to be unable to break things out until one of their other current projects ends. Dr. Felsen has also checked on some ideas related to gas sampling and monitoring. Quite a few volcanoes produce a variety of gasses that can be detected at the surface, prior to an eruption. Gas venting is commonly related to magma emplacement beneath a volcano, but the records he *has* been able to obtain, from intermittent gas monitoring stations in Yellowstone, are inconclusive. It seems that continuous movement of magma at shallow depth, over the course of historical records, has resulted in continuous minor venting, such that no significant changes can be noticed."

"Thanks to both of you for trying, Surya. I still have a few avenues of investigation that I need to pursue, and I should be able to get back to you by the first part of next week. The trouble with a large caldera such as Yellowstone is that there isn't any *historical* precedent. Some of the most *violent* historical eruptions have *not* shown any identifiable pre-eruption warnings."

"I know, Sam. Remember, I came from Indonesia, which has the largest number of historically active volcanoes in the world, although none are currently known to be on the scale of the Yellowstone caldera. However, the Toba eruption, about 74,000 years ago, was probably about the same size as the last one in Yellowstone."

"Surya, I think all three of us are on the same thought plane. I know that this is important, but we can't jump the gun and get people panicked. We must provide supportable conclusions and projections, not undocumented or weakly defensible speculation. I'll talk to you next week."

Sam hung up the phone and then thought intently for several minutes. He retrieved Surya's e-mail and the attached satellite images and looked at them carefully. Surya was right about the changing snowmelt pattern in Yellowstone. He deposited the images in a file he was building on Yellowstone and called Dave Clement.

"Dave," began Sam, "I need your help on a rather sensitive, but as yet *unconfirmed* problem. Can I get your confidential help?"

"Sure, what's up?" answered Dave.

"Well, do you remember my question from yesterday?"

"Yes. Why?"

"I've been working with two other geologists, and we

think we may have indications that a volcanic eruption in Yellowstone could come in the near future. The problem is that our data is just not definitive enough yet to go public with. That kind of statement could cause some people to panic. And if we made such a prediction and were wrong, I think we would be open to a variety of intense chastisements."

"All right...I can understand the situation, but what do you want me to do?"

"Dave, the information you gave me is suggestive of some regional uplift in the vicinity of Yellowstone, but it is not conclusive for a variety of reasons. Do you know of any sources where I could find out for sure if measurable uplift has been happening over the last ten years or so? And is there any way to identify possible uplift within Yellowstone National Park over the period of, say, the last six to nine months? I'll pay for any costs you incur while answering those questions; just let me know the damages before you commit me to spending. My resources aren't unlimited."

"Okay, Sam...you have my word, and I won't break you. In fact, I might have relatively easy access to some useful data. I'll call you back...probably this afternoon."

"Thanks, Dave. I'll be waiting to hear from you."

⇌

Actually, *Sam was very troubled.* His study of Yellowstone had begun as a casual tangent in his geologic interests. Now it was second on his mind only to Liddy, and it was a major driving concern. He knew that Yellowstone would erupt someday—it could happen in the near future, or not for thousands of years. *What really bothered him*, however, was that *other* people or government agencies must certainly also be aware of the situation, and that *they should be warning people* if what he now perceived was, indeed, true. Sam wondered why no one was talking publicly about the unusual geologic activity in and around Yellowstone. *Surely someone else had noticed*! But sadly, no other scientists or agencies had been paying attention.

Sam sat for a while and contemplated: What is the U.S.

National Park Service doing in Yellowstone? Didn't the USGS have some responsibility there? Was the WOMG totally blind to the largest geologic hazard in the State of Wyoming? Was the Central Emergency Management Group unaware of the danger? Was there any government money being spent on analyzing the potential for such a serious disaster, rather than being so hung up on the questionable details of global warming or, according to some opposing viewpoints, global cooling? Millions of dollars can be spent monitoring the amounts of particulate matter and greenhouse gases caused by power plants, but *one relatively moderate volcanic eruption can spew out more pollution than man has produced since the start of the industrial age*. It was arrogant or wishful thinking to believe that *human activity* was the prime cause of environmental changes!

Sam's reflection was interesting, but his biggest concern was first *confirming*, or more hopefully *negating*, what his data appeared to show. If his present interpretation—*that Yellowstone could soon erupt*—continued to be reinforced by more data, then how could *he* alert the public if the responsible agencies failed to give a warning? Like it or not, public safety often boils down to *individual responsibility*. It appeared that a great burden might soon rest on Sam's shoulders—one that would require him to act on his own in order to save others, risking ridicule if he was wrong.

Back at the beginning of the present century, individuals, rising to responsibilities that were thrust upon them, did not hesitate to act. When terrorists hijacked airplanes and destroyed the World Trade Center in New York City, countless firemen, police, and citizens sacrificed themselves to save others. That same day, some passengers on one of the other hijacked planes saw their duty as individuals, voiced a prayer, and jumped into action. No one told them they had to do it; they just saw their obligation to try to save lives and went for it. They were all heroes.

Sam didn't see himself as *heroic*, and he certainly didn't want to become a public figure. He was trying, in his mind, to rationalize speaking out. Sam then recalled the history of the surprise attack on Pearl Harbor. Before the United States became involved in World War II, if certain individuals (who had received warnings that Pearl Harbor might be attacked), had stood up to the fog of bureaucracy, the outcome might have been different on Dec. 7, 1941. But as it was, warnings that entered the bureaucracy in several places never made it out to the persons in positions who could have done something to prevent the tragedy. *Individuals and their actions do make a difference*!

Courage is needed to speak out in public with an unpopular idea, and to inevitably face public and private ostracism. Social attacks against the proclaimers of unpopular ideas can last for years, or for a lifetime if one's ideas are proven to be wrong. Sam doubted that the idea of a volcano going off in Yellowstone National Park would be welcomed by anyone. It could spread fear, panic, disruption of business, and probably would have some political consequences as well. Never before had Sam stood up in public to say things that could affect thousands of lives. He wondered if he could gather up enough courage to do so, if required.

Sam's cogitation was broken when his telephone rang. It was lunchtime, and Liddy was calling to find out what their plans might be for the evening. "Sam...Camile and I were planning to attend a horse club meeting tonight. They're having a guest speaker who'll be giving a slide show on horse packing in Yellowstone. Are you interested?" asked Liddy.

Anxious for some relaxation and entertainment, Sam responded, "I sure am! Would you like me to pick the two of you up for supper beforehand?"

"Oh, no," she replied. "I'll drive. Camile and I thought you might like to eat over at my house before the meeting. How does that sound?"

"It sounds great! You must have known I needed a break. I've been hitting it pretty hard today, and I sure could use your company."

"And I yours, Sam. The workload at the station gets stiffer every day. It seems to take forever for Eric to hire some extra help! Just come on over after work...okay?"

"I'll be there. Thanks, Liddy!"

Around four o'clock, Sam received a return call from Dave Clement. Dave had found a potential wealth of raw data. He told Sam, "It's in the form of Global Satellite Survey Data (GSSD). Special satellites have been recording detailed geodetic data for at least fifteen years. But the problem is the huge volume of material...*it covers the entire Earth*. It has never been reduced and interpreted for small specific areas. It seems this has been due to budgetary constraints that plague the USGS and other agencies that might have been able to make use of it. The region around Yellowstone is one of those areas that took a back seat to studies that are more closely tied to large population centers, *and* to areas that are projected to be affected if global warming causes any rise in sea level."

"Oh man, Dave! What are we looking at as far as time and cost?" responded Sam as if an avalanche of paper was about to hit him.

"I don't know yet, Sam. I think the information is there, and I may be able to reduce enough of it to find the answers you're looking for. It's electronically available through the government for an access fee of $250 if you have the proper software, but the reduction time may be on the order of a couple of weeks. I won't have the amount of time necessary to reduce the data here. But if you'll allow me to recommend a program that's sold through several surveying suppliers for about $800, I can help set it up for you at CTC, and you can crank through the data almost continuously. I know that's a lot of money, but you could probably get through the analyses faster than I could. I'll even take some extra time to help you get started on the right track. If you're as concerned as I think you are, then I'm concerned too."

"Thanks, Dave. Let's go with that. I might even be able to get the college to cover the costs. But I'll pay for it out of my own pocket if necessary. How soon could we get started?"

"If you want, I can get things going now, and we could install the software over at your office tomorrow evening. I won't have time during my regular work hours for that part of the project."

"That'll be super, Dave. Maybe I can get Liddy's help too. She's a lot sharper on computers than I am."

"Well, this will require a few *sharps* on computers! The program isn't simple, but I could probably train you to handle it. If she has the experience, it will take a lot less time to produce results. Once you do get some answers, let me double check them before you make any wild assumptions. There are possibilities to easily go astray with this data and software. By the way, how long have you been seeing Liddy? Are you two getting serious?"

"We've known each other for just less than two months, but yes, I'd say it's getting serious. However, I think we both need a little more time before making any life-changing decisions. I'll ask her to help us if she's available. Why don't we meet at my office tomorrow evening about six?"

"Sounds good, Sam. I'll pick up the software and see you there."

Sam hung up the phone and then went looking for Ralph. At the main office, he was told that Ralph would be gone until the following Monday. The finances for this project might have to come out of his own pocket, after all. He wouldn't find out for sure until Monday, but he forged ahead anyway. Sam returned to his office and finished the day helping several students with their most recent geology assignments.

During the drive to Liddy's house, Sam's tension eased and he looked forward to a restful evening. After finishing supper, Sam, Liddy, and Camile attended the monthly meeting of the *Windy Trails Horsemen*. The business portion of the meeting took about forty minutes, touching on planned trail maintenance in the northern Laramie Range for the coming summer, and a packing demonstration for a 4-H gathering in May. Immediately following the business meeting, the guest speaker presented a slide show on packing into remote sections of the Beartooth Mountains and the primitive areas of Yellowstone. The slides of Yellowstone showed features of the park that are rarely seen by humans. Images of isolated deep canyons and waterfalls, flower-painted meadows, geysers, and gray bubbling mud pots intermingled with shots of wildlife that included bison, grizzly bears, elk, and a wide variety of birds. The slides depicted a splendid wonderland open only to those who dared long trips into the wilderness.

A feeling of doom momentarily passed over Sam as he

thought of how this enchanting place might suddenly cease to exist. He didn't want to believe that it could happen, but the recent geologic events pointed toward that possibility. It would occur sooner or later, like a recurring bad dream. He recalled previous conversations with Liddy and Camile about the possibilities of a pack trip into Yellowstone during the upcoming summer. *Would it be possible? Was it even safe to think about it? Would next year be too late? Or would Yellowstone remain unchanged for the next thousand years?*

After the meeting, they returned to Liddy's where Sam had parked his truck. Before leaving, he told Liddy about his talk with Dave Clement, the ground elevation concerns, and how he could use some computer expertise. Liddy replied that she would be more than happy to help him with his geodetic survey analyses.

⇌

The following evening, Liddy met Sam at his home for a quick meal, after which they drove over to Sam's office at CTC. Dave Clement showed up about five minutes later, greeting them with an armload of software and reference manuals. The three of them gathered around Sam's computer while Dave loaded software and explained procedures. After a few minutes it became obvious that Sam was totally lost, but Liddy understood almost everything. She was taking notes only on those items where she would need a memory jog. Sam, deferring to her superior abilities, requested that she take charge. Discussing the situation as they went along, Sam impressed upon Dave and Liddy the serious implications that their efforts were likely to produce.

It was close to eleven when they finally finished, and the program was up and running. Liddy created and initiated a small sub-program which would allow almost continuous data downloading and sorting, subservient to daily routine programming interruptions. The system was now in order such that Sam could check on it and re-address data entry as required. Filtering and checking the massive amounts of data was now almost automatic. They might actually be able to synthesize elevation contour changes from the reduced data as early as the weekend, or at least by Monday, thanks to Liddy's help. Dave would still have to assist with that, but all three of them were encouraged by the prospect of early interpretations.

⇌

Sam needed to re-initiate the data entry program once on Thursday afternoon, after the power had flickered off for a longer period than the backup supply could maintain. He and Liddy checked the downloading and processing on Thursday and Friday evenings, and again on Sunday afternoon. Liddy had become as concerned as Sam about the possibility of an eruption in Yellowstone, and she did a little research on her own into volcanoes and their effects on climate and life on earth.

She found that most explosive volcanic eruptions of any size have been shown, *conclusively*, to affect climate. Dust and aerosols from these eruptions, when spewed high into the stratosphere, have invariably caused cooling trends. Late in the last century in the Philippine Islands, Mt. Pinatubo (larger than St. Helens, but still small in the scope of volcanoes) produced a brief, but noticeable, cooling effect. The much larger eruption of Tambora in 1815 was followed by world-wide temperature drops.

But Liddy found much more worrisome, even *shocking*, interpretations related to a *prehistoric* eruption. About 74,000 years ago in what is now Indonesia, the eruption of Toba was estimated to be similar in size to the Yellowstone eruption of around 600,000 years ago. Although no major extinctions from that time period are known to date, studies of human genetics suggest that the world's human population crashed during that time. Estimates suggest that *less than 10,000 people survived a population bottleneck that may have lasted as long as 20,000 years*!

Although not a proven cause of humanity's troubles at that time, studies relating to nuclear winter scenarios, coupled with known climatic changes from volcanic activity, point to the eruption of Toba. The Toba eruption correlates with a relatively rapid period of global cooling, leading to glaciation during a warm interglacial period. The *volcanic winter*, caused by Toba, may have accelerated or accentuated climatic change already taking place. Interpretations of paleoclimatic data from various sources indicate that world-wide temperatures dropped by five to nine degrees F overall, and as much as eighteen degrees F during the growing season! *No wonder humanity only narrowly escaped extinction about 74,000 years ago!* Such temperature drops would be *disastrous*, even for our modern technological society!

Liddy found this fact *staggering!* She showed the information to Sam, with an underlying hope that he might somehow explain it away. Maybe the source she referenced was not credible. *"Sam! This can't be possible! Can it?"*

"Liddy...*that* is my nightmare scenario!"

"Yellowstone couldn't be that bad, could it?" lamented Liddy, almost pleading with him. "I'm just beginning to understand that geologic processes are *continually* active. But, I'm still having trouble thinking of geologic cataclysms as something that can happen *now*, in *our* time. It just seems like they should be limited to *remote locations in the distant past or future!"*

"I'd like to think that too, Liddy," answered Sam as he gently reached over and pulled her closer. "But I've seen some of that information before, and I recognize the reference as a credible source. The certainty that humanity was almost wiped out 74,000 years ago *increases* with every new published study. And the volcano Toba, as a cause, was suggested around the turn of the century. Toba's eruption was roughly the same size as the last big eruption in Yellowstone. Those researching the problem invariably cite Toba as a major, *if not the determining factor*, in that climatic change that resulted in the population bottleneck."

"Will the same thing happen when Yellowstone erupts?" asked Liddy gravely as she let her head settle against his chest.

"Liddy," began Sam, stroking her long, silky hair, "try not to be so worried. An impending eruption of Yellowstone is not a certainty! We have some evidence that points in that direction, but there are still a lot of things that we don't know. Wait until we have more information. Even if it did go off, there are still many other possible eruption scenarios that are much less devastating than those of Toba or Yellowstone's earlier activities."

Data downloading, sorting, and filtering was almost complete Sunday afternoon, so Sam arranged to have Dave meet them Monday evening to begin interpretations.

⇆

On Monday morning, Mike and Ginny were waiting for Sam at his office door when he arrived at seven-thirty. They were both excited and began talking immediately before he even opened his door.

"We just had to find out for sure," rattled Ginny as Sam unlocked his office and they followed him inside. "So we headed back to Grizzly Cave on Friday after class. We managed to get into the cave by ten o'clock Saturday morning. Mike re-photographed the survey points, being careful to set exactly the same lighting angles to accentuate the rocks, as seen in the first set of photos, and to show the surface of the water."

"I guess I just had the light angle wrong on that second set of photos," added Mike.

"After taking new pictures, as you can see here," continued Ginny rapidly as she handed the prints to Sam, "we ran our survey again. We also checked our survey markers for looseness. No markers were loose and we could find no clay or anything else that could cause them to become raised up. Both our survey and our photographs show the cave to be *tilted to the east by about one-half inch over a distance of 1300 feet since last October!*"

"You two have done a commendable job," complemented Sam with a smile. "Even if you had made an initial survey calibration error, these photographs visibly show the relative water level changes. Could I get copies of your photos and survey data, and do I have your permission to discuss your work with some other people?"

Mike handed Sam a folder stating, "Here, these are your copies. We'd be honored if you referenced our studies."

"Thanks," accepted Sam as he took the folder. "If you visit my office tomorrow, I may have some complementary data to show you."

Mike and Ginny then left for their class as Sam headed for the office of the Geoscience Department Head. He then made a pitch for finances to Ralph Escobido and gave a brief explanation of his perception of the Yellowstone situation. Ralph listened intently and expressed concern, as he approved the already committed expenditures. Ralph suggested that as soon as Sam had completed his studies and confirmed his interpretation, he should prepare some sort of news release, on CTC letterhead, to inform the public of the potentially dangerous situation. Sam promised Ralph that a summary report would be ready by Tuesday, assuming that their computer compilation was successful. Ralph Escobido slowly began to understand the broad scope of Sam's concerns. He too became troubled at the thought of an eruption so close at hand!

That evening, more than three hours of work, by Liddy and Dave, produced a series of *eye opening* topographic change contour maps. The maps clearly showed *a consistent uplift across the entire region* over the course of the fifteen years for which they had data. It was highest in the center and tapered to the limit of measurability near the edges at about one-half inch. This area of uplift extended from west-central Montana on the north to southwestern Wyoming, near the Colorado border, on the south. Significantly, it appeared that a broad area of maximum uplift was centered on the projected position of the Yellowstone hotspot. Wide regional doming now became a *measurement* rather than *speculation*.

Even more significant was a bullseye pattern of topographic change lines centered on the Yellowstone caldera. These lines demonstrated an uplift of *more than four feet* for the entire caldera since last August, and *almost fifteen feet* over the previous five years! This caldera swelling extended into the surrounding country and appeared to taper out at a distance of about sixty miles. When superimposed on the regional map, it appeared as a blister on top of the regional uplift.

Sam and Liddy, from their reading and discussions, both understood the implications of this discovery. After talking with Dave, he understood as well. Ground swelling, in response to subsurface magma movement, has preceded many historical volcanic eruptions, but *no studies have ever shown uplift as extensive as they were now observing*! The uncertainty factor was, however, still embedded in the fact that no one had ever *seen* or *documented* a major caldera eruption *even close* to the size of those recorded in the geologic history of Yellowstone!

Dave now fully appreciated Sam's sense of urgency in compiling the data for presentation to those agencies responsible for public safety. Unprecedented uplift surrounding the Yellowstone hotspot, coupled with ground heating and caldera swelling, was frightening to comprehend. Magma movement beneath the surface undoubtedly caused the ground swelling in the vicinity of the actual caldera. However, the mechanics of regional uplift, due to the presence of the Yellowstone hotspot, still could not be explained—neither could the full implications of wide regional uplift be determined. But all of their data pointed toward the likelihood of continued earthquakes throughout the region and *very strongly* toward the possibility of an impending eruption at Yellowstone.

The three questions that Liddy and Dave asked Sam were the same three that he now asked himself: *"Is the eruption of Yellowstone certain to happen?"* Sam was getting convinced of this, although he still maintained that slight degree of doubt that accompanies most geological predictions; *"When could it go off?"* This was of prime concern for both personal as well as public safety; and an answer to the last question, *"How large will the eruption be?"* could only be based on the geologic records of past events. Granted, there had been a few small oozings of magma many years after a major eruption. But the record of unbelievably large explosive activity at roughly 600,000 year intervals, the last being more than 600,000 years earlier, coupled with the present rapid regional uplift, appeared to set the stage for *volcanic devastation on a scale unknown in the historical records of humanity.*

CHAPTER 11

Controversy

▼

On my right hand the rabble rise up; they knock me down and pave the way for my ruin - Job 30:12

The last days of April were dry and warmer than normal for this time of the year. As Sam worked diligently, trying to decipher the conundrum of Yellowstone, he sensed that the warming weather was a prelude to a bubbling caldron that he could not yet see. On Tuesday morning he held a telephone conference with Chris Felsen and Surya Ganisalim, for the specific purpose of summarizing their findings. Sam's recent and conclusive evidence, depicting current regional uplift and additional rapid localized swelling of the Yellowstone caldera, convinced them that they needed to take action quickly. Chris suggested that they send out a coordinated statement to the appropriate agencies, in order to make people aware of what they perceived to be an extremely hazardous situation. Sam and Surya agreed with Chris, but they also decided that phone calls to the various agencies should be made promptly. Sam asked another instructor to fill in for him at his morning class, and the three of them used the conference call and data link between WSU and CTC to compile their report.

Sam presented his uplift data to Chris and Surya, and he explained the additional independent confirmation derived from a cave survey by his students, Mike and Ginny. Surya reciprocated with his plots of earthquake activity and noted those attributable to magma movement. Sam then asked if the two maps could be superimposed on the screen, and Surya completed the task as they talked. Combined, the maps showed that the frequent, seemingly random earthquakes over the last several months were *confined to the area of regional uplift.* Chris noted immediately that the pattern of earthquakes and highlighted faults conformed to his idea of where stress relief might occur, *if* it was linked to the rapid regional uplift. If the stress was extremely deep-seated and related to the hotspot, even the position of the Point of Rocks dike fit the pattern, as interpreted by Chris. The problem was that only a very minor amount of stress from the regional uplift seemed to have been relieved. *The swelling of the ground, in and immediately adjacent to the caldera, was projected by Chris to be the most likely area of future stress relief*!

It took the three of them about two hours to compile a logical two-page summary description and map of the Yellowstone situation, to be sent to any potentially concerned agencies. The summary listed their findings that included: *current regional uplift, rapid caldera swelling, increased heat noted at the surface above the caldera, continued indications of magma movement, stress relief earthquakes and faults related to the regional uplift, and the projected stress relief focus at the Yellowstone caldera.* They further demonstrated the historical unpredictability of large caldera eruptions and the potential for such eruptions to affect a very large area with both an eruptive blast and deep ash deposits. Their report mentioned possible complications from the ash fall such as collapsed buildings, transportation problems, blockages of streams, and climatic change. They very carefully cited the data that they had acquired and requested that immediate attention be paid to the problem. Overall, the three geologists tried to avoid seeming to be alarmist, while showing the pressing need for concern. They explained their belief that an eruption was imminent, but because of geological uncertainties, they could not specify *when.*

Sam showed the summary to Ralph who then quickly approved it for use with the CTC letterhead. This was in conjunction with Chris and Surya's statement on WSU letterhead. All three of their names and signatures would appear at the bottom, along with the names of their respective institutions. Primary on their list for distribution was Wyoming's Central Emergency Management Group (CEMG), which was attached to the Governor's Office, and the Park Supervisor for Yellowstone National Park. Sam would call the CEMG, then fax them the summary. Chris would do the same for Yellowstone. At the same time, Surya would fax their summary to the Wyoming Office of Mines and Geology (WOMG) in Cheyenne and to the United States Geological Survey (USGS) in Denver.

When Sam called the CEMG, a secretary politely told him that warnings of any emergency *not already in progress*, or of *potential* emergencies, had to come from the appropriate responsible agencies. She explained to Sam that just as a weather emergency warning needed to originate with the United States Weather Bureau, a geological emergency warning needed to come out of the WOMG or the USGS. Yes, they had received Sam's fax, but it needed to be approved by the WOMG or the USGS before they could do anything about it. "When did you say this *might* happen?" the secretary asked. Sam started to explain the uncertainties of predicting an eruption, but then he decided that it might be more productive to just talk to the WOMG or the USGS.

Sam called the WOMG and asked to speak to Department Chief, Gordon Aughey. Gordon was not in, but since it related to hazards, Sam could speak with Bill Burnhard. Like many bureaucrats, Bill was a pleasant-sounding, smooth talker on the telephone. Sam had not met him, but he was aware that Bill had produced the erroneous statement, in February, about the Point of Rocks dike.

"Good afternoon, Mr. Burnhard. I'm Sam Westone from Casper Technical College," began Sam. "My colleagues and I have been studying the Yellowstone hotspot and caldera, and we've discovered some startling indications that Yellowstone has the potential to erupt in the near future. My associates have faxed you a brief summary of our findings that I would like you to look at. As you're probably aware, an eruption from a caldera such as Yellowstone has rather devastating potential. We're concerned about the emergency management aspects of such an eruption. Since we haven't heard of any involvement by government agencies, we wanted to know if you were aware of the situation."

Bill recognized Sam Westone's name. He still carried a chip on his shoulder about the way he had been put down by Sam's presentation during KWYN's February television special on the dike. He began, "Well, Mr. Westone, I just received the fax from a Surya Ganisalim about ten minutes ago, and it seems to be a rather rash statement. You declare this as a conclusion reached by yourself and two others, but I see no mention of the USGS, which would surely be aware if such a situation existed. It's been over 600,000 years since Yellowstone had a major eruption...there haven't been any major changes in geyser activity or strong earthquakes that would suggest that it is about to happen now. Your paper seems to indicate some uplift in the Yellowstone area, but that information doesn't appear to be confirmed by a reputable researcher in that field. Are you a registered surveyor or a volcanologist?"

Sam began to reply, "I'm neither a surveyor, nor a volcanologist by profession, but..."

Bill interrupted, "*I figured that*! Until you can come up with someone who's attached to a reputable organization...to verify your somewhat wild assertions...we just *cannot* get people excited by a *loose cannon* in the geological community! I'll examine your information, but I suggest that you look for some sort of verification, *before* trying to create panic by your unsubstantiated predictions of catastrophe...*Good day!*"

The phone clicked off, and Sam just sat there for a moment, bewildered and amazed. He hadn't expected to have an easy time making his point, but he never anticipated the *rude brush-off*. Sam had heard that the Governor's office was searching for a new director for the WOMG, and he *hoped* that whoever was hired for that position would be able to stir up some attitude readjustment in at least *one arrogant member* of the WOMG staff.

Sam then called Chris Felsen and found out that Chris had also received a brush-off. Yellowstone National Park was shorthanded in regards to their scientific staff, due to budget cuts. At the present time they lacked a chief geologist. It was also Yellowstone's policy to receive advice *only* from their own park geologists or from the USGS. All geologic studies within the park, by individuals or institutions, must be coordinated through the USGS.

Chris had then made four calls to the USGS. He related to Sam, "The USGS told me that the seismic network in Yellowstone National Park has shown them nothing to get excited about. They stated that indications of magma movement appeared to be similar to mild sporadic activity prevalent during the last half of the twentieth century. They also said that the snow *always* melts early in Yellowstone, and that it should be of no concern. As to addressing uplift, the USGS geodetic operations have been shut down for several years, *except* for monitoring along densely-populated coastal areas and near some west coast volcanoes, such as Mount Rainier, Three Sisters, and Mount St. Helens."

"The last person I talked to at the USGS asked that I send a copy of our findings to a Mel Bergschrund, who is in charge of a section tasked with evaluation of geologic hazards. They gave me his mail-stop address, but I couldn't get a phone number. The people I talked to say that it probably would be at least six months before they can even think about looking into our concerns. They also said not to get too excited, however, because if it *is* going to erupt, 'there will probably be some sort of large earthquake or other warning preceding it.' *They can take action at that time, but they can't schedule anything now.*"

Chris continued, "Gosh, Sam. I knew that the USGS had gone downhill after they were forced to merge with the Biological Survey (USBS) during the 1990s. But I had hoped that their overall condition hadn't fallen as far as their perceived credibility. You just can't have biologists telling geologists what to do if you want to keep the geology in true perspective. *What do we do now?* I suppose the three of us could just go ahead with our own press release. *Something* should be done to warn people. Even if it doesn't erupt immediately, at least the subject will be out in the open where it can be discussed."

"I agree," replied Sam. "My department head, Ralph Escobido, has already approved of what we're doing. He also has the background to understand the significance of the situation. Let's expand on our two-page summary as if we're presenting a *technical discovery* to a *general audience*. I think we need to point out some possible hazards, without seeming to be *too* alarming. But we should also stress the uncertainties in the timing of geological predictions."

"Sam, *you've got it*! Let's both try to write it up today, then Surya and I could get loose to visit you this Thursday, say around ten in the morning, to combine our efforts into one paper. I think we could have something released by Friday."

"My schedule looks open on Thursday, except for classes; I could probably get a substitute teacher again. Once we get our combined summary completed, I'll see if the television station will release it for us. Come to think of it, maybe I could get Liddy to videotape a presentation rather than just handing them a paper, although we'll need the written material to give to the newspapers. Liddy could probably also help us set up the presentation in the best possible format, as long as it meets with her boss's approval. KWYN has been pretty supportive of any efforts coming from CTC. I'll see you Thursday, Chris, and I'll let you know if we can get a video going."

Sam now realized that since he couldn't get the proper agencies to recognize the possibility of an imminent Yellowstone eruption, it had become his duty to warn the public. It frustrated and worried him because he knew that in geology, uncertainties abound. It was possible, although he did not believe likely, that all the precursory activity could suddenly cease, and that long-term dormancy for the caldera would slowly return. If that turned out to be the situation, he and anyone else who had spoken out would be branded as "Chicken Little," crying, "*the sky is falling!*" After all, someone is always predicting the end of the world.

⇆

Sam spent that evening with Liddy, discussing the situation they now faced. His resolve was helped by Liddy's support and encouragement. She was concerned about the possible tragedy for humanity if Yellowstone did erupt, with after-effects similar to those of the Toba catastrophe 74,000 years ago. It would be necessary for Sam to stand up in public and make statements that many people would either not understand, or if they did, they would not want to believe. *Sam also wanted to ask Liddy to marry him*, but if he was branded as a "wacko," he did not want her to suffer the aspersions that surely would be cast upon them both. That sort of negativism would be particularly hard on her as a television newscaster at KWYN. She could even lose her job as a result. He would have to wait just a while longer to ask her.

Sam prayed about his situation. Prayer often led him to solutions or to actions that he might not have chosen had he not asked for divine guidance. In his personal quest for courage, Sam remembered some words from Isaiah:

> *"The Lord God helps me;*
> *therefore I have not been disgraced;*
> *therefore I have set my face like flint,*
> *and I know that I shall not be put to shame;*
> *he who vindicates me is near.*
> *Who will contend with me?*
> *Let us stand up together.*
> *Who are my adversaries?*
> *Let them confront me.*
> *It is the Lord God who helps me;*
> *who will declare me guilty?"*

Sam and Ralph Escobido talked to KWYN News Director Eric Larson on Wednesday morning, requesting some airtime to address recent findings about Yellowstone that would have both educational and public safety implications. Eric had seen tremendous benefit to KWYN in terms of an increased viewing audience from the last time Sam had been featured in a geology-related special. Now, he promptly agreed to allow Liddy to interview Sam, Surya, and Chris for a special Yellowstone-related news release, whenever it would be convenient.

That morning, Sam relayed this success to Chris and Surya, asking them to dress appropriately for a television interview on Thursday. Chris was very enthusiastic about the scheduled videotaping, but Surya, on the other hand, was a bit camera-shy. However, Chris reminded him that it would be good practice for the presentation of his dissertation. They would be ready and would bring some oversized printouts of Surya's seismic data, and could even produce an enlarged printout of the geodetic contours, if necessary. Sam appreciated that, since CTC did not have oversize printing capabilities. The large diagrams would fit well in a video presentation.

⇋

    Thursday morning, Surya and Chris entered Sam's office on schedule, just as he was returning from his morning class. He offered them coffee and explained that they could work in an empty conference room, and that Liddy would arrive around noon for the videotaping. All they needed to do was organize and smooth out some of the details of their presentation, based on the summaries they had compiled. KWYN would allow them a total of twenty-seven minutes in which to make their presentation. They would have to reduce some of the more complex ideas into terms understandable by the average television viewer. However, Chris did express his concern that a review of geologic findings was normally done out of the public eye. But that could require an extended period of time before the results could be made publicly known, and at the moment, *time* was the commodity that seemed to be in short supply.

    They all agreed that they would just have to put up with any adverse fallout that might come their way. A written version of their findings, along with references, would be submitted to the *Wyoming Geological Association*, hopefully by the end of the following week, for inclusion in papers to be presented at a scheduled October conference. The paper would also be submitted to the *National Association of Geologists and Geophysicists* of which Chris was a member. Chris's and Sam's past experiences in publishing suggested that the worst thing that could happen in their professional circles would be *a few bruised egos*. However, the potential to save lives was more significant in their minds than any personal ridicule they might have to face.

Liddy arrived with her video equipment before noon and quickly set up in the college's conference room. Ralph Escobido was also present to watch the proceedings. Liddy explained to both Chris and Surya that if they should make any mistakes, they should simply hold up a hand and pause momentarily, then continue. She would be able to edit immediately after the taping, and they would be able to participate in the editing to make sure that what they intended to say was clear. After talking with Liddy, Surya was much more relaxed in front of the camera. She had a knack for helping people to feel at ease while taping them.

Their presentation would begin with Sam's introduction of the Yellowstone situation, including some geologic history of past eruptions. Chris would then explain the types of geophysical and remote-sensing studies used by their *team* to arrive at their conclusions. Next, Surya would present his seismic data and profiles. This would be followed by Sam's explanation of the geodetic study, then Surya's data on rising ground temperatures.

The taping progressed rapidly and Chris presented the data overlays that reinforced the individual conclusions, reached from each of the complimentary data sets. Chris put forth his interpretation of the geologic stresses that had been expressed in the earthquakes recorded over the preceding months. He also discussed the probable causes for the more recent quakes that now appeared to be concentrated in the Yellowstone caldera. Sam presented a summary, cautiously explaining, "We believe our geologic interpretations indicate an impending eruption, but the *timing* is anyone's guess."

Sam then elaborated on potential dangers such as eruptive blasts, ash falls, mudflows, the absence of pre-eruption warnings, and possible resulting climatic changes. As a note on potential local ash depths, he cited a reference he had found the previous evening that had measured an ash bed just west of Casper. That ash had come from Yellowstone's last violent eruption and was almost a foot thick. Sam finished by reiterating, "Pressures within the earth could be relieved internally, and the projected eruption might not occur, but *we believe that to be unlikely.*"

During the course of the presentation, Sam gave credit for

help to Ginny Pryor and Mike Hulett for their survey in Grizzly Cave, and to Dave Clement and Liddy Hill for their help in generating the geodetic interpretations. However, although he had made use of their data, he emphasized that *he and his team* accepted the sole responsibility for the projection of an impending eruption.

After the taping, Liddy related to Sam, "I appreciate your concern for me, but I will stand by you and your conclusions, no matter what the result, after this news short is put on the air."

"Thanks, Liddy," sighed Sam. "You don't know how much your support means to me." Sam held her hand tightly in his and smiled at her before they both resumed their work.

Editing was completed less than two hours later, before Chris and Surya left for Laramie. Sam had been unable to find someone to teach his two o'clock class, so he was not present for the final editing. After Surya and Chris had left, Liddy sat in on the last half hour of Sam's class and then spent the rest of the day with him.

⇌

The following Monday morning, Mel Bergschrund stared disinterestedly at the latest report to land precariously on top of the potential paper avalanche that he referred to as his "in-basket." Mel was one of the career managers who had been moved into the USGS when it had endured a forced merger with the newly created National Biological Survey during the 1990s.

His office was in an older section of the Federal Buildings complex west of Denver, Colorado. He had worked in that same office for years and had only one more year until retirement. Mel struggled to prioritize each paper *crisis* as the cascades of important reports, proposals, and questions were daily disgorged onto the ever-present piles on his desk. Over the last ten years, his management style had degenerated into the challenge of farming out each piece of incoming mail to appropriately skilled underlings, then approving responses and reports flowing back up, across his desk, to people in higher positions. On top of this paper shuffle, Mel also had the responsibility of tracking his section's ever-diminishing budget.

Mel was neither a geologist nor a biologist, but he envied them. They were so focused on certain segments of specific disciplines that they didn't have to worry about the overall budget or keeping upper level management satisfied. He recalled his first week on this job—he had been *slighted* by the people he had replaced. They had referred to him as a "carpetbag manager." *And they may have been right.*

Those old boys being put out to pasture had usually started out as field assistants to geologists and then had worked their way up to field and research positions or to managerial slots. They knew their material and could pull the essentials out of reports and investigations, based on personal experience. But Mel thought he had it tougher. He'd had to learn everything by reading, hoping he could distill the important information or find the right person to provide him with answers in order to make appropriate decisions. If he made a mistake, or if someone steered him wrong, then it was *his* neck, not theirs. He had at least six inches of paper to deal with every single day, and another twenty e-mails to answer! He hoped he could put up with it for just one more year until he retired.

At least today's mail provided some entertainment for Mel. The last two reports to land on his desk looked like some *political infighting* or *ego arguments*. One, signed by three geologists from Wyoming, says that "Yellowstone is going to erupt," and nobody seems to know about it. The other one, dated a day later, comes from the Wyoming Office of Mines and Geology and contradicts the first. Neither of them really requests any kind of assistance, although the first one asks the USGS to look into the situation. Mel recalled that somebody had phoned last Tuesday about Yellowstone, and the secretary who took the call thought it might be a joke.

Mel wasn't sure where this *Yellowstone stuff* got started, but he did get a phone call on Thursday from a geologist in Yellowstone National Park. The guy was requesting information about recent geologic activity up there. Apparently the park superintendent had asked him to call the USGS, since the *chief geologist* position in the park was vacant, and the chief's duties temporarily fell to the next lower level. The poor fellow was new to Yellowstone and specialized in developing interpretive exhibits and pamphlets. He seemed nervous and was probably looking for reassurance from us that no disaster was on the threshold.

Mel had told him not to worry because "the USGS stays on top of such things." This was his usual pat answer for concerned citizens on subjects that to him seemed to be far-fetched. After all, *don't geological forces move rather slowly over long periods of time*? At least that was the impression that he got from his staff. Mel had transferred the call to a geologist, Red Gossan, who must have answered all of the appropriate questions. At least the guy hadn't called back.

Mel looked again at the two reports. They were probably the ones that had started all of the hubbub. He didn't think he would hear much more about it. But if he did, then he would *elevate* the subject in importance. He doubted that this would be one of those things that would blow all out of proportion, like the *lynx habitat* or *endangered fish* controversies. Since Red Gossan had fielded the telephone call, Mel would send both reports on down to Red and his assistant, Mary Amundsen. He'd let them figure it out.

Mel attached a *"What do we do?"* note and dropped both reports into a yellow inter-office delivery envelope, addressed to the only two geologists in his section of fourteen employees. Red and Mary were both competent geologists; they had never pointed him in the wrong direction.

⇌

At six-thirty that same Monday evening, KWYN News showed their pre-announced special entitled, *"Yellowstone – Are We In For A Change?"* KWYN had begun advertising the upcoming special on Friday, resulting in a higher than normal viewing audience. The telephones at KWYN began ringing non-stop before the end of the program. The following morning, phones also rang at both the CTC Geosciences Department and at the WSU Department of Geophysics and Geology. Some callers were concerned about safety, but a large number of the calls were from businessmen who speculated that the statements made by Sam and Chris would hurt their tourism-related income. Some had already received cancellations for the upcoming summer tourist season.

One caller to WSU threatened to withhold some long-term funding unless an immediate retraction of the presentation was made. Sam and Chris knew all too well that they had violated the first commandment of institutional science that stated, *"Thou shalt not criticize the sacred views held by a long-honored institution, nor by those who fund an institution, nor their favored computer models, nor their data bases, nor their methodology, nor shalt thou surprise them."* Sam and Chris had opened up a *can of worms* by pointing out a dangerous problem that had been overlooked or ignored by government bureaucracies and that had definite economic repercussions. Chris Felsen actually began to receive some censoring admonitions from the WSU Board of Trustees and, more disconcerting, telephone threats from some private individuals. Sam also received personal warnings.

Surya had been portrayed as a *student* of Chris's, thus escaping the heat of public outrage. However, he did not evade the vitriolic response of the WOMG that was, of course, led by Bill Burnhard. The WOMG issued a statement on Wednesday, partly in response to the concerned calls that they had received, but largely from Bill's desire for vengeance after being publicly humiliated in February. At this uncertain point in his career, Gordon Aughey didn't care what an official WOMG statement said. The WOMG statement accused Sam and *"the belligerent Ph D and his misdirected student"* of being the *"SS of Geology,* trying to incite panic for a few moments of public attention." The WOMG release further stated, "none of the data presented has been subjected to peer review within the geological community and is therefore *suspect,* both in content and in conclusions." The WOMG statement was read on KWYN's evening news that same day, only two days after the special report by Sam, Chris, and Surya had been aired.

Even the superintendent of Yellowstone National Park, Josie Welborne, got into the act. That Thursday, she sent a video to KWYN, in response to their Yellowstone special. Eric Larson aired the short video statement, since he felt that viewer ratings would increase if such a controversy remained in the news. Josie's short video showed her near the new Park

Headquarters at West Thumb, accompanied by her husband and their two children who were frolicking on a playground in the background.

Her remarks followed a script prepared by her public relations officer…"I have checked with the United States Geological Survey, the premier authority on geology in the United States. They are the source that we in Yellowstone use to direct our geology-related concerns. They have informed me that they have *no* knowledge of any impending eruption here in Yellowstone National Park! They say that indications of magma movement beneath Yellowstone have been known since the middle of the twentieth century and are not unusual. If Yellowstone were headed for an eruption, we would be seeing changes in our geysers, along with major increases in earthquake activity. Since neither one of these things is occurring, I do not believe that we can expect any adverse volcanic activity. If anyone has any questions about their safety, please visit or call me, or my staff, at Park Headquarters in West Thumb. *I'm sure that I will be the first to know if an eruption is headed our way.*" Then the camera slowly zoomed out, showing Josie smiling and her happy family playing in the background. Her statement first aired on Friday during the late morning news show.

Because of numerous requests, KWYN repeated Sam, Chris, and Surya's Yellowstone special, but because Sam had taken the lead, they referred to it as *"Sam's."* It was repeated that Saturday, on the following Monday, and again a week later. Each time it was shown it was followed immediately by Josie Welborne's video statement and then by the press release from the WOMG. KWYN also included audio interview clips of Bill Burnhard denouncing Sam and Chris and their interpretation, and of the head of the Wyoming Central Emergency Management Group disavowing any knowledge of an impending eruption. This combination of Sam's Yellowstone special, along with Josie's video and the other dissenting statements, appeared in the national news on the Tuesday following the second KWYN showing. The USGS, however, issued no announcements related to the matter.

At the USGS, Mel Bergschrund caught Sam's Yellowstone special on the national news at the end of the same day that he received a written request from Josie Welborne to investigate the situation. *Yellowstone had now risen in priority* on his list of important projects to address. However, no offer of funding accompanied the request. Mel had some latitude in his small budget, but *he needed to be careful.* This seemed important, but it might go nowhere.

Mel had deadlines approaching for both the *Colorado Front Range Flood Hazard* study, and the *Wasatch Mountain Front Earthquake Stability Hazard* study. Both areas supported large populations and had significant safety concerns. But, maybe he could squeeze in just a small amount of funding for Yellowstone as well. After all, the one report by Mr. Westone was *very alarming* in its unbelievable conclusions. On top of that, there might be some biological concerns that could kick loose some funds, at least for an initial evaluation of the situation.

On Wednesday morning, Mel realized that both of his geologists were in Salt Lake City attending meetings concerning the Wasatch Mountain Front project. They would not return until Monday. He left memos for both of them to examine, as soon as possible, the material that he had sent to them earlier. He wanted them to focus on any possible reality that might be related to this *new*, but hopefully small, *"Yellowstone Volcanic Hazard"* project. Mel then called Josie Welborne at the park headquarters to let her know that his USGS section was investigating and that he would keep her informed.

⇌

Editorial remarks appeared in most Wyoming newspapers, on both sides of the issue, and Tuesday's network news story fueled the national press for various commentaries on Wyoming and Yellowstone for several weeks. Included were a few *off-the-wall* editorial comments by some religious and environmental fanatics, but the general rambling centered around potential revenue losses and the omnipresent media personalities trying to outdo each other with *scientific opinions.*

Following their usual formats, if a media personality

agreed with what was said, it was referred to as a *"brilliant analysis."* However, if a commentator held a viewpoint contrary to the material presented, as in the case of Sam's discussion on a Yellowstone eruption, it would be branded as *"controversial."* Because many interests did not want to recognize Sam's analysis of the situation, nor the inconveniences represented in the associated hazards, he was often given a one-line dismissal..."*Mr. Westone's opinions represent a rather controversial viewpoint, not normally associated with the mainstream of science."* Other commentators would back-jab with *innuendos* while putting on a superficial air of *authoritative civility.* "We (they always used 'we' rather than 'I'...to give the appearance of a *majority* view to their agenda) would *never* refer to Mr. Westone as a 'kook', even though his views border on the extreme in a situation that needs further study." The attacks on Sam were made without any attempt to contact him for rebuttal, and he had no alternative other than to ignore them.

The continuing news media coverage of the debate about Yellowstone helped Mel Bergschrund elevate the importance of an evaluation of Yellowstone. However, his supervisors were emphatic that if the politically directed Wasatch Front and Colorado Front Range studies were not completed by the end of the first week in June, a congressional inquiry could result. Several representatives and senators had made commitments on those public safety studies. The low population density around Yellowstone, combined with an unproven hypothesis about a volcanic hazard, did not justify taking time away from on-going studies. Floods along the Colorado Front Range and unstable slopes along the earthquake-prone Wasatch Mountain Front had both resulted in some loss of life and significant property damage over the years! Mel did as he was told, but he still waited for responses from his very busy geology team of Red and Mary.

Wyoming State University, under financial pressure from alumni, made no further statements, but Chris Felsen firmly refused to retract the statements he had already made. Chris was hoping for a speedy review of the joint papers submitted by himself, Sam, and Surya. Sam was also anxious for their paper to be reviewed, hopefully to return to them some public credibility.

Eric Larson, in tune with his viewing audience, asked Sam if he would mind being interviewed for a news program and was glad when Sam agreed. KWYN and Sam's *letters to the editors* of several newspapers were the *only* news media available for him to address remarks made against him. Eric also interviewed Bill Burnhard and several businessmen from the Cody area. When stacked together, these dialogues produced an entertaining program. This news special was broadcast on a Thursday near the middle of May, less than three weeks after the first Yellowstone special.

Sam's interview began as he reiterated his initial findings. Then, in response to criticisms of *Chicken Little* behavior, he explained, "predicting a major volcanic eruption is not quite like predicting the probability that the earth will be hit by an asteroid. You don't know when or where an asteroid may hit, but there is some *probability* that it will happen...*not a certainty*. The Yellowstone caldera has erupted in the past at relatively long, but almost regular intervals. We are certain that it will erupt again, and we know generally *where* it will erupt: *in* or *near* the caldera. Our only uncertainties are the *timing* and the *size* of the eruption."

The businessmen from Cody condemned Sam as trying to scare people with "*something that is as nebulous as human-caused global warming,*" and with bringing about "*economic disasters as devastating as the shutting down of area gold mining, in the 1990s, by radical environmental interests.*" Bill Burnhard animatedly berated Sam's presentation with a flood of irrelevant bureaucratic verbosity, coupled with attacks of a personal nature. Although Bill felt that he had quashed Sam's arguments, most viewers thought of Bill as a somewhat "fanatical politician" rather than a geologist.

Aside from the actuality of the attacks against him and his analysis, Sam lamented the obvious lack of objective logic represented in the words of those who criticized him. As a teacher, he wished that *logical reasoning and questioning* were taught more in schools—*not* the blind questioning of authority, but the sincere scientific evaluation of material presented, accompanied by examination of the credibility of reference sources. *Why do so many people appear to reject such an approach to problems? Where is logic taught in our basic educational institutions?*

An odd mixture of pedagogic authority and concerns for making students feel good seemed to Sam to have replaced *unfiltered* honest thinking. Both inside and outside of the classroom, and particularly in political situations, Sam had observed that the term *"fact"* had taken on a new meaning. If a person or group disagrees with certain facts, then the facts are either ignored, emotionally discredited, or new ones are fabricated. Sam realized that this wasn't a *new* problem, but our modern society, through the use of printed and electronic media, has elevated this craft of obfuscation and distortion to an art form. Sam dearly wished that those who questioned his reasoning would do so in a logical way so that a better interpretation could be built, if one existed. *It would be better to build upon knowledge, rather than to use opinions and pet agendas to entirely destroy individuals and their ideas.*

⇌

On Friday morning, Liddy arrived at work very early and was surprised to find that video technician, Robert Busch, had suddenly quit his job for a new position in Colorado. Liddy was informed that her weekends off were cancelled until Robert could be replaced. Because of this further reduction of the station's staff, she would now have only Mondays free, just one day per week. All of the staff would need to work yet longer hours to take up the slack. This was just *one more assault* on her *frazzled nerves*! She too was receiving backlash due to her close association with Sam. Some of the KWYN staff had been teasing her, asking her how it felt to be dating *"Chicken Little."* Liddy would respond only to defend Sam's geological analyses. But mostly she tried to ignore the pokes at her and Sam.

Liddy was feeling in a slump when she arrived home that afternoon. Camile tried to cheer her up, but her efforts only loosened Liddy up enough that she cried for ten minutes. After the outpouring, Liddy felt better, but depression still clung to the edges of her mind. She believed that Sam was right and was just trying to do his duty as he saw it. She also knew that Sam did not want to be in the public spotlight. *Couldn't other people see that? Why were people being mean to her as well?*

It was late in the afternoon when Sam arrived at Liddy's. He had been taking a beating in the news and in editorials, particularly since no overt physical signs of impending eruption had yet shaken the Yellowstone region during the three weeks since his public warning. He had been concerned about the personal attacks on himself, but now he just joked about the various sorts of *"experts"* dishing out verbal insults. As Sam greeted Liddy, he could see that she had been crying. His light-hearted attitude brightened up her outlook. Sam assured her that if she would promise to stay cheerful, he would either fix supper for her every Saturday and Sunday or take her out to dinner. He joked around and finally made her laugh. Then he told her to stay in her house and not come over to Camile's until he returned for her in about twenty minutes.

Liddy wondered what was up, remembering that Camile had rushed off just minutes before. When Sam returned and escorted her to Camile's, she found a table set with flowers, candles, and wine, accentuating an elaborately decorated cake that had been made by Camile. Liddy's mind had been so clouded by distress that she had forgotten her own birthday! Sam placed steaks on Camile's grill, to be served with baked potatoes and salad. Sam and Camile both sang *"Happy Birthday,"* while Grieg added a few colorful howls to complete the chorus. It was a memorable evening, highlighted by Sam presenting Liddy with a beautiful fleece jacket depicting a *running horses* pattern, and by Camile relating many of her past and rather humorous experiences with her numerous furred and feathered friends, past and present. When the party ended, Liddy's mood had risen up out of the pit, and she knew she could put up with her adjusted work schedule and any hard knocks from her co-workers, as long as she continued to receive help from such dear friends. Together, she and Sam would weather the tribulation.

It was now nearly a month since Sam's initial

Yellowstone special, and the third week of May was progressing. With an absence of spectacular happenings to keep the public or the news media's attention, the flurry of interest in Yellowstone appeared to be fading. However, certain individuals and groups remained quite attentive to the situation. Because of some loss of income perceived by a group of businessmen from Cody, West Yellowstone, and Red Lodge, a suit was filed in federal court against Sam Westone and Chris Felsen, naming also their respective institutions of Casper Technical College and Wyoming State University. The suit sought a *"cease and desist"* order against making any more statements related to a potential eruption of Yellowstone, and it requested twenty million dollars in damages for the cumulative business losses that they had allegedly already suffered. This made the headlines and generated numerous letters to the editors of newspapers across the region. The fiscal damages that were sought seemed to be aimed more at the *deep pockets of public institutions* rather than at reimbursement for *actual* financial injuries.

No action was immediately forthcoming, and no gag order was issued against Sam and Chris. But several days later, one of the more aggressive "businessmen," a Yellowstone backcountry concessionaire with shoulder-length blond hair, boldly confronted Sam and Liddy in a Casper restaurant as they were having dinner. Reminiscent of a quick scene out of an old grade "B" western movie, the meddlesome fellow addressed Sam, "Are you the idiot profeshor who's trying to put us out of businesh with your inshane whacko lies about Yellowshtone?" Then, before Sam had a chance to respond, the man violently pushed over the table where they were sitting, spilling water glasses and silverware. Liddy's chair, to Sam's left, tipped over, and she fell to the floor as the man simultaneously made a lunge at Sam.

Other customers jumped to their feet as Sam fended off a blow from the man's right fist. It had been years since Sam had practiced any martial arts, but he was quick. Sam's adrenaline surged as his defensive reflexes kicked in. Anger welled up within him at this attacker who had most certainly injured Liddy. Sam jerked his head to the left as the man's fist passed his right cheek. Then Sam, with the speed and intensity of a grizzly bear, grabbed the man's wrist with a pulling and twisting motion. His fluid and unbroken maneuver yanked the man downward and off balance, forcing his arm away to Sam's right and then bending it behind the man's back. The opponent's body surged violently forward and toward the floor in the direction that he had been moving, both from his own momentum and from the hard pull that Sam had added. With the sickening crunch of a human head and body impacting heavily against the hardwood floor, the scuffle ended as quickly as it had begun. That was the first time in his life that Sam had ever had to defend himself from a physical attack.

Sam's assailant, later shown to have been inebriated, was knocked out cold from his sudden inspection of the restaurant's oak décor. He suffered a fractured skull along with a dislocated shoulder. He was charged with *assault and battery* and *public intoxication* when the Casper police arrived three minutes later. The assailant, through political connections, managed to keep his name out of the newspapers, although Sam, subject of a pending lawsuit, was mentioned as the "victim." Liddy suffered a mild bump from her fall, and she and Sam were both considerably shaken by the experience.

The restaurant manager apologized profusely to Sam and Liddy and to the other customers for the incident. They had never before had fights in their establishment and wanted to maintain their reputation as a *family* restaurant. To smooth things over, they offered to give free meals to all of the customers who had witnessed the altercation, and they made a special effort to ensure that Sam and Liddy were comfortable. Wine, provided with dinner, helped to achieve that end. However, after the meal was over, the restaurant's owner discretely but forcefully asked Sam and Liddy not to return again until after the lawsuit against Sam had been resolved. Sam had expected some *minor* public animosity, but *physical assault* and *banishment from a restaurant* were not within the realm of his expectations.

Other actions, by diverse groups within the public at large, also surprised Sam. A couple of *fringe* religious groups believed that Sam had prophesied the end of the world. They pestered him with phone calls, e-mails, and letters, hoping that he would give them the final word when *"everything was going to blow."*

A *New Age* group believed that *"magnetic lines of power"* were converging on Yellowstone, and that they would be the recipients of that energy if they stood in the right place at the right time. This group also flooded Sam's e-mail and telephone with meaningless messages. And, if that wasn't enough, another group was pushing for public and private funding to save the animals with a sort of *"Noah's Ark,"* in order to remove grizzly bears and other animals, until the danger had passed. The pestering from these people got so intense that Sam had to obtain a new unlisted telephone number, and his office e-mail became unusable.

$$\rightleftharpoons$$

Sam and Chris had spoken out to warn the people of Wyoming about what they perceived to be a *very real* and *clearly dangerous* geological situation in Yellowstone. In return for doing their moral duty, they were being regularly chastised in the news media. Since no alarming geologic activity had occurred, and their warning was now more than a month old, the public was losing interest, and Sam was even beginning to wonder whether he and Chris and Surya had misinterpreted their data to arrive at erroneous conclusions. But each time he was tempted with such thoughts, a complete review of his data brought him back to his original conclusion—that Yellowstone *would* erupt soon.

Attacks from specific people were becoming louder, particularly from Bill Burnhard. Bill now made it a part of his regular schedule to give luncheon or dinner talks, around Cheyenne and the state, to civic-minded service clubs and to women's groups. He would cast aspersions on Sam and Chris, and in very smooth but faulted logic, discredit their prediction for a Yellowstone eruption. Neither Sam nor Chris were inclined to beat the bushes for speaking engagements to defend their viewpoint, but when asked, they presented their case in a professional manner, avoiding any public attacks on their nemesis, Bill. Sam resolved that he would weather the storm against him, no matter how long it took.

⇌

During the last week of May, Sam Westone finally received some positive feedback. A Wyoming State Senator from Lander asked Sam to apply for the position of *WOMG Director*. The senator, Fred Aspenwood, was impressed by Sam's ability to stand up and say what needed to be said about Yellowstone; he thought he also detected in Sam a sense of duty and commitment that had been lacking at the WOMG for quite a few years. Fred had a geological background and believed that Sam was correct in his predictions. He said that if Sam would apply, he would do all that he could, through his political contacts, to see that Sam was selected. He also stated that the position was a political one—an appointment within the government bureaucracy. There was no currently preferred candidate, and someone needed to put the WOMG in good operating order. Sam told Fred that he would consider it, although he was quite happy with his current position.

Sam thought intensely about the WOMG position. He would rather be a geologist than a bureaucrat. However, in such a position he might be able to initiate some changes for the *good* of Wyoming. That seemed like a noble thought and he again reminded himself that *individuals make things happen.* Governments and bureaucracies do not solve problems; they merely implement the will of the individuals who control them. However, those who strive for bureaucratic power and accompanying wealth often maintain it for themselves and become liabilities. Sam realized that individuals very often seek public offices believing that they can change the world for the better through their limited exercise of power. Some of them actually succeed, while holding on to their personal values and morals. But if their ethical compasses are not firmly oriented to begin with, they eventually become corrupted by the power they seek, and then stagger beneath the desire to acquire more. The thirst for power then consumes them, and friends they had at the beginning of their power search no longer recognize them as the same person.

Sam wondered if his motivation to even think about such a position was truly based on a strong desire for beneficial changes or for self-promotion. *Objective* self-analysis is always difficult. He figured that positive changes in the system were foremost in his mind, but if he ever began to think of the advantages of official power, then it would be time for him to quit. Sam submitted an application to the governor's office later that week. He considered that whoever did the selecting would either write him off when they saw his name, or find his resume agreeable. Sam would be happy whether he got the job or not. If selected, he would rise to the challenge. *He did not want to tell Liddy about this yet.* He didn't want to worry her with an idea that he might seek a job away from where she now lived and worked. He also decided that he would not take the position without Liddy accompanying him. *He would ask her to marry him by mid-June*, at the latest, but he was waiting for the *right* place and the *right* time.

⇌

Beginning about 1:30 p.m. on Tuesday of that same week, both Sam and Surya noticed the start of a new series of earth tremors in Yellowstone. The tremors seemed to be similar to those that they had earlier interpreted to be magma movement. They occurred primarily northwest of the Yellowstone caldera, but also showed up beneath the caldera itself and somewhat to the southeast of it. Depths were variable, from a shallow 2.8 miles downward to more than twenty-six miles! These were *much deeper* than any previous earthquake swarms!

Surya still had not been able to resolve system differences between his array and the seismic array existing in Yellowstone National Park. This gave him some difficulty in interpretation, but it was still far better than data from either system by itself. His components presented a three dimensional view of Yellowstone, while the Park's seismic stations gave specific points with which he could adjust minor details, in order to better interpret what was happening beneath the surface.

Surya's interpretation showed that a poorly defined boundary extended downward to great depth northwest of the caldera. Along this boundary, shaped like the curved surface of part of a steep, inverted funnel, *magma was moving upward under the caldera.* Neither the speed of magma movement, nor the relative volume of the magma, could be determined from his analyses. Chris Felsen concurred with this interpretation, and he and his student both believed that some sort of eruption could be expected from the vicinity of the Yellowstone caldera very soon. The continuing question for them was not *if*, but *when.* This was Sam's interpretation also.

The three of them knew that, historically, most volcanoes gave some type of warning prior to eruption. They just hoped that any such warning would be in time to allow the evacuation of Yellowstone and the surrounding areas. The three geologists could not even begin to project how much of the region would need to be evacuated. They knew that the lack of historical precedence for the eruption of a caldera the size of Yellowstone would mean that geological warnings could easily be, and probably already were being, misinterpreted. However, the most *sobering* fact was that a small, but significant, percentage of historic volcanic eruptions gave no immediate indications prior to eruption. Unfortunately, *those few eruptions that occurred without prior warning tended to be the largest and most violent!*

CHAPTER 12

Dance of Destiny

▼

The swarm of deep-seated tremors continued through the end of May and on into June. Curiously, no statements from the various agencies, expected to address public safety issues, were forthcoming. The National Park Service, the USGS, and the WOMG remained silent, as did the Wyoming Central Emergency Management Group. Any media interest in Yellowstone seemed to have disappeared. Even most of the caustic comments addressed toward Sam and Chris in the news media had subsided. But Sam and Liddy remained vigilant. They had long since decided to cancel any plans for exploring Yellowstone during the summer.

At the USGS, Red Gossan and Mary Amundsen worked a busy schedule of meetings and summary compilations for three solid weeks before they had time to sort through their in-baskets. Upon discovering the report by Sam, Chris, and Surya, accompanied by the WOMG release, they both agreed that Yellowstone warranted attention. In fact, they had decided that weeks ago, upon hearing Sam's statements in the news, but they had been too bogged down with other responsibilities to pay much attention to the problem. The report's contents needed to be examined thoroughly before any conclusion could be made. However, if Sam's facts were confirmed, then the argument for a potential Yellowstone eruption would appear solid.

Red and Mary found that the WOMG statement contained nothing of substance to refute the position of the three Wyoming geologists. Red was able to perform a brief check of the USGS seismic records and verified that there *was indeed* recent voluminous magma movement under Yellowstone. Based on Red's investigation, Mel Bergschrund issued an official USGS news release at the end of May, confirming that, *"an uncommonly large amount of magma appears to have been moving beneath Yellowstone within the last month."* The statement made no interpretations as to what that meant, nor did the USGS issue any warnings to the public. Their release also refrained from addressing the statements made previously by Sam and Chris, or by their detractors.

Concurrently, a heavy spring storm produced a devastating flash flood that flushed through a deep canyon west of Boulder, Colorado. Fifteen people were killed, and damage was counted in the hundreds of millions of dollars. Mel's geologists were forced to drop all other projects and concentrate on finishing their Front Range Flood Hazard study ahead of schedule. They were to work closely with local government entities in order to enhance safety in flood-prone areas.

Although Mel and his geologists were unfortunately held back in their attempts to examine this new Yellowstone problem, Mel did call Josie Welborne. He informed her about the magma movement and promised to let her know of any additional findings by the USGS.

Sam and Chris's preliminary court hearing, in the suit filed against them, was set for Wednesday during the third week of June. The only note of redemption that had come, beyond data they had generated themselves, was the short news release by the USGS.

In light of that news release and to address concerns by Yellowstone area businessmen, an informational meeting was organized that would be held in Cody the second Saturday of June. Saturday was chosen so as to capture some local influential activists who would not be able to attend during the week. Under the able leadership of Louis Costalotti, a short, rotund attorney from Cheyenne, the businessmen and their lawyers had formed the *Friends Of Yellowstone Area Businesses (FOYAB)*. The Saturday meeting was planned by FOYAB, and because of its ostensible *fact-finding* nature, it was co-sponsored by Yellowstone National Park and Josie Welborne was a scheduled speaker.

Louis Costalotti had no business interests in Cody, but he did have political ambitions. He also perceived possible financial gain from the pending lawsuit against two state institutions, CTC and WSU. If he could help the businessmen strengthen their case and then be retained by FOYAB, he would make money *and* become widely known across Wyoming for his *legal skills*. Although billed as a "fact-finding" meeting, FOYAB's main thrust was through their lawyers, under Louis's leadership, to build a case for their *lost revenues* lawsuit.

Along with Josie Welborne, Yellowstone's only current geologist would attend the meeting. Josie hoped to identify safety concerns and determine if park visitation would be reduced this tourist season compared to previous years. She did not want to close the park for any reason if it could be helped. Her gut feeling was that this concern about a volcanic eruption was just another one of those wild ideas that never materializes into reality. It was *her* park, and she wanted to do what was best for the park and its visitors. She requested that Mel Bergschrund from the USGS and a representative from WOMG be in attendance. However, Josie was a bit misled about the purpose of the meeting.

The meeting was well advertised, and several interested environmental groups announced their intentions to attend. FOYAB made requests to CTC and WSU that Sam and Chris be present to discuss their data. However, since a suit had been filed, attorneys for CTC and WSU rejected the idea of either Sam or Chris attending. Eric Larson wanted to send a video reporter to the meeting, but because of the staff shortage at KWYN, he would have to rely on an arrangement with a station out of Billings for coverage of the event.

The Rocky Mountain area representative for the Reef Group also learned of the meeting. His area of responsibility encompassed Wyoming, Colorado, Montana, Utah, Arizona, New Mexico, and Idaho. It was an important region. Along with looking after various types of minerals, he also scouted out individuals and organizations that might qualify for financial help *if* their activities played into any of Reef's interests. Environmental groups were always looking for mining projects to thwart. However, some businesses had also helped Reef's objectives at certain times. Both groups would be represented at this meeting; it would be a fertile field for possible *recruitment* or *assistance*, depending on one's point of view.

⇋

Surya's computerized three-dimensional interpretations gradually coalesced into what seemed to be a large tapered cylindrical body, or perhaps a dynamic region of disconnected semi-fluid bodies. These somewhat nebulous bodies were scattered above the Yellowstone hotspot that was pressing upward toward the caldera. The region appeared to have some internal, almost vertical circulation that became less defined with depth. However, the edges of the region were interpreted to extend downward greater than eighty miles! Its internal characteristics became less identifiable in its lower reaches, but its outer boundaries could still be determined to slope steeply downward and outward. Surya hoped that with eventual seismic reflections from some larger quakes, he might be able to truly define the character of the Yellowstone hotspot.

⇋

The month of May and the first part of June dragged on relentlessly for Liddy. Her working hours seemed long and endless and she would often be exhausted at day's end. However, her spirits were refreshed during the short bursts of time she could spend outdoors. Spring was her favorite time of the year and it had arrived early, eating up the last remnants of snow, and bathing her nostrils with the sweet fragrance of fresh green grass. Those few brave, early tulips that had huddled against the south side of her house, for warmth and wind protection, now bloomed in profusion along with several other varieties of flowers. Every day after work, this little haven energized her soul with its splashes of flaming color. Liddy's garden was one of her refuges from the business of the world.

Her spirits soared when she thought of Sam. She was with him most evenings now, but they seemed all too brief. He held true to his promise of fixing dinner for her every Saturday and Sunday, occasionally with Camile's help. On her Mondays off, Liddy either went riding with Camile or visited Sam in his office between classes. After the CTC semester finished in mid-May, Sam would ride or hike with her on Mondays.

Liddy really needed more time off from her job. Since her work schedule had been tightened, she hadn't even been able to visit with her parents in Buffalo. KWYN had yet to hire any new replacement personnel, and they did not seem to be trying very hard to do so. At Sam's urging, she demanded that she get at least one weekend off. In early June, KWYN finally relented and allowed her to have the second weekend of the month.

⇌

Working overtime, Red Gossan and Mary Amundsen finally finished their Colorado Front Range and Wasatch Mountains studies ahead of schedule, on the first Friday in June. The following Monday, as Mel had requested, they began in earnest to try to verify the conclusions reached by Sam Westone and Chris Felsen. *It was not an easy task.* Previously unexamined computerized records needed to be searched, but most of the expertise at the USGS, in seismic research and geodetic evaluations, had been temporarily transferred to west coast locations. But by putting heart and soul into the task and rechecking cited references, the two geologists were actually able to *verify most of Sam and Chris's findings.* However, because of their inexperience with geodetic measurements, they had to convince a co-worker in that field to evaluate their elevation change analyses. He agreed to come into his office on Saturday, and would, he guessed, have their information checked by late morning.

⇌

Liddy's free full weekend off work had finally arrived, and she and Sam loaded his truck with hiking gear, food, water, and of course Grieg, and headed north for the Bighorn Mountains. They planned to hike in the vicinity of Powder River Pass and then stay overnight with Liddy's parents in Buffalo.

Upon arriving in Buffalo, Sam topped off his truck's gas tank before driving up U.S. Highway 16 into the mountains. They had originally intended to exit I-25 south of Buffalo, to take the gravel road up Crazy Woman Canyon, but Sam and Liddy were caught up in conversation and drove well past the turnoff before they realized it. *Sam, in particular, had much on his mind.* To the west of Buffalo, the highway followed Clear Creek steeply upward through the boulder-covered slopes of Mosier Gulch, finally cresting a wide open hill sprinkled with flowers. The rugged backbone of the Bighorns stretched out before them in the sun, a snow-capped line of bright granite cliffs and cirques. Here they paused briefly to soak up the view and take photographs before meandering southward through forested slopes and then again west and upward to the top of the pass.

The weather was notably clear and thunderstorms were not predicted to move into the area until afternoon. Thick snow still lay along the road in old isolated drifts, but where it had melted away, glacier lilies hugged the damp areas deserted by the retreating remnants of winter. In the drier open meadows, delicate wildflowers covered the ground. Sam parked his truck off of the highway and next to the guardrail, a few hundred feet east of the highest point on the road. At an elevation of 9666 feet, Powder River Pass and its surroundings offered incredible views to both the east and west where the plains spread out almost 2700 feet below them. To the east, the mountains fell away suddenly into the sun-washed Powder River Basin, and the Pumpkin Buttes and Black Hills floated on the distant skyline. To the west, nearby ridges obscured some of the lower canyons along the mountain flanks, but the far distant view across the Bighorn Basin was exceptionally clear, such that individual peaks of the Absaroka Mountains, hugging the eastern border of Yellowstone, were easily visible.

⇌

That very same morning, the geodetic specialist at the USGS in Denver, with the assistance of Red and Mary, hastily tackled the Yellowstone elevation data. He appreciated the intricacy and beauty of survey data, but felt that surveys should be left to provide control for more sophisticated, but overall easier techniques. By ten-thirty that morning, he was able to verify the elevation changes over the broad area around Yellowstone and was *shocked* by the results! He had been closely monitoring the Three Sisters area in the state of Oregon, and he could hardly believe that *far greater* changes had taken place in and around Yellowstone, and unbelievably had gone essentially *unnoticed*! He then showed Red and Mary a simple demonstration of a technique called "satellite radar interferometry." This would serve as a separate confirmation of their results. Radar-generated images, recorded months to years apart by satellites, can be compared to reveal deformation patterns over broad areas with remarkable clarity. Merely retrieving a few images from computer files, then comparing them, reiterated within another twenty minutes, the *drastic changes* that had taken place in Yellowstone!

With this startling information in hand, they immediately tried to contact Mel Bergschrund at his meeting in Cody. They could not reach him, but left a message for him to return their call as soon as possible. Their findings, confirming Sam and Chris's warnings about a potential Yellowstone eruption, *begged for attention* from USGS managers. Their interpretation would also probably require a second confirmation of the urgency of the situation by USGS volcanologists. Since Mel couldn't be reached, they tried calling the USGS branch chief at his home. They caught him just as he was preparing to leave on a fishing trip. After listening to Red and Mary explain the situation, the branch chief contacted two of his senior volcanologists who were working on the west coast. He opened up a conference call for all who had been involved in this Saturday morning exercise. After twenty minutes on the phone, coupled with electronic exchanges of graphic material, the branch chief concluded that *a warning was justified*. He further decided that a news release that day should be accompanied by an order to evacuate Yellowstone National Park. He asked Red to explain the situation to Mel, whenever he called back. The Branch chief then phoned both the Federal Emergency Management Agency and the Wyoming Central Emergency Management Group, who would coordinate the issuance of warnings and an evacuation order.

⇋

The FOYAB meeting in Cody opened that morning at nine o'clock in a conference room at a large motel. Louis Costalotti acted as a moderator and provided introductions. The first speaker and duly elected head of FOYAB was a local outfitter with the unlikely, and self-selected, name of *"George Strongarm Custer."* His birth name had been Bruno Cornelius Drover, but he changed that to something he thought would be more *memorable* for his clients. His drinking buddies just called him "General." With shoulder-length blond hair, he presented himself in dress and flamboyant mannerisms similar to what he believed might have been expected from the *famous* general that inspired his name change. It was an act that tourists loved and one that appealed to potential clientele.

George was still nursing a dislocated shoulder and a skull fracture from a "wreck out on the trail" (he claimed), three weeks earlier. He paused by the microphone for minor applause before he began speaking. George presented a concise, although apparently inflated, statement of financial losses. He then pounded the podium with his fist and asked loudly, with an air of authority, *"Has anyone actually seen any evidence that Yellowstone is a danger to anyone?"* The conference room was silent. He pounded his fist again and then stated, *"I made my case!* Next?"

The *General* was followed by a litany of *lost revenue* statements, prepared by a parade of local businessmen and women, up until the eleven-thirty lunch break. The chorus was broken only once by a brave environmental activist seeking assurances that ecological values would be protected in the Greater Yellowstone Ecosystem, whether a volcano erupts or not.

not.

Josie Welborne was scheduled to speak immediately after lunch, followed by Bill Burnhard of the WOMG, and then Mel Bergschrund of the USGS. Josie was disappointed with the meeting. It had not shed any light on the volcanic situation, and she was regretting even attending at all. She now planned to head back to the park immediately after her talk. Brief conversations with both Bill and Mel indicated to her that *she would learn nothing more here*. She'd had calls to her office forwarded to the cell phone in her purse, but typical of a Saturday, she had received only one call, dealing with a problem bear.

⇌

Sam, Liddy, and Grieg walked downhill to the southeast from Powder River Pass, purely enjoying the scenery and each other's company. The wide expanse of blue sky was accentuated by wispy, white ripples near the eastern horizon. Intense rays from the sun heated the meadows and rocky outcrops, releasing an earthy fragrance that filled the still air and hinted at the renewal of life after the passage of winter. The heady scents of spring, accompanied by buzzing insects and bird song issuing from small clusters of brush, filled Sam and Liddy with hypnotic joy. As they strolled into an especially colorful meadow, its blanketing spray of blue and yellow flowers filled their senses.

Sam took Liddy by the hand and led her to the middle of the flower-carpeted meadow. He said nothing, but Liddy sensed his determination and focused energy. When they stopped, he turned to her and firmly wrapped her in his arms. Their mutual embrace filled them with passion for each other, and their long kiss seemed to change the whole world. It was for them like the end of a geologic age and the birth of a new era. All of their past life had led them to this cusp in time, and from this moment a shining new path would guide them in directions that they could only guess. It was as if their very souls had been blended for some divine purpose. Love flowed in and around them, throughout their minds and bodies, and into the rocks and the earth. They and the world around them were *one*. Sam and Liddy held each other tight—not wanting these moments to end, and both hoping that time would stand still. *Neither dared to speak.*

Their precious sojourn in the meadow changed, as they knew it eventually would, when a cool breeze rippled the flowers and Grieg pressed his nose between them. They knew now that their lives would be eternally intertwined, and that no thoughts would be kept for either one alone. As Sam released his embrace and tenderly gazed into Liddy's eyes, he whispered, "I have something for you." He reached into his shirt pocket and unwrapped a small shiny object. Then, taking her left hand in his, he placed an engagement ring on her finger. It was made from the rough diamond he had found in the Point of Rocks dike and from gold that he had panned himself. With a questioning look, *the answer already known*, he asked, "Liddy, will you...?" But before the question was finished, Liddy quietly shouted, "*Yes! Yes, dear Sam!*"

With arms wrapped around each other's waists, Sam and Liddy dreamily wandered together across the meadow. The bright sunshine was nothing compared to the radiant glow of their happiness. Grieg followed along, bounding through tall grass and flowers, sniffing rodent burrows, and snatching bites from remnant snowdrifts. After taking several self-portraits among the flowers, they wandered up closer to the pass at the crest of the range where they had left Sam's truck. The blue sky was now becoming studded overhead with budding white cumulous clouds. They sought a spot to eat lunch, preferably where they could sit on a large warm rock with an unrestricted view to the west.

But before Sam and Liddy arrived back at the parking area, Grieg suddenly began to whine as if he had been severely injured! He ran frantically between Sam and Liddy, then in the direction of the truck, then back to Liddy, whimpering continuously. His head hung low, his tail was tucked tight between his legs, and his eyes reflected a *penetrating fear*. It was eighteen minutes past noon. An expanding silence then came over them and the air ceased its movement. The birds quit their flights and abandoned their songs, as if sucked into the earth. A strange emptiness seemed to surround them and they both felt an eerie chill—*a chill of fear that could not be dissipated by the warm sun.* Then they felt the ground move beneath their feet in a gentle, almost seasick rolling motion that caused them to sway. The rolling lasted for seventeen seconds. When it finally stopped, they raced the remaining distance up the ridge towards the truck. Upon reaching the hillcrest, their view to the west opened up, and *Sam and Liddy froze in their tracks*!

⇌

The lunch break during FOYAB's "fact-finding" meeting was a beehive of positioning, power brokering, and petite conversation. The Reef Group representative bought lunch for the environmentalist and sympathized with the cause. He then excused himself to rub elbows with Louis Costalotti and George Custer. The art of developing influence and *appearing* sympathetic to diverse issues was something he had worked at for years. The Reef Group benefited repetitively from his pageantry of persuasive perfection. He was a valuable asset to the Reef Group and his six-figure income reflected his importance to that organization.

Josie Welborne lunched with her park geologist and Mel Bergschrund, the only other federal representative there. The three of them unanimously agreed that it had been a waste of their time to attend this rendezvous of *self-centered, greedy wolves.*

Bill Burnhard dined with George Custer and Louis Costalotti, who picked up the tab for lunch. Although Bill provided fuel for the pending lawsuit, his predilection for heaping coarse denigrations on Sam and Chris caused his lunch partners to sigh with relief when he finally left to inflict himself on Josie Welborne. Bill apparently believed her to be in a position of influence that might help him in the future. He also noted a local photographer moving in her direction—*a possible chance to be caught in a photo opportunity.*

Bill reached Josie's table at the same time as the photographer and introduced himself to both. "Good afternoon...I'm Bill Burnhard, with the Wyoming Office of

Mines and Geology. I've been evaluating safety concerns related to the potential for an eruption in Yellowstone. I can assure you that the geologic evidence I've seen indicates that no such event is likely to occur…mind if I join you?"

Josie was not in full appreciation of the gathering, and felt uneasy, more so after Bill introduced himself. Her initial video statements, from four or five weeks earlier, now seemed to her rather strong and self-confident, and she was less sure of the situation. Nothing had really changed, except that she was annoyed with the lack of concrete facts presented by anyone talking counter to what Sam Westone and Chris Felsen had presented. Also, Mel had told her that some of Sam's′ interpretation had been confirmed, specifically the magma movement. The remainder of the data was still being evaluated.

Josie's thoughts were interrupted when a waiter asked if Mel Bergschrund was at the table. Receiving an affirmative response, he handed Mel a note asking him to call Red Gossan immediately at the number provided. Mel recognized it as one of the USGS extensions in his Denver office building. Mel started to excuse himself in order to locate a phone, when Josie offered him the use of her cell phone. Mel thanked her and called from the table. Red answered on the first ring and excitedly told Mel, "We just finished checking the data from Sam Westone and Chris Felsen…*they are totally right!*" Mel's face turned pale, and he struggled for breath as Red continued, "*They are right! We've confirmed every bit of their analyses.*"

Josie, seeing Mel's expression, leaned forward to hear and asked, "*What's wrong?*"

Bill edged closer so that he too could clearly hear Red's voice as Mel held out the cell phone. "*All of it is right!* Two of our west coast volcanologists confirm the findings. The branch chief has contacted FEMA, who will be making a press release. *They'll soon be issuing an evacuation order for Yellowstone Park.*" Bill's and Josie's faces turned ashen as a *listening silence* rippled outward from the table where they sat. The whole room suddenly swayed and cracked, and Josie lurched forward across her table as people and furniture crashed across the floor. She could barely hear Red's voice as the phone waved wildly in Mel's hand. Josie tried to keep her balance and not land on Bill, who was already sprawled on the floor, shouting the obvious…*"Earthquake!"* Red's voice continued, *"We don't know when th…"* It was cutoff in mid-sentence as the local cell phone tower ceased operation.

People were screaming, and some had been injured! In panic, most of the people made stumbling dashes through the dimly lit mayhem toward the guiding emergency exit lights. Josie zigzagged around overturned furniture and out of the dining room just as the rolling motion ended. Bill, Mel, and her park geologist stumbled along behind as they followed the red carpeted hallway, littered with fallen pictures, broken plaster, and dangling light fixtures. They then merged into a disorderly herd of humanity, forced along in a crushing and frantic flow that eventually disgorged them from the south entrance to the inn.

The disheveled group congregated along the street just outside and looked around, trying to assess their situation. Bill groaned long and hard and then began spouting off, to no one in particular, *"Man! That was some earthquake!* I'll bet it caused a few landslides and maybe even destroyed some buildings!"

Josie glared at him with a look that could have peeled the paint off of a new car. Bill saw it and took a step backward away from her, knocking Costalotti off balance as Josie hollered, "You'd just better hope that's *all* that got damaged by the quake!" She stepped toward him, and he backed up farther. Louis carefully moved out of her way, while the "General" and several other bystanders now paid close attention. *"Mel, here, just got cutoff from the USGS branch chief in Denver…"* Mel bobbed his head in acknowledgement as Josie continued, *"and they just verified the conclusions of Sam Westone and Chris Felsen, that Yellowstone is in serious danger of erupting!"*

Bill's thoughts, having been temporarily diverted by the earthquake and by the attention he perceived to himself from his comments to those around him, now focused on Josie's sobering words. He slowly began shaking his head from side to side without speaking, as a child in kindergarten might do when scolded by a teacher for acting badly.

Josie persisted in her attack without interruption, *"Weren't you paying any attention? They'll soon be issuing an order to evacuate Yellowstone!"* Nearby, Louis's face turned white as he listened. "Mr. Burnhard…if you'd spent a little more time trying to help understand the situation rather than tearing down others to fluff up your own sick ego, we might have found out about this sooner! *That earthquake might've been strong enough to trigger an eruption!*" Bill sagged to the ground in embarrassment, fear, and apparent confusion.

Louis, now in a nervous fit, interrupted Josie with a pummeling of questions and comments, "How soon do they expect it to go off? Are they sure it'll happen? What's being done about public safety? You people can hang around here...but *I'm leaving! I've got a business to take care of!*"

Josie looked at Bill and then at Louis in disgust, as she would at a drunk who had just vomited on her feet. Several other FOYAB meeting attendees were paying close attention to the small scene. Some shifted on their feet, and a few mumbled to their friends as sirens from emergency vehicles wailed in the background. Then, as the sun winked out behind a dark cloud racing overhead, a deafening roar blotted out all other sound.

Like a long forgotten word, spoken suddenly and loudly to a crowd that silently awaited its coming, the volcano that was Yellowstone burst forth. That long lost word, unintelligible to most who heard it, shouted a farewell to nature's jewel—that concentration of vegetation, wildlife, and wonders known to the world as *Yellowstone.*

CHAPTER 13

Storm

▼

Therefore we will not fear, though the earth give way, and the mountains be carried into the midst of the sea. - Psalm 46:2

"Oh, *my God*!" gasped Sam in horror. *"No…No!"*

"Heeuhh…" inhaled Liddy as the air seemed to stop in her throat, and her chest felt almost too heavy to breathe. *"Look at that!"* she shouted, but the shock of what was happening turned her voice into no more than a faint whisper. Then again, shakily, but louder, *"It's Yellowstone! It's erupting!"* In fear, Liddy felt her knees start to buckle beneath her. Her eyes began to water, and she felt sick as her vision blurred until she wiped her eyes on her sleeve. Then she saw with an unusual and almost surrealistic clarity, while cool-headed Sam evaluated the situation, making mental notes as if observing some common, but complex, geologic field problem.

The thin haze on the blue horizon gave way as a turbulent dark volcanic storm boiled up beyond the crest of the Absaroka Range, which lay 120 miles distant. The grimy beast swelled up rapidly as if discharged from an underground hell chamber. Its ghastly, brown cauliflower shaped tentacles swept sideways and upward to immense height. Liddy, weak in her stomach and wobbly on her legs, began taking pictures with her digital camera: one shot on wide-angle, then a series with the settings on maximum telephoto. Her digital camera could record up to six minutes of continuous video, or 1000 detailed still photographs. Because of the long distance to the subject, the series of stills would show as much as a video, and she would be able to record for a much longer period of time. Her years of digital and video training kept her attention focused, although she had never been so afraid in her life. She was trembling almost uncontrollably, but the auto-stabilization device, incorporated into her camera, kept the pictures from blurring as she shook.

⇌

Captain Frank Smith of United Airlines Flight 3738 was one of the first people, along with some of his crew and passengers, to notice the eruption of Yellowstone. But most of them did not really comprehend the event as it all happened too fast. The jet was flying at an altitude of 34,000 feet, on a route from San Francisco to Winnipeg. Frank commented to his copilot that he never realized a Yellowstone geyser could be seen from that altitude. He had actually only seen the very beginning of the eruption, before the nose of the plane obstructed his downward view.

About nine seconds later, the copilot and a few passengers noticed that a brown turbulence had suddenly obscured their view of the ground. The copilot mentioned this to Frank, who became startled as he looked downward, and then immediately activated the seatbelt warning. He spoke into the intercom, "Ladies and gent..." But Frank never finished his words. The rising cloud of debris flattened the plane from the bottom as if it had been slammed into the ground at twice the speed of sound. The blast continued skyward as the combination of heat, force, and rapidly moving debris removed any trace of the passenger jet's former existence.

⇌

Josie Welborne's family, relaxing in the new park headquarters complex at West Thumb, never noticed the eruption. Neither did countless thousands of other innocent souls who died that day in Yellowstone. Tourists and park employees alike had little chance to glimpse, even for a brief moment, an awareness of their situation before the violence overcame them. In those short moments, probably none comprehended the eruption or had a chance to utter a single word of prayer.

The Park Service had installed several Webcams at strategic locations within Yellowstone National Park; these allowed people worldwide to view the main attractions of the park in real-time. Unfortunately, they were all hard-wired to electrical power and telephone lines. The hard-wired connections were one of the first things to break when the triggering earthquake struck. If they had been self-contained and solar-powered, with direct satellite connections, then the world would have seen some close-up details of the start of the greatest volcanic eruption in the history of mankind.

⇌

Surya Ganisalim was in his office, writing on his dissertation, when he felt a slight motion in the Geophysics and Geology building. He was working through the weekend, trying to get ahead, as he wanted to take a full week off to go backpacking with friends in the Uinta Mountains of northern Utah. He knew immediately that he was feeling an earthquake, and because of the extended time of the rolling motion, he suspected that it was significant.

With his half-eaten sandwich in one hand, he began tapping keys on his computer to bring up the data stream that would be pouring in from his seismic array. It took a moment to load, but then his real-time display, in a three dimensional depiction, showed a wide zone of subsurface activity more than twenty-eight miles north to south, and almost forty-five miles east to west, beneath the Yellowstone caldera. It also showed some kind of disturbance extending from the surface downward to depths of more than twenty-five miles on the north side of the caldera, and to about twenty miles beneath its south side. These disturbances seemed to be somewhat linear, and they intersected the edges of the magma chamber that irregularly occupied the region from about three miles down to about ten miles. Maybe the fault or faults responsible for the quake extended unusually deep?

Surya almost choked on the bite of food in his mouth, then swallowed hard. He jumped to his feet knocking over his chair, spilling coffee and food, while shouting, *"Yellowstone! Yellowstone erupted...It's blown away!"* The only other student on that floor of the building, startled by the tremor followed by Surya's yell, stumbled in panic into Surya's office. Surya looked at him questioningly, not remembering that anyone else had been in his vicinity, and then the reality of what had happened hit him.

At that moment, Surya's display became distorted, indicating a data connection deficiency. The display then lost its three-dimensional character and reverted to a simple seismograph trace. That trace lasted about seven seconds before the computer flashed off, then back on again, as the building lights dimmed. A moment later the power quit, followed by a few small flickers indicative of a power return that never materialized.

The computer memory had captured the magnitude 7.8 triggering earthquake, and the almost immediate deactivation of Surya's network connection to Dillon, Montana. It also recorded the start of the eruption to the point at which the combination of earthquake and eruption disrupted the power grid sufficiently to cause surges, brownouts, and eventual shutdown. The power shutdown affected a large portion of both the western U.S. and Canada. Those few moments of data that Surya had captured and interpreted, combined with data and interpretations collected over the previous months, secured a successful completion for his dissertation. Not only that, but when his data and interpretations were later publicized, Surya received numerous job offers from both industry and government agencies.

⇆

Time seemed to stand still as Sam and Liddy watched in fascination and fear. Sam took several color slide photos and carefully studied the changes taking place before his eyes. In the minute and a half since they topped the ridge (a total of about three minutes since the start of the earthquake), they watched the ominous, low brown cloud expand to cover more than thirty degrees of their horizon, followed closely by a secondary towering turbulent cloud that now rose to an angular height of about ten degrees above the horizon. At their distance of close to 160 miles from the Yellowstone caldera, that represented a distance along the horizon of about ninety miles, and a height, guessed by Sam, approaching twenty-five miles!

The cloud engulfed the Absaroka Mountains on the western horizon, and then their view of the Bighorn Basin progressively vanished beneath the dark spreading turbulence. An unnatural silence, accompanied by a heightened sense of awareness that seemed to be both focused and oppressive, *like watching a silent movie in slow motion*, enveloped them. It would later be more aptly related to the expanded sense of time experienced during a personal trauma, similar to what a soldier experiences during intense combat.

Sam's truck was parked near the east end of a highway pullout, about thirty feet lower in elevation than the top of the pass. Six other vehicles were parked closer to the pass along the pullout. Several other people had been wandering around the area, and now they were all looking in awe at what was happening to the west. Liddy continued to take pictures as Sam watched the amazing scene unfolding before them.

A curved, almost transparent disturbance, somewhat like a ripple in a smooth pool, was moving across the Bighorn Basin toward them and ahead of the brown cloud. It appeared to be spreading outward from the cloud's origin, probably at the Yellowstone caldera. Its curved leading edge was distorted in places by mountains and hills, and its depth could not be determined. A rising thin and turbulent dust cloud, moving along the ground, accompanied it. Its speed was fascinatingly, almost hypnotically fast. Sam suddenly understood what he was seeing. Transfixed for a moment, he shook his head as if to clear it, and then yelled at the top of his lungs, *"Get below the ridge! It's a shock wave!"*

He grabbed Liddy, who looked at him in confusion as he tucked her under his arm like a sack of grain. He then sprinted eastward for about fifty feet. There, at the edge of a steep east-facing embankment, he jumped, carrying her down below the hill with him. After three large bounds, he stumbled to his knees. Sam shoved her face down to the ground, yelled at her to close her eyes, and then laid down on top of her, hiding his head as best he could and covering hers with his hands. Grieg followed, piling himself tight against Liddy and Sam.

Almost immediately, a *deafening boom* that gradually changed into a *continuous roar* swept over them. Simultaneously, the sound was accompanied by a wind gust that Sam estimated to be well over *one hundred miles per hour!* Flying dust, gravel, and a mix of other debris pelted and stung them. A weather recording instrument near an old fire lookout above Meadowlark Lake, several miles west of Powder River Pass, was retrieved a week later during the continuing search for survivors. It had recorded a sudden temperature rise of from 65 to 105 degrees F, and a wind gust of 171 miles per hour, before the instrument failed completely.

Even after all the reading he had done about large volcanic eruptions, Sam still found it unbelievable that the shock wave could carry this far—well over 150 miles from the site of the eruption. This was probably the farthest distance from the eruption that anyone on the ground was seriously injured or killed by the shock wave that had, for a variety of reasons, been directed to the east and south. The Bighorn Mountains shielded the towns along their east side, and the shock wave was attenuated to no more than a strong gust of wind sixty miles farther east. The shock wave actually came from the first of two closely spaced blasts. The *secondary* burst of the eruption was more substantial, but it had been directed almost straight upward, affecting the countryside to a lesser degree, but equally in all directions from its origin.

As the wave passed, hurricane force winds lashed the area, followed quickly by a rapid increase in temperature to near *one hundred degrees F*. A nauseous sulfurous smell accompanied the hot gale. Then, as the leading edge of the low cloud passed and the wind slackened, a blink of sunshine caught Sam and Liddy briefly. Five minutes later, this little gap in the sky filled in with fine ash and the shadow of a dense, dark cloud, banishing the last sunny rays of hope. Liddy was shaking uncontrollably, while Sam was pumped with adrenaline in a fight or flight response! He felt little, although he was bleeding slightly from scratches on his arms and a bruise on his head where a fist-sized rock had caught him.

There was now a brief and penetrating silence, broken only by the faint cry of someone injured or scared and the moaning of an approaching gust of wind. This was followed again, after thirty seconds, by a second rolling thunder-like sound. The rumble steadily increased in volume, and like the first blast, became loud enough to hurt the ears—but rather than ending, it just kept reverberating. Taking Liddy by the hand, and giving Grieg a pull on his collar, Sam climbed back up the embankment.

The view across the Bighorn Basin no longer existed. In a shaky trance, Liddy automatically snapped three more pictures, including one of the overturned cars by the highway. Sam looked around quickly to see if he could help anyone. He saw only a crying child, maybe three years old, lying behind a large boulder. The little girl's cries were the only ones he heard, and only because their pitch was so different from the rumbling sound.

Sam picked up the child and then he hurriedly led Liddy a hundred yards down the slope to the east where his truck, protected by the crest of the ridge, had been sheltered from the direct shock wave. However, the blast had still retained enough force to shove his truck partly up against a metal guardrail, and the few trees that Sam could see near the ridge had either been cut off or leveled.

Sam, clutching the child with one arm and entering through the driver's door, helped Liddy get into the passenger seat. He then gave her the child and put Grieg in the back, under the camper shell. A heavy blackness rolled over them as if doom would pour forth from the heavens. A roiling thunderhead, generated from the air forced upward along the mountain flank, violently unleashed its fury on them as the on-rushing cloud of brown ash mingled with it and strengthened it into an unearthly and fearsome spectacle. A barrage of lightning danced around them and cannonading thunder shook the firmament as it fought for dominance over the roar of the eruption. Muddy drops of rain began to fall through the dust and ash that now swept across Powder River Pass.

In order to be heard above the battle din of nature, Sam yelled at Liddy to stay put. He then ran back up toward the place where the little girl had crouched behind a large boulder of Precambrian gneiss at the edge of the parking lot. He carefully looked in and around the wrecked vehicles on his way to the sheltering rock. But he could discern neither signs of life, nor injured people, nor bodies. The lightning flashes gave brief clarity to the unworldly scene. That large rock had probably harbored the *only* survivor. He looked around and called out loudly, "*Is anyone here?*" No one answered. The sound of nature's rage overwhelmed everything. Even if any other persons *were* alive, they could not hear him.

The noise continued to increase, as did the depth of the darkness and the intensity of the muddy rain. Sam voiced a quick prayer, asking safe deliverance for Liddy, himself, and others caught in the volcanic storm. He yelled again and still heard nothing other than the ferocity of the apocalyptic tumult that now descended from above. He wanted to search for more survivors, no matter how slim the chances of finding any. However, he knew that they must leave the area immediately or risk the possibility of being buried in ash.

That decision to leave was one of the hardest that Sam would ever make. The thought that he might have been able to save even one more person haunted him. He ran back to his pickup, backed it up to get clear of the guard rail, and drove eastward down the highway toward Buffalo. Sam drove as fast as he felt was prudent, while keeping his wheels on the road and avoiding scattered trees and limbs that littered the highway from the blast wind that had swirled erratically across the lee side of the mountains. Muddy rain greased the pavement and visibility was difficult.

The first burst of the eruption had initially moved outward at over twice the speed of sound, slowing and becoming subsonic at a distance of seventy-one miles. The attenuated blast flattened almost all timber on the west side of the Bighorn Mountains, except those small patches that were protected in a few deep canyons. It also razed many of the towns in the Bighorn Basin, temporarily sparing only those that were sheltered by mountains or ridges. Powell, Lovell, Greybull, Basin, Meeteetse, and Worland all disintegrated with a total loss of life.

Because the initial blast was directed southward and eastward, many nearby towns in Montana escaped early destruction, only to eventually suffer burial by falling ash. Most of Thermopolis survived the initial torrent, and amazingly so did much of Cody, due to the protection of topography. Thermopolis eventually succumbed when ash piled up to great depths; all structures there collapsed as the ash accumulated beyond any building's ability to support the massive increase in weight.

Cody met with *complete annihilation* less than half an hour after the eruption began, when a thick and turbulent *pyroclastic flow* of hot gas mixed with ash and pumice cascaded eastward out of the rising eruption and down the valley of the North Fork of the Shoshone River. That debris cloud, over 200 feet thick, and with a temperature of about 750 degrees F, raced down the valley at a speed of more than 160 miles per hour. Buffered and lubricated by the entrained gas, it wiped out the small settlement of Wapiti in an instant and then turned the surface of Buffalo Bill Reservoir into high-pressure steam as it passed. The energetic steam layer beneath the cloud forced the flow upward, causing it to spread as it crested Cedar Mountain and Rattlesnake Mountain before cascading over the town of Cody. The steam from the reservoir, coupled with the flow path being blocked by Cedar Mountain, forced part of it southward and back up the South Fork Valley. The searing heat of the pyroclastic flow instantly killed all in its path, sparing the residents of that valley the slightly more tortuous death of being buried alive, when ash from the eruption piled up over the course of a few hours to more than fifty feet deep.

A similar flow billowed downward and outward from the caldera to the southwest. Its range was extended when it became buoyed up with additional steam as it passed over Jackson Lake. That pyroclastic flow wiped from Jackson Hole the towns of Moose, Teton Village, Wilson, Jackson, and its Snake River subdivisions. The towns of West Yellowstone and Gardiner, Montana did not survive the initial blast. The area of total destruction encompassed parts of Wyoming, Montana, and Idaho, much of which was buried in ash that varied in depth from six feet to more than sixty feet. Due to wind effects on deposition, later satellite measurements, when compared to pre-eruption topography, showed ash depths no greater than about sixty-five feet. The deepest ash piled up just west of the former site of the city of Cody.

⇌

Unbelievable to Sam as he drove down the highway, some weekend traffic was still headed uphill *toward* the looming disaster. Sam flashed his headlights off and on—a feeble warning, at best. A few other vehicles were also headed down and Sam now concentrated on his driving to avoid a collision. The road was not only slippery from the muddy rain, but the sides of the road were difficult to see.

Liddy, who had strapped the little girl into the jump seat in the back of the small, extended cab pickup, was still shaking. She was able to function somewhat, but she seemed to be in an *automatic* or *mechanical* state of mind and felt light-headed. She pulled the cell phone from her pack, and quickly dialed her parents' number. The phone produced only silence broken by irregular static. The batteries checked out okay, and there should have been an easily accessible cell phone tower nearby. In a hyperventilating string of rapid-fire words, she yelled to be heard over the outside noise…*"Sam! Sam! The phone doesn't work! We should get hold of my mom and dad!"*

Sam reached over without looking and squeezed her hand reassuringly…"We will! Either the cell tower is down or the dust and rain are attenuating the signals. I'll try the radio." He turned on his two-meter rig, set the frequency at 146.52

simplex, and called "KA7HBS, KA7HBS, KA7HBS...this is KC7QE."

Sam waited five seconds but heard no answer.

"*Is it that bad that we can't get through?*" asked Liddy, almost as rapidly as before, and biting her lip as she finished.

Sam tried not to show that he too was shaking with fear. "Liddy, *we're in a rough spot...there's no doubt about it.* But we both need to calm down so we can work our way safely out of it. Take some slow, deep breaths and try to relax a little. I'll try again." He called into the microphone, "KA7HBS, KA7HBS...this is KC7QE."

This time he was rewarded, "Hello, Sam...this is KA7HBS. *What's happening?* It's as dark as night here, and the power is out. We had an earthquake, and it seems to be raining mud! Are you and Liddy alright?"

"*Yellowstone has erupted! We're heading down!*" replied Sam. "We're okay...*but things may get worse!* Warren, *you must leave Buffalo now!* Drive to Liddy's in Casper and we'll meet you there. *Don't wait for us! Go now!* We're traveling from the west, heading toward the east. It's pitch dark here too, and from what you say, we may not see light again. We'll take the road down Crazy Woman Canyon so we can get out of the area faster. We may be out of contact with you while we're in the canyon. Keep your two-meter rig on. *Go now!* We'll call on five-two when we get below the canyon."

"Okay, Sam...we'll leave right now," Warren replied. He said something else, but the signal faded as Sam's truck dropped behind the ridge to his left. The muddy rain probably contributed to the disruption of Warren's two-meter signal. Liddy mechanically snapped a few more pictures in their headlights as they drove. She gradually calmed down a little as she sat sideways and tried to comfort the scared little girl strapped in the jump seat behind her.

⇐

Before the eruption, extremely high pressures had built up beneath the Yellowstone caldera, due in part to recent magma emplacement. This had been observable in both the substantial uplift in Yellowstone, and in the minor, but noticeable, uplift in widely surrounding areas. Sam and Surya's interpretation of the Yellowstone earthquake swarms that had occurred over the last several months had been correct—the swarms *had* resulted from magma movement. The pressure buildup had been held in check by the thickness and weight of the overlying rock and by the confining strength of the surrounding rock.

The magma chamber beneath the caldera had been adjusting itself for more than 600,000 years. Time had allowed resident magma to become vertically zoned into areas with slightly differing compositions and amounts of dissolved volatiles. Slightly heavier materials, with lesser gas content, had settled down toward the bottom of the magma chamber. Viscous silicic magma, containing the largest amounts of volatiles and gas bubbles, accumulated at the roof of the magma chamber, gradually but dramatically increasing pressure. This gas pressure, when combined with the push from the influx of new magma from below and the upward force from the hotspot itself, had developed a situation analogous to an over-inflated balloon. All that was needed to *pop the balloon* was an event that would open a fracture and release the pressure through the less than three miles of overlying rock.

The event that triggered the eruption was a magnitude 7.8 earthquake, focused on a series of west to northwest trending faults, just northwest of and intersecting the edge of the Yellowstone caldera. Like a carbonated drink that has been shaken vigorously and then opened, the earthquake triggered a massive degassing within the magma chamber. This was accompanied by a simultaneous breaching of the chamber roof along ring fractures that bounded its edges.

The northwest caldera edge fracture actually failed first, about one full second before failures of ring fractures, east and southeast of the caldera, were in motion. The fractures filled almost instantly with the violent eruption of material. In another 2.5 seconds, secondary fracturing of the magma chamber roof south of Sour Creek Dome, in the caldera itself, helped to direct the initial part of the eruption toward the east and south. The opening up of major fractures in this area, accompanied by the removal of part of the magma chamber roof, facilitated the dumping of much of Yellowstone Lake directly into the magma chamber at multiple locations.

Yellowstone Lake, with 136 square miles of surface area and an average depth of about 140 feet, supplied slightly more than *three and one half cubic miles of water* to the developing situation! Additional water was supplied by Heart Lake, Lewis Lake, and Shoshone Lake. Some of that water was transformed into steam to drive the eruption as water fell into the magma chamber. Part of it, before it could fall, was vaporized by up-rushing material to mix with the clouds of ash, which later fell as muddy rain. Water that was not consumed in steam or joined with airborne ash was mixed with debris near the ground to become *lahars*, or volcanic mud flows. In the absence of volcanic action or some other situation, the volume of Yellowstone Lake alone could have supplied enough water to devastatingly flood a portion of nearby Wyoming and Montana.

The water that poured into the breached magma chamber almost instantly turned into superheated steam and provided unimaginable pressure. That pressure, combined with the continuing exsolution of gasses from the magma, resulted, three minutes after the initial eruptive blast, in a secondary and more powerful eruption directed straight upward. By the time the first eruption cloud had reached a height of twenty miles, it was overtaken by the second eruptive blast, which then carried fine ash and moisture to a height of thirty-five miles.

The first pulse of the eruption lofted *68.5 cubic miles* of ash and related debris—*roughly 100 to 200 times more material* than was erupted by Mount St. Helens in 1980! But that first pulse was dwarfed by the second eruptive pulse which began three minutes later and blew out an estimated *211 cubic miles of material in less than twenty minutes*! Smaller, scattered eruptive outbursts, over the next six hours, produced another three cubic miles of ash, followed by the almost passive extrusion of seven cubic miles of rhyolitic lava. In total, *the eruption of Yellowstone violently vented 279.5 cubic miles of ash and other debris,* followed by *seven cubic miles of lava.* This is slightly *more* material than was interpreted for the 600,000 year-old Lava Creek ash, but only about *half* of the amount produced in the Huckleberry ridge event of two million years ago.

Early in the eruption, removal of part of the magma chamber roof precipitated a rapid decompression of the magma downward, initially at several tens of yards per second. The process eventually died out at a depth of more than one and one-quarter miles within the magma. This decompression continuously propelled violently expanding material upward, like a giant inverted rocket engine, for just over eighteen minutes. Lessening amounts of dissolved volatiles, accompanied by exhaustion of the supply of steam from lake water and an increasing depth of built up debris, eventually stifled the process. After that, the eruption degenerated into smaller sporadic and scattered explosive outbursts of material that lasted for another six hours. Falling debris then mingled with extrusions of degassed rhyolitic lava in the collapsed southeastern portion of the caldera, over the subsequent five hours. The area of the ring fractures near the edges of the caldera, particularly on the north side, remained as sites of minor steam and ash ventings for another two months.

⇆

Sam turned east off of U.S. Highway 16 and drove down toward the narrow canyon of Crazy Woman Creek. He was glad that he had filled his truck with fuel in Buffalo, just before heading into the mountains that morning. Immediately after leaving the main highway, he pulled over briefly to scrape accumulating dust and mud from the windshield and from his face. Liddy brushed mud from her head and from the face of the little girl. Sam dug out three old bandanas from behind the seat, securing one across his face, and giving the other two to Liddy for her and their passenger. The thick dust that had quickly metamorphosed into muddy rain permeated the cab of the truck, and any air movement created an odd juxtaposition of both mud and dust. The situation reminded Sam of trying to mix powdered cement with water, then sneezing into the mess while trying to clear his face with wet hands. Everything stuck where you didn't want it, and you had the worst of both dust and mud at the same time.

Sam turned on the truck's AM-FM radio, but was greeted only by severe static from the continuing electrical storms. Nervous and jittery, while trying to maintain an outward appearance of calm, he shoved a tape into his cassette player, only to have it grind to a stop after two seconds, its vital components clogged with debris from Sam's hands. *No way around it*, thought Sam, *this drive is going to make for a very long day!* Then he forced himself to smile, hoping to calm Liddy and to keep her from getting discouraged.

Liddy felt weak and dispirited, but in a way, she was resigned to whatever befell them. However, in the grungy darkness lit only by the weak light of the instrument panel and erratic flashes of lightning, she smiled back at Sam, hoping to encourage him and to hide any despair that might otherwise show on her face. *They had each other*, and that helped remind them of the timeless vision they had so recently shared in a flower-filled meadow. Their forced smiles were mutually encouraging, although each thought that the other was being more optimistic than either actually felt. They were both afraid and shivering, but not from any cold.

Sam pulled back onto the road, and they began their descent from the mountains through Crazy Woman Canyon.

CHAPTER 14

Canyon Descent

▼

The sky grew black with clouds and wind, and there was a great rain.
- 1 Kings 18:45

A short way down into Crazy Woman Canyon, Sam stopped to clean his windshield. In the swirling winds, the increasing torrent from above varied rapidly from the consistency of damp abrasive dust to that of dirty rain and back again. There seemed to be more mud in the air than rain, and his windshield washer reservoir was now empty and needed to be refilled. The temperature had dropped to around sixty degrees F, probably close to what should have been expected in the canyon at that elevation. Sam refilled the washer from extra jugs of water that he normally carried in the back of his truck, and he made sure Grieg was surviving the ride. The dog was cowering and shaking, but gratefully accepted a pat on the head from Sam as he replaced the water jug.

The never-ending *in and out of the truck* routine had become a messy chore for Sam. He and the driver's seat were both caked with mud as he got back in and continued to drive. Mud stuck to the door, as well as to its hinges and latch. He hoped that it would continue to close securely for the duration of the trip. They lost elevation rapidly as they slid down the road between the steep rocky slopes and granite outcrops in the upper part of the canyon. Actually, Sam thought that it was probably good that things were muddy. If the ash had been totally dry, the dust might have already choked his vehicle to a standstill. At least they were still able to move.

The darkness was *thick* and *complete*. With the truck's headlights, they could see no more than about fifty yards through the falling goop and often only fifteen yards. So far they had met no other vehicles on the Crazy Woman Creek road. Sam guessed that the fishermen who frequented the area must have had the good sense to flee, either when the earthquake shook them, or when the thick debris cloud arrived overhead. *The falling ash probably spoiled the fishing anyway.*

Another vehicle seen on the road might have been a source of emotional comfort, but it would have the serious potential to either block the road or inhibit their advance down the canyon. Sam already felt that their progress was discouragingly slow due to poor visibility. He hoped that they would not encounter anyone else on the road. He had only a vague and disheartening idea of how long the ash might continue to fall and how deep it could pile up. Sam felt the strong need to move ahead and to get out of the area as fast as possible.

Several times Sam had to stop and remove small trees or boulders that barred their way. A pry bar from the back of his truck worked well on some of the boulders, but for others, he needed to use his *come-along* hand winch, attached either to trees, large rock outcroppings, or even to his pickup. In the process of winching one boulder to the side, Sam suddenly noticed that the level of the stream had risen at least six inches above its normal bed and was spreading across the road in low places. The muddy rain was increasing in intensity, and the danger of both flash flood and mudslide was looming large in Sam's mind. He drove as rapidly as he could, trying to keep his increased worry from being detected by Liddy and the little girl. But his almost frantic movements, as he pushed and levered rocks and small trees from their path, coupled with his hard-set jaw, conveyed his growing concern to Liddy.

At each stop, Sam would again clean the windshield. In order to conserve the fresh water in the back if his truck, he used water from the creek next to the road to remove the continuing build-up of mud. His gold pan substituted for a bucket, dipping the now dirty water from Crazy Woman Creek. The muddy water did almost as good of a job as had the windshield washer, and one pan-full took most of the larger lumps off in one splash. However, it was messy and Sam was getting soaked and just a bit chilled as well.

After the fifth obstacle removal and windshield cleaning in a mile and a half, Sam thought that it had been no more than perhaps three-quarters of an hour since they first felt the blast of the eruption. In the gloomy blackness that accompanied their fear and excitement, it was hard to judge time. Sam hadn't thought to look at his watch when the rapid turn of events had begun. The sound of the wind and falling rain now replaced the loud roaring as the dominant external noise. Even the sporadic thunder seemed muffled in the background. They had not even noticed when the outside sounds had changed. It suddenly occurred to Sam that, although he had talked briefly to Liddy's father on the two-meter radio, he and Liddy had not spoken a word since then. Time was distorted, stretched out, and immeasurable. "*Liddy, are you all right?*" he said with a start.

"Ye...yeah!" she answered rapidly. "I th...think so. Just sc...scared!" Her teeth were chattering. "And overwhelmed!" she added. "You saved me. I saw that cloud c...coming, but I was ju...just so mesmerized or scared, or both, I...I couldn't move." Looking at the girl in the jump seat, she added, "And n...now we have someone else to look after as well." The little girl was shaking and occasionally whimpering. Liddy picked her up, wrapped a jacket and her arms around her, and held her tight. "Sam, maybe we c...could put in a tape and have some music?"

"Sorry, but the player's broken. I tried it just before we started down the canyon."

"Oh. I g...guess I noticed that, but it didn't really register. How about the radio?"

Sam turned it on and scanned both the AM and FM broadcast bands and found that he could receive nothing on FM and only static on AM. " Sorry," he said. "The static is killing any AM signals, and I'm not sure the radio is even working on FM!"

"Maybe we could sing a little," suggested Liddy, as she looked at the girl in her arms. "Sam, help me out. We sang, *"Precious Lord, Take My Hand"* in church awhile back. I know the words...I'll try to keep my voice steady."

Sam wasn't afraid to sing, but he couldn't carry a tune in a bucket, not even a mud-filled one. He needed someone else to take the lead; then he could stumble along making appropriate sounds. Knowing this, Liddy began and Sam joined in. She changed some of the words to fit their situation:

> *"Precious Lord, take our hands, lead us on through this land,*
> *We are tired, we are beat, and we're worn.*
> *Through the storm, through dark night, lead us on toward the light,*
> *Take our hands; precious Lord, lead us home.*
>
> *When our way's filled with fear, precious Lord, linger near...*
> *When the day is tiresome and long,*
> *In the canyon we stand, guide our truck through this land,*
> *Take our hands, precious Lord, lead us home."*

The singing helped to calm them both and definitely soothed the girl on Liddy's lap. Liddy smiled at Sam's discord, and some of her stress was briefly relieved. They repeated the song and then Liddy continued to hum a variety of simple tunes to the little girl. Her humming seemed to have a great calming effect on the girl, and holding her helped to soothe and strengthen Liddy.

A moment later, they rounded a corner in the narrowest section of the canyon. In front of them the road was obstructed by a large, fallen block of limestone. Sam, out of habit and familiarity, noted that it was part of the Ordovician Bighorn Dolomite, with its characteristic deeply pitted weathered surface, although his observation was of no importance to their situation. *It was one solid piece of rock—about ten feet high, twenty feet long, and ten feet wide!* Obviously this rock had been precariously balanced higher up, and the earthquake had shaken it loose. Sam was now regretting that in his adrenalin surge from the eruption shock wave, *he had forgotten about the earthquake.* Maybe he should have stayed on the highway instead of taking the shortcut through Crazy Woman Canyon! *But it was too late to go back now!*

Sam's hands began to sweat. He usually thought clearly under pressure, but he had never been in a predicament such as this. Also, he had never before held the responsibility for someone else's welfare in an obviously hazardous situation. The little girl was essentially helpless, and her parents quite likely did not survive the blast. Sam did not know her name, where she was from, or where her relatives might be. He also did not know how far they needed to travel to escape the falling ash that had the potential to deeply bury a large part of the western United States. He would have to worry about those details later. The immediate problem confronting him was *how to get past this rock!*

Okay, Sam, he thought. It's time to concentrate on logic, and ignore the superfluous details. *What is our best move?* All choices probably have some drawbacks. Better ask Liddy! *Two minds are better than one!*

"Liddy, *the road is blocked!* Do you have any suggestions?"

"Uh, no Sam, *unless we can drive through the creek,*" she answered.

"Thanks, Liddy," answered Sam with relief at her obviously simple answer to what he had perceived as a more complex problem. "You stay in here while I check it out. Perhaps you can find out who our passenger is while I'm out...I'll be back in a few minutes."

With a large flashlight in hand, Sam got out of the truck and reflected, *why didn't I think of that?* He walked to the edge of the large rock and then down a short embankment to the creek. Ash covered the surface of the water that now ran muddy rather than clear. Sam waded in to test the depth and to search for hidden rocks that could cause his truck to hang up. The water was bitterly cold and nearly two feet deep, but Sam thought it might indeed be possible to drive around the end of the large rock by going through the creek.

The gap between the canyon wall and the fallen rock was quite narrow. Sam spread his arms out wide to measure, and he could almost touch the rock and the wall at the same time, but for about an inch. *Their passage would be tight!* Sam was now glad that he drove a small pickup rather than a full-sized one. There was no way a full-sized pickup could have passed between the rock and the south canyon wall! Thinking objectively, Sam mused—this will put us between the proverbial *"rock and a hard place."*

Sam waded back and forth through the water, shuffling his feet to search for hidden rocks or deep holes, until he was completely past the road blockage. He found one hefty rock in the water that he was able to roll downstream and out of the way. He found two others near where his truck would have to climb back up the bank to get out of the stream and onto the gravel road. With Herculean effort, he was also able to heave these off to the side and out of the path he thought his truck would take. Sam was now thoroughly soaked and chilled, and he was beginning to acquire a new layer of mud to replace that which he lost in the creek.

The road below this point looked clear, at least as far as he could see with his flashlight's limited beam. Ash and mud continued to fall, coating his face, filling his eyes, and covering the landscape with soft, slippery mire. The farther down the canyon he could drive, the better. The possibility of a flash flood in those narrow confines concerned Sam greatly, and he hoped that they would soon be able to escape from the canyon. If the ash continued to fall, there would be a possibility of mudslides.

Satisfied that his truck could probably make it through the tight spot, Sam returned to Liddy, and she introduced him to "Rachel." Trapped in his soggy clothes, Sam was shivering from the cold of the creek and from the extended tension of their situation, but he did have a thinner covering of mud than before. He managed to sound confident, although he didn't feel that way when he said, "Hello, Rachel...I'm Sam. *You're going to be okay.*"

Displaying some absentmindedness, due primarily to stress, Sam then had to get back out of the pickup again and clean off the windshield with water from the creek before he was able to continue driving. Climbing back in again, he shifted into four-wheel drive, low range, and slowly steered his truck over the bank into the water. He lined his truck up with the gap between the vertical rock wall and the massive fallen block. Easing forward carefully, he felt the water pushing the truck in the downstream direction as the flow increased in the constricted gap. "Not quite the *African Queen*," joked Sam, "but I think we can now appreciate what a difficult journey really is."

Liddy gripped the handhold above her door with one hand and then tightened her other arm around Rachel. She noticed that their vehicle clearance was going to be very close on both sides. They felt the scratching and scraping as the right fenders dragged across the rock wall. At the same time the mirror was torn from the driver's door by the edge of the huge rock on the left.

The truck bounced hard on its frame and jerked suddenly to the right. Rachel screamed as a rock projection cracked the passenger window. Luckily it didn't break, and the truck bounced back to the left. Both rear fenders now caught, and *Sam felt the vehicle coming to a stop!* Quickly, he hit the accelerator. There was a brief pause while the truck seemed to be suspended in the water, its wheels spinning, before it tilted forward and then suddenly surged ahead with the sickening, painful noise of *metal being folded by rock.*

They were through, but the water continued to push the truck in a downstream direction. Sam spun the steering wheel sharply to the left to avoid being trapped below a steep embankment that he knew his truck could never surmount. In the deep water, the pickup responded as quickly to his steering efforts as a heavy barge would on the Mississippi River.

The wheels bumped on the stream bottom, spun wildly and then caught traction as the truck lurched upward to the left. *Sam gave it full throttle!* With wheels spinning and then suddenly regaining traction, Sam's truck surged up onto the gravel road. Momentum carried it across the road where the truck bounced its left front fender off of another rock next to the north canyon wall. As Sam cranked the steering wheel hard to the right, Rachel screamed again and began crying at the noise and violent twisting motions. *"We made it!"* shouted Sam as he brought the truck to a stop.

Liddy, shaken by this most recent escapade in their grueling odyssey, again hugged Rachel close for mutual comfort. Things were happening to them over which she had no control. She was drained of both physical and emotional energy. She would help Sam with whatever she could, but their situation was in his hands. She could think of nothing that she could do different to help them to escape from their predicament.

When Sam had asked her to marry him this morning, she had, in her mind, already pledged to be with him always *for better or for worse.* She trusted him completely. And now she prayed silently for him and for divine guidance to lead them to safety. She could not see how they could survive without God's help! She prayed for Rachel, for her parents, and for everyone. She prayed that they would again feel the warmth of the sun, undimmed by clouds of ash. Through her prayers, she began to relax. She could now think more clearly and objectively. The world outside of their truck appeared to become detached and almost unreal. *But she knew it was real, and she could deal with it now.* Rachel, sensing Liddy's growing calmness, settled down as well.

Sam stepped out to survey the damage. No truck parts appeared to be in danger of scraping the tires except for the left front fender. Luckily, the headlights still pointed ahead. Sam retrieved a long digging bar from the back of his truck. He then levered it against the turned front tire and pried the fender out to make sure it would not rub against the tire. *He could not afford a flat now!*

After replacing the bar and giving Grieg a reassuring pat, Sam doused the windshield again with creek water and similarly washed the driver's side window and muddy door latch. Climbing back inside and wiping his face, he noticed that both Liddy and Rachel had relaxed somewhat. Sam then continued guiding his truck down the narrow road that followed the canyon bottom.

Their truck was pelted twice with a rattle of falling stones, dislodged by runoff from the cliffs above. Each time, the unexpected noise made them jump. At first they feared that the eruption itself was throwing larger material their way. But even as they realized the source of the falling rocks, it was of no comfort against their fear of a cascade of larger rocks that could cause them serious damage. The second pelting by stones, falling from the unseen canyon walls above, was worse than the first. Larger flying rocks actually left a few deep dents in the hood and roof of the truck, but the windshield glass survived and they remained unharmed, although their frazzled nerves left them badly shaken.

Sam was not the type of person to keep his truck in immaculate condition, but he did like to keep it relatively clean, and himself as well. What he wouldn't give to get out of this aggravating abrasive mud! It clung to his clothes, to his hair, to his face, and to his boots! It abraded the back of his neck and it had worked itself into the juncture of his jeans and shirt where it felt like coarse sandpaper against his skin. It also built up as a smooth packed residual layer on the driver's seat. The inside of his truck now had an overall dingy gray appearance. He had wiped the instrument panel clear several times already, and he would soon have to wipe it again.

Every time Sam got out to work on another roadblock or to clean the windshield, he was plastered with another coating of mud. He couldn't remember when he had been as gritty as he was now, unless maybe when he was a kid playing in wet bentonitic soils in the North Dakota badlands. At that time, his mother had used a hose and a large bristle scrub brush to clean him. He remembered what an unpleasant experience that had been. Now he would pay a handsome price to be hosed off and scrubbed with a stiff brush!

The next couple of miles were painfully slow. The road was partially blocked by fallen trees and large boulders that presented a slalom-type course in the center of the road. It was obvious from the presence of ruts, which were buried to mere traces beneath accumulating ash, that at least one other vehicle had descended the road before them. Several boulders had paint scrape marks on them, and some appeared to have been pushed or pulled to the side just enough to allow a vehicle to pass. However, the intensifying ash fall and rain, acting on rocks and vegetation clinging to the canyon walls above them, continued to place new obstacles across their path.

One tree, about six inches in diameter, completely blocked the road as they neared the canyon mouth. It was very springy due to its numerous small branches and was jammed three feet above the ground directly across the road. Sam's only recourse was to cut it with the bucksaw that he had luckily left in the back of his pickup. But *sawing that tree in a sea of mud was a near impossibility!* Everything was a slippery mess and he couldn't see well because of the mud and sweat plastering his eyelids. It worked its way across his forehead and dripped from his matted hair. The small branches on the tree collected more mud and caught the saw blade about every third stroke. The unstable tree bounced and rolled slightly with each stroke of the saw.

Turbid water was now lapping across the road and around his feet as he worked to cut the tree from their path. Sam hurried as much as he could, but his haste contributed to poor coordination, making the sawing more difficult. The water, or mud (it was hard to tell which) was now rising steadily and noticeably, dramatically increasing Sam's personal stress with their predicament.

Because the tree was suspended by its ends and sagged in the middle, Sam had to cut upward from the under side of the trunk to avoid pinching his saw blade. He fumbled with the saw several times while he cut, and then finally, the tree broke in two. He finished severing it completely with quick strokes from the topside, across the remaining stringy bark. Sam managed to pull one end of it out of the way by using a tow strap attached to his truck. As the flow across the road rose up to mid-height on his truck tires, Sam drove forward. He slid the vehicle past the remaining trunk butt, and they finally continued their slow slog through the muck toward the canyon mouth.

The road wound along the sloping canyon side just above the stream for most of the final stretch out of the canyon. However, it made one last dip across the creek, over a small wooden planked bridge, before leaving the canyon and swinging wide across more open country. As they drove down a short slope toward the bridge, muddy water could already be seen washing over it. A pile of debris pressed up against the bridge, forming a dam behind it. Sam knew the danger of crossing such a bridge, but there was no other way out of Crazy

Woman Canyon! He hesitated momentarily. He feared that any missing or broken planks would provide holes for his wheels to become trapped in if he drove too slowly. But at a higher speed, he might hydroplane across them. If the vehicle hydroplaned, he could also loose control with disastrous results. The ensuing splash, when his truck hit the water, could kill his engine. Either way, *he had to cross quickly or they would become trapped!*

Sam gunned the engine and they raced forward. Although short, it was a very old bridge, and Sam thought it wavered slightly as his front wheels crossed the first planks at its edge. Spray from the speeding vehicle obscured their view of it, and the tires hydroplaned, causing him to skid left at a slight angle to his approach. He had made a choice and *he hoped that he had made the right one.* Just as they passed the end of the bridge, he turned hard to the left and they skidded around a sharp bend in the road.

Coming almost to a stop, Sam glanced back in the dim reflection of his headlights to see the debris pile fold over the bridge as it collapsed into the raging current! *They had barely made it out of the canyon!* If he had arrived just a few seconds later, they undoubtedly would have been washed away or stranded!

It was nearly three o'clock in the afternoon and the ash, away from the stream bottom, appeared to be about four or five inches deep when they finally exited Crazy Woman Canyon. The muddy rain had lessened, and the falling ash now seemed drier as they left the mountains behind. Luckily, their route had been subjected to less mud and rain than had some other areas. But they still had another seven miles of gravel before they could reach the pavement of State Highway 196, south of Buffalo.

Unfortunately, they would have to cross Crazy Woman Creek again a few miles farther on, but the gravel road would be straight for several miles while the creek twisted and turned across a much longer distance. With their speed much greater than that of the rising flood, they should have no trouble staying ahead of it. On top of that, they were now out of danger from objects blocking the road! Sam felt absolutely beat, but it was still a long way home and he wasn't about to slack off in his efforts to deliver them all safely.

Liddy tried to call her father on the two-meter radio while Sam concentrated on finding the road through the gloom. The darkness seemed to be a permanent and oppressive, suffocating blanket that muted the world around them. It shut out all light except for the feeble beams emitted from their vehicle's headlights. And even those, which one could not look directly into during the day, were unnaturally reduced in intensity and snuffed out by the voracious blackness.

"KA7HBS, KA7HBS...this is N7GED," called Liddy. The radio still worked, and even though bent, the antenna had not been broken off of the roof of the cab.

Warren responded immediately with a noisy and broken, "KA7HB_ thi_ is __7HBS near Kayc__. We're _outh of ___cee _ut __ copy fine. _ow ___you?"

Liddy replied, "Daddy, we're out of the canyon, headed toward the highway...keep going...we'll catch you in Casper. KA7HBS...this is N7GED."

The only response they heard was, "Okay Liddy _e _____ep__iving_____s____"

"I think he copied you," said Sam. "I hope the ash lets up as we go south."

"I think you're right," replied Liddy. "I'm feeling a bit better now. Sorry I freaked out on you so bad. I was so afraid; I couldn't help myself. We'll all be fine now, won't we Rachel?"

"I'm s...scared!" cried Rachel. "Wh...Where's mommy and d...daddy?"

"We're all scared," answered Sam. "But we'll be okay, and we'll look for your mommy and daddy as soon as we get to town. Don't worry about being scared; I think I was probably more scared than either of you. We'll take care of you, Rachel."

Sam was almost beginning to relax a bit as they approached their final crossing of Crazy Woman Creek. The concrete bridge was draped with a thick blanket of ash. It, however, stood out in vertical contrast to the rest of the landscape, because its modern guardrails interrupted the suffocated valley with guides to the roadway. But to Sam's dismay, the leading edge of the rising tide from further up the creek had already reached the bridge.

Their narrow escape at the canyon mouth had apparently been another surge in the flood that was still headed in their direction. Some unknown blockage was causing water and ash to flow across the top of the bridge. This flow was as yet only a few inches deep. However, the curving approaches to the bridge were under water. They needed to escape across this last bridge, but *Sam could not see where the road was in order to get to it!* The water was not only muddy, but a thin layer of ash floated on top of it! Without actually probing the mess, it was impossible, in the dim headlights, to distinguish between ash covering the ground and the thin layer floating on water!

Sam slowed his truck to a crawl, and they inched forward, hoping to stay on the road as they aimed for the space between the guardrails. Suddenly, both front wheels of the truck dropped off of an unseen edge and the truck's frame landed hard on the road surface. Sam instinctively hit the brakes. His engine was still running, *but they were stopped cold,* and Sam had hit his jaw on the steering wheel when the truck fell. Rachel began to cry again.

Sam rubbed his jaw and muttered in disbelief, "I don't see how I could have missed the road. Sit tight for a minute while I check it out." He then stepped out into the darkness. Liddy again comforted Rachel, but had to fight back tears and clench her jaw to keep it from chattering. She felt almost defeated at this latest in the seemingly unending string of obstacles that they had faced.

Sam was also feeling discouraged, but he forced himself to think of each barrier to their progress as an individual problem. If he tried to imagine all of the hazards lurking ahead, it would be harder to effectively address each one along the way. Like any other large project that he had ever worked on, this taxing journey needed to be tackled in increments, one small step at a time.

Sam carefully waded out in front of his truck. With his feet he felt the washout into which his front wheels had fallen. It was knee-deep, but only about two feet across. Apparently, they had not missed the road, but *part of the road itself was missing.* The washout needed to be crossed in order to continue on to the bridge. Sam returned to the cab and explained to Liddy, "It's a washout, just a bit larger than our wheels, and I'm sure we can get across, but I need to walk over to the other side to check for any other hazards. Wait here, Liddy, I'll be back in less than five minutes." He smiled reassuringly at her, then closed the door and walked toward the bridge with his large flashlight in hand.

Liddy watched him fade from view as he passed the far side of the bridge. She had great confidence in him, but what if this was one situation that they just couldn't win? *What will I do if he doesn't come back?* She tried to force her mind away from such thoughts. She checked the clock on the instrument panel; *he'd been gone two minutes.* What was taking so long? Oh, Sam! *Where are you?* She held Rachel tighter.

Three minutes, and *still no sign of him!*

Liddy prayed.

Four minutes had now passed!

Suddenly, she thought she saw the glow of a light toward the far end of the bridge! A moment later, she saw Sam walking toward her. She heaved a sigh of relief. A moment later, Sam opened the truck door. Liddy grabbed his hand, just to *feel* him. "Sam, I got worried about you. Will we be able to cross?"

Sam leaned into the truck's cab and gave her a muddy kiss. He forced a smile from beneath his sticky veneer, "Yes, we'll be able to cross, *but you'll need to drive!* I can hook my come-along to the bridge rail, but you'll have to give it some throttle to bounce across this ditch. The far approach to the bridge is also under water, but I was able to walk to dry ground. Strap Rachel in tight and slide over here. I'll wave my light when I want you to start forward. Once you're moving, *don't stop until you get on the bridge!*"

Sam put the transmission in low-range, then closed the door and retrieved the hand winch from the back of his truck. Luckily, he had a long cable and tow strap for it. He ran the tow strap from the truck toward the railing and then attached his hand winch between the strap and the railing. Taking up the tension, he pulled the truck forward until its front wheels pressed hard against the edge of the washout. He then signaled to Liddy, and the front tires began to spin against the wall of the submerged gully. Sam rapidly applied more tension on the winch, and the fast spinning wheels ate away at the edge. The front end of the truck began to rise up.

Then all of a sudden the truck lurched ahead as the winch cable and tow strap went slack. The rear wheels fell down in the hole, then the truck bounced violently, skidding sideways as it sprang out of the hidden trap. Liddy yanked the steering wheel to the right to avoid Sam as he jumped to the side. She then had to swerve left again to avoid the rail on the right and then brake hard as she skidded onto the main part of the bridge. Sam quickly retrieved his hand winch and tow strap, and then tossed them loosely in the back with the frightened dog.

The water appeared to be rising rapidly as Sam replaced Liddy in the driver's seat. He piloted them forward through the murky water to the left of reflector posts that marked the right edge of the road. After another hundred yards, they climbed a low hill that finally took them out of the flood plain of Crazy Woman Creek. Sam wondered again if he had made the right choice when he had selected Crazy Woman Canyon as their escape route. The difficulty had been intense and at times the obstacles had seemed insurmountable! They had yet to reach the highway that would hopefully get them safely to Casper. But Sam felt that the worst was now behind them as the threat of flood receded with their increasing distance from the mountains.

CHAPTER 15

The Ashen Trail

▼

They meet with darkness in the daytime, and grope at noonday as in the night. - Job 5:14

Sam and Liddy felt intensely relieved when they finally reached the pavement of highway 196 and turned south. Sam again took a moment to clean the windows and pour more water into the windshield washer. The highway was less muddy, and Sam could see well enough to drive at almost forty miles per hour. The four to five inches of ash blanketing the road made driving feel as if they were traveling through a farmer's field, freshly prepared for planting.

The highway toward Kaycee was in good shape, and they saw no other traffic. The absence of ruts in the uninterrupted gray mantle indicated no previous passage of other vehicles. There were a few connecting roads that could have routed them to the paralleling I-25, but Sam thought that this obviously untraveled stretch of pavement might allow them to make better progress than they would on the four-lane highway, especially if many other people were also trying to escape from the area. In actuality, most people did not even consider evacuation, but rather attempted to get to their homes to see the crisis through while caring for their families.

Ten miles down the highway, the engine in Sam's truck began to cough and sputter. He slowed as he tried to discern what the problem might be. Then the engine died completely. As they rolled to a stop, Liddy questioned Sam, "Will we be able to get it started again?" Her look of concern was like that of a boater who has just realized that the craft is sinking.

"I sure hope so," answered Sam wearily. It felt to him as if their fate balanced precariously on a sharp edge, and any small action by him could easily result in either their safety or their destruction. He tried to think clearly and carefully. He was physically drained and the uninterrupted mental stress of their narrow escape from Crazy Woman Canyon had shredded his nerves. He imagined they would reach safety when they got to Casper, but on the other hand, *what if they would have to travel even further that day?*

It reminded Sam of hiking through the mountains without a map or any knowledge of exactly how far one needed to walk to get to a destination. The first steps are lively and full of energy. But as the miles mount up, concentration becomes focused on pacing toward a final unknown goal. Slacking off or resting causes stiffness, and the end is not as easily reached. Sam resolved to maintain his momentum, no matter what! Rest would have to come later. But for now, mental determination was needed to keep them out of trouble and to get them home.

With an upbeat voice that he hoped would provide encouragement to Liddy, he said, "Sit tight while I take a quick look under the hood." Sam stepped outside into the midst of a smothering cloud. The falling ash had become dry and the penetrating powder nearly choked him. Over the course of the last few miles, the windshield washer had actually begun to contribute to their visibility problems, rather than help. The handkerchiefs they covered their faces with were useful, but with the increased dryness, they began to feel an agonizing soreness in their throats and nostrils.

From the back of his truck, Sam retrieved several large cotton rags. He gave two rags to Liddy to double over the bandanas they already wore. As he held one over his own face, he used another to thoroughly wipe the remaining mud from the windshield. Sam then opened the hood carefully. *No wonder the engine had stopped—the air intake was completely blocked!*

Using a stiff bristle brush, Sam cleaned the heavy ash coatings from around key engine components. He then brushed and blew as much of the gray grit as possible away from the filter access and air intake. Huddling under the partly closed engine compartment hood, he carefully opened the air filter container and dumped out an accumulation of ash and trapped debris from the paper filter. After carefully replacing the filter and its cover, Sam retrieved a few supplies from the back of his truck. Then, using two rubber tie-down cords, he secured a double layer of cotton rags across the engine's air inlet as a pre-filter.

Sam closed the hood and slapped the new layer of dust from his grungy clothing, before climbing back into the driver's seat. "Did you get it fixed?" inquired Liddy hopefully.

"I think so. The air intake was completely stuffed with grit. We're out of the mud for the moment, but dry ash might be a greater problem for the truck."

Sam applied the starter and the engine turned, but it didn't start. A second cranking also failed to start it, or even to make sounds indicative of success. Sam began to sweat, while whispering, *"Come on! Come on!"* as he cranked the engine a third time. Liddy began to pray silently just as the engine emitted a promising cough. Sam pumped the foot-feed lightly, and then engaged the key for a forth try. This time it coughed twice, sputtered a few times, and then purred back to life. Liddy shouted, *"Hurray!"*

Tiny Rachel echoed with, *"Hurray, hurray!"*

They became more optimistic as the truck carried them southward again. Sam began to look for milestones that they could celebrate as they were passed on their way toward Casper. He knew that small successes on a long journey would be uplifting. When they reached I-25, about twelve miles north of Kaycee, Sam shouted, *"Hurray, Hurray! We're on our way!"* Rachel immediately perked up at Sam's vocalization, and Liddy, with a new lightness in her voice, asked, "Are we really in better shape on the Interstate than on the two-lane highway, Sam? You seemed to have handed us a bottle full of optimism!"

"We may or may not be better off, Liddy," replied Sam. But if our spirits are raised up a little, we should be able to think more clearly."

"You're right, Sam," commented Liddy with an air of acceptance. "We can't change the mess we're in, *but we do have each other.*" Although the outcome of their predicament remained in question, Liddy actually felt a brief interlude of peace—they were together and they were moving forward!

The faint barking of a dog startled Sam until he realized that it was their passenger in the rear of the truck. "*Doggy!*" declared Rachel, with emphasis and fascination. Liddy answered her, "Yes, Rachael...there is a doggy in the back of the truck. His name is *Grieg.*" Rachael looked toward the back window of the pickup. Liddy turned in her seat, but could not see Grieg's nose pressed up against the forward window of the camper shell. Rachel hollered, "*Doggy!*" and continued to look behind her, reaching her hand in his direction. Unfortunately, sight of the dog was prevented by the darkness and the coating of caked ash that stuck to the window of the cab. Grieg barked again and whined in painful isolation from his loved ones.

"Sam, why not bring Grieg up here? He sounds so lonely, and he could entertain Rachael," entreated Liddy.

"Sounds like a good plan, but I don't want to stop the truck unless we have to," Sam responded. "Next time I have to stop and get out, I'll bring Grieg to the front."

They saw several vehicles parked on the entrance and exit ramps to the Interstate. They were apparently waiting for better driving conditions. At this location, ash depth was over five inches. Sam felt he should warn people to leave the area, so he pulled over next to one of the parked cars, relayed his warning, and then asked the driver to pass the word to the people in the other vehicles. Sam pulled back onto the highway and drove south. I-25 was not nearly as busy as Sam had imagined it might be. As they finally passed Kaycee, Sam shouted, "*Hurray! We're past Kaycee. Hurray!*" Liddy and Rachael echoed with another, "*Hurray!*"

They continued south for another three miles to a hilltop where Sam stopped to again clean the pre-filter to the engine air intake. As he did so, he paused briefly in the darkness to listen to the lonely moan of the ash-laden wind. It reminded him of a winter snowstorm, and he suddenly began to shiver. He felt profoundly isolated from the rest of the world, until a forlorn whine from Grieg reminded him of his promised task. He quickly carried the dog to the cab, setting him behind the front seat. Grieg's joy overwhelmed them all. Rachel laughed with excitement as Grieg's sloppy tongue slathered her outreached hand. Sam and Liddy laughed too and it felt so good! Sam figured they needed Grieg as much as he needed them!

As they began driving again, Liddy asked," How long do you think this ash fall will last? Do you think we'll be safe in Casper?"

"I wish I knew," answered Sam. "You saw our guesses, but anything is possible. I just hope it doesn't last *too* long. That *population bottleneck*, caused by Toba about 74,000 years ago, is something to think about. Lets pray that nothing like that happens again!"

"But won't our modern technology save us from a total collapse like that?"

"I sure hope so," answered Sam. "There's a lot of people out there who think that we can control weather and climate. But there's no irrefutable evidence to back up their assertions. However, I *do* think our technology will allow us to cope much better than our ancient ancestors did."

"Probably so," remarked Liddy. "Just our high-tech clothing and housing alone are so far beyond what was available to the ancients. I'd guess that the human spirit, overall, is difficult to suppress, and we'll muddle through, no matter how bad it gets. We only know what's happening *here*…to *us*. Maybe we just happened to be on the down-wind side of the eruption, and *the sun is still shining in Montana?*"

"Liddy, I *love* your optimism! You're right. We don't know the extent of what happened in Yellowstone. I'm sure we'll find out eventually. Let's just hope that your *wild-eyed* geologist was overestimating its size!"

"Well, my *wild-eyed* geologist, I love you, no matter how large or small the eruption was!" laughed Liddy.

"I love you too, my beautiful television engineer! *And* your fine layer of ash as well!" declared Sam.

They glanced at each other in the dim light, filthy from head to toe with gray grit. Then in unison, they both said, "*What a mess!*" and started laughing.

Rachel hollered, "*Mess!*" and laughed along with them.

This was only the second time that either of them had laughed or smiled in sincerity rather than in encouragement since before the earthquake, more than three hours before. They now truly believed that they would survive, and that they would be together for a long time.

The west wind began to intensify, and visibility was again deteriorating. The wind kept some areas of the pavement almost clear of ash, but the drifts in other places were building up like those of a serious snowstorm. Despite some bare sections of road, visibility limited their speed to no more than forty-five miles per hour on clear stretches and much less where drift formation prevailed. It was no longer possible to even guess how much ash had fallen. The stretch of highway from Kaycee to Casper had always seemed endless to Sam, but now the distance had increased in his mind. Searching for the road, through blowing and drifting ash, produced every bit as much eye strain and fatigue as did driving in a blizzard at night.

After another fifteen miles, Sam slowed and then stopped. Someone was standing next to a small car by the side of the road and was waving a flashlight. The man walked over to Sam's window, identified himself as a tourist from Japan, and asked for help.

"Please give a ride to my wife and son if there is no room for me as well," he pleaded. "Our rental car has stalled, and we are all very thirsty. I fear it is dangerous to stay here."

"I'm sure we can fit all of you in," said Sam, "although it's going to be tight. And we *do* have extra water."

Liddy nodded, adding, "We can squeeze two in the cab, but one will have to ride in back with our dog." Sam noted Liddy's reference to *our* dog. He reached over to touch her hand, and Liddy squeezed his hand solidly in return.

Sam transferred Grieg to his old perch in the cramped quarters under the camper shell. He then helped the man, Taka Matsumoto, slide in next to the dog. Sam gave him water to drink and cotton rags to cover his face to aid breathing. Meanwhile, Liddy assisted Taka's wife, Kiyoko, and their twelve-year-old son, Koji, into the tiny jump seat of the club cab, gave them water and rags, and then climbed back in, continuing to hold Rachel on her lap. Sam cleaned his pre-filter again before resuming his driving. The truck was now very cramped, and it reminded him of a bunch of college kids, packed tight in a small vehicle, on a weekend outing.

Kiyoko, wedged sideways in the jump seat with Koji, explained that they were on vacation from Kushiro on Hokkaido, where Taka worked in public safety. They were driving from Billings toward Cheyenne when the ash cloud overtook them, choking their rental car into a stall. They were not aware of any nearby volcanoes, but Taka had recognized the volcanic ash for what it was. Sam explained to Kiyoko about the eruption of the world's oldest national park. Liddy then elaborated on their experiences in escaping from the Bighorn Mountains and their current attempt to get out of the area where Sam was expecting some of the heaviest ash fall.

Sam stopped four more times to clean his pre-filter and to make sure that Taka was doing okay under the camper shell. They were only eight miles from Casper when Sam was finally able to contact Warren on the two-meter amateur radio—the ashfall severely attenuated VHF radio signals. The familiar voice on the radio, like a ray of light shining through the blackness, triggered another round of "hurrays" from Sam, Liddy, and Rachel.

"KC7QE…this is KA7HBS," Warren responded to Sam's call. *"We're sure glad to hear you*! The power and phones are out, and the TV station is broadcasting on emergency low power. People are being asked to conserve water. We have about fifteen gallons on hand, as does Camile, and she has a generator for pumping from a shallow well, if need be. Other than the fact that Yellowstone has erupted, we haven't heard any news, and no one seems to know how bad the situation is. How was your trip down?"

"KA7HBS…here's KC7QE. It's been slow, and my truck has had a rough trip. We're fine, but now there are six of us, plus Grieg. We picked up passengers along the way. Liddy wants to know if Camile is alright."

"Yes, Sam, she's fine. Luckily, her son and his family were down here visiting for the weekend, so they're safe as well."

"That's great, *Dad*," replied Sam. "Liddy and I want you to know that we are engaged to be married!"

Warren was nearly speechless. "W*ow*! This hellish day seems to be looking up, Sam. *What wonderful news that is*! Tell Liddy her mother is crying...and *smiling* to boot!"

Sam returned, "We'll tell you the whole story when we see you in about fifteen minutes. *73* for now. This is KC7QE, clear and listening."

⇆

They reached the north edge of Casper at six-thirty—exhausted, famished, and filthy from their long ordeal. The wind was blowing strongly from the west at twenty to forty miles per hour, typical for some of the windier days in Casper. The air was so saturated with ash that the wind created a turbulent dust storm, lowering their visibility to less than one hundred yards. It appeared to Sam that the ash accumulation here was less than farther north, but some problematic deep drifts were forming. Although the sun would not set for another three hours, no light could penetrate the atmosphere surrounding them.

After pulling up in front of Liddy's house, the motley group slowly exited Sam's beat-up and mud-caked truck. Sam and Liddy were drained and weakened in body and spirit. It was as if they had tried to carry the world on their shoulders, staggered under the weight, and then when they could carry it no further and it was about to crush them, the burden was suddenly lifted. No other day in their lives had contained such a range of emotions, from the heights of ecstasy down to the deepest depths of fear and despair. The dreadful enormity of what had happened that day had not yet had time to linger in their minds. Like refugees fleeing a war zone, they had been preoccupied with their fight for survival. Now they could only think of rest and food and the safety of others.

As they all crowded into Liddy's house, Grieg promptly plopped down in his favorite corner, while the human faction cleaned the dirt from their eyes and then produced some quick introductions. The scene reminded Sam of a group of cavers who had just exited one of the long and dusty caves of northern Wyoming, craving soft chairs, cold beer, and warm sunshine.

Sam knew that, for now, sunlight was too much to ask for, but a cold beer could wash the grit from his throat. As if reading his mind, Warren handed him a beer from an ice chest and shook his hand saying, "Welcome to the family, *Son*." This was followed with good wishes all around, and brief accounts of some of the harrowing predicaments that plagued their escape to Casper. Clinging to Liddy, Rachel asked again for her mommy and daddy. With moistening eyes, Liddy responded, "Don't worry. God is with your parents. We'll keep you safe."

Taka then asked for a flashlight and motioned Sam outside. He shined the light up on Liddy's roof, explaining to Sam that the drift forming up there needed to be swept off to prevent structural failure and collapse. Due to his job experience in Japan, Taka had knowledge of the potential danger from the accumulated weight of volcanic ash on a roof.

He elaborated to Sam, "If you have just three inches of ash covering a section of roof that is twelve feet by thirty-six feet, you will have 108 cubic feet of ash that can weigh between three and eight tons! If your structure was not designed for such a heavy load, it may collapse. And," he added, "we don't know how much ash will fall, nor whether it might become saturated with rainwater. That would make it even heavier! Structural damage still occurs with most ash falls in Japan, although we have reduced the numbers by educating the public."

Sam thanked Taka for the warning and then went back inside to ask Liddy for a ladder. She didn't have one, but Camile did, so Sam and Taka walked over to her house. Camile hugged Sam and expressed her relief in his and Liddy's safe return. Then after appropriate greetings and introductions were passed around, they borrowed a ladder and two brooms. Camile's son, Eduardo, retrieved a third broom and joined them in their efforts. They first swept ash from the roofs of Camile's house and barn and then cleaned off Liddy's roof. Taka explained that they should check the roofs periodically to make sure that ash was not building up too thick over any large area.

Eduardo had set up Camile's emergency gasoline generator, but candles and lanterns were being used in both houses for light. He did not want to turn the generator on until absolutely necessary. He had rigged up an air intake filter, but he wanted to be conservative in the generator's use, just in case the situation lasted for more than a few days. Practical Camile always kept plenty of extra food in her pantry. There were boxes of various canned products, rice, pasta, grains, and dry milk. With such a stash, she could feed several people for many weeks. Water, however, needed to be rationed carefully for the unknown duration.

Sam and Liddy, her parents, Rachel, and the Matsumoto family gathered around Liddy's table for supper. The dirty bedraggled group, their faces reflecting the yellow glow from the candles, accompanied by one electric camp lantern, created in the room an almost medieval atmosphere. Having achieved their own immediate safety, the fate of others rested heavily upon their thoughts. A part of the world that they had known: the towns, the people, the animals, and the vegetation, may no longer exist! This was a room of survivors. The earth was being buried, but as their candles strained to push back the night, a gleam of hope flung its tendrils across the room.

Liddy's father spoke a brief prayer of thanksgiving and asked God to watch over those who suffered and those who had died. Warren then asked Taka if he would like to offer any other words according to his religion before they began to eat. He suspected that the Matsumoto family might have other than Christian religious beliefs.

Taka replied, "I thank you for rescuing us. I thank you for your courtesy, your hospitality, and your consideration for strangers who may hold beliefs that differ from your own. You found us thirsty and destitute by the side of the road, and you gave us water. You took us with you when you did not know us. You have brought us, strangers, into your family home to feed us. We too are Christians, a part of the Christian minority in Japan. But you have shown us the true meaning of Christianity. You have provided us, travelers from another land, with hospitality that we may never be able to repay. For my family and myself, I thank you all." Then he wept in gratitude as he led them in the *Lord's Prayer*.

After they had finished supper, Sam decided to drive across town to clear the ash off of his own roof. Taka offered to help him. Following some discussion, they decided that because of the small size of Liddy's house, the Matsumoto family would go to Sam's to stay, while Liddy's parents and Rachel would remain with her for now. They would be able to keep in contact on ham radio, via two-meters, particularly with Warren's mobile rig and Sam's home station. They would maintain schedules on the half hours and on top of the hour at 146.52 MHz.

At Liddy's request, Sam agreed to make one short side trip to the KWYN studio. Liddy quickly wrote a brief public service announcement to hand to whoever was in charge at the station. The announcement was a summary of Taka's warning for people to keep ash swept off their roofs to prevent collapse. She also wrote a note about Rachel and her missing parents. Perhaps they had escaped somehow. She wanted the station to broadcast the fact of Rachel's safety and to help reunite her with her parents, if possible.

After again cleaning the ash from his truck's pre-filter, Sam and the Matsumoto family left Liddy's around eight o'clock in the evening. The ash was still accumulating, and Sam's headlights struggled to penetrate the darkness. It should have been daylight, as the unseen summer sun would not set for another hour or so. The thought was depressing. *Would they see the sun the following day, or even the day after that?* Sam didn't know.

Sam delivered Liddy's announcement to the television studio where a crew of three people were manning the station. They were operating on emergency low power of 1000 watts rather than the normal 100,000 watts. The station crew was glad to receive the information, and two of the employees immediately headed for the flat roof of their building with push brooms and a snow shovel. The roof-cleaning announcement would be broadcast regularly until the danger had passed. That simple statement undoubtedly saved many Casper homes and businesses from collapse.

As Sam and company drove down the mostly deserted streets of Casper, faint luminous flutters of light from candles or lanterns in windows blinked at them as they drove by. In Sam's heart, the hope of a new day wavered off and on with each flickering light, but at the same time the dim glows enhanced the eeriness of the dead, ashen world outside.

Upon reaching Sam's house, he and Taka hastily went to work removing the deepening deposits from Sam's roof. Sam turned on some emergency lights and settled Kiyoko and Koji in the living room and kitchen area. He then checked his generator, back-up batteries in the radio room, and emergency water supply. He possessed about ten gallons of water, plus two more in the truck. There was still water pressure in the line, so he filled another five-gallon container. Since electricity was unavailable, Sam could cook with a camp stove in the garage if he was careful about ventilation. But cooking would not be necessary until the following day, when hopefully the ash fall would diminish.

Sam and the Matsumoto family used a sparse amount of water to clean themselves in his garage. It wasn't enough for a thorough job, but by using some shop brushes before using the water, the effort made them feel a lot better. Sam was relieved to finally remove the caked mud from his face, ears, and hair. After slipping into some fresh clothes, he found clean but poorly fitting clothing for the Matsumotos. Conversation with Warren, via two-meters, revealed that a similar cleansing ritual had taken place with Liddy, her parents, and Rachel.

Accompanied by Taka, Sam walked down to his basement ham radio station, where Taka informed him that he was familiar with amateur radio from his civil defense work. Sam then turned on his HF radio, and using battery power, he tried calling on the Wyoming emergency frequency of 3.923 MHz. But he was greeted only by loud static, caused by both thunderstorms and the static discharge of ash particles blowing across his antenna. On VHF, he located some simplex emergency activity on the Casper repeater output frequency. Apparently, no area repeaters were functioning, and most hams were probably too busy taking care of their families. The Wyoming Central Emergency Management Group had advised people to stay at home, not only for safety, but to prevent excessive damage from ash infiltration to the workings of their vehicles.

Sam felt as though he had spent the entire day at hard labor. He slept soundly that night and did not hear Taka cleaning off his roof in the early hours of the morning. Upon awakening to darkness when it should have been light, he became momentarily disoriented before remembering the traumatic events of the previous day.

After dressing in fresh clean clothes, Sam walked stiffly to his kitchen, noticing that Taka and his family were already awake. After lighting a candle, he offered them a simple breakfast of cold cereal, bagels, and milk. As soon as Sam had finished eating, he quickly went down to his ham shack and his early radio schedule with Liddy and Warren. Since HF propagation was still impossible, he could gather no more news about the eruption. However, his discussion with Liddy revealed their needs beyond simple shelter. *He and Liddy wanted to be together*! Sam's larger house had plenty of room for guests, so Sam decided that *everyone* should stay at his house.

He drove over to Liddy's to get her, along with Rachel, Grieg, and other supplies that would fit into his truck, while Liddy's parents drove their own vehicle to Sam's. Camile and her son Eduardo agreed to keep Liddy's roof clean.

Telephone service, both land line and cellular, did not function in the Casper area. Two-meter ham radio communication was relied on to report local conditions, while HF radio communications, which could have informed them about the situation across the country, remained nonexistent for the remainder of the day.

Sam and his newly extended family and friends spent the day talking and speculating, looking over books and maps by candlelight, writing letters, and taking pictures for posterity. They tried to formulate plans for the aftermath—a day when the ash would stop falling and the cherished sun would again reappear. Huddling in the uncertain dark and waiting for the unknown outcome of a disaster is best done, if possible, with friends and family. Sam and Liddy, so utterly grateful to be alive and together, calmly accepted their present situation and waited patiently for the return of the sun's precious light.

CHAPTER 16

Damages

▼

The inhabited cities shall be laid waste, and the land shall be made a desolation. - Ezekiel 12:20

The heavy descent of ash continued until late Sunday afternoon, after which a lighter dusting drifted downward from the heavens. Subdued daylight did not return until Monday, and the sun's rays remained dim, as suspended particles of volcanic ash inhabited the skies for weeks. Blown to extremely high altitudes, the very finest particles eventually circled the globe, dramatically reducing the amount of solar heat reaching the earth's surface for years to come.

On Monday morning, in the pale red sunlight, a Wyoming Air National Guard transport plane flew north out of Cheyenne, following the route of Interstate-25. The craft held a Central Emergency Management Group observer and a volunteer combat video crew. They were sent by the governor of Wyoming to make an initial assessment of the devastation. This was the only plane authorized to fly anywhere over Wyoming, Montana, or Idaho since the eruption two days earlier. No one was sure how long the plane could fly before airborne ash would grind its engines to silence.

The plane angled west to Casper and then north toward Buffalo and Sheridan. Although the volunteers on this flight knew the risks, they intently strained to see and record the destruction that lay stretched out below them. The land looked as if a dull-gray blanket had been draped over the corpse of topography, muting its features, but hinting at the violence that had so recently passed. An immense and eerie emptiness, stretching for countless miles, surreally dominated the drab, dead world below. Occasionally, structures or broken trees protruded above the gray expanse of ash, hinting at the life that once flourished there.

Buffalo could not be found!

Farther north, remnants of Sheridan jutted up above the lifeless waves of a dead sea—a skeletal mosaic of ruins that now marked its former existence.

The aircraft then banked westward and climbed up over the Bighorns. As it crested the range, all hints of previous life vanished. It was as if their plane was transported through space or time to another world in another galaxy, or to a time on earth before life existed. A gripping sensation of fear and loss descended upon and permeated the aircraft.

No one spoke.

Nothing recognizable could be seen in the otherworldly ocean of nothingness that was the Bighorn Basin! Only lifeless ash hung in the atmosphere and carpeted the world below. A complexion of ghastly, gray pallor covered the face of the earth, accentuated on ridge tops by the reddish glow of a mid-day dying sun.

The plane lumbered westward toward the buried graveyard of Cody, an empty hearse passing over a battlefield where no trace of dead remained. The vast desolate basin then gave way to a rugged place of somber shadows as the aircraft gained altitude in its flight over the Absarokas. Clouds of steam and ash could be seen ahead, sporadically belching upward from the broken land that was once Yellowstone. A brilliant cinnabar glow between gaps in the gaseous effluvia indicated molten lava oozing from an unseen wound in the earth. This place was unknown to the pilot who had flown across it many times before, and the smell of sulfur crept into the plane to sting his nostrils. He then saw swirls of dust and vapor rise and tumble as the pallid form of a horseman reared and lunged to charge toward the aircraft. Sparks from the hooves of the steed shot out and faded as brief glimpses of molten lava dived behind the rising clouds. Flashes of lightning highlighted the heads of both horse and rider, and the pilot felt a paralyzing fear deeper than anything he had ever known.

A quick desperate glance at his crew told him that they too beheld some awful vision. Whether it was the same brief illusion that he had perceived, or some other nameless thing, he did not ask. He banked the aircraft sharply left and then circled to the southeast, away from the yet active and fearsome spectacle of Yellowstone's newly formed caldera and whatever else it concealed. That maneuver reminded his crew of a soldier turning his face away from a grizzly scene of recent battle. A psychological pall hung over the return flight until they again saw signs of life as they approached Casper.

Upon returning to Cheyenne, the flight's video was made available to news outlets, and short clips appeared that evening on all of the major television networks. KWYN obtained its first sporadic information, relating to the wide extent of the disaster, via satellite links. On Monday evening their regular incoming news feeds had been completely restored, and they too viewed the unbelievable devastation recorded by the airborne video crew. As the primary ash cloud slowly dissipated, people with emergency power began to receive the national news networks also. The horrific scenes shook everyone who saw that video. Sam and Liddy both thanked God for the miracle of their deliverance from that hell on earth.

⇌

As visibility rapidly increased on Monday, so too did rescue efforts. Amateur radio, through its pre-established and practiced emergency procedures, came into the forefront of much of the news associated with rescue work. Before the eruption, few people, outside of law enforcement and emergency services organizations, were aware that ham radio was alive and well across the nation. But in their time of need, the public suddenly realized that those "ugly" towers and antennas, often accused of interfering with favorite network soap operas, now supplied life-saving communications! Locally and nationally, the Amateur Radio Emergency Service and the Radio Amateur Civil Emergency Service handled thousands of health and welfare messages. They also established temporary communications links for law enforcement agencies, National Guard rescue units, hospitals, the Red Cross, and numerous refugee shelters. Amateur radio was key in relaying public service announcements and general disaster information to news outlets from various agencies and rescue groups.

Liddy managed to return to work on Monday, only two days after the eruption, to help relieve the employees who had manned the station over the weekend. There would be no more teasing her about *"Chicken Little."* The station employees, like everyone else who had lived through it, were numb and dumbfounded by the magnitude of the catastrophe.

Several stories played out at KWYN and in the national media, where surviving hams in some of the hardest hit areas had been able to direct rescuers to the trapped and injured. These stories, usually relayed from law enforcement agencies, were followed in near real time as the rescues took place, sometimes over the course of days. As college classes were suspended indefinitely, Sam, with Warren's assistance, spent nearly two weeks helping with amateur radio emergency communications, using either his emergency backup power or commercial power after it was restored. Liddy videotaped emergency communication scenes from Sam's ham shack as well as from the shacks of several other Casper ham operators. Those brief spotlights on amateur radio became a part of KWYN's disaster coverage and subsequently aired on national networks.

Liddy's digital pictures, taken from Powder River Pass, proved to be the best ground-based images of the Yellowstone eruption. If other photographs had been taken as close to the eruption as Liddy's, they were never recovered. The KWYN audience was treated to Liddy's pictures three days after the tragic event. The national news picked up on her pictures later the same day, and they were seen regularly by worldwide viewers for several weeks.

Satellite images of the eruption were first seen on stations in areas far removed from the wide zone of devastation, and they were spectacular! More than fifteen Earth-monitoring satellites had recorded the scene as the roiling cloud of destruction rose up and spread outward! Those images were probably viewed by every geology student in the world for the next thirty years.

As information slowly became available, Sam learned that his previous predictions pertaining to the extent of destruction fell far short of the mark. His estimates of ash volumes and other physical projections were in the ballpark, but the high death toll and the agony caused to the population, along with secondary disruptions of lives, infrastructure, business, economy, and government, were well beyond his capacity to visualize. Many were the untold stories of personal heroism, both in Wyoming and across much of the region. Those unknown tales of human suffering, bravery, and compassion were forever buried beneath deep layers of volcanic ash.

> *Every man was a hero,*
> *Each woman sought her family's needs.*
> *History records almost nothing*
> *Of thousands of brave, selfless deeds.*

As Sam picked up Liddy at the station, after her third day back on the job, she informed him, "Your choice to take us out of the Bighorns through Crazy Woman Canyon must have been divinely inspired! If we'd followed the highway, *we never would have made it.*" Liddy was becoming weary and numb from the onslaught of bad news that she had been reporting, but tales from her home country hit her especially hard. "I just saw a report and video from a search and rescue helicopter that flew up the main highway west of Buffalo. Landslides blocked the road completely when the earthquake struck, and about fifty cars and trucks were trapped and buried. *There weren't any survivors*, Sam!" She reached out to him and wept.

"Oh, Liddy!" heaved Sam in sorrow as he held her tight. He was exhausted from his efforts with emergency communications. His ham radio had brought him accounts of rescue successes that lifted his spirits, but it had also related news of tragedy that made his heart sink. "If I'd only known how bad it was going to be," he continued, "I'd have been more persistent in speaking out. I would *never* have taken you there if

I thought we might be in danger!"

"You couldn't have known, Sam. *Nobody* could have guessed," comforted Liddy in return. "You warned people directly and honestly. *You did your best!*" She wrapped her arms around his neck and kissed him. It was late when they climbed into his pickup and drove down the dark streets toward home.

In the weeks that followed, the media replayed again and again the early April video statement put out by Josie Welbourne (with her children playing in the background). It represented not only the unfortunate personal dramas associated with the eruption, but demonstrated how the arrogance of officialdom, combined with complacency, could result in such an overwhelming tragedy. Warnings had been given to the public by Sam and his associates, only to be torn apart and ridiculed, and then dragged to a slow death, while government agencies continued to be caught in the net of policies, budget cuts, and red tape. They hadn't the energy, incentive, or patience to deal with a distraction that seemed too unreal to materialize.

⇆

Electrical power and telephone services were restored to Casper by Thursday, as well as to most of the areas where less than one foot of ash had fallen. Ash that had fallen in company with rain continued to coat power lines in some areas, shorting them to ground. In other places the built-up weight had been sufficient to break both power lines and supporting poles. Such ash coatings needed to be removed by crews before power could be restored. But in a few places, beneficial high winds kept poles and power lines clean. Unfortunately, due to wind and weather patterns, the area buried by greater than one foot of ash was extensive, taking in parts of Wyoming, Idaho, Montana, South Dakota, Nebraska, eastern Colorado, Kansas, Missouri, Iowa, and Illinois. Most of the continental United States received at least one inch of ash and very fine dustings were eventually noted throughout the entire world.

The ashfall was the *most widely destructive component* of

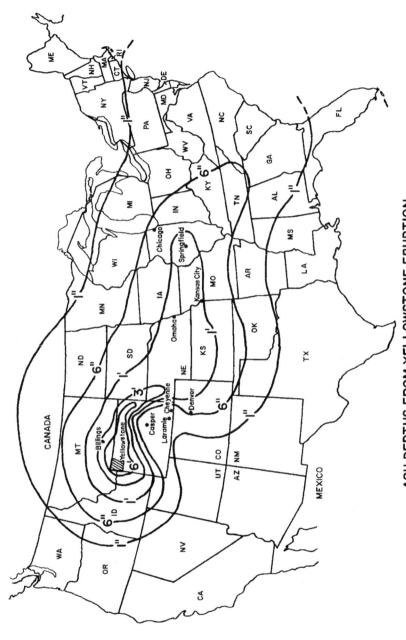

ASH DEPTHS FROM YELLOWSTONE ERUPTION

the Yellowstone eruption—its effect on humanity was *overwhelming* and *worldwide*. After rapidly cooling, the volcanic ash buried, smothered, and crushed vegetation, animals, buildings, and people. It combined with both rain and surface water to form devastating mudflows. It muddied and then slowed rivers and streams, choking aquatic life. When the mixture of water and ash became too thick to flow easily, it blocked the rivers like ice dams in a spring flood. The rivers then spread out behind the blockages, inundating the countryside. When the rising tides built up enough pressure, they over-rode and broke the temporary dams, sending even more devastating waves downstream and across areas historically immune to floods.

Of the larger cities in close proximity to the caldera, Billings, Montana was the hardest hit. More distant urban areas such as Omaha, Kansas City, and Springfield, Illinois also suffered under the terrible muddy onslaught. *The infrastructure and the population in the heartland of America were smashed into ruin*! The death toll, reaching biblical proportions, extended as far east as Kentucky and was estimated in the hundreds of thousands, *but this was only the beginning.*

Energy resources that once flowed from the Powder River Basin, on coal trains and in pipelines, ceased to supply power plants and refineries with raw material. Because of the deep ash deposits and damage to infrastructure, it would be many years before the Powder River region again exported this life-blood of America. The choking off of energy supplies came at the start of a *new ice age*, compounding the problems of a hurting nation.

Temperatures plummeted almost immediately after the eruption. This was due to the blocking of the sun's radiation by ash suspended in the atmosphere. During the summer, occasional bouts of frost plagued many agricultural areas. Early snows arrived in late August at unlikely places such as southern Arizona and the Carolinas. The world climate endured a major setback in its race, perceived by some, toward global warming. All marginal cropland failed, putting millions of acres out of production. As food supplies became limited, the threat of starvation haunted the world.

Casualties related to the *secondary* effects of drastic

climatic change extended to all corners of the globe, and they eventually *exceeded* those more directly related to the ashfall. The years following the eruption were the coldest in the historical records of the northern hemisphere. For many years, worldwide temperatures averaged five to nine degrees F below the previous fifty-year averages. *All of the greenhouse gasses generated by man could do nothing to stop the little ice age resulting from the eruption of Yellowstone!*

But decades later, when the climate again began to ameliorate, the fertility of volcanic soils showed their value. New strains of winter wheat and other grains and vegetables multiplied the output of America's croplands to volumes never achieved prior to the eruption of Yellowstone. The capacity of the breadbasket was dramatically enlarged, and feast eventually followed famine. After many years, America again began exporting its bountiful harvests of grain to feed the world.

$$\rightleftharpoons$$

Liddy Hill was again bogged down with overtime work at the KWYN studio. Within the two weeks that followed the eruption, she had dragged herself through twelve sixteen-hour days in a row, with no projected relief in sight. Sam remained at home where he and Warren continued to act as net control station operators for ham radio emergency communications. Liddy's mother, Dorothy, took care of Rachel and prepared meals. For more than a week after the eruption, the Matsumoto family stayed at Sam's and helped out where they could. Sam then ferried the appreciative family to Cheyenne where they made airline connections. Only one lane of I-25 was open between Casper and Cheyenne, but traffic was light. Fortunately, Sam was able to acquire enough gasoline for the trip. However, fuel supplies would be expensive and difficult to obtain for some time.

The Matsumotos' flight was one of the earliest scheduled out of Cheyenne, and it set a pattern for drastically increased air traffic from Wyoming's capital city. The Casper airport remained closed through July, until swirling ash was no longer the major hazard to aircraft takeoffs and landings. The

Cheyenne airport, due to the vagaries and vicissitudes of wind patterns, had actually received less ash accumulation than had Denver's airport, and it temporarily became a very important air transportation hub.

⇌

Only three days after the eruption, the President of the United States declared two-thirds of the lower forty-eight states disaster areas, and the Federal Emergency Management Agency mobilized to coordinate rescue and recovery activities. Both the National Guard and units of the regular military were called in for rescue activities. The large death toll of both humans and livestock brought on the spread of disease, and martial law was instituted in many areas where local governments had been wiped out.

Transportation and communications failures, along with the sudden erasure of consumers, businesses, and assets brought the country to the brink of economic collapse. Worldwide economic depression set in as well, due to the internationally interconnected nature of business coupled with the agricultural failure brought on by global cooling. However, economic fear and uncertainty were offset by a national conscience that pulled people together in a spirit of community. Not since the start of the war on terrorism, at the beginning of the twenty-first century, had national unity been so incredibly strong.

The Reef Group lost one of its major players at the FOYAB meeting in Cody. This diminished its influence within the national political arena, thereby lessening security in many parts of the organization. But for the Reef Group, this was merely a *temporary* setback. Most people, including Sam Westone, had never even heard of the Reef Group, nor realized that it had influenced such a wide sector of U.S. society.

Radical environmental concerns, similar to those of a religious persuasion (there often being little difference between the two), supplied the local and national news media with entertainment material for their audiences. When Yellowstone erupted, a few fanatics were ignorant enough of natural processes that they voiced their "utmost concern that the government had allowed this to happen, without first filing an *environmental impact statement.*" They actually believed that the eruption was a *secretive nuclear* or *geothermal power experiment* gone amiss. Their more knowledgeable contemporaries understood the natural processes, but wanted an environmental statement completed before bulldozers could be used to clear debris in the recently enlarged *Greater Yellowstone Ecosystem.*

But the U.S. Congress, in one of its most logical moments in living memory, let the Yellowstone National Park boundaries stay where they were. They then gave direction to the National Park Service to study the area for ten years, before coming up with a plan to place new roads and facilities that would be in harmony with the recently altered topography, geology, and thermal features. Based on earlier studies of the Mount St. Helens eruption, Congress also declined to allow other than *natural* revegetation processes to take place within the park. Similarly, it rejected requests for other than natural reintroduction of the formerly indigenous grizzly bear and the once re-introduced wolf.

⇌

Other countries acted individually in response to the disaster according to their priorities and national characters. Canada moved swiftly to salvage her own troubled areas and to aid as much as possible those of her neighbor to the south. Mexico, with its economy under rapid expansion for more than eight years, took the lead in sending financial aid and skilled rescue workers. Several countries from various parts of the world sent food, medical supplies, and rescue workers. Japan and Mexico took the technical leads in assisting with U.S. rescue and recovery efforts, in part due to their own experiences with volcanic disasters.

The United Nations merely debated what to do. The United States immediately curtailed all of its foreign aid programs in order to care for its own ailing population. In consideration of its own crisis, it then requested that the UN take over its commitments for humanitarian aid to other countries. However, the UN resolved that any requests by the United States be ignored until it agreed to be subservient to new UN environmental regulations and restrictions.

On another side of the international political spectrum, several countries jumped on their perceived opportunities for gain in the absence of U.S. strength. One Asian country typified such actions, and tried to storm into one of its neighboring countries to "quell an uprising there." War also broke out in the Middle East, and with a mosaic of shifting alliances, no one was really certain who was on whose side until it was over.

Although the interior of the United States was in shambles, most of the active U.S. military remained in fighting form, particularly the Navy. Regular military units were pulled back from domestic rescue duty, and well-prepared National Guard units worked efficiently with the foreign assistance groups. This was a *complete surprise* to the belligerent nations who had assumed that such a domestic disaster would cripple America's resolve to keep them in check. Retaliation and military assistance, in both the Middle East and the Far East, were swift and furious under the direction of a strong U.S. President. Both scenes of action were brought to standstills in less than a month, although heightened tension in these areas continued for many years.

⇌

Liddy's endless days of overtime work at the station stretched into weeks, and her job was becoming almost unbearable. Ever since Vance Trounce's death in February and Robert's resignation, she had been requesting that KWYN hasten to hire additional help and shorten her work hours to a reasonable schedule. But station manager Eric Larson continued to sing the same old tune…"*Just hang in there, Liddy!*"

"Sam, I don't know how much more of this I can take!" complained Liddy. "I want to move on with my life! I want to be with *you* and not be so exhausted by work that all I do in my spare time is sleep. I'd like to watch over Rachel too." As Liddy spoke, she realized that newly discovered maternal instincts were becoming greater than her desire for a successful career had ever been. Her introspection of that sudden discovery almost hushed Sam's response.

"You don't need to stay employed if you don't want to, Liddy," empathized Sam. "We can get by *just fine* on one salary. Rachel has been kept busy and entertained by your parents and my radio shack, but she really needs *you!*" Sam had exhausted every avenue available to find missing persons, and he had listed Rachel with every organization working to re-unite families that were separated by the disaster. "Liddy, every group I can think of is working on Rachel's case."

"Sam," interrupted Liddy, "I refuse to just turn Rachel over to some agency after all she's been through!"

"No, Liddy, *we won't!*" he responded. "If no relatives can be found to take her in, we'll just have to apply for adoption...and...I imagine it would probably be easier to adopt Rachel if one of us was available to care for her full time."

Liddy sighed with relief. The strength of her attachment to Rachel amazed even her. "Well, since the critical part of this disaster is winding down, I think my obligations as an employee at KWYN are *over*, Sam."

The next morning, Liddy handed in her resignation. She figured that if the television station went down the tubes for a few weeks, people could get their news elsewhere. Besides, there would eventually be other media engineers more than willing to take her job. For Liddy, it was all a matter of priorities, and she knew now *what really mattered* in life!

⇌

No one had been working at the WOMG on the Saturday in June when the Yellowstone caldera erupted. Nor did anyone attempt to report to work on the following Monday. Bill Burnhard died tragically as a result of the eruption that he had so vehemently dismissed. Bill's pre-eruption statements under WOMG letterhead had dropped that organization's credibility to a new low in the eyes of those in Wyoming who had managed to live through the disaster. Out of Wyoming's population of roughly one-half million, more than 100,000 souls had perished, and the survivors were not happy that they had received no *official* warnings prior to that terrible calamity. The WOMG would not survive another budget cycle unless public trust through new leadership was restored.

A few weeks after the eruption, Sam received a phone call from the Wyoming Governor's Office, to be followed up by a letter, requesting that he accept the position as director of the Wyoming Office of Mines and Geology. Sam responded that he would have to consult with his fiancé, but he would give them his answer shortly.

⇆

Not everyone had been caught off guard by Yellowstone's eruption. Andrew Merlott was working his placers with a newly completed sluice when he felt the ground move from Yellowstone's triggering earthquake. Although he couldn't see to the north, things just seemed a bit odd to him, so he sought shelter in his trailer. Andy had watched Sam's Yellowstone special on KWYN television, and he'd figured that any predictions from Sam Westone, *him being a prospector and all*, had to be right!

Andy had taken preparations that even Sam might have thought to be excessive, although they proved to be appropriate. He had shored up his trailer house with some of the timbers and cribbing that he planned to use in his new adit. He didn't want his home to collapse in the event of a heavy ash fall. After all, it was his *home*, and he knew from experience how terribly heavy dirt could be. The ash reached about eight inches deep near Atlantic City, but Andy rode out the storm just as he had survived in other situations. *"It's pretty tough to keep a good prospector down,"* he laughed.

Epilogue

▼

For there is the hope of a tree, if it be cut down, that it will sprout again and that the tender branch thereof will not cease. - Job 14:7

A tiny seed, borne on a warm, dry August wind, sailed and spun erratically eastward until it slipped into the calm of a small valley. Abandoned by the updraft, it spiraled downward and lodged in fine dust at the base of a rock. It was but one of many seeds that spread out across the barren landscape left in the wake of the most powerful explosion in the history of mankind. Other seeds also made the pilgrimage to those desolate wastes, arriving in the droppings of birds, or clinging to the fir of animals that ventured short distances from surrounding areas of cover. A few had even survived the blast, miraculously protected by stumps, rocks, or thin soil cover. Outside of the caldera, tiny animals and insects weathered the storm in underground burrows. Thus, with the coming of moisture and the changing seasons, life in Yellowstone and the surrounding country slowly began to renew itself.

New beginnings came not only to the natural world, but also to those people affected by it. The survivors of the eruption slowly but surely rebuilt their lives, starting anew if necessary. Sam and Liddy and Rachel began their lives together when the mountains shook and the darkened sky rained ashes, fear, and destruction. But like the steel from the forges of Damascus, their harrowing odyssey bound them together and brought out in Sam and Liddy virtues that neither alone had possessed. As the flowers and grasses that sprang from the ashes of Yellowstone, they too blossomed and flourished.

In late August of that year, Sam Westone and Liddy Hill were married under the veil of a reddened sky in the mountains west of Cheyenne. That high spot escaped much of the devastation caused by heavy ash deposits. Local strong westerly winds and fortuitous heavy rains following the ash fall washed clean some of the more exposed elevations. Liddy's parents, Rachel, Camile Brown, and several other relatives and friends attended the ceremony set in a glen of aspen trees surrounded by massive outcrops of pink granite. Temporary custody of Rachel was awarded to Sam and Liddy until all efforts to find and identify any living relatives were exhausted. Sam and Liddy Westone then officially adopted Rachel in April of the following year, although they always celebrated her birthday in June.

Sam accepted the position as Chief of the Wyoming Office of Mines and Geology, and he began working there in September. The very first phone call that Sam received in his new office came from a public pay phone in Rock Springs. A prospector named Andy Merlott just wanted to thank him for his early warning about Yellowstone.

⇌

*The forces of geology
never sleep...*

APPENDIX I

Glossary

▼

This glossary is provided to refresh the memories of those who have studied or have an interest in earth science and geology. We hope it will also help those without such a background to better understand the details of the geology and other technical material discussed in *Yellowstone Farewell*.

anticline – a convex upward fold in rocks, containing stratigraphically older rocks toward the core of the fold

antiform – an anticlinal-type structure where the age sequence of the rocks has not been determined

apex – the highest point of a mineral vein relative to the surface, or the summit of a fold

ash – fine volcanic dust

ashfall – the precipitation of volcanic ash from an eruption cloud

auriferous – containing gold

basalt – dark, usually extrusive, igneous rock containing plagioclase; may include accessory magnetite, hematite, ilmenite, apatite, olivine, quartz, and glass

caldera – large basin-shaped volcanic depression, often caused by the collapse of the roof of a magma chamber

catastrophism – sudden, brief and violent changes in the earth's geology and biology, as contrasted with slow, but steady changes over long periods of time

continent – any one of the earth's major land masses, including both dry land and continental shelves

continental crust – the type of earth's crust that underlies the continents, less dense than oceanic crust, and generally granitic in composition

continental drift – term for original theory proposed by Wegner (1910) addressing the apparent movement of continents, now replaced by plate tectonics theory; as with most theories, refinements of ideas continue to evolve

crust – the outermost layer of the earth, defined as being above the Moho, and representing less than 0.1 percent of the earth's volume

crustal plates – one of several blocks into which the crust is divided in a scheme of global tectonics; movements and interactions of these plates are responsible for earthquakes, volcanoes, faults, folds, mountains and rifts

CT-scan – computed tomography, also known as CAT-scan (computerized axial tomography) —a method of using a computer to combine images from multiple x-rays to produce sophisticated cross-sectional or three-dimensional pictures of the internal organs, and can be used to identify abnormalities such as tumors

diamond – isometric carbon mineral with a specific gravity of 3.52 and a hardness of ten; octahedral crystals are the most common form; colorless or attractively colored crystals are sought-after gemstones

diamondiferous – containing diamonds

dike – a tabular igneous intrusion that cuts across the surrounding rock

dunite – an ultramafic intrusive igneous rock made up primarily of olivine and may also have chromite, magnetite, clinopyroxene, ilmenite, and apatite; garnets and platinum possible

DX – a distant radio station, usually in a different country

fault – a fracture plane or zone in rock along which there has been displacement

gabbro – massive, coarse-grained, dark-colored intrusive igneous rocks with approximate composition equivalent to basalt, principally plagioclase (labradorite - bytownite) with greater than fifty percent clinopyroxene, may also contain magnetite, ilmenite, chromite, and apatite

garnet peridotite – coarse-grained igneous intrusive rock composed of olivine, pyroxene, and pyrope garnet, and occasionally spinel and diamond; nodules in kimberlites are considered to be fragments of the earth's upper mantle

geothermal gradient – the rate of increase of temperature with depth in the earth

gneiss – a planar textured, medium- to coarse-grained metamorphic rock with alternating dark and light colored bands

GPS (**G**lobal **P**ositioning **S**ystem) - a worldwide radio-navigation system using satellites as reference points

granite – generally light-colored intrusive igneous rock containing quartz, potassic feldspar, plagioclase, biotite, and muscovite, and may include several other minerals

greywacke – dark gray to brown, poorly sorted, irregularly thick-bedded, angular sandstone with a dirty or muddy matrix

hotspot – a persistent area in the upper part of the earth's mantle that is hotter than its surroundings, and is expressed through the crust by high heat flows and volcanic activity

igneous – a rock or mineral that solidified from melted or partially melted material

intrusive – magma emplaced within pre-existing rock

kimberlite – greenish to black brecciated ultrabasic, potassic intrusive; traditional host-rock for diamonds originating in the earth's mantle; contains serpentinized olivine, chloritized phlogopite, calcite, pyrope garnet, ilmenite, chromite, chromian diopside, and other minerals

lamproite – ultrapotassic, mafic intrusive or extrusive igneous rock that may contain diamonds

Laramide Orogeny – a time of mountain-building and geological deformation typical of the eastern Rocky Mountains, beginning during the late Cretaceous and lasting until the end of the Paleocene

lithology – the description of the physical character of rocks (lith = stone, ology = study)

mafic – describes dark igneous rocks that are rich in minerals containing abundant magnesium and iron

magma – naturally occurring melted rock material

magma chamber – a reservoir of magma within the earth's crust that acts as a source for volcanic materials

mantle – the layer of the earth below the crust and above the planetary core

mantle plume – rising heat from deep within the mantle and the hypothetical cause of a hotspot

matrix – groundmass or fine-grained interstitial material between larger grains or phenocrysts

metagreywacke – metamorphosed greywacke, often dark mica-rich quartzite and schist

metamorphosed – term applied to a rock that has been changed at depth within the earth's crust by heat, pressure, or chemical action and without completely melting, thereby altering its structure and mineralogy; prefix 'meta' applied to original rock type, if known

metasediments – sedimentary rocks that have been metamorphosed

mid-ocean ridge – a continuous sub-sea mountain range extending through the middle of the North and South Atlantic, Indian, and South Pacific oceans, and is a spreading center between crustal plates where new basaltic oceanic crust is continuously extruded

mineralogy – the study of the formation, occurrence, characteristics, and classification of minerals

Moho – the boundary between the earth's crust and the mantle is called the Mohorvicic discontinuity, named after the Yugoslavian seismologist who discovered it in 1909

nuisance value – the economic value paid to remove or eliminate an activity that is in the way of another activity or project, regardless of the legality of either project

oceanic crust – the type of earth's crust that underlies the oceans, more dense than continental crust, and generally basaltic in composition

olivine – olive-green to yellow, hard, medium heavy, magnesium iron silicate mineral, often in clear crystals, found in dunite, lamproite, peridotite, gabbro, and basalt

pay dirt – earth or rock material, that when mined, will yield a profit to a prospector or miner

pediment – a relatively planar, gently sloping erosion surface, often veneered with gravel and other alluvium

peridotite – see garnet peridotite

pile-up – numerous radio amateurs from a wide variety of locations around the world, all trying at once, on one frequency or on a small range of frequencies, to call one particular amateur at a remote or unique location

plate tectonics – conceptual model of global tectonics based on the movement and interaction of crustal plates or blocks

pyroclastic flow – an explosively vented mixture of mostly fine-grained unsorted particles of rock and high temperature gas that turbulently moved down-slope in a manner similar to an avalanche; also called ash-flow

QRP – amateur radio Q-signal meaning to reduce transmitting power, popularly indicates transmission using less than five watts; a Q-signal is a group of three letters used to briefly convey a standardized statement or question using Morse code

rhyolite – light-colored, extrusive igneous rock containing quartz and alkaline feldspar, and may also contain volcanic glass, biotite, and others; extrusive equivalent of granite

sedimentary – classification of rocks deposited as sediments, either chemically precipitated or composed of debris weathered from pre-existing rocks

seismic wave – an elastic wave produced by an earthquake, explosion, or other vibration

shear zone – a tabular zone in rock that exhibits movement along many parallel fractures that may serve as conduits for ore-forming solutions

shield volcano – volcano built up by flows of very fluid basaltic lava and appearing as a broad low dome

silicic – silica-rich magma or igneous rock

spinel – isometric mineral ($MgAl_2O_4$) that often appears as small perfect octahedrons

subducted – one block or plate of the earth's crust descending beneath another

subduction zone – elongate region, notably along a continental margin, where one crustal plate descends relative to another

syncline – a concave upward fold in rocks, containing stratigraphically younger rocks toward the core of the fold

tectonics – geologic study of the broad regional structures in the earth's crust, their origin, and their development over time

tomography – procedure where internal body images, at a predetermined plane, are recorded by means of the tomograph, which is a computer-driven device that builds the image from multiple x-ray measurements

tuff – compacted deposit of volcanic ash and dust that may contain as much as fifty percent fine nonvolcanic sediments

turbidite – a sediment or rock deposited on the floor of a body of water by a rapidly moving bottom current, more dense than the surrounding fluid because of stirred up entrained particles, and characterized by graded bedding and moderate sorting

ultramafic – rock composed of a high percentage of mafic minerals and usually less than about forty-five percent silica

vesicular – containing many small voids caused by gas bubbles trapped in magma at the time it solidifies

volcanic – relating to the processes, rock types, structures, and features of a volcano

volcano – an opening in the earth's surface through which magma, ash, and associated gasses are vented; usually in the form of a conical hill or mountain built up by erupted material

WWV – National Institute of Standards and Technology (U.S. Dept. of Commerce) broadcasts precise time and frequency information continuously from station WWV in Ft. Collins, CO, on frequencies of 2.5, 5, 10, 15, and 20 MHz

xenocrysts – crystals that are genetically foreign to the igneous rock in which they occur

xenoliths – rock pieces that have been incorporated into a melt from surrounding rocks and are included in an igneous rock, even though they may have no direct genetic relationship to that particular igneous melt

zeolites – general term for a complex group of minerals derived from alteration of feldspars and other minerals; characterized by easily reversible water loss

APPENDIX II

References

and

Suggested Supplementary Reading Material

▼

American Radio Relay League, 2002, The ARRL Operating Manual: American Radio Relay League, Inc., Newington, CT, 416p.

Baigent, Michael, and Leigh, Richard, 1989, The Temple and the Lodge: Arcade Publishing, New York, NY, 306p.

Foxworthy, Bruce L., and Hill, Mary, 1982, Volcanic eruptions of 1980 at Mount St. Helens - the first 100 days: U.S. Geological Survey Professional Paper 1249, 125p.

Hausel, W. Dan, 1998, Diamonds and mantle source rocks in the Wyoming craton with a discussion of other U.S. occurrences: Wyoming State Geological Survey Report of Investigations No.53, 93p.

Hausel, W.D., 1991, Economic geology of the South Pass granite-greenstone belt, southern Wind River Mountains, western Wyoming: Wyoming State Geological Survey Report of Investigations 44, 129p., map scale 1:48,000.

Hausel, W. Dan, and Sutherland, Wayne M., 2000, Gemstones and Other Unique Minerals and Rocks of Wyoming - A Field Guide for Collectors: Wyoming State Geological Survey Bulletin 71, 267p.

Hausel, W. Dan, Sutherland, W.M., and Gregory, R.W., 1995, Lamproites, Diamond Indicator Minerals, and Related Anomalies in the Green River Basin, Wyoming: in Wyoming Geological Association Guidebook, Fifty-second Annual Field Conference, Aug.19-22, 1995, p.137-151.

Hill, Chris, Sutherland, Wayne, and Tierney, Lee, 1976, Caves of Wyoming: Wyoming State Geological Survey Bulletin 59, 230p.

Holy Bible, various dates and translations by numerous publishers.

Hose, Richard K., 1955, Geology of the Crazy Woman Creek Area, Johnson County, Wyoming: U.S. Geological Survey Bulletin 1027-B, 118p, 1:48,000 scale map.

Keefer, William R., 1976, The Geologic Story of Yellowstone National Park: U.S. Geological Survey Bulletin 1347, 92p.

Love, J.D., and Christiansen, A.C., 1985, Geologic Map of Wyoming: U.S. Geological Survey State Map, scale 1:500,000, 3 sheets.

Roberts, Philip J., Roberts, David L., and Roberts, Steven L., 2001, Wyoming Almanac: Skyline West Press, Laramie, 5th ed., rev., 562p.

Roosevelt, Theodore, 1888, Ranch Life and the Hunting Trail – Illustrated by Frederic Remington, Reprinted 1995 by Random House: Gramercy Books, New York, NY, 187p.

Sarna-Wojcicki, A.M., and Davis, J.O., 1991, Quaternary Tephrochronology, *in* The Geology of North America, vol. K-2,

Quaternary Nonglacial Geology: Conterminous U.S., Geological Society of America, p.93-116.

Sigurdsson, Haraldur (Editor), 2000, Encyclopedia of Volcanoes: Academic Press, San Diego, CA, and other locations, 1417p.

Smith, Robert B., and Braile, Lawrence W., 1993, Topographic signature, space-time evolution, and physical properties of the Yellowstone-Snake River Plain volcanic system - the Yellowstone hotspot–*in* Geology of Wyoming: Geological Survey of Wyoming Memoir No. 5., p.695-754.

Sutherland, Wayne M., and Hausel, W. Dan, 2002, Preliminary Geologic Map of the Rattlesnake Hills 1:100,000 Quadrangle, Fremont and Natrona Counties, Wyoming: Wyoming State Geological Survey Open File Report 2002-2, 2 plates, text 28p.

U.S. Geological Survey, 1972, Geologic map of Yellowstone National Park: U.S. Geological Survey Miscellaneous Investigations Map I-711, scale 1:125,000.

Warner, Philip, 1996, Famous Scottish Battles: Barnes & Noble, Inc., New York, NY, 160p.

Suggested Sources
of Information

▼

The following are suggested sources of information concerning geology, ideas, places, and concepts addressed in this book. This list is only a brief beginning, but if you wish to learn more, these sources can get you started.

American Radio Relay League
225 Main Street
Newington, CT 06111
Ph 888-277-5289
http://www.arrl.org/ - website
Source for information on amateur radio, licensing, instructional materials, and publications.

National Speleological Society
2813 Cave Avenue
Huntsville, AL 35810-4431
Ph 256-852-1300
www.caves.org - website
Dedicated to the exploration, study, and conservation of caves.

National Rifle Association
11250 Waples Mill Road
Fairfax, VA 22030
www.nra.org - website
Source for information on safe use of firearms and related legal issues.

Power Pak Systems, Inc
P.O. Box 7076
Laramie, WY 82073
Ph & FAX 307-742-6852 Cell 307-760-5284
Email wl7cma@fiberpipe.net
www.fiberpipe.net/~ppsi/ - website
A source for portable emergency power supplies and communications.
But keep in mind – Disaster Preparedness Is No Joke!!

University of Wyoming
Department of Geology and Geophysics
P.O. Box 3006
Laramie, Wyoming 82071
Ph 307-766-3386
http://home.gg.uwyo.edu/ - website
The place to study and learn about Wyoming's geology and geology in general.

State of Wyoming
The Cowboy State
http//:www.state.wy.us/ - website
Information source concerning Wyoming's tourism, hunting, fishing, industry, agriculture, government, and cultural events.

U.S. Dept. of the Interior, Bureau of Land Management
Wyoming State Office
P.O. Box 1828
Cheyenne, WY 82003-1828
Phone 307-775-6256
http//:www.wy.blm.gov/ - website
Source for Wyoming public land management information, maps, and mining claim rules and regulations.

U.S. Geological Survey Information Services
Box 25286, Federal Center
Denver, CO 80225
Ph 303-202-4210
http://volcanoes.usgs.gov/yvo/ - Yellowstone Volcano
Observatory website
http://volcanoes.usgs.gov/ - U.S. Geological Survey Volcano
Hazards Program website
http://earthquakes.usgs.gov/ - U.S. Geological Survey
Earthquake Hazards website
Sources for geologic information and publications.

Wyoming State Geological Survey
P.O. Box 3008
Laramie, WY 82071
Ph 307-766-2286
http://wsgsweb.uwyo.edu - website
*Source for Wyoming geological information, expertise, maps,
and publications.*

Yellowstone National Park
Information Office
P.O. Box 168
Yellowstone National Park, WY 82190
Ph 307-344-7381
Email yell_visitor_services@nps.gov
http://www.yellowstone-natl-park.com - website
http://www.yellowstone.net/webcamlive.htm - Old Faithful
webcam
Visit and learn about America's premier national park!

About the Authors

▼

Wayne Sutherland has lived and worked in Wyoming for most of his life. He received undergraduate degrees in both Geology and Education, as well as a Masters degree in Geography from the University of Wyoming. He has over twenty-five years of experience working in geology, natural resources, and environmental management for both state and federal government and private industry. Wayne is presently a geologic consultant who has recently held contracts with the Wyoming State Geological Survey, mapping geology and exploring for diamonds and metal deposits. He has co-authored publications such as *Caves of Wyoming* and *Gemstones and Other Unique Minerals and Rocks of Wyoming*. Wayne, callsign NQ7Q, is an active amateur radio operator, involved with radio club activities and civil emergency work. He has made contact with over 300 countries, via ham radio.

Judy was born and raised in the Red River Valley flatlands of eastern North Dakota, where her passion for the outdoors began during childhood wanderings in woods along the banks of the Goose River. She attended college in her hometown, but in her quest for *bigger hills to climb*, she moved to Wyoming in 1973. She worked in a library, studied Equine Science at a small Wyoming college, and then completed her BA degree in Art from the University of Wyoming. Judy's avocations include oil painting, nature photography, horse training, vegetable gardening, and classical guitar and piano. Over the years, she has assisted her husband with geologic fieldwork and cave exploration and mapping. She and Wayne have also worked as volunteers for the USFS and USBLM, receiving the *Volunteers for the Public Lands* national award for their work in photographic monitoring of one of Wyoming's largest cave systems.

The Sutherlands are outdoor enthusiasts who have walked and skied hundreds of miles across much of Wyoming's backcountry. They have explored and surveyed in Wyoming's largest caves, ascended many of Wyoming's highest peaks, and backpacked extensively throughout the Bighorn and Wind River ranges. Wayne and Judy belong to various organizations that promote responsible backcountry use and resource conservation. They also promote energy-efficient house construction and have designed and built two passive solar-heated homes in Wyoming.

YELLOWSTONE FAREWELL
ISBN 0-9723999-0-9

Check with your local bookstore, or order directly from us.
Send $18.00 U.S. plus $4.00 shipping and handling to:

Spur Ridge Enterprises
P.O. Box 1719
Laramie, WY 82073
USA

	Number Of Books		Price		Total
Yellowstone Farewell	_____	X	$18.00	=	_____
Wyoming Sales Tax required for sales shipped to Wyoming (see list on back)					
books _____		X	tax _____	=	_____
U.S. Shipping & handling @ $4.00 first book plus$1.00 each additional book					_____
Foreign S&H rate greater based on 2 lbs (907 g) shipping weight					_____
Total Amount Enclosed					_____

Bank certified check, or money order preferred. No credit card orders via mail.
Credit card - Order directly from our website – www.yellowstonefarewell.com

Ship to:

Name: _____

P.O. Box or
Street Address:_____

City, State:_____

Zip Code:_____

Country:_____

Books shipped immediately upon receipt of payment, after your check clears our bank. Please be sure to include shipping address and zip code.

Quantity discounts available for bulk purchases of this book. For further information, contact Spur Ridge Enterprises, P.O. Box 1719, Laramie, WY 82003. E-mail: spur@yellowstonefarewell.com

2002 WYOMING SALES TAX

Co.#	County	Tax Rate %	Tax / $18 Book ($s)
5	Albany	6	1.08
9	Big Horn	5	0.90
17	Campbell	5.25	0.95
6	Carbon	5	0.90
13	Converse	5	0.90
18	Crook	5	0.90
10	Fremont	4	0.72
7	Goshen	5	0.90
15	Hot Springs	5	0.90
16	Johnson	6	1.08
2	Laramie	5	0.90
12	Lincoln	5	0.90
1	Natrona	5	0.90
14	Niobrara	6	1.08
11	Park	4	0.72
8	Platte	5	0.90
3	Sheridan	6	1.08
23	Sublette	4	0.72
4	Sweetwater	5.5	0.99
22	Teton	6	1.08
19	Uinta	6	1.08
20	Washakie	4	0.72
21	Weston	5	0.90